The characters, places and events in this book are fictitious. Any similarity to real persons, living or dead, is coincidental and not intended by the author.

Cover image by Hutchinson Fire Department of Hutchinson, Minnesota.

CRICKLEWOOD GREEN
by
Eric Borys

October 24th

Engulfed in fire, the SUV blew a singular stink of man's Hell. A combusted conjure of plastics, rubber, fuel and electronic circuitry, caustic enough to dry-heave a vulture inside out. All makes, models, shapes and sizes burned the same, as Tyce remembered. No difference between the bomber's dusty BMWs and the hapless, bombed Army six-by trucks. Here in the Michigan rain the forgotten smell - a souvenir of Tyce's war year – had cast him to another state of mind.

Tyce leaned back from the rifle's scope and brace at his shoulder, blinking, as if from a hypnotist's wake-up. Unpinned from the optical's zoom everything seemed miniature; the sideways wreck and the road's downslope mile, corridored by trees blushed crimson, amber and gold. Tyce relaxed, conscious of his breathing. Cramps announced themselves – his kneeling thigh, his right wrist. Sound returned. The fat *thap* of leaf drops onto his poncho. Tyce palmed the hood back, twisting to look up and behind. The top of Cricklewood Green's pinkish-tan wall was visible in fragments behind the treetops, the attacker's view of a castle to storm. Oh, the riches and wonder inside. If they only knew.

An eye-bugging spasm in his lower back forced Tyce to turn forward again. At the road's blockaded crest, the afternoon drizzle had snuffed the crashed SUV's burn to steam. Match-size flames still blipped inside, but the frothy, oily blaze was exhausted having eaten the tires to the rim and wilted the red chassis to a blackened shrunken apple. This gave Tyce a clue to the time, probably an hour. By windshield glare, Tyce was not sure if his first two shots had killed the SUV driver before the spike-strip chain yanked the speeding truck onto its passenger side, momentum skidding it into the concrete barriers like a dumped hockey player. The impact triggered a weak one-two explosive charge and eruptive flourish of bluish fire flung out the windows and across the staggered line of obstacles. They had packed flammables inside. He'd seen the Hajjis try it against Mosul roadblocks with high explosives and no better results. There, another car or two would typically follow - to rush the breach with more bombs. But these attackers came on foot.

Minutes after the crash, four of them emerged in Tyce's scope, creeping along the tree line on each side of the leaf-pasted blacktop. Scruffy white men in mixed-bag deer-camp camo with various ARs and short packs in two-by-two leapfrog style, possibly imitating movies where they had seen this work. Run, crouch and aim. Pause. Run, crouch and aim. Pause. Their interval was consistent. Tyce inhaled, leading them, waiting to red circle the next man when he stopped.

Pink Floyd…

You.

Yes, you.

Stand still, laddie.

Tyce exhaled and squeezed. One shot to each man in mid-crouch. Left side of the road. Drop. Then right. Drop. Whatever body armor they may have worn was butter against Tyce's Springfield. The pudgy running man on the right side jittered in the wet and slipped on his ass. As the man rolled and baby crawled for the woods, Tyce put one into him center mass, limbs slipping out like a collapsing tent. The fourth one on Tyce's left side, nearly straight on, had some training. He hit tree cover fast and fired steady, toward the barricade, toward the burning. The resulting cracks of .223 around Tyce were faint, wild. Tyce was at ease in his hiding.

Another state of mind. Once again, he was young Sergeant Tyce, E-5. Though that never was him, really. During his war year, Tyce was already a second-time-around old man reservist. Called-up, bad luck, wrong place and time. Now, once again.

Through the rifle scope, the tree-hidden man's profile huffed vapor at his stiff pals across the road. Not liking the shot, Tyce waited, unsure if more of them were maneuvering through the trees. He could see no obvious radio on any of the bodies, nor hear any steps or shouts, only the rain's sizzle and the soft curr of fire. For instants, he glimpsed edges of the fourth man's knee or elbow, but Tyce knew he had only 29 rounds left for the Springfield. In the dripping minutes, Tyce became certain the man was alone. Then, in a rustle, the man rolled and dived into the undergrowth. Jerking the optical with the movement, Tyce blindly fired once into the magnified distortion of branch, vine and shadow. Suddenly Tyce became unsure, of anything.

Thus he remained, for however long, tuned, aiming down the road. Probably an hour, tuned to Sergeant Tyce, and the smell of man-made Hell. The lumped bodies in the roadside grass didn't trouble him. Death was boxed, along with his fear. In this state, tucked-in with his sight line clear of smoke, he wanted more of them to come.

Tyce set the rifle in his lap. He flexed and breath-warmed his numbed fingers, swigged some water and pressed the earpiece radio mic.

"Second Squad to Barracks."

Though alone, Tyce didn't want anyone listening to know it. Twirling his wrist, Tyce wiggled and snake-popped his spine.

"Second Squad to Barracks. Come in."

"Y-Yeah. Tyce?" Lorna said. She sounded frightened - still rattled from yesterday, no doubt. She had to hear the gunfire from inside the walls, no doubt the truck's explosion.

"Yes. What can you see?"

"Nothing. Nobody. Just trees."

"Camera ten. Pan it from each side, slow. You know how."

"No. Nothing moving. The same car's there. Maybe a truck further back on Orton. The same ones. I've got it zoomed all the way. No people. But I can't tell for sure."

"It's OK. Pull back and pan slowly. Then the other ones. Watch the walls. You know where we're coming back in, right?"

"Yeah. I know."

He boosted to a crouch, stretched his left leg and worked the knee.

"You OK-K, Tyce?"

"Yeah. Everyone's OK." She couldn't get it.

"Tell Jason and Jeff we've got hot chili for them. Tell Dave, Rick fixed the machine gun."

Tyce smiled. Jason? Jeff? Rick? She was still with it. Still Lorna, a tart riddle. No, yes, no. A stammer was cutting her voice since yesterday, like a faulty radio.

"Copy that, Lorna. Over and out. Stay off unless you see something moving."

"G-Got it …copy."

Another *what-am-I-doing-here* minute and Tyce stood. He back-slung the Springfield and from a dry tuck in the branches unrolled the shorter, lighter M-4 carbine from its plastic covering. The M-4 the better tool for up close and fast. From the fringe of the wood line he stepped down toward the SUV, weapon up, scanning. When his National Guard ass had been pressed into road security teams in Iraq they shot pissed-off full magazines into the wrecks to make sure. Crossing the road and rounding the side of the blackened cement barricade, Tyce thought he could see bone structure through the truck's burst-open windshield. Two steps closer and he laughed. The toggle of aluminum shoulder points and arms. A rod stump of pink melted head and plastic flesh. A mannequin. Why? No wonder the spike strip flipped it. They'd must have locked the wheels off and sent the SUV up the straightaway. It hadn't occurred to Tyce until he saw it now, but who would have been the poor bastard they sent to kamikaze it? Who drew that straw? Things were strange now, but not that strange. This was smart, actually. Tyce wasted shots on the driver, not the engine block.

Watching and listening, he finally circled to the back. A flung-out white can had rolled to the blacktop edge. His toe thumped it, full. Spies Hecker 5505 - paint thinner. A corner of a Detroit Red Wings sticker remained intact on the bumper. He recognized the petroleum fire's feathery black loop around truck, like the burn-in of a crash-landed angel.

The rain thickened again. Chilled, Tyce pulled the poncho hood over, peering down the road to its vanishing point beyond the distant piles of his faceless kills. He never saw the Hajjis faces, either. Wondering about the fourth man and his own exposure, Tyce back-stepped behind the wreck and cement barriers. After dark Tyce would return to search the men and drain the unexploded can. He was certain more would come.

A moist golden leaf fell away from his poncho. It was the best custom camouflage any phony sniper could want. Six-year-old Sandra Rose had gathered fresh leaves and helped Lorna and her mother attach them to Tyce's olive drab poncho with art-class spray glue. She wanted to help make him 'invidible'. Sweetest kid. He'd saved some peanut butter cups to give her but he couldn't.

Allergies.

A few days ago, one of the women in Cricklewood Green - Joyce - asked him how he was doing. It depended. Young Sergeant Tyce - E-5, clear eyed and 22, Akido-fit, (Ch)Airborne, Expert in rifle - felt squared away. Tyce the cramping, creaking 51-year-old ex-reservist? The homeless LifeForce Security guard? That guy was fucked.

***

Labor Day – September 4th

Even though it was a put-on, a flipped bird to the assholes across the pond, barefoot Ray Dudek's heart swelled as he pulled the blue-on-white United Auto Workers colors up the flagpole. A thing unexpected when the warm breeze snapped the flag stiff. He felt pride. Ray had marched in the Woodward Labor Day parade a few times. Well, once anyway. The aches constantly zapping his 67-year-old body didn't rate questions anymore, but pride took a moment to recognize. Ray rang the cable cord against the aluminum pole in a kind of benediction. It echoed over the water and morning quiet.

UAW. Labor Day. Anymore - tubes clogged, hinges replaced, legs gone bony in his baggy grey shorts - Ray never thought about the line. But today in his cool shade piece of backyard the last punch-out, nearly 20 years ago, came back to him. It had been the Friday before Labor Day weekend. Four of the old guard at Sterling – Ray, Burke, Sarnowski and Pruitt – conspired to take their Screw You final shift together. They snuck hits of Pruitt's Wild Turkey all morning, then the surprise lunchroom goof of shrimp cocktail brought out by one of the ladies from upstairs. A few of the younger people hung around while the old farts joked and tossed tales around the green plastic wheel of meat. Grubby fingers digging the pinkish sprouts into the sauce. One last time, running down all the long-gone pricks and fools, the hangovers and accidents. Nubs - remember him?

Looking up at the flag, another memory overcame Ray. The way some weird thing fucked up a nice dream, waking you up wrong. Wrong the rest of the day. Ray remembered Mickey's face – McWilliams was his name. He pictured Mickey's shaved head glinting under the shop overheads, standing too close.

"The museum of natural history," Mickey said, taking a piece of shrimp for himself. "No more of your shitty music. No more 'Brown Eyed Girl'."

Mickey chewed, eyes on the four clustered in front of the Pepsi machine. Mickey glanced backward at the indifferent younger men and women sipping and eating. "The dying breed. No more free Viagra. Or do you guys use them pumps?"

The harshness in Mickey's goggled eyes was vivid. Bits of white meat and red sauce on his lips and beard. His tattooed hand smeared it off.

It was no secret. Everyone at the plant who had to show up on Tuesday knew what the four men were walking with. Buy Out. The last of the Detroit Buy-American, Solidarity 1970s, Better Idea, Good-Old-Days money. The auto layoffs and collapse were well underway by then. For the Tuesdays, there would be no shrimp. Before the four men split away for their cars that evening they made plans. All four knew they were lying as they made them. Ray had not talked to any of the three since.

For a few seconds the memory was sweet. Now the damn face was going to stay in his head the rest of the day. Anymore, the bad shit just came and stayed. At night in his dreams, Ray was afraid. Clumsy.

Ray's attention moved over the pond to the big homes and long backyards. The brown, sponge-looking rocks around the pole ouched Ray's feet into a hot-step to the paver walkway. Wincing, he followed it down to the water. The spread rock, gravel, stacked stone and paver bricks were Sherri's idea. All that Southwest jive. She'd plant cactus if she could. The sun cast a brassy shimmer on the pond. This time of morning Ray still missed the Luckies. Nothing like the first cigarette of the day.

About 1,000 feet across and half-mile long, the teardrop man-dug pond, fatter at its north, was the center of Cricklewood Green. No more than four feet deep, its three-legged donut fountain at the middle kept a constant spray to snuff the algae and mosquito eggs. Ripples lapped at the edge and Ray's toes. Twenty homes on twenty-one lots ringed the pond, house fronts outfacing the blacktop loop. Many of the former state land's old-growth trees dotted the backyards. Most everyone had decks, some timber-rail fences, a few little gazebo things. The landscaped bushes and natural trees bordering the huge yards made things pretty private.

One Jimmy Buffet-type joker, farther down by the tennis court and pool – Buziki? Bruzny? The one with the big-mouth wife and flakey daughter – had laid out a big patch of sand. Like it was a beach, with his picnic table and umbrella. Most of the back lawns were putting-green jobs, spritzed by the wives' gardens. Distant plots of creeping purple, squared off packs of red, orange and so on. Even the vacant homes were kept groomed by the association - Sanders, Hapgood and the other douche-bags. They weren't happy about Sherri's rocks. Screw them and their association and their "erosion". Erode this.

The flag-snapping wind from the south. Forecast of another hot one, high of 91. Labor Day. In the last of his east-side lot's retreating shade, Ray squatted at the water's edge and rim of rock garden, looking for some imperfections. He saw none. Let it erode. It was his yard. Sanders' anti-union crack last week was too much. Thurston Howell motherfucker. Ray ordered the UAW flag that night. His ear keyed in to the fountain's hiss, like endlessly frying bacon. Another thing Ray missed.

Ray opened the back-deck's slider, entering the cushion of central air. Acoustic guitar strummed on the satellite radio. Sherri sat at the granite kitchen island in front of her laptop, still in her orange and black silk robe.

"Did you see it?"

"Do you want me to make you anything?" Sherri looked up. "Wipe your feet."

"No." The coarse mat scrubbed his soles.

Ray heard her typing as he went to the sink. He pumped the soap, washing his hands.

"I'll have some fruit, I guess."

Sherri pulled her robe closed, walking to the stainless refrigerator. The laptop binged.

"Type your daughter and say I'll talk to her later."

Ray stood at the island, mashing and rolling the paper towel in his grip, squinting at the screen. "I don't do this text thing."

"You knew how to order your damned flag."

"That's different."

"It's $35."

"Not even."

"Right. $34.50."

He watched her wash the pear, peach and melon and retrieve the cutting board. The cupboard slammed. The computer binged again.

"Just type – 'talk later'. Please, Raymond."

Ray's fingers pecked the message, sending. Easing onto a stool he grimaced at the icy sting of his sciatic nerve.

"How is she?"

"Well the school's not going to admit Malcolm until he gets the shots. I'm sick of hearing about it. Just like Mark. No matter what you say they have a reason why you're wrong. What she wants is for me to tell her she's right."

"She's always been that way, Sherri. There's gotta be an answer. A reason for everything." Ray said. "Did Mark say when he's coming back?"

"I expect today. I do believe at one of his friends is working." When Sherri was irritated a Southern exactness barbed her specch.

She slid the plate to him. "Here. Did you take your pills already?"

"Yeah. Where did Mark get the money to go?"

"I don't know. I don't care. I presume it was a cheap trip. He took some hamburger, some eggs. Guns, of course. I didn't pay much attention." Sherri Mullins stood back against the sink. Ray smirked, admiring her luminous blue eyes and plump form. Crossed arms bearing up her still-great tits. Sixty-three and Goddamn Sam. Sherri's shortish hair was mussed, dyed a soft red with a shock bang of white grey. Their sunrise sex had been powerful but abrupt. They were lying there, talking, when she rose up quick and without a word, leaving the room in a swooping trail of sunbeam, silk black and orange. Ray had sat up, swung his legs over and scratched. He wondered what he might have said. After nearly seven years together, he was still falling through trap doors.

His daughter, Colleen, talked to Sherri a few times a week. Ray was glad for the link to his daughter. Malcolm was a newborn when Colleen and that husband of hers moved to Sacramento. The new little girl was probably almost four. Way back when, Ray's wife's cancer left him and his two teens without a translator/referee. Mark and Colleen each took off after high school, an unconfessed relief. Phone calls around Christmas, sometimes Ray's birthday. Sherri bridged something with Colleen.

Mark was something else. Always was.

Mark arrived four months ago, laid-off and broke, only weeks after Ray and Sherri moved in to Cricklewood Green. Neither said it, but the 34-year-old hadn't been missed since Friday. Mark's absence gave Ray an unclenched awareness of his own home. Rooms felt different. Even sex had a renewed, freer, louder twist.

Over the last two days Ray thought on his and Sherri's years together in Nashville, before he talked her into the great bargain of Cricklewood Green. Ray swallowed some melon, eyes averting to the lap top when its swirling pattern went black.

"Hannah and Joyce invited us to their house tonight for drinks. They're having a get-together."

"Huh?" Ray looked up at her.

"Hannah. And Joyce. They've invited us over."

"The lady doctor?"

"Yes."

"The dykes?"

He knew by her pause, the deep sniff. One foot was already in it.

"Yes, Raymond. The dykes."

"Who's all gonna be there?"

"I don't know. I'm going. You're invited." She walked away as he was about to ask for a fresh coffee.

Hearing her ascend the stairs, Ray finished the pear. He wondered if Sanders had seen the flag yet.

*****

Her idea, the squat-ceilinged attic/office was walled and carpeted in glossy, asylum white. Sanitarium white. Four small, square windows centered each side. The pillbox apertures could not open, but with the NASA binoculars Robert Sanders could survey along the black shingle and red tile rooftops, to the pond and opposite side's backyard trees, to the spoking driveways and ring of blacktop, into the deep layer of trees and undergrowth hiding the development's wall. From his western view the carpet of treetop horizon flattened as three shades of green. He resisted the urge to get up from the keyboard and look. It was too early.

   He glanced up again, over his shoulder. Though it brightened the cell to livability, the skylight bubble irritated Sanders. Until recently, he'd never understood the abstract cliché. *Did you ever feel like you were being watched? By what? By whom?*

   Now he knew.

   Sanders spent his mornings here at the machine, appointment-style, coffee, corresponding, researching, reaching out, keeping up. At 61, his nascent engineering "consultancy" rarely paid. Mostly it was volleying the possibility. Currently he was begging a contract for the concern of an Ohio township's sewer expansion. Exhaling, Sanders removed his glasses to blur the screen. The township supervisor's Friday e-mail had a barely coherent, collegiate informality. It flamed Sanders up the neck. Pitted against other men for the work, Sanders had already bent on the request to scale down his fee and analysis. He suspected the township body would pay him to sign off on the plans unseen. Whatever would sell the bonds. Sanders' finger deleted his curt reply, but he felt better having typed it. He imagined an office of countrified bureaucrats. His finger blowing the whole thing up.

   Metaphor.

   For a man not inclined to metaphor, Sanders felt as of late, distastefully, he was slipping wholly back into adolescence. To Sanders the Engineer, books were historical accounts and technical manuals. His television practical news or silently-suffered cooking programs when attempting closeness with his wife, Barbara. Within the last month, perhaps longer, metaphor propelled his mind with gibberish. Comparison and fantasy. Blowing the whole thing up.

To "consult", Sanders the Engineer was now Sanders the Brand. His logic and devotion to his trade had seemingly betrayed him. He loved physics, numbers and engineering for their truth. Four thousand pounds of pressure is nothing else. Thirty feet is thirty feet. Correct and error. But now the words truth and lie inverted. Sanders the Brand had to sell himself. Underneath their metaphors, they would ask why they should buy. Sanders could not tell them. The cheerful "advice" books Barbara left on his desk were disposed of without mention, the same way they arrived. Sanders attempted to read one. Its suggestions akin to cult indoctrination ("look at your face in the mirror and write five positive adjectives that come to mind") and as logical as Sanders becoming a rock musician.

He re-hooked his glasses and clicked to the chess page. Of the two games, the match against CaptWill88 from Houston was progressing the most in Sanders' favor. Sanders' gambit with his knight paid off, isolating the man's bishop. CaptWill88 had lost control of the center and typed a compliment. The match against ArthurPD was a matter of time, but Sanders refused to resign. Arthur was a fine player, a rank higher, and Sanders appreciated the chance to learn. Sanders moved his knight left, threatening a pawn. Arthur was not on-line this morning. It would keep.

With a glance at the clock, Sanders wheeled back from the monitor, picking up the NASA binoculars. Going to the east window, metaphor piled on, calling back from his youth. Prisoner in the tower. Monte Cristo and no tunnel. Rapunzel. Field glasses to the eyes like General Patton. *You magnificent bastard.*

Labor Day. A holiday. Of course, she slept late.

If anyone ever asked, Sanders would have said the most appealing feature of this view was the expanse of sky. Thin, high and fast clouds today, before endless blue. The woods and trees and the green he could take or leave. A Jersey City kid, nature meant nothing to him. His favorite time and place of residence had been the inland San Diego area. McDonnell-Douglas and Ford Motor Company. (Not "Ford". Ford Motor Company). He appreciated the order and space of the near-desert. His wife did not. She had vacationed in Michigan as a child. Her reverie for it sent Sanders into the flypaper of his present.

He moved to the south window, abutting the stairway door. He could see Cricklewood Green's gate and the security guard's building. Off to the right the pool, tennis court and the community room. To Sanders' left the single road from the gate went north 130 yards before splitting at a cluster of high hardwoods, becoming the blacktop loop belting the homes and pond.

Stepping back to the desk, Sanders felt the cup's coldness, setting it down. CaptWill88's move chimed but Sanders could not sit. He went to the south window again. Nothing. Then turning and stepping to the north aperture, binoculars following the road. Nothing. At the east window a fluttering white and blue flag caught his eye before the jolt. He focused, tracking left. It was primal. The urge to call out torn apart in his throat, second-guessed.

She had broken pattern. Running north on the east side, she was nearly around the top of the pond. She always started on the west side, her home, and *then* she went north. Always! Sanders would watch her same warm-up, the exact same, every morning. He could watch her approach up the west road for at least 15 seconds. Her young body coltish but supple, breasts pneumatic, cored in muscle. A body yearning to be touched – explored and pleased to a singing reaction – in the same way an arrow's form yearned to fly. He followed from window to window as she rounded the top of the loop, losing the picture only in the tightest pockets of treetop and roof. Finally she ran out the gate, past the wall, into the three shades of green.

East today! Why? The...wrongness...seized him even as he took in her impossible legs, buns like rubber balls in the red shorts. The frustration wouldn't cease. Aware of his foolishness, Sanders was positive he had missed something life changing in the lost minute.

******

Her mouth had stopped but Lorna Brusine's brain kept sirening. *Shutup!Shutup!Shutup!Shutup!*

Behind Lorna the front door boomed shut, cringe-freezing her in the driveway. She peeked backward in terror of her mother maybe charging after her, full Italian with a knife.

Clutching her water bottle, Lorna pressed the bend of her wrists to her temples, eyes closed, trying to stop the storm. She needed to pattern and everything was wrong. Beyond wrong. Water first, then stretches, then water again, then check the songs. Now, FUCK! *Shutup!Shutup!* It was like trying to cook in the dark. Pieces. Fucking bitch did it on purpose. Today of all days. Of course, she did.

At the end of the driveway Lorna counted. Counting, bending, stretching, trying to pattern. Drink of water. Count. Pushing against the mailbox post her muscles aroused like razor-stropped leather. Lorna breathed in the sweet, molty azaleas at her feet. Pink. Pink and her black Chucks, tied tight.

Counting, eyes shut, Lorna filled her lungs. She reached to the phone strapped around her left bicep, starting Patti Smith's voice in her earbuds. Lorna stood straight, nodding, legs and lungs finding it. Step-step…step-step…. click click, click click, catching the song's rhythm with her heart and feet.

Exhale.

Open.

Look to the right. Look to the left.

Yes. Left. A new pattern. Her brain didn't rebel. Maybe the Nemerthin was working, with all the adrenaline and screaming and bullshit? Like a shock therapy.

Change it. *Go!*

Running this direction, Lorna fresh-noticed the tree trunks, thicket grass and leafy stick overgrowth on her right side. Hide the walls from them. They loved the wall – why else would you live inside it – but who wants to look at it? Otherwise one day you'd be yelling at the gardener or you'd walk into your sterile un-used front room with the ugly, unsittable chairs, look out the window and wonder why you were such a dried up, old, unhappy bitch. And then you'd see the pinkish/orange stone wall and feel like a prisoner.

Lorna passed the fenced pool and red brick clubhouse. The tennis courts were further back by the corner, separated by vast lawn no one ever used. Somewhere on a cached website or in boxed brochures there had to be families frolicking and flying kites on it. Lorna could imagine her mother charmed by the pictures and wearing down her father. Her master-plan investment. *"You're forgetting it's MY money, Jerry."*

Breathe…stride…breathe…stride. Good song - *Hey Joe, where you going? I shot her. I shot her.* Her best friend Hailey loved cool music, playing Hannah tons of weird old songs from her Grandpa and Dad. Stuff you could really ride when you ran. Hailey and Staci texted Lorna last night. Classes starting Tuesday. Tomorrow. The new roommate, Jess, was cool but the apartment wasn't the same. It wouldn't be the same. *Miss you, L.* After she posted the news in July, Lorna had to take her page down. Everyone's messages too grim, as if quitting college was dying of cancer in prison on Mars.

No, no. Stop it. Keep going. Breathe, stride. Ride it. Go. The sweat. Good sweat.

Coming on her left was the V-wedge split of the entrance road and half-dozen high trees, the pond glow-dancing between dark columns of trunk. There were squirrels in the wedge last summer, zipping around in the dirt and dogshit. Driving toward the wedge trees was the first thing Lorna remembered about moving in. A roasting hot day and there were all these squirrels. Lorna thought the pond was real for a second until she saw the ugly fountain. She remembered imagining the squirrels were robots, part of the presentation, like the asylum in the Ellexxa Future books. In autumn someone poisoned all the squirrels. Probably Hapgood, her mother said. Her mother collected enemies and Hapgood, the association guy, was a fresh coin at the time. Her mother acted upset but wasn't, really. No one cared about the squirrels, but it was a chance to argue. People in this place loved to argue. Too bad animals couldn't catch V-14. There'd be no blame.

This was weird. She was staying angry.

At the split Lorna veered left/north, head swiveling right, on instinct for traffic. She glimpsed the black iron-bar entrance gate and the security guard building everybody called the Barracks. Nothing coming.

The song ended,. New music rising in level and throb - The Make-Up. She matched the pace, sniffing with the kick rhythm on the exhale.

The blacktop felt soft under her feet, cool burn coming on, tightening her ribs.

Two vacant homes passed on her left, For Sale signs since last Labor Day, maybe longer. The houses were next to The Grave - the empty lot. Her Dad said the house was leveled and grassed over after the family in it died of V-14. A professor of Lorna's believed theories of the V-14 virus lying dormant in homes were floated to boost the construction and real estate business. *We must build new. The old houses will kill you.*

Hannah and Joyce had guests. An SUV with New York plates in their driveway behind Hannah's blue Saab. Passing the streetlight pole, Lorna saw Hannah hosing the flowers in front of the porch, pink ballcap over her short, silverish hair. Lorna's face snapped forward, but it was too late. Hannah knew Lorna saw her, a wave meant to call her over. She kept going, pretending. Hannah and Joyce were cool. They were the only ones Lorna knew besides the Narlows. Lorna had gone running with Hannah a few times, but it was too many rules - stretch this way, pace this way. To

Hannah running was medicine, not dreams. Kept times and judgment.

When Kim Narlow found out Lorna wasn't leaving for school the sighed pity was mondo phony. The real goods – babysitter down the block! – Kim expressed through their daughter. *"Guess what Sandra Rose? You can still see Miss Lorna now! Isn't that wonderful?!"* Passing their house, she glanced over for Sandra Rose, hoping to see her dancing up in a window or stomping in the blow-up pool, but the white two-level was as tight and dark as the vacants. The Make-Up song ended and surged into Carnosaur. Big drum thrash, third gear. The tingling spidered across her back. Exhale on the fourth beat. Fight the ache. Lorna kicked up the pace, reaching.

She was getting close. All the mental fuzz-buzz freezing, breaking off her with the expanding pain. The good part would be there. Always.

Another quarter mile and she passed though the fatigue, when the top of the road bent south. Sunlight through the leaves pulsed on her eyes. Free to cruise and coast, beyond it all, she ran on. Orgasms were close, but just a peek of it. This was it. Her thumb reset the music. Drifting, soundtrack stuff. Classical. For dreams.

At the gate she had to recede a little, stomping in place until it rolled open. To move it along her head snapped right, seeing one of the guards standing in the glass doorway of the Barracks. She recognized him from the bar. Steve. Nice smile. When she served his beers he would look away as she challenged him to hold it. Always alone, he pretended not to know her, paying and thanking in nods. At least he wasn't one of those who wore the black T-shirts with predatory animals on them – eagles, wolves, bears. Now in cop mode, thumb hooked in his gun belt, Steve held firm, watching her. The mustache actually kind of worked on him. As it ground open, the gate's bars and Steve's night-blue uniform broke her dream. Labor Day weekend had been the start of the Jackpot killings. Six years ago? Yeah. Labor Day, for sure.

Lorna ran out, tapping the volume higher. Over the bumpy dirt drive, past the trees and tangle she hung to the right, out and down the blacktop slope the mile to Orton Road.

Jackpot. It flushed through her cleared mood like squid's ink. The killings happened nearby - Lake Orion, Grand Blanc. Three different families, eight people dead. Holiday deaths. Labor Day. Halloween, Christmas. Named later for the leader, a mutant named Jackpot Armstrong, and his pals, one guy and three teen girls. Seriously, he had the actual Florida birth certificate name of Jackpot Armstrong. Clean and pretty monsters, they dressed and acted like Bible Study kids. Clapping and singing as they drove around in a white van on their mission. Cops even let them go once. In court they had no memories of the killings. Their other personalities committed them, evil possession.

Six months of anxiety, worse each time, like a bad tooth. The Labor Day crime scene photos got leaked to millions of views. The pictures were intense – the Bohen's bodies arranged at the dinner table, blood figure painting and crypto riddles on the walls. For a whole week everyone tweeted and texted. Then nothing. Then the mutilated Indian couple on Halloween – news tweet text. On Valentine's Day a girl's body was found, less than a mile from where she was running right now. 'Manson' you heard a lot from older people. Some maniac from 50 years ago. Somehow, everything was 'better' 50 years ago, even the maniacs.

Now Lorna was bonded to it. The killings and the Valentine's Day girl were Cricklewood Green's spine and reason for living, reason for sucking. Her mother knew the third foreclosure, fire-sale bail-out developers who finished the place. The wall, the cameras, the Barracks. Security was touted instead of next-frontier luxury. Cheap, too. It bonded all of them here. Arguing, frightened and cheap.

The Brusine house? Check.

She ran on. In the pinched edge of Lorna's vision, surrounding trees became a vast, fluttering corridor of green she felt wrapping behind her and collapsing. Enveloped, all was blank behind her. The ink cleared.

Down at the road X, peaked, her legs stopped. In the intersection, Lorna absently circled, head down in the bright hot, wiping. She offed the music and the clashing, grinding whiz of the insects seemed woven into the row of power poles, the high wild grass and warped wire fence. The north/south asphalt of Orton Road and the west-bound two-lane, toward more woods and Essex, wavered to an overheated mirage blur. The smile came to her. The sensation was good. She had run out of herself.

She trotted back up the incline, maintaining, past the billboard for Cricklewood Green. Upscale Homes for Sale. "*Return to You.*" 24-hour guard-gated enclave.

At the top Lorna waved at the gate camera. Wondering if she were the only pedestrian whoever did it, Lorna walked past the waist-high concrete barriers on each side of the lane. Steve was not at the glass.

Slow-stepping up the road, going left, Lorna's dwindling bask evaporated. The dread pushing. Welcome back. The pills, running. All of it useless. Each time, Lorna kind of believed this was the one. Maybe she could hold on to the peace. But as soon as the dream was gone, it was gone. Patterns, storms. You couldn't be free until you did it again.

Once, at school, Lorna was stupid enough to snort a line of Pink T after some weed edible and got badly fucked up, in terror she'd never come down. Hailey was her saint that night, hushing, hugging and rocking her, over and over. "It's only the drugs, Lorna. It'll all be over. It's only the drugs. It'll all be over."

What if it *was* only the drugs? Her brain was this defect, busted mirror you could patch with Cerestine or Nemerthin - for a while. *And BTW? You're nuts, Lorna, but all these other people aren't.*

A thick burn splatted up Lorna's throat, like a lizard's fly-catch tongue. At the driveway she stopped, hands to hips, head down. Return to You. Drips down her back and face. Mailbox. Post. Azaleas.

Pink and black.

****

None of Steve Dominski's choices satisfied. Not even Lorna, bouncing in place thirty feet away. To turn from the glass door would mean watching Mandel jerk off on his phone. Not actually jerk off, but that probably happened, too. Steve could have watched the camera monitors. Technically his job but, technically, eye-fry, brain-fry, no thanks. It wasn't Steve's nature to think past a job, but today they were someone else's choices. As if he wasn't supposed to be in this spot, this place. Someone was in his seat on a jet, flying somewhere. Worse yet, the seat was empty.

Steve got the glance from her and double-clicked the gate command. In the Highwayman, Lorna barely spoke while majoring in communication. Green eyes, dark long hair, lips, hips and left arm full-sleeve tats - double daring. The Highwayman five-night regulars came and stayed for her bar-length prowl. Lorna wiping the wood and digging bottles from the ice, knife-drawing the church key from her jean's back pocket, popping tops, collecting silver. Lorna seemed to treat them like a zoo experiment, dropping winks and quips, testing how long and how much could be drawn from the pack. Steve guessed going through life with every guy wanting to fuck you had to be kind of weird, so why not? He wondered why she wasn't back up at college already. Well past it at 33, Steve still related to the seasons like school; excited for spring, a little down for Labor Day. Lost chances.

He pushed back from the glass door, feeling the gate's rumble through the thick pane. There was no sign on the entry door. Not Cricklewood Green, LifeForce Security or the address. It could have been a laundromat, excepting the windowless, brick-over-concrete superstructure. Bunker fit better than Barracks, but that's what everyone called it.

Security was on Steve's mind, since last night's news feature on Channel Seven. Five years after the Jackpot murders. Steve had not thought of the girl in a long time. In the dark, on his couch, drinking the last swirl of his last beer before bed, Steve wondered why no one ever interviewed him. First officer. He wouldn't have said yes. But, still…

"Do you ever think about this door, Garrett?"

Mandel was leaning back behind one of the two desks, as best he could in the short chair, working the thumbs. In his early twenties, Garrett Mandel was custard-pale, liquid blue eyes and sharp limbs. A sparse downy mustache, unfertilized and unloved. His expression was usually struck, as if the world perpetually shouted "Hey! You!" to his turned back. Peltier called him Cousin, certain a blood relative's pull was Mandel's sole qualification for LifeForce. Steve knew a cousin of Mandel's. Garrett and his cousin Jody were from up in Gavin, the bigger town to the northwest. In high school, Jody had driven his car off a creek bridge near Essex one Saturday night, returning soaked but unscathed to the bonfire party. From then on everyone called it Jody's Bridge. Whomever greased Mandel into LifeForce, it wasn't Jody.

"What?"

Mandel's short-sleeve uniform shirt drooped around his skinny arms, the bottom of a tribal tattoo showing like a lizard's fly-catch tongue.

"Did you ever think about this door? It's just a pane of glass. These thick-ass walls and a glass door. Who planned this?"

"Whattaya mean?"

"It's not very secure. Everything else in this place is planned. Who chose glass?"

"I don't know. Cuz' someone's always supposed to be here," he said, looking at the panel of sunlight framing Steve. "They'd have to know what we got in here. Try it and your ass'll get shot. Would you?"

Steve didn't answer. Mandel was back into his phone.

Much about the job didn't add up if you pulled at threads. The Cricklewood Green contract guaranteed three guards on post at all times. Two men to respond to calls inside the wall, leaving one guy on camera and radio (behind the super-safe glass door). But the guards were first obliged to call the Sheriff's office in Gavin before a response. See intruder, call Sheriff, then chase/cuff/shoot. When Steve was an Essex cop he could hammer it from Cedar Street and be up to this area, six odd miles away, in four minutes. The Sheriff's office patrolled Essex now and always had a car near town. So, three guys? You get a domestic up here and they're gonna call the Barracks? They'll call the Sheriff. Then you'd have to deal with that. *Hey, Dominski. Didn't you used to....?*

No one was crashing that gate without a tank. No baby-eating monsters were creeping miles through swamp wood ravines to climb a thirty-foot wall. And if they did, most residents were armed. Jackpot was freak past. It wouldn't happen that way again.

But LifeForce was a job. Yes, sir. Glad to do it. Three men sounds correct to me.

Steve passed through the kitchen area, turning left, back past the holding cell, to the bathroom & shower. After Essex went into the breadline, the state disbanded its six-man police force. Steve tried going back into his father's construction business, but it was bad all over again. Uneven levels, frays and flush the goddamn screws already, dumb ass. His brothers picked open buried embarrassments during breaks. When the crew - guys younger than Steve - started coining nicknames for him those LifeForce Security commercials came in loud and clear. Essex didn't even have a firehouse anymore. Call Gavin. Call the township.

Having passed his bonded LifeForce assignments down in Kalamazoo and Wyandotte on great evals, Steve was now Corporal, cherry-posted in Cricklewood Green, ten minutes from where he grew up. One night, years ago, Bob Hernden told him something from behind the cruiser's grid.

"Crime and punishment, officer. Good money in those," he said after a belch. "Stick with either one and you'll never starve." Then he threw up all over the back seat.

Now Steve was Senior Officer on post today. Labor Day.

Who says bad habits don't grow wisdom?

Steve washed up and exited the john with its single shower. The holding cell next to it had been used only once to Steve's knowledge, in a midnight photo session (The fired guard's girlfriend had a website). Steve followed the hall on a long right, though he could have quick-turned right into the office area with Mandel, the desks and the camera station. In the hall leading to the kitchen area, the HVAC/water heater/power room and supply/gun walk-in were on Steve's left. Its steel door sealed airtight and a satellite phone was among the goodies inside. Two Kevlar vests. A Remington shotgun, desert-war surplus M-4 rifle and extra .40 ammunition were locked in a safe separate from the shelved paper, hand-radio rack, Culligan jugs, office and bathroom supplies, snow shovel, rock-salt bag and cornered mop bucket. He passed into the kitchen/break room. Crowded by the refrigerator, wall-hung TV and round table, the space was an ass-bumper for more than three people. Cracking a can of soda, Steve clicked the TV for some noise. A few flips and he stopped on an old Eastwood western, watching a minute of trumpets and chimes before setting the remote on the table, leaving the sweaty Mexican to die in the sand.

"You do anything good over the weekend?"

Mandel's face lifted. "Sheeit. I thought my Moms was crazy. But my Nans is just as nuts, dude."

"What happened?"

"I don't know." Mandel sat forward, setting the phone on the desk. "You remember me telling you how my Grandpa died? Well a couple months ago they finally sold the cottage and the boat and shit. And my Grandpa wanted to make sure his kids all got the money from it. Just them, and that's cool. So, my Moms and my aunt and uncle all got a buncha money. And my Moms. Man."

Mandel's head shook out a bad taste.

"She's just been pissing up her cash on bullshit. Stupid shit. My brother told her. I told her. It's not like she should have a TV show but, like, she's sick with it. I swear. Last week I go there. UPS. She bought a fucking cotton candy maker. Yeah. Would you even know where to buy one? There she is on the computer, all day. She bought this electronic… fuckin'…toy robot dog that barks and rolls over. She's got a fuckin' *real* dog. Cotton candy. I can't think of her ever buying us cotton candy."

"Man, Garrett. That sucks."

"I know. It's her money. But, she's gotta save. And it's like, we're telling her, *'you gotta lay off it. You gotta go out. Leave the house. The flu's all over with. It's OK.'* But then like a week ago I called my Nans and told what I thought about it, right? Like, she should say something. In a nice way. Then the other day Nans messages everybody. My Moms, aunt, uncle, me. Everybody. Come to the house on Saturday. We're having a cook-out. She wants to tell us something. But it's cool. Up front she says it's not medical, nothing to worry. I figure, cool. We're gonna clear it up with everybody there. Come to Jesus for my Mom and all that.

"We all drive to the lake, get there and my Grandma - Nans… she's got this fuckin' boyfriend she wants everybody to meet. This spook named Darius. Smiling in his white shirt and suit jacket. Shakin' everybody's hand. Knows all our names. My brother. *'So, you're a big rig driver, I hear'.* You believe that?"

"Who is he?"

"Says he's a professor. Flew here from fuckin' *Baltimore*." Mandel's thumb jerked left. "She met him on the internet. My Nans is 68, dude. Crazy."

"Is he younger than her?"

"I don't care if he's black. Straight up. I wouldn't trust him if he looked spittin' image of my Grandpa. She met this fucker, like, in, January? And they're going to Punta Cana for two weeks. Wherever that is."

"Puerto Rico, I think. You think he's lying?"

"I think he's a professor of slinging bullshit. She's 68. And she ain't rich but, she ain't poor. Know what I'm sayin'?"

Steve drank. "Did he fly up on his own?"

"Oh, he looked and talked all proper. But what else would you do if you were a con man? Right?"

"Maybe it's OK. Maybe they like each other."

Mandel lipped his disgust.

"What did everyone else say?"

"My Moms loved him. Of course. *'Oh, so where do you teach? Where you from?'*. And he's got snacks laid out. And he's grillin' for everybody. *'Would you like some more wine, Evelyn?'*. My uncle knew what was up, but the rest of 'em? Me and my uncle were polite but if he thinks he's movin' in he's got another thing comin'." Mandel's head wagged, chin out in a step-off mug.

"Did you check him out?"

"Oh, he's on a site. Looks like a college site. Says he's got a book. Shit, I can build a web page. I can build a page for a book. Fake articles. Guys like this, they go all around the country scammin' old ladies."

The gate beeped Steve to the console. Lorna again, waving to be let in. Behind him Mandel had walked to the kitchen. Steve stood in the archway, watching Mandel fill a cup of Culligan, the fat jug gurgling.

"I'll tell you one thing you're lucky for," Steve said. "At least your grandmother's taking care of herself. My Mom and Dad had to put my grandmother in Swistak. Just the smell in the lobby would give you nightmares."

Mandel drank, dulled eyes orbiting to the TV. "Nah. My Nan's is the ass-kicker. But my Mom will end up like that. Betcha."

"She'll be fine."

Mandel walked back to the desk. "Shoulda went canoeing is what I shoulda done," Mandel said. The surprised expression came back over him, like an ended song, unexpected. Depleted, Mandel thumped back into the chair, reaching for the phone.

Steve sat. The two monitors clicked through a rotation of the 18 cameras and worked by touch screen. You could zoom, pull back or high-res one camera to a single 24-inch screen or let them click in blocks of 2, 4 or 6. When Steve sat at camera he kept the police-band radio faint or switched off. It was still within his right hand to pick up the mic and respond to calls.

Steve wasn't sure yet about the new guard, Tyce. LifeForce wasn't above transferring a spy and Tyce had a strangeness about him, a fucked-up humor. He kept calling Cricklewood Green '*The Village*' and saying he was '*Number 6*', expecting you to know what he was talking about. Today Steve was thinking less and less Tyce was any kind of spy. He was supposed to clock in at 8 a.m., still absent. A man short.

"Hey, Garrett."

"Yeah?"

"What did Tyce say?"

"I told you, said nothin' He'd be late. That's it. Good day to do it. He knows Peltier ain't coming by on a holiday."

Steve popped around on the screens. Empty yards, sun and wind-waved trees. He wheeled back and stood, staring out the door.

Everyone had to thumbprint in, so Tyce would be fucked on his monthly eval no matter what and he'd only been on post a few weeks. But, still, Tyce was ex-military and Peltier, the district First Sergeant, had been a Marine. A nearly full-blood Chippewa, Peltier was six-foot and V-trunked with small black eyes seeded above acne-pitted cheeks. Peltier's voice soft-wrapped a dry wit and he used both to upset people's balance. What started as a conversation over a shared snack could gently pitch into a dead-eyed reprimand. Or what felt like a cross-armed lecture one afternoon could become the bawdy story of an R&R in Thailand.

Whatever. Peltier would deal. Tyce wouldn't be Steve's problem.

In the kitchen Steve clicked channels until he didn't see them. How nice would it be to have a grilled meal on a deck by a lake? Drink wine with a friendly professor and a family. Talk. Have a nice afternoon.

He was looking forward to telling Peltier about it. Peltier might start calling Mandel 'Grandson'.

Steve slipped the phone from his pocket, tapping, swiping glass for anything new.

****

How *many* times had he been stuck on this highway? In these same circumstances, in a holiday afternoon traffic jam? Mark Dudek could sort of remember them but couldn't really. Harder you try, the blurrier it gets.

From the back seat, Mark Dudek surveyed the profiles in the left lane and then the two scowls in the Nissan behind him. Guy and girl. Shades, sunburn, swigged waters. The passenger girl's bare feet on the dash. Nearly everybody around him was on their phones. What if they were all calling or texting in to report the accident? But there never was one. Crawl and crawl for an hour until the end and there was never anything there. His Dad used to talk about it when Mark was a kid. A long time ago the government used to tell people to head Up North if there was a nuclear attack. Balls, his Dad would say. You ever see people going Up North or coming back on Memorial Day? Fourth of July? Then imagine them running for their lives with everything they had. The Russians wouldn't have to bomb.

"Look at these assholes." His Dad would gesture out the window at the sun-gleamed, inching cars, Lucky Strike in his mouth, eye squinting above the smoke curl. "We'd all kill each other on I-75."

How *many* times had Mark heard that? Next to these very same grass inclines on either side of this ass-to-nose moo parade. How many times had Marked looked on *that* green highway exit sign? It had been going on that long. It reminded him of the Gai-Kwon comic. Where happenings are static and eternal and different people just inhabit them. Like, the traffic jam when he was in second grade was still happening, always happening, just like this one now. You just pass through it. When you leave it, it's over for you. But not over.

Why is memory so fucked? Why do you keep what you keep? Mark could remember the traffic-jam day smelling of car exhaust and his Dad's sweat. Tiger baseball, his mom with a white hankie, patting her forehead. Today the airtight AC cool mixed around the fire-smoke smell in all their clothes with the speaker's whiplash drums and grind. Mark couldn't tell what would imprint. And all for what? None of it helped, all these memories or what would be memories. You keep going through it. Why doesn't anything change? What Mark needed to know or remember was never there. He was the same, then as now...

Timmy's fingers held out a joint from the passenger seat. Mark leaned forward for the pluck, drew deep and placed it back. Reclined on his duffel, he caught stray vowels underneath the music's fury. Darren's stubbly profile jawed, bony arm draped over the wheel. Unable to see Timmy, Mark imagined Darren an insane person, talking to himself.

"Horr...slow...mo. Kno...."

Thinking of the girls' bare feet twisted Mark to the rear window. She and driver dude were both still texting. That's how they'd go nuts in this traffic. Take away the phones. They held people together during V-14. The phones and the net never failed. It was a fact. Service during the flu epidemic was better than any time before or since. Mark knee pressed the passenger seat. Again. The last of the joint came back up in Timmy's hand, just out of reach. Darren wouldn't pass it, wouldn't even look at Mark. He leaned forward again.

Dehydration pressed Mark's skull after he exhaled the smoke. Mark had one warm-ass Dr. Pepper left. No more water. He unscrewed it and drank, butting the roach on his boot bottom and dropping it to the Accord's floorboard. The buzz tingled and Mark's irritation with Darren, Timmy...memory, all flaked away to the coming shower, ice cream. Bed.

He hadn't gotten off in three days, his camo fatigue pants tightening in the slightest anticipation. Mark's beard itched, but the Purple Kush contented him to close his eyes and ignore. He would not come this way again. Fuck 'em both. Maybe it was the end of something, finally.

Timmy's camping invite on Friday morning had elated Mark, excusing him from the sad clown inventory of what he would have to sell to pay his Dad and pay the storage unit on the 15th. His Ruger nine, hopefully not. The Glock nine could go. Definitely the Mossberg 12-gauge could go. Mark's AR and all its Lego parts were already sold off – extra grips, trapdoor stock, the spare upper. All of his .223 ammo with it. Ugh. Mark's unemployment ("Unenjoyment") was gone and there was no way his storage stuff would fit in the house. Sherri would shit a kitten. Even though the weekend away was with Darren, on his land – no, fuck that, his *parent's* land – Mark needed to not see Sherri or his Dad for a few days.

Timmy mooched over to Darren in the past year because Darren could do more for him. After Mark got laid-off, Darren had weed. Darren still had a game system. Darren had beer and new toys, job stories and a girlfriend Timmy prayed – preyed – he could get cute-friend pussy shrapnel from. Things happened to Darren. Mark didn't mind. That was just Timmy.

It was an hour and a half trip up to the spot, 40 acres off the Pine River. Not bad at all. Outhouse. No electricity, but it was quiet. No Ranger Ricks. In the last sliver of Friday's daylight they set up the tents under the soft-bed pines, near the picnic table and well-pump. The talk was easy, after-dusk cracking and dragging the firewood, fuck-muttering through branch snags. The first beers and the jokes were pitched and backhanded like it was the next hour of their last face-time in the spring, before Mark's eviction. They lit the campfire to music, smoke and more beer. Hits from Timmy's bottle of Beam. Then host-boy's toys came out. Darren retrieved it from the trunk, a stainless baby-briefcase looking thing. Those kinds of cases never contained anything good in any movie Mark ever saw.

Powered up on the picnic table, the curved tablet Whelp-T streamed last week's "*LA Madness*" episode in foot-high hologram. Darren made wiggy, faggy gestures with his left hand.

"I feel like a wizard."

Timmy laughed while Darren detailed the magnifying and color adjust features. *See, the curve was the trick to the 360 resolution. But, what's even coolerrrrrrrrrr is....* After ten minutes of ooh-ahh, Mark walked past the fire's aura to cool relief on his face. A three-quarter moon defined the clearing and parked Accord, the moon-whitened trail splitting the woods going north. Polaris up there. You could navigate from it. An owl sounded off. Mark breathed in and smiled. He hoped for another hoot and got it, exhaling.

When Mark returned, Darren and Timmy were seated at the fire, talking of lottery money fantasies and what they would do if. Turning the speaker down, Mark took beer requests. He returned from the cooler with three wet, bottom-cold cans.

"We should write a movie," Mark said, handing them off.

"About what?" Darren said, hand out. "Thanks."

Timmy stood, setting his can next to his canvas chair. "Do a horror movie. Because you can make 'em cheap and they make bank."

Timmy stepped to the edge of the dark and turned his back. The arriving crackle of his stream sounded over the music.

"Only if you want to." Mark sat, wiping his hand on his camo fatigue pants. "It's gotta be a great idea. Something fresh."

"Or time," Timmy called back. "Movies that fuck around with time always work."

"My girlfriend tried doing it. It's insane." Darren's eyes were into the embers, chin tucked. "But you're right. Lightning bolt. That's how it has to be."

"I know. Exactly," Mark said. "She met people though, right?"

"Sort of," Darren said. "But it's like imitation friendship. Those people bullshit for a living. It's like, they're lying to you and they don't even know they're lying to you."

Timmy passed the Jim Beam around before he sat. "But she met the guy who made the zombie movie, though. Didn't she get close to getting something, like a deal?"

"Yeah. And that's the thing." Darren said, although he never said what the thing was. "Everyone watches movies, so everyone thinks they can write one." He drank from the pint and passed it. The fire hissed and popped. "It's life work to do it."

Mark gulped a swallow of whiskey. Boosted by the burn, he perched forward as best he could in the canvas chair, fingers splayed on his calves.

"OK. You tell the story of V-14."

Darren brushed the dark bangs from his eyes, concentrating on the radiant center, serious-like. Mark saw doubt. "OK."

"Take all of the information, the real information, and put it in a connected way. You show the thread of it. I know there's tons of blog stuff and documentaries. People know what they're told. But they haven't seen it. How easy it was. How it all knocks together."

"How does it start?"

"Mexican flu. First cases were in Southern California. Not Mexico. No cases were documented in Mexico until after they were found in New York and Texas and North Carolina on January 11th. All the same day. The first Mexican case wasn't until January 13th. LA was already in the dozens. The whole border lockdown was a show operation. All the raids and the tests were total misdirection. To distract people while the virus spread. Blame the Spics. Keep everybody fighting about bullshit."

Darren shook his head. "No no. How does it start? First scene. What are you showing me?"

"Right, right. OK. The Santa Anas. Santa Ana winds. You had Kip Prevost, that hiker. He saw Army trucks in Diablo Canyon on New Year's

Day night. All the crews in NBC gear and those giant turbine fans he described. They're releasing the virus in the wind. Can't you see it? The trucks driving in the dark. The right music."

"Kip Prevost is the hero?"

"No," Mark said. "It's not that kinda movie."

"No," Timmy said, pointing. "Do it. Then he tries to warn people, going all over. Make him CIA or something. Like, he was on vacation when he saw it."

Mark stood. "No. Show the timeline of the cases. Jump scenes."

"Timeline? Dude," Darren said. "Like you said, there's documentaries everywhere. And, man, Mark, nobody cares about V-14. I had cousin die from it. I'm not saying no, but anybody who lost someone? They're not gonna watch a movie about it."

Picking up a long branch, Mark dug it into the hots, blooming fireflies. "Ok, then. Jamestown."

Timmy chuckled. "I knew that was coming."

No denying. Jamestown had been something. Mark beer-saluted whatever Jamestown needed to be, finishing his can.

Darren's face raised, the color of sunset. Shadow rutted his brow

"Same thing. No matter what side you pick it's a loser. All I'm saying is what I know. You better have a movie star signed to it. The first ten pages we need a hero. In the first twenty pages he'd better meet a girl. By page thirty you have the conflict clear." His wizard hand waved. "First Act. It's what they're going to tell you."

"What do you know?" Mark glared at him. "You've never done it. It was your girl. Not you. And she didn't do it either."

Darren stood, moving away. "Hey, I'm not saying don't do it. Just don't waste your time, is all." Darkness absorbed his shape.

"What you need," Timmy said, "is you pull the right kind of stunt. See, you get famous first."

Spelled into the embers, Mark blink-realized Darren standing next to him. Darren dug a metal cylinder into the slot of a small wooden block. His lighter flamed and he drew in a mighty pull of weed, the cylinder tip glowing.

Darren handed the kit to Mark.

"Tim's right. Jamestown. That Sergeant Gillian. Guy's a multi-millionaire now." Darren said, chokey. He let the cloud go. "You see the bourbon commercial he's in?"

"Fuck him. The flu was just the test," Mark said. He packed the cylinder and lit it.

"Aw, come on, Mark." Timmy's head bobbed around for something close and liquid before realizing the can was tucked in his crotch.

"The run up," Mark said, spitting the smoke. "Don't know about you guys. But I'm gonna fight."

Timmy giggled. "Run up my ass and fight for air."

Darren's laughter echoed off the trees. Mark stabbed more sparks with the branch. "Yep. Fuck the constitution. Whatever. People are used to 'evacuation' camps already."

"When everyone's in the camp who's gonna buy the Pepsi?" Darren said. "The Toyotas, the flat screens. Puppy Chow. Hate to tell you, but money runs the world, dude." Darren walked around the blaze and sunk to his chair, rubbing his face. His eyes flared out against his fatigue. "You got a gas mask?" he said, trying to one-up.

"Yep."

"He does, too," Timmy said.

"Tank? Helicopter?"

"They did alright against 'em in Jamestown." Mark tossed in another log. The poke stick rolled in his grasp, auguring the soft, glowing bed of coals.

"Till they didn't," Timmy said.

"Two hundred and fifty years ago we'd be sitting like this. Some woods in New Hampshire. The British are going to take our rights, tax us. And you guys would have said, '*aww, what are you gonna do about it?*' Your jobs and toys and whatever, but…"

"We're gonna write a play." Darren said. "For the Boston Theater."

Mark met his face. Darren didn't waver.

"Lemme ask you something, Mark," Darren said without stopping. Classroom style. "Say your movie gets made and goes monster. You clear fifty million. What we were talking about before *you* got here."

You was pointed. *You* stung.

"Still gonna live in your parent's basement and give it all to the widows and orphans and grannies? Mark's Flu Fund for the Government Victims? Even a little bit? Bullshit. You wanna get paid. Same as everybody. Don't come off like you're Joe Patriot and I'm some scumbag."

Standing, Timmy swayed. His tossed can hissed on the coals.

"Fuck this static." He stumbled into the dark.

A reply fattened on Mark's tongue and dry-died, forgotten. Dropping the stick onto the fire, Mark walked to the moonlight, weaving on toward the river. Completely cooked, Mark seemed to time slip, uncertain how long he'd been at the water. The moon reflection entranced him. Millions of miles away but ripple-dancing in the exact spot he was standing. The moon guided his zombie-shuffle back to camp and he felt blessed by it, happy alone. Mark unzipped his tent, stripped bare and faded out in a pale X atop his sleeping bag.

******

Kim's suggested invite of Vern Hapgood to dinner was logical, Asian-wise. But Mike Narlow thought his wife's idea was a better second step. Seal the deal. Over a cold-called meal Vern would wait for Mike's performance, Mike tense to give it. Mike had been mainlining Asian Business Strategy for the last fourteen months, three of them in Beijing. Let me be American for once, Mike thought. Blunt and Vern Hapgood. Two matching words. We'll circle, we'll sniff butts. We'll shake. Simple.

Walking the sun-simmered blacktop loop, hands pocketed in his cargo shorts, Mike breathed-in the peace. He passed from humid but cooler domes of big-tree shade to open areas of lawn fairly vibrating with heat, saw-bug rev in the wooded overgrowth. The surrounding katydids and cicadas hijacked his thoughts to the alien, jabbering chaos of China. Mike nodded, smiling. Going back was an easy challenge in the moment. One he could take. He had this. Clean air, clean sky. This was his.

Passing the Vanderkam's house and another for-sale vacant, Mike rounded the north end's soft corner and wide-lane view to the fountain. Getting closer to Vern's house and its giant willow, he could hear loud talk radio in the open garage, glad to be spared the salesman's knock on Vern's door. Passing Vern's Escalade in the driveway, Mike took off his sunglasses entering the epoxy-floored dimness. Vern was seated near the right bay, sandpapering the grey-primer fender of his 1969 Camaro shell. At Vern's age - early 60s probably - Mike doubted it would ever get finished. A strong floor fan atop the washing machine was blowing on the large man's left side. In a white sport shirt unbuttoned to his bulged, river-stone of a belly and long khaki shorts, Vern's broad, bearded profile glanced in Mike's direction, dipping the sandpaper into a bowl of water at his hairy bare feet. He faced his work and continued to rub.

"Hello Mike."

"Hello Vern. How goes it?"

"Not bad. Enjoying your Labor Day?" He looked up quickly in acknowledgment, if not welcome. Mike noticed a half-smoked Macanudo cigar edged atop the washer and a sweaty can of Bud.

"Yeah. Got some sleep. Grilling salmon for the girls later. I'm back to China this week."

"Really? Would you like a beer?"

"Sure."

Vern's mostly bald head remained steady. "Help yourself."

Mike retrieved a can from the cornered fridge, stocked with brew, cans of soda and a whole Honey Baked ham. There was no other food inside it.

"What can I do for you?"

The radio host was denouncing the Federal Reserve.

"Do you know anything about Lathrup Realty?"

"Nothing in the specific, beyond what I know about all realtors." Vern dipped and sanded. "Fragile egos. Mostly sleaze. You have to remember, these are people who have failed at every other endeavor in their life."

"Well, I've looked at the listings here and they all show as under contract. There's no phone number and any emails I send, I never get replies to." Mike said, unpocketing his phone, bringing the page up. "In fact, all of Lathrup's listings except two vacant lots in Kalkaska show as under contract or pending. The listing agent is Greg Sweet?"

"Yes. That's the name on the signs."

Blunt. "Well I'm interested in one of the houses, next to me. 318."

Vern's profile twisted to his right. A parrot-like eye seeking Narlow over his shoulder.

"To move?"

"No. I'm interested in buying and renting it out."

"You'd have to contact Greg Sweet. And, as you may or may not know, renting is against the by-laws of the association. It violates the agreement you signed."

Vern stood up off the stool, splatting the balled sandpaper into a wastebasket.

Mike nodded a beat, feigning consideration before sipping.

"I understand, Vern. But from my end these homes have been vacant for the better part of a year," Mike said. "The last sale was in April? I'm willing to assume the risk. I have confirmed, credit-checked tenants in mind. What do you think?"

"It wouldn't be my decision."

"Well, here's my obstruction, Vern. You head the association. I can't reach Greg Sweet. I can barely find out anything. Lathrup doesn't return any messages. From what I've researched UB Group owns the note on all the vacant homes. All I have for them is a PO Box in New York. I bought from Horizon Group. I thought the property was still Horizon."

"It's not."

"Who owns the paper on this development, Vern?"

 Vern nodded. He picked up his beer.

"It is complicated." Vern exhaled. "As I understand it, the first consortium cut the deal with the township. They lost it in the crash in '09. The second group built most of the homes. They went under on bad paper. There was a third group, but the deal collapsed. I don't know why. Then Horizon bought the development. That's what I was part of. We got it to market."

Mike nodded.

"Horizon to sold to UB Group fourteen months ago."

"Why weren't the homeowners told?"

"You most certainly were, Mike. Everyone was mailed, and emailed, the information. Maybe ask your wife?" Vern guzzled the beer, then wiped his bald dome.

Mike blinked. What was the movie line from '*Scarface*'? *Do I come back in? We start over?*

"Alright. Who do I talk to at UB Group?"

"I report via email. This information will be in your letter, by the way. I've communicated to three different property executives in the last fourteen months. Each of them has been seemingly more inefficient than the last. Once I was at the end of an email chain - when we had to replace the water softener? I've researched, myself. The source of the e-mail pinged back to a server in the Czech Republic. So, to your point, I don't know who UB Group is. You won't get answers from them. They'd most likely direct you to me. But you're free to do what you want."

"OK, Vern. Here I am."

"Yes. And I've told you."

"But UB Group kept you on?"

Vern smirked. "I suppose I'm their Lord Jim."

Mystified like a man arriving at the formal in his boxers, Mike hadn't a notion how to parry that one. *Lord Jim?* A fleeting image of the Doors singer in sweaty leather. Come on baby light my fire. Well, if this wasn't Deep Heet in the KY. Mike Narlow was in China again in a garage in Michigan. The puzzle within the puzzle within. So much for blunt.

"It's not like I'm going to rent to a bunch of spooks and low-lifes, Vern. They're a responsible couple."

Vern trashed his empty can and picked up the cigar.

"I wouldn't think that at all, Mike."

"It's…I get the feeling you know more than you're telling me."

"Yes," Vern said. "Don't you know more than you're telling me?"

Stepping over the workbench area, Mike plucked a blue grease pencil from a jar. He turned over an old receipt and scrawled a number. "What do you think?" Mike said, sliding it over. "Yours for making it happen."

Vern picked up the pencil and jotted a few words.

"What the fuck, Vern?"

The cigar flared above Vern's Zippo flame. "Indeed, Mike. What the fuck? I still have no idea what you want from me."

"I want to buy a house here and rent it out. Period."

"I can't help you. I'm not a realtor. I'm not with Lathrup. I'm not UB Group. I own my home. We're the same." He gestured casually with the hot end. "You seem to want a nepotistic advantage I cannot give you. An advantage that would then allow you to break a by-law you agreed to follow. I don't know Greg Sweet. I've never met the man." Vern puffed.

"He may not exist. It's certainly possible with these kinds of people."

Mike nodded. "Wow. I thought we were friends."

Vern looked away a moment as if adding, weighing. Mike knew Vern made his money in developments, contracts, real estate law. His scarred brow shaded in concentration.

"You're a good neighbor, Mike. We have a good rapport. You have values I admire. I suspect you're good to your family. But people mis-qualify friendship. They use it as an excuse for corruption."

Mike walked toward the daylight. "Whatever you say, Jim."

****

Hannah Sutherland's father didn't necessarily hate Jews. He casually insulted them the way he did everyone. No malice. Just Archie Bunker, two-and-two fact. The Sutherlands didn't know any Jews in Grand Rapids. But, Hannah remembered as a child listening to her father argue late into a summer night with the neighbors. Israel and Syria and Golan and Sadat and Palestine. Her father's Cutty-abrazed shouts in fierce defense of Israel and the Jews. She was so mystified she briefly forgot her anger at being kept awake so long after midnight. *Where did all that come from?* As it got later, the adults in the kitchen got louder. She could smell their cigarettes up in her room. God, how everyone smoked back then.

Understanding none of it at the time, Hannah wondered why her father seemed so upset. She'd never heard him speak these things before, nor again. Finally, when someone turned the radio up, Hannah marched downstairs in her Winnie The Pooh footie pajamas, unplugged Neil Diamond and kicked them all out. It became Family Legend recounted every holiday when things carried on too late. *Everyone quiet down and behave or Hannah will close us down*, her mother would slur with a hug and a sour cheek peck. Now when Hannah listened to people carry on with phony outrage about Them or That, she closed her eyes and whispered

"Israel" for some instant grace, or perhaps instant karma. Hannah ended up marrying a Jew. For the punch line – make it a Jewess. What would Dad have said about that?

Out on the deck tonight, the crowd was debating the Pannasco Supreme Court decision, the legacy of the flu, the problem in Algeria and the coming election. Alone in the kitchen's blipping candlelight, Hannah sipped her wine, watching the gem glints on the bottles, packed atop the granite like shoreline penguins. To her 54-year-old ears it all still sounded the same. But she would not stop the music – halfway into Joni Mitchell's *'Court and Spark'*. The selection was Hannah's sly choice. Tonight was Joyce's time to hold court. And spark? Well, take the Type-A, lanky Midwestern tomboy and pair her with the short, plump, New York wiseass and stand back.

Old money, Joyce Snyder had run a third-world children's health non-profit and Hannah fell in love hearing her at a symposium in Manhattan. Back then, Hannah was a pediatrician toying with abandoning her Michigan practice for UN jungle charity. Her father's recent death, passing 40 and lonely nights had sunk Hannah into a repugnant self-pity. Spark fixed her. Hannah came out as a Michigan State undergrad but had never been in love - charged or challenged by it - during the decade-plus constructing her Self. Whooshed years recalled as a spliced-time dream told to her by a stranger. Then this confident, loud woman with the wild, graying tresses fixed on Hannah from the podium. Those giant Sophia Loren eyeglasses - and those lips. Foregoing privilege, Joyce had held the fly-bitten babies and carried the water, Peace Corps and far more. She had no time for self-indulgence.

"Suffering does not fix narcissism," Joyce said, rebuking a stammering Hannah at the reception, one hand flagging for a Chardonnay. "Then where will you be? Your head and heart better be with those children. Your reasons for being there will mean less than nothing to them or the families. You had better be there 100 percent for no reason at all. Only because it's the right thing to do, and you *have* to do it."

Joyce's turned back rattled Hannah with anger and turned her on like a skyrocket. Before Hannah left she got Joyce's card. The first texts were terse, but Hannah felt the play in them. Two weeks later Hannah was back for a weekend. A month later Hannah was getting her New York State ID, applying for her medical license and they were repainting the bedroom. Hannah's dynamo dream woman could discuss *Anna Karenina* or caulk a bathtub in 20 minutes. Plays and Paris and New York adventures. In Hannah's conscience, the dirty-faced kids were not heard from for another decade, until V-14.

Two close friends died. Three others the couple knew slightly. Hannah was drafted by Presidential Emergency Order #8 and served three months in a Bronx hospital. One peak week in May over 7,000 people died in New York City. With no alternative, barges of body bags were towed to Governor's Island. Joyce held a particular distaste for the way the virus was named - V-14 – like some Nazi *wunderwaffen*. As with the flu of 1918 it primarily killed those 20 to 50. Fathers and mothers, managers and crew chiefs, foremen and head nurses. Worst for Hannah were the fathers and mothers. Devastating.

Some city quarantines lasted weeks. Service apps flourished. Supplies could be ordered, left on locked docks in stores or LifeForce guarded ware-stations, retrieved by coded drivers, paid for by chip card, delivered to doorsteps and sprayed with anti-bacterial before brought inside. Thefts and killings and pocket riots went on, but the End Times never showed. Routine emerged. Many could work, communicate, eat, drink, and suck-in any entertainments they liked and never vacate their box at the top of the stairs.

Except for looting, New York was spared the violent unrest prairie-firing the middle of the country that spring. Thousands of armed heartlanders were certain V-14 was a Government plot. This conviction spread after the first vaccine faltered and 20 percent of the inoculated were still getting sick. V-14 was prematurely declared contained and it briefly got worse because the quarantines and restrictions were loosened. Knowing they were Right, some heartlanders fought when the government and military tried to enforce quarantines or contain fresh cases into camps.

Jamestown happened.

In the area around Jamestown, Tennessee, residents held off the Tennessee National Guard and US Army for 11 days after the town was ordered to be tested and the sick residents relocated. With guns, shape charges, car bombs and other weapons they killed dozens of troops, destroyed tanks and shot down a helicopter and a drone before surrendering. More rebellions spread with varying degrees of lesser success. Law was swift and tidal upon them. In the end, most people wanted to live, unhurt, plot or not.

When the pandemic was declared over, 1.3 million were declared dead in the United States, 20 times that worldwide. No one believed it that low, truly. The shocked numbness lasted for Hannah through the fall. But Joyce saved her once again. The day after Thanksgiving two years ago, they lounged in front of the terrace window. Clouds like layered blue-grey agate crawled over the East River. The women recounted past holidays, snug in their blanket, close skin and warm mugs. Joyce told Hannah later it was an easy decision. Hannah's eyes had animated for the first time in months, she said, when recounting her Michigan childhood.

"Then let's go," Joyce said.

"Maybe we'll do it over the holidays. We could see my brother in Illinois, too."

"No, I mean let's go. The air, trees, house, a yard. The dog you always wanted."

"But, when?"

Joyce picked up her phone, screen dilating to life. "Now. Three bedrooms? An office and then a guest room?"

On March 17th· they moved into Cricklewood Green for the rebirth of Spring. Many other residents moved into the development around the same time. Insanely low prices. Optimism and marble baths. Hope and cherrywood cabinets. Return to You and central air, soapstone, Pergo floors. The Possible and balconies, full finished walkout basements, central vacs, coffered ceilings. At night on their decks, people listened to owls and the white-noise comfort of the fountain, smug behind the gate and unseen wall, the Victorian streetlamps spaced like nightlights. After the flu, people were nicer for a while.

A year later, Joyce was darting resentment at Hannah over being an hour from decent food and the half-speed conversation with the "Huck Finns". Antagonizing the association because she liked the fights, Joyce didn't even *want* the damn fire kettle. But Hannah loved it all. The pond, the birds; walking the state-land trails. The Miniature Pinscher, Max, which Joyce (told her so) adored as well. But Hannah left to her office in Rochester Hills every day. Joyce had only the house. Joyce didn't walk because there was nothing to walk to. Hannah had adapted to Manhattan like a native, never considering the reverse wouldn't work for Joyce. The conflict was metastasizing into their bed.

Two NYC friends, Roger and Darla, arrived on Saturday, leaving tomorrow for Mackinac Island, on to the Upper Peninsula, the Falls. Listening in the hall as they unpacked, Hannah visualized Darla's sneer.

"It's gorgeous. But you're in the middle of fucking nowhere."

This Labor Day weekend would help, but not enough. Tonight, Joyce's voice was clear and fast above the conversation, her laughs like precise cymbal crashes. Besides Roger and Darla, Cathy and Annie drove up from Troy and were staying the night. Their neighbors Sherri Mullins and Kim Narlow from up the street were also around the kettle. But Hannah's favorite guest was 78-year-old William Gallo. He lived alone at the northmost point of Cricklewood Green – the fat top of the teardrop - with a grand view down the water from his master balcony. Small framed with ivory hair, Hannah imagined William as a gentle altar boy aged 70 years by a wizard's curse. Gallo was a former Michigan state representative, a gimlet and Town Car Republican. Joyce loved to joust politics with him after a Sunday dinner. William's voice never rising and Joyce's salvos candied by blown kisses and winks William received with down-eyed smiles. Gallo had never married. When travel came up he spoke fondly of a man named Andrew who had accompanied him across Europe, once to the pyramids.

Outside, the deck conversation deflated. Pouring herself another, Hannah could feel the countdown before someone - Kim Narlow - slid the screen open and walked in.

"Hey lady. I was wondering where you went." Star pins of light found Kim's cat eyeglasses, glowing on her sharp, clean cheekbones and the tips of her newly short hair, half 1980s punk and half mall-mom. Small and sleek, Kim Narlow had been a naughty topic in the women's home. "What's goin' on?"

"When everyone starts solving world problems it's time to change locations. How are you doing, Kim?"

"God, I should have left a half hour ago. Narlow is gonna kill me." Kim's cheeks twisted in a smile. Her eyes a crisp pink from the aromatic smoke that had been passed around outside. "Roger is really funny."

"He is. I miss him. It's good to see him and Darla again," Hannah said. Tricks of the candles or imagined movement diverted Hannah's attention to the living room and the front door, coppery streetlight filling its etched glass.

She looked back to Kim's stoned contentment. "I'm glad you're having fun."

"I am. It's great. Well, I gotta pee before…anything." Kim wheeled, giggling and low-winging her arms to feel her way down the dark hall toward the office and half bath. The hallway shelf candle had gone out. Hannah moved to replace it when a staccato of barks from Max stopped and turned her. His tone signaled trouble. Except for William and Joyce, all expectant eyes went to Hannah in the slider doorway. William stared into the kettle flames. Dressed to charm in her white and blue mosaic caftan, Joyce rose to pull Max back from the deck's edge.

"Shh, it's nothing. Nothing's gonna hurt you, Sweetie."

Near the foot of the three-steps down to the lawn, Vern Hapgood stood with his leashed Alsatian, Baron. A long cigar glowed against his beard. Max's barks aroused other neighbor's dogs, their barks relaying through the darkness.

"Hello Vern," William said, facing Vern off his right shoulder. He toasted his glass of ice; Hannah realizing how lit William was. Sherri stood to walk inside, passing Hannah.

"Turd in the punchbowl," Sherri said.

Hannah grinned.

Hapgood removed the cigar. "Hello Bill."

The dogs faced off in low growl. Hannah walked out in her pink sweats and bare feet. She had not dressed to charm. "You're late, Vern."

"For?"

"We burned the evidence," Hannah said, setting a handful of sticks into the four-legged iron kettle. Joyce cradled Max, facing Vern and his animal. Baron jerked at his leash, Max yipped once more before Joyce hushed him. Joni Mitchell crooned the mellow counterpoint.

Hapgood yanked the leash. "No!"

The German Shepherd's legs folded, dropping its black and tan bulk to the grass. Hannah moved next to Joyce, filling the stepway to the lawn. Eclipsed from the firelight the color faded from Vern's significant shape. Hannah guessed him 6'3 and about 270. A layer of fallow softness barely concealed the steel core of the man. A core which must have served Hapgood well when he was an orderly at Indiana's Logansport State Mental Hospital in his 20s, so others had said. The sticks cracked and popped in the kettle. Warmth rose on Hannah's back.

"What are you doing here?"

"I'm making sure you remember the agreement you signed." Hapgood gestured with the cigar. "If it were me this wouldn't be the ideal receptacle for a campfire. Particularly if I had set it on a wooden deck."

Seemingly satisfied in everyone's discomfort, Hapgood puffed, uttering "Come". The dog stood and they both absorbed into the night like smoke. Kim and Sherri came out with the clink of Baron's chain still rippling. Joyce and Hannah's amped recounting of Hapgood, Barbara Sanders, contracts and legal crud gradually dissipated both women's adrenaline. People stood, the screen door slid and slapped. Drinks were ordered and poured, snack plates refreshed. When Hannah finally sat, William Gallo admired her a long moment with a bent smirk, taking her exhale and swallow of wine as a cue.

"I vividly remember meeting Vern, you know. And I didn't even speak to him until years later," Gallo said. He sat forward and accepted the fresh Dewars from Sherri with both hands. "Thank you, dear. We may have shaken hands, were introduced. It was a fundraiser in 2000, I think. It was before 9/11. And after the dinner they brought out a comedian, a young fellow, for the entertainment. He was young. Very nervous. And unfortunately, he wasn't very funny. Not offensively so but just… not funny. Vern started heckling him. Gradually, it became this onslaught. Just downright abusive. But I remember we all just…sat. No one said anything. We all did later, of course, to each other. The young man tried to ignore it and perform but he finally left the stage. Just, shaken. You could see."

"Did you say anything to him?" Sherri said. "Afterward, I mean."

"Oh, no. I heard later he walked right to the parking lot and drove off." Gallo stared into the fire. "I don't know if he was even paid. But, we sat there while Vern tore this poor boy down. I remember the comedian looking down at us, from face to face. Sort of expecting someone to stop it. We did hire him, after all."

"That's sad," Kim Narlow said.

"It is. But...Vern is someone people wanted their side. He was well-connected. He delivered." Gallo looked off his left shoulder at Kim. "People make allowances when they want things."

Inside the kettle, twigs cracked and popped. Around it, silent faces were the color of sunset, shadows rutting their brows.

*****

In the unforgiving bathroom light and the faucet's white-noise splash, Tyce pushed at his left incisor in the mirror, hoping the fucker wouldn't budge too much. It didn't hurt terribly. His cheek and eyelid were past swollen, the eyelid bluish as if a robin's egg were under the skin. The burst lip was worse. Five stitches, red and fat. Tyce turned his head in degrees, squinting by reflex to somehow make it better. *It wasn't that bad.* No, it was. A crescent of bruise on his left occipital but thank God he rolled in time. His left forearm had taken the rest of her blows, bruised and sore, before he could get to his feet and disarm her.

Tyce throwing her into the bedroom wall was pure reaction and the one cop gave Tyce a vibe of belief. She didn't have a mark and Tyce's mouth was bleeding drops in addition to the bulging purples on his face. I mean, fuckin' A. Did you ever wake up out of a dead sleep with someone whaling on you? *Whaling on you?* With a plug-in alarm clock? The other cop had his hands full with her, attempting to account for her side and blocking flailing, reaching limbs.

Not Tyce's worst 6 a.m. ever, but close. It could have been a knife.

While Tyce held her in a hammer lock to the bedroom floor her screamed curses rang cottony in his sleep-dumb ears. Then the smell of the burn reached his nose and he looked up to see the fire's glow off the bathroom tile. Tyce jumped up and pinballed through the hallway. The bathtub was full of Tyce's burning possessions. He hit the shower arm full blast and hurriedly doused the two-foot flames. The nightmare of her running form gaining on his back like a train.

She had tossed Tyce's clothes, phone, computer pad, assorted books, documents and other roasted unknowns into the tub, squirted the charcoal fluid and lit the match. The night before, after going through the car wash, Tyce put his wallet in the console of his truck because it was too cramped to get it back in his pocket. At least he had those contents - IDs, bank and credit cards. The keys to the kingdom of respect which could at least rent him a room until he got footing.

Judging the tooth sound, Tyce walked out of the motel bathroom and sat on the bed in front of the TV noise. The cops had been cool, considering. In his girlfriend's blizzard of insults and rage she confessed to lighting the fire. When the cops pointed this out to her and mentioned arson, her demeanor cooled. She refused charges against Tyce. Arms cuffed back, on his knees and sputtering red slop, Tyce refused as well. The embarrassment still smoldered. There he had been - shirtless, cuffed, dazed and bleeding like some reality-show trailer monkey. Now he was some cop's bar story. And what she did to his face. Jesus….

The rest of the morning was spent evacuating his unburned clothes and necessities from her house. Tyce doubted he'd go back for his TV or anything else. All he needed in truth fit comfortably in the motel room. He would just have to move his firearms with him in the truck when he went to work, if he still had a job tomorrow. Tyce was bonded ten more months to LifeForce, owing a ton of money if he violated contract. By luck she hadn't burned his laundry-hampered uniforms. But his old job contacts were ashes. Before he was laid-off, Tyce had finally gotten out of The Shops. No more widgets. He was front office, traveling, visiting plants and making decisions. Tyce cared. Plant safety meant something to those guys on the machines - and their families. Tyce came home clean. Who knows where he'd end up if he got canned tomorrow? Back to Name Tag city. Cut knuckles, grease. The endless shit-talking, grudges and front-lobe rot of The Shops.

Numbers. When they laid him off. *The numbers,* they said. That was all they needed to say.

On the other side of the TV he peeked at Frankenstein in the bureau mirror. Frankenstein shook his head at Tyce's sorry ass.

How did she find out?

Did it matter? Same story, chasing pussy. He'd fucked-over another one. A good one, too.

Tyce groaned and dropped backward. He really thought he would have gotten good at this shit by now. Still he felt appropriately hurt. Labor Day, after all.

***

Tuesday, September 5th

It had cooled off last night. Cloud-mottled, tangerine sun was lifting the eastern overcast and shined the high, ferny grass in the roadside culverts, beaded with dew. The obscured ball of sun flicker-popped on Tyce's eyes from between passing trees. An approaching sign for Essex warned him to reduce speed to 35 – radar enforced. He knew better. Everyone did.

Tyce's truck followed the swoop of Kent Road northbound, passing Essex' outlying houses. High-porched, wood-frame bungalows with overhung roofs. The yard clutter some snootier types would take for careless, but Tyce knew to these people it was all practical. The people who lived here – from Here – noticed any thing or face out of place the way a castaway knew what washed up on their beach every morning. Dominski said a few hundred people still lived in and around Essex, maybe a few more now since the D-Plex opened. They held on to things.

He passed the first flat-glass storefronts and the end of the crevassed sidewalks. Most of the store windows were blank/black. Polite. Lease or Rent messages would be salt. Mockery to everyone who knew better. At the intersection of Kent and Heller Lake Road, one of Essex two traffic lights repeated yellow. It was barely 6:30. Tyce wasn't due until 8 but couldn't take another 20-minute nod and shock wake, visions of overdrafts dancing in his head. Shaving, he noticed the moon of bruise around his eye had grown but the swelling receded some. From his lip alone there would be no denying it. A glance at the ugly in the rearview roiled his stomach further, too wound up to eat. Would he be back at the motel in time for *Price Is Right*?

He stopped to turn right, east, onto Heller Lake Road. A baggy old guy walking a smallish rottweiler stood in front of the BP station, squinting at the sun. The sign boasted a Pepsi special and 4 pieces of fried chicken for $3.00.

Tyce was in no way ready for Peltier.

Heller was the main strip, downtown, as such. Two-story building fronts hugged the narrow-walked street. Every few had evidence of life; insurance office, Fox Hair and Tan. Carol's Restaurant, a dentist. Chinese food. Mike's Hardware. Most of them had the things you couldn't get at the D-Plex. The drug store was closed. Vacant P&D Market thanked you for 29 years from behind dirty windows. Along Heller the offshoot streets running north and south branched to squat, aluminum-sided homes on long, unfenced green lots. A few ancient, hulking willows obscured driveway cars.

Despite the red "J" sign in the window, Tyce had stopped into Teddy's Gun and Outdoor once to price ammo. He'd been in his LifeForce uniform and the vibe was frosty. The "J" was the symbol of the redneck uprising in Jamestown during the flu. The image came from a picture snapped during the siege. One of the rednecks had two-finger smeared a "J" in blood on the side of a roached Tennessee Guard M-113. (J for Jamestown? But maybe Jesus? Justice?). Now it was the brotherhood flag of the Us. LifeForce being another Socialist, gun-seizing, World-Government tentacle of Them. He'd driven Heller almost every day since getting assigned at Cricklewood Green, but this was the first time he'd noticed the American flag upside down in Teddy's window. Tyce wondered what news he missed in the past two days.

Bob Dylan was Tyce's unlikeliest of co-pilots this morning. A grimed and cracked-case stowaway CD inside the truck console, under the ketchup packs, fuses, maps and oil change receipts. Tyce couldn't remember how he'd gotten the disc or who made it for him. But Tyce was glad for the spare, strummy music. Commercials and moron morning radio sent him digging. His other music was now burned circuitry.

Aside from the BP and the corner bar, Teddy's was probably the fattest business in Essex. Gun sales after V-14 were, well…epidemic. Teachers, preachers, office girls and coffee boys were carrying. A fear working its way through the national veins, thick and faintly nauseating but the patient bore it, hopeful of cure. An appropriately Dylan thought this morning, with enough small-town twang. Tyce smiled, upping the volume. The music helped him feel leveled for the first time in 24 hours.

Heller Lake Road swung north at the corner of the tallest building in Essex. A classic arch-windowed, red-brick 3-story anchored by the Highwayman Bar and Grill. Kidde-corner southeast, a pack of black-necked, white-collared geese strutted and flapped by the stream of Miller Park, far back from the faded city-father signs, playground steel, picnic tables and baseball diamond. Tyce accelerated north past the closed Giant Grocery and strip stores, windows smeared white, the name a shadow of bolder blue where removed letters had blocked the sun's grey fade.

The acre parking lot was now a flea-market every weekend. He passed the shuttered Essex village office and the plywood mothballed police station next door. Down an adjacent side-street the harsh brown steeple of a church loomed over the tree tops. The Burger King zipped by, some more roadside homes and off-shoot streets. In Fender's Gas and Garage lot a pack of sick and slouched For-Sale cars faced the road, dew turning to grimy sweat on the sun-glossed windshields.

Tyce shifted and accelerated. Heller became cloistered by thick woods on both sides. End of radar enforcement.

North another mile, the woods broke open some before the intersection with Oakton Road, revealing the massive, slate-grey D-Plex. The orange tips of the toothpick-like light posts still burned bright. Distantly, it reminded Tyce of the American bases in Iraq; an alien cluster of sodium light and right angles framed by sky. The D-Plex was the only fresh fruit, fresh flowers, fresh meat and blue jeans for miles. It even had a health clinic. Weekends, D-Plex had its own safety patrol (LifeForce guards, actually) to whistle and herd-wave the cars packed with hot dogs, toilet paper, peat moss, Indonesian T-shirts, anti-freeze, plug-in clock radios, foam flip flops, motor oil and birthday cakes. All your shopping under one roof, radiating like a sun, or eating like a black hole.

Tyce took the right turn onto Oakton, eastbound. *Easy there, Bob.*

Living in Michigan almost 20 years, Tyce preferred it over his birthplace near Buffalo, New York. This was a weird part of the state, an area prone to swampy lowlands. Its woods and undergrowth were crossed with streams and creeks and gloomy stump ponds. Higher ground was built upon, Essex and Gavin and Cricklewood Green. Socked-in summer humidity, winters with a wasteland quality; unlike the more Nordic regions to the state's upper northwest firs and ski resorts. Weeks ago on a hot August dusk after work, Tyce had gone exploring and drove to his goal within minutes. He was lost, parking in a dirt crossroad surrounded by trees. Like an X in a twenty-foot tall corn maze, dimensions of leafy shadow obscured any landmark or vantage. He stepped out of his truck that evening in the buggy, airless silence, slightly afraid of the desolation that vibrated with life at the same time. Tyce enjoyed the funny surprise of it, feeling his senses grasp for comfort and order past the unease. A lick of long-gone combat buzz. Very cool. One could drive and turn and drive and turn among fallow, high-grass fields and woods, seeing nothing to assure in the relentlessly flat sameness. Lost, only fifteen minutes from I-75 if you knew the way.

After the five-some miles of mostly wooded straightaway, Tyce stopped at the sign and clearing around the intersection before Cricklewood Green. Oakton Road became Orton Road, turning north toward thickening woods and the state land. Southbound it became Deerfield Road, taking you lower to bridges and swamp and the reedy paths around Trunk Lake. Tyce crossed, slowly passing the development billboard, (*"Return to You"*) up the private access blacktop to the Green. Just before the dead-end turnaround Tyce made the short left to the gate, slowing for the two gentle folds in the dirt strip. He guessed the logic of the folds was to prevent anyone from ramming the gate with any speed. The sensor read his pass, rolling the gate open. He parked in the short lot, exhaled and walked up the ramp to the glass door.

The three night-guards didn't acknowledge him. Allen, the black dude, had his back to the door and camera console, arms draped over his chair's top. He was spectating on the jive volley between Venegas and the third guard. Tyce thought he was Pakistani but had not met him. Tyce sensed all three were stoned.

"Man, you got people starving in gutters over there and cows just walk by. Nobody touches them? I'd get a machete and it's dinner time. What?" Venegas chuckled darkly, thick arms crossed.

"You are Mexican, yes?" The third guard said. He was slight, with small hands and a precise mustache. "A Catholic country. You have no sacred animal?"

"Sacred animal in Mexico is one you can't catch. If not, it's goin' in the pot, yo."

Laughter.

The machine read Tyce's thumb print and beeped. 6:48 a.m.

"You ever wanna go back to India?" Venegas said.

"Ho ho. No way, Jack. I'd rather go to the moon than back there."

"You could stay on one of them bases up there," Allen said. He unwrapped a small candy, placing it in his mouth.

"What base? You are crazy, Joseph."

"You think they went up there all them times and just took rocks? They built all kinds of shit up there. Where do you think they all went when the flu was on? They were still flying space shuttles up there."

Allen folded the wrapper into the tiniest square. The overhead fluorescents reflected off his glasses.

"All I know is if I go to the moon, my ass ain't coming back. I could make it on one of them bases. Definitely," Venegas said.

"You know what else?" Allen said.

"What?"

"They got shit under the ocean, too."

****

By 10 a.m. Cricklewood Green was a beehive. Dominski sent Mandel with the pool crew, arriving for the day-after Labor Day draining and closing. Lawn crew trucks came in a staggered convoy, every three minutes or every time Tyce wanted to piss or get a coffee or close his eyes a sec. The riding mowers skipped Tyce's attention to the camera monitors so often he reduced the two screens to single images of the gate. He snapped the police-band radio off. Fucking Dominski.

Fed-Ex, then UPS two minutes later. A D-Plex delivery. A swallow of coffee, then a maid service ringing in. Tyce logged each incoming vehicle tag and logged each tapped entry code, cross-matching the approved list. Detectives would heap appropriate scorn on the logs if they were ever called in for clues or evidence. The maid's typed code failed. The fourth one this morning, another separate log and report.

She pressed the intercom again. "Hello. Merry Maids."

"Steve?" Tyce said.

"Let 'em in," Dominski said, his crotch and reek of Axe spray too close to Tyce's nose.

Tyce typed the tag and time. He looked up at Dominski, a what-the-fuck flare to his eyes. Dominski was watching the monitor.

"I guess when the Association was running everything they had one cleaning service, one lawn service." Dominski said. "It was easier."

"Why don't we just leave the gate open?"

"I don't know." Dominski slurped his coffee and stepped for the kitchen. Neither Mandel or Dominski mentioned his face or asked about the weekend. Tyce was already being forgotten.

Peltier arrived talking, around 10:30. His tone into the cell phone was crisp and supplicant. Words like 'negative' and 'exceptional'. Axe smell came up behind Tyce again.

"Yes, sir. Friday. That's a definite," Peltier said.

Peltier pressed the thumb scanner.

"I agree. I anticipate that, sir."

A grey, boxy work truck with louvered, locked cabinets on its sides rolled to the gate. "Hudson Properties" decal on the door. It idled, windows up.

Tyce searched the tag list and the schedule to no matches. Peltier and Dominski quipped and chuckled to each other, voices phased out in Tyce's ears.

Tyce pressed the intercom.

"Can I help you?"

A doughy, shaved head slipped out the lowering driver's window.

"Hudson."

"Enter your code, sir."

"We're here for your monthly." The boomed laugh from the cab was faint through the speaker.

"Let him through," Peltier said. "It's legit."

Tyce opened the gate, typing again. Halfway through the gate's rumbling closure it jarred and opened again for a resident's exiting car.

"Good morning, Tyce," Peltier said.

Tyce gave him the full Frankenstein. "Good morning, Sergeant."

Peltier's squinty, ticked blink looked like he'd been flicked in the nose with a cotton ball.

"Hudson is here to check the pumps and the power room. We have to let them in. Get the keys. I'll show you."

Grabbing the hooked key ring, Tyce met eyes with Dominski. He gave Tyce a short nod, like you would give to someone on the street wearing your same hockey team jersey. Dominski was one of those guys. A Jobber. The guy in the shop who leaves the empty cardboard tube in the john because nobody told him it was his job to change it.

Tyce followed Peltier down the ramp. They walked the left-west road, passing the fresh-clipped infield between the Barracks and the pool shack and clubhouse. A huge blue hose led from the pool, flowing to a nearby storm drain in the road. Tyce could see Mandel's skinny ass smoking and gesturing with the pool crew. Peltier glanced left and Mandel turned his back as if tagged. A snap in his posture, Mandel's left hand flicked down and his shoe squished the cigarette flat in a teenage reflex.

"What do you think of him?" Peltier said.

"Mandel?"

"Yes."

"I don't know. I haven't spoken to him much."

"Do you trust him?"

"He hasn't given me reason not to," Tyce said.

"I don't. Not in the sense I think he's a thief. But he doesn't lead me to believe I could rely on him."

Tyce said nothing.

The zip and grind of mowers and trimmers made Tyce wonder how much these guys made. They probably didn't have to worry about much. At the first house on the right, the one with the fake beach and the pink potted flowers at the driveway mailbox, volleyed yelling came through the open windows, male and mixed female voices. Peltier's palm raised and Tyce stopped with him. Peltier drew breath at the shouts. Tyce felt it off him, endocrinetic, chemical. A man who reacted to the distress sounds of women. Like a capped flame, the noise stopped. Tyce sensed someone watching them inside the grey stone two-story, abutted by an equally high maple. Head swiping in dislike, Peltier walked.

"All the time. One day something bad will happen in that house."

Peltier's silence strained Tyce. The desire to please and explain overcame him and his jaws ached with revulsion over it. Sunlight throbbed his temples, where his melted sunglasses should have been.

Barbara Sanders was in a gesturing conversation with a small brown man holding a weed trimmer. The thin, tall brunette wore black-frame sunglasses and a baby blue sweat scarf. Her hands smoothed the air, expressive at the lawn. The man's capped head averted, nodding.

"Let's talk about it," Peltier said.

"Well, yesterday morning, about six, my girl and I...our neighbor came pounding on the door. Blood all down her nose, flipped out, hysterical. Her boyfriend was loaded. He beat her up, trashed the place. She asked if I would go there with her to get her stuff."

"You didn't call it in?"

"Nobody ever accused me of making good decisions, Sergeant."

It wasn't quite a laugh, but Peltier reacted enough to press Tyce on to the other side of the high-wire.

"She went in first and he got me from around the corner with a lamp. Crazy scene. I got up, pulled him off her. We went at it and I finally choked him out."

"What did the cops say?"

"Well, they weren't called. She begged me not to. He's on probation. It didn't look too bad at the time. It was impulse. I thought I was doing the right thing. Like I said."

Peltier snapped a look at Tyce's profile and faced forward.

"You didn't say that."

Tyce waited for the rest.

"I called you last night, Tyce. And this morning."

Peltier's pace increased.

"My phone got smashed. I did call in yesterday. About 10, I think." Tyce said. "From the ER. I talked to Mandel."

The sergeant looked off to his left, at the woods. "How long were you in the military, Tyce?"

"Four years the first time, out of high school. Then almost four in the Guard in my 30s." He cleared his throat. "Iraq then."

Peltier shook his head. "Bro. You didn't learn to lie better than this? By the time I left the Corps, I could lie like a motherfucker. I could straight-face tell my Gunny I could piss cherry wine and damn near believe it myself."

Tyce said nothing.

"It's a day, bro," Peltier said, catching his eyes a moment. "You called in. You did it right. No worries."

The Hudson truck had parked in the blacktop turnaround's shaded edge. Approaching, Tyce could hear the bald, dough-faced driver's phone call. He lifted a leg to bumper, tugging at the long black shorts obscuring a colorful tattoo winding up his calf. Someone on the other end wasn't understanding. Doughboy didn't have the money yet. Passing him, Tyce and Peltier crossed into shade to the squat, windowless brick structure among the trees. The other Hudson worker was leaning against the steel door, down into his phone. He was a smaller guy, mustard-yellow uniform shirt unbuttoned to the heat. Computer pad strap-slung across his hip, the young man's easy-going face looked up not at all in a hurry.

"Hey, Henry," he said.

"Jason. What's good?" Peltier said. Tyce unlocked the door to an ooze of musty heat and the steady burr of the well pump as the men recounted nothing-muches. Both entered past Tyce, Peltier flipping the overhead switch. The inside concrete's white tint had nearly soaked in or flaked away. The shack was about 25 feet across and 15 deep with two screened vents high on each side. Tyce recognized the V-10 electrical generator to his left, a Baghdad Green Zone special. The white propane tank next to it was the size of a prize heifer. He correctly surmised it as the back-up spoken of in his orientation tour – kicking on to power the well-water pump, Barracks, cameras, streetlights and gate if need be. On his right, the tubular hulk of the well pump and water filter system.

"Jason, this is Tyce. Tyce, Jason. They come every first Monday to pretend to check this shit."

"Jeez, man. You alright?" Jason said. He didn't linger more than a moment before getting to his work. He opened a panel on the well pump to a broad set of dials and digital gauges.

"Amateur MMA."

"Yeah? I had a cousin who tried doing that. He lasted a couple fights before he got his jaw broke." Jason plugged his pad's USB into the monolithic, whirring green machine and tapped. "Sucked his dinner though a straw for three months."

Leaning in the jamb, Tyce turned away from the dissection of Sunday's Lions' victory over the 49ers. The sun had crested the trees on the east side of the pond. Doughboy at the truck was a black silhouette merging into a long shadow on the turnaround, hand to ear, stepping in small circles. After ten minutes and take-it easy, Peltier wanted to walk east, do a lap of the property. The grind of the mowers grew, faded and grew as he and Tyce passed the long yards.

"Why do they do that?" Peltier asked.

"What?"

He gestured at a vacant home's for-sale sign.

"Reduced price. No one can come here without an appointment. There is no one to see the sign. A buyer would already know the price is reduced. Why a sign at all?"

They walked on around the bend, south.

"Probably for the residents," Tyce said. "Couple always wanted the kids to move next door. They see the sign. Reduced price…"

"Maybe. I wouldn't live here, even if I could, you know? Steroid houses. You know what I mean? Big, but I feel like I could push that wall over. No bones, no strength. I was here back when they didn't even have the guard house. Winter time you sat in your truck all night with heat going. No joke. They had, I think, eight houses built. Maybe three occupied. Place felt like a graveyard at night."

Tyce's empty stomach curdled, the cut grass making him nauseous.

"Mandel said he needs to take a day off Saturday. You take his shift, yeah?"

"Yes, Sergeant. Will do," Tyce said.

"Relax, bro. It's all good."

****

Sherri guessed Mark's payback would come unexpectedly. Mark was predictable to the extent all men were, but Sherri had come to recognize he had a woman's timing and delivery. Bickering with Ray, Mark kept a margin a righteous innocence behind a nimble slash of blame. Ray's guilt was easily stirred, but Sherri has no time for the well-past grown child's crap. In yesterday's quiet dusk, before Mark clodded through the door, she had almost forgotten him. Then, returning from Hannah and

Joyce's, she tripped over his stinking duffel bag still blocking the foyer. It was, in a word, enough.

Tuesday morning Sherri decided, with fall approaching, it was time to wash the down comforters. Her steps on the basement stairs were deliberate, every light switch flipped up with the blade of her hand. Illuminated, Mark's corner hovel was a damp-smelling kudzu of boy sloth, malignant and spreading on the bare concrete – piled bed, sofa, giant TV and electronics. The computer desk invisible under monitors and crap. A hobby desk abutting it piled with soda cans, diabolical-looking implements and firearm pieces. Plastic milk crates stuffed with cords and cables. Cardboard boxes, wooden boxes. Army green ammunition cans full of God knows what. Scattered papers - bills, pink overdraft statements, receipts. Tossed pants turned inside out, pockets stark white. The bedded mound didn't stir.

He seemed to sleep through the wash but the tennis balls in the dryer – to keep the feathers from bunching – finally roused him. When Sherri went to check, the outline of Mark's bunched hulk was tapping away at the computer. With the speaker's rap song spitting a barked hail of 'fucks' and 'bitches' she stepped backward up the stairs.

Ray had already left. The back and leg pain usually broke down his goodnight meds by about 6:30. He frequently drove to Trunk Lake and its paths for his doctor walks. Never in the complex. *Ain't giving nobody no goddamn parade.* When Mark was gone, Ray slept calmer and longer.

Sherri stood at the glass slider, watching the pond. The drum thumps and faint obscenities in the basement vibrated her feet. She went upstairs. A little make-up. She slipped into her flip flops. Take the point and leave the table a winner, for now.

Sandra Rose Narlow answered the door in an oversized frock of spangled, shiny gold. It reminded Sherri of a 1920s flapper Halloween costume. Knowing Kim Narlow and Sandra Rose, it probably was.

"Misheri!"

"Good morning, Sandra Rose."

"I'm gonna have ornch marmalade. Would you like some?"

"No but thank you. May I come in?

Six-year-old Sandra Rose turned and bolted, bare feet thumping the hardwood. Sherri followed into the cool hall, closing the oak door.

"MOOOOOM! Misheri is here!"

The maid's familiar pony-tailed head peeked around the great room's archway. Sherri and the maid absorbed their surprise in silence. The Hispanic girl's face disappeared rodent-quick and Sherri could not see her in the great room as she passed. Sherri had fired the maid service in June. Jewelry went missing but she did not mention it in her call to cancel, not wanting anyone fired. It may have been Mark.

"MOOOOM!"

"Sandra Rose! Come eat. Right now!"

Shrill TV cartoon dings and screeches rang off the kitchen's granite and tile, up and back down the peaked ceiling. Kim Narlow looked at Sherri cross-eyed, lips agape. Kim gave the orange-smeared wheat toast a coup de 'grace slice and handed the plate down to Sandra Rose.

"Twenty more minutes of Charisma Cat and then we're starting on your lessons. Eat and then go find your tablet."

"OK," The girl took the plate running down the hall.

Kim clicked the yammering countertop television off, but the adjacent living room's TV continued. Another TV echoed somewhere back in the house.

"Sorry. I don't even hear it anymore, I swear. Five grand and she's yours," Kim said. "What do you say?"

Sherri pulled a stool away from the island. "Throw in the Mercedes and you're talking."

Kim still wore last night's wine – lazy jaw, short hair whisked. Her black Harley Davidson T-shirt creased and faintly funked. Kim smirked, drinking canned soda. "God, I had too much fun."

"How long did you stay?"

"I don't even know. I was the last one to leave. Me, Joyce and Roger stayed up by the fire." Kim thumb and index finger looped to an 'OK' and she brought them to her lips, toking the invisible joint. "I haven't done that much in a long time. I'm sorry - you want some coffee? Anything?"

"No thanks. You should have seen my second husband. I used to wonder how he even got high. It seemed like he never wasn't."

"The band guy, right?"

"Yep. I tried some again last summer but it's just too strong anymore. Y'all kids can have it."

Though no one was listening who cared, Kim leaned in.

"What do you think about Joyce and Hannah?"

"Yeah. It was a little odd, wasn't it? You couldn't get them to sit next to each other until asshole showed up," Sherri said. "Hannah's never life of the party, but something was bugging her for sure."

"Well, after you left, she was talking to Darla and -

"MOOOOOOM!"

Her mouth poised to yell, but Kim inhaled it with closed eyes, snatching calm in the held breath. Kim's eyes opened, skyward, listening. Nothing more came except cartoon clang, but when Kim fixed back on Sherri her face was void, gossip forgotten, waiting. Sherri filled in. They talked of new TV shows, flowers and weather. Mike's trouble with Vern, Sherri and Ray's trouble with Vern. Upcoming vacations.

"Is Mike still going back to China?"

"Mmhmm. Thursday. For three weeks."

"Well you and Sandra Rose are more than welcome to come by for dinner, anytime. You need anything, just ask."

Kim's eyes lowered. "I didn't show you what I got last week."

"What?"

She left the kitchen and walked upstairs. From her stool, Sherri could see the anchoring photo triptych of Kim's brother above the granite fireplace and TV in the living room. Black and whites of a young man in a baseball uniform, posed with Kim as children and the earnest graduation pose. The memoriam card. Mourning them was so difficult. The epidemic was a collective misery, but it unwound so bloody slowly, making all the death impersonal, somehow. There was no real way to mark the agony of two hundred days and no blame. A national V-14 Grief Day struck Sherri as ridiculous. Two anniversaries to dread – your own "real" one and the obligation of everyone else's. Time would snow it all under. Ask someone about AIDS. Or polio.

Turn the damn TV off already.

Kim returned to set the laptop on the granite. She keyed the short clip and seemed to back up, as if it would ignite.

On the screen, a young Chinese woman in a smart grey suit spoke in poised, lightly accented English. Yan would be visiting America for the first time in December and greatly anticipated meeting Kim and Sandra Rose after hearing so much about them and seeing their photos. Mike was a very bright and insightful (?) man. A joy to work with (??). Yan hoped she and Kim could become good friends.

As rest of the message fogged in her mind, Sherri foresaw the future conversations she would have about it. The anecdote this morning would become, sometime when Sherri would be discussing the skirmishes between men and women. A high card played at some Cabo spa lunch or during drinks on the promenade deck overlooking the sun shining blue through an Alaskan iceberg. Top this, Sherri's tone would say. *The husband's side-piece sent a video to the wife!* At the same instant, a cringe shuddered the older woman, a sagging empathy as she recognized the Chinese girl's haircut now copied on Kim Narlow.

"So, what do you think?"

Sandra Rose bounded into the room, cheeks marmalade smeared.

"What did you do to your face, little girl?" Sherri said, nearly standing off the stool. The relieved volume of her own voice surprised her.

Kim Narlow picked the girl up from her left side, deftly closing the video with a pick of her right hand like a faerie's charm. She kissed the giggling child's forehead, dotting on the tip of her nose to miss the mess. After three Mojitos, Sherri could admit she didn't like children much. The first husband was game in that stormy, teenage year but Sherri knew better. The second husband was certainly a seed planter but nobody's gardener. With him it was *see-you-next-week* tours and another hit song was always too close but too far. By the time his career and their marriage crashed, Sherri was fine with and without. Sherri suspected she would have been a good mother. A memory for lessons and a patient teacher. She watched Kim wipe Sandra Rose's face, bouncing her.

"Messy. Messy girl."

Sherri's Aunt Fran appeared in her mind. "Talk baby talk to a child and you're asking for a lifetime of diapers," she used to say. Stiff, high hair and jet of smoke expelled from the corner of her crimson mouth.

The memory of her Aunt became a hulking Mark Dudek. A lifetime of diapers.

The maid had moved to the kitchen archway, silent, waiting to clean the clean kitchen. Kim lowered Sandra Rose, telling her to go play. Twenty more minutes and then school lessons.

"Thank you, Margarita. We'll be out in a moment," Kim said, rolling the R's to keep the girl's name from sounding like a drink order.

In the living room, Kim switched the TV to good-morning talk and ignored it, asking about Ray's coming operation in October. Her response rote, Sherri's eyes drifted to the many more framed photos surrounding the fireplace. The room was similar to her and Ray's but the Narlow's ceiling was higher, domed, the walls a light peach. They were picture people. Mike Narlow was indeed handsome, a Mediterranean brusque. A recent photo showed his middle pushing out against his colorful biking leathers, compared to the lithe torso of his fraternity beach-party pose. The young man, cap askew, holding a beaming 20-ish and tan, long-haired Kim Narlow across his chest like the conquest she no doubt was. One dark eyebrow was dipped in eternal conspiracy with you – left to imagine what happened later.

Sherri sensed the maid's scuttles back over her shoulder. The Narlows also had a walkout deck through the sliders. Sherri suggested they move out there, where, maybe, there would be nothing to remind the women of anything.

****

Pacing the scrub grass and powdery earth, Sanders' emotions finally coalesced to shame. Despondency beget the anger, fueling the hubris, finally exhausted, to this. His exhales were without wind. Sighs he couldn't force. If Sanders had ever felt this diminished the memory was so smothered he hadn't the strength to confront it. Voices carried on, out of the car's open windows, mocking him. He felt the weight of the thing in his back pocket as he circled the Prius, wandering. So much for cell phone technology. *What did it get you, smart ass?* Ah, to have the will to throw the damn thing away....

All around the tree-curtained cloister was the detritus of vice, urges. Sanders stepped amidst empty beer cans, bullet casings, fast food wrappers faded by rain and weather. Booze bottles, crushed soda cups with straws like snorkels. Mounds of ashtray butts had been dumped wholesale out the sides of parked cars. Decayed, charred trash inside a blackened campfire smudge. The ugly slash of a condom in the weeds.

One scatter was so mysterious Sanders bent to see it closer. A dozen tiny grey cylinders, click-clanking under the nudge of his cross trainer. They looked for all the world like oxygen tanks. Gas? Liquid? He couldn't imagine what perversity they enabled.

Back straightened, Sanders looked down through the foliage at the distant monolith of the D-Plex, its parking lot islands of short, planter trees and cars in column. The hinted, straight dark band of Oakton Road was obscured by the trees and overgrowth. Likely they came up to this ridge clearing for the obstruction, to see surprise coming before it crept up the hidden dirt rut off Oakton Road. A small, oblong stage for urges.

He was the same. The same as them. Shame, as them.

The morning's bright sky had flattened grey with afternoon clouds. The car radio's voices continued behind him. Sanders resisted turning them off. Belief in himself would have to start somewhere. If he bluffed long enough perhaps it would self-fulfill. The management book said so.

Earlier...

The prescriptions were not ready. Inefficiency or not, Sanders knew his pique had as much to do with delayed prescriptions as the murder of an Austrian archduke did with the First World War. Sitting out the wait in a plastic scoop chair, hands clasped, Sanders looked from the heart health and diabetes posters to the D-Plex wanderers. In noisy packs or bumping two-by-two, the shopping center's inmates gnawed and pawed. Free food samples and even torn-open bags of chemical chips. Ignorant, over-fed, de-evolved. Institutional. Their ambling children bawling, communicating in screeches. Here a Tuesday afternoon in September, barely past 2 pm and they weren't in school? Sanders could find no connection in any passing face. His attention snapped away from them up to the black-glass bubble cameras girded to the corrugated roof, then down to his shoelaces. But like a picked sore, he came back to the irritant - the inmates. Primates. We went to space, God-damn you. What our past's thinking, devoted men had accomplished meant nothing to them. Graspers all. Nothing more. Their reach extended to their genitals. If the builders of this world could see them, would they give a damn? Throw in the towel? Sanders' thoughts went uglier and he minded his breathing, removing his glasses. He knew the resentment would start working on his own self - a fat host of failures, there. At last, Sanders name was called, his card scanned and the pharmacy tech handed the crinkly bags to Sanders without seeing him.

Inside the car, behind the door's sealing *whoomp*, Sanders' breath left him. He realized he'd been holding it since the hand-off. He couldn't inflate his lungs. No, not couldn't. Wouldn't. His brain refused. A family passed by the windshield, the small fat child banging the wheeled cart into a car while the mother texted. The older male, fat, tattooed, looking off into space, holding the young girl by the hand. The future. There you have it. *Who would feed them? Where would the energy come from?*

Breath came to him in a collapse. A realization. He could only start the car and drive back to his tower. There was no other option for him. No other possible destination for Sanders on this planet. Sanders hadn't the strength to weep.

He turned the key and the car radio came to life. Full of conviction. The radio host was sounding off on the same things. The death of the American spirit. A nation of servants, sloth. A charge returned to Sanders. His foot revved the engine. A resolve and a security coming with it, yet he didn't want to move just yet. With the motor and the radio, the car had become a capsule of boundless possibility, confidence. All of it, all of them out there, could not touch him. Sanders' lungs gusted with the vent's cool air. The callers reported with assurance. *Yes. Yes, Goddamn it!* The sketches of explanation he'd toyed with in the store came back to him with direction. Sketched lines becoming bolder blue and defined. Sanders couldn't recall ever feeling the way he did about the cell phone in his pocket. It never had such purpose and connection. He buckled in, levered the car to drive and slow-coasted out of the parking lot.

Creeping east along deserted Oakton Road, Sanders formed detail and support of his case. Angles of dispute were considered and overcome with alteration, streamlining. The soundness of his ideas assured, Sanders slowed the car a mile or so past the D-Plex. There was a dirt incline up into the trees he'd noticed dozens of times. No sign at the entrance, nothing posted. He turned right and low-geared the car up the rise.

It was first-date trepidation. A cousin of what Sanders felt watching the Brusine girl. He swatted down the metaphor, a gnat of his youth. The dirt road put him onto a grass and dirt platform with more woods and hillside behind it. Perhaps it had been someone's home lot, once planned and overgrown by time. By engineer's reflex he adjusted the car between invisible lines and shut it down. He felt too warm, but even when Sanders rolled the windows down, the capsule held.

Sanders clicked his pocket pen. Without a pad, he peeled the prescription bag open, smoothing the clean white over the arm rest. He set the bullet points. It took several minutes of skipped deadlines – after this caller, after the next commercials, read it just once more. He dialed and wished for water. Hell, even better a shot of something strong. Paper in his left hand, phone eared, about to report from today's tar pit of Them.

A call-screener picked up, telling Sanders to state his business. Sanders blurted his first bullet point. Provoked, the screener gave him a right-on. He asked Sanders' name and location and told him to please hold. The patched-in five second delay between the phone and car radio sent Sanders' shaky hand to cut the volume.

Feeling hot, Sanders considered stripping out of his shirt. He farted and awkwardly opened the door with his left hand, bumping it closed with his thigh. Paper in hand, phone to ear, he looked through the breaks in the foliage down to the D-Plex and its parking lot.

"Next, Robert from Michigan. Sound off, my friend."

He greeted the host and paid the compliments. He was no Daily Communicant to the show, but he knew to do that much. Sanders' bullet points easily hit home. The great inventors. Omaha Beach. You couldn't even call these modern people children because children were curious and evolving. The future of the men who went to the moon was being devoured by bludgeoning, masturbating monkeys.

Huzzahs and amens from the host.

An aside about himself - Sanders the Engineer. He mentioned the

Shuttle (to prove what he knew what he was talking about). Romans built still-standing bridges and aqueducts, he said. Logic was now discarded. Fools rewarded.

Preach brother, preach. He got the ding ding ding.

Then it slipped...

Too much about Sanders the Engineer, his struggle to find a job among Them. The host pounced. Wait a minute. Everyone cuts their own deal in this life. No whining. No pity party. No one owes you anything. Sanders' frantic defenses were blubbers of Me and I. Us became Them.

Blame yourself. Your excuses are your own. He got the toilet flush. Sanders got cut off and was lost in space.

Shaky, Sanders opened the driver's door and sat, feet in the powdery dirt. The callers and host continued to savage him. One said the Space Shuttle was a bus that drove billions of taxpayer's dollars – entrepreneur's dollars, job creator's dollars – into the waste of outer space. Huzzahs and amens. Sanders was another who lived off the public tit, bawling when it dried up. Unqualified to make it on their own. Poor me.

He walked away from the car, the crashed capsule, stuffing the phone into his back pocket. Technology. *Where did it get you, smart ass?* He stepped aimlessly around, marooned. This is where he would spend the rest of his life. It all coalesced to shame. He felt like a child who handed all his pocket money to the carnival game and no prize – sucked in, shucked in. Metaphor and a childhood memory swatted him. All of them at the lunchroom table, laughing at his Valentine to her.

Suddenly the car radio clicked off. His head swerved, staring at the car. He felt woozy at the infinitesimal possibility he telepathically disabled it. Sanders noticed a peculiar, enveloping silence. Previous unaware sounds and frequencies were thunderously absent. His attention averted to the left, forward. The massive green D-Plex sign had gone dark.

******

When it happened, they both looked up at the white cork ceiling like cats. Whose great hand turned out the lights? Nearly dark but for narrow cuts of gloom through the blinds, the room's teal walls blanched grey. The boy's skinny butt in Sponge Bob briefs crinkled the examining table paper. Hannah heard murmurs from the lobby.

Hannah's fingertips rested on the boy's knee. "Just wait here a sec. OK, Mitchell? I'm going to see what's wrong."

The boy nodded, grim face grimmer.

Careful to gently close the door, Hannah followed the hallway to the standing, dumbfounded faces of Marion, her office manager, and the boy's mother, Mrs. Stamer.

"My cell phone went out, too," Stamer said. "It's…something." Passing, Hannah smelled her Trezor & bath scrub. Marion stepped back from the counter.

"I was just sitting here," she said, a front-loaded excuse. Her always-cold, purple sweatered arms spread from her sides. Hannah could feel the mother moving behind her, toward the exam room.

"Mitchell. Mitchell, get dressed."

Hannah pulled the blinds open, brightening the reception area. Hannah lifted the counter phone to a dial tone and handed it to Marion.

"Marion, call DTE. There should be a flashlight in one of these drawers if you need it." Outside was nothing but parked cars, short hedges and the white stucco row of one-story glass fronts reflecting grey sky.

Turning, Hannah watched the young mother tucking Mitchell's shirt into his tiny khakis.

"It may be a short outage, Mrs. Stamer, if you'd like to wait - "

"I doubt it. The phones are dead. Tie your shoes. Come on."

"I wasn't finished but I think his ears only need to be cleaned. I doubt there's impairment."

After pressing and poking her phone screen in vain, the woman's brown eyes clicked up, seeming accusatory. Black brows crisp, like bird wings in glide. Her free hand hitched the boy's arm. "Fine. We'll be in touch. Come on. Say goodbye."

In tow, the boy peeped a meek "bye".

"Bye, Mitchell."

"God bless you, Mitchell." Hannah hoped the closing glass cut off the blessing. After the pamphlets, Marion had been warned. Before Hannah's frown reached Marion she was already tapping the number.

"It's dialing."

In her mid-60s, Marion was a loose-ends, only-son-on-the-West-Coast, wife of a retired auto exec. An entree-sized Jesus fish magnet adorned her Lincoln's trunk. When Joyce visited the office her first and only time, Marion remained excessively polite. Joyce, being Joyce, laid a cheek-hollowing, goodbye tongue kiss on Hannah that pushed Marion's smile to the point of shatter. Every Thursday as she left, Hannah was promised prayer on Sunday. But Marion was detail sharp and terrific with moms, trumping easily the spacey, college-grad girls Hannah initially ground through like cheap pencils.

Walking outside, Hannah saw the tail-end of Stamer's SUV hang right, disappearing around the building. A peculiar, stagnant gloom had crushed the bright morning. It had become a day to peel off in hopes of something fresher. From out of *Princess Brides,* a tan, sun-dressed brunette trotted to her red Cadillac, another useless phone crowding her fob hand. At the click, the horn tooted once and the brunette folded inside the open door. The car swooshed to life. Already, a far-off siren wailed.

Theirs was among a maze of mostly vacant two and three office/ boutique shop strips, isolated by islands of hedges, low-sculpted trees and blacktop switchbacks which stumped clients GPS' (*"Sorry we're late, but…"*). The sort of place where you would hide a rich man's psychiatric hospital. Though the building's address said Holly Ridge Court, Hannah wasn't sure what the law jurisdiction was, this far from any town or homes. From her white coat pocket Hannah checked her own phone. The circle spun. Acquiring. Acquiring.

The tan girl in the Cadillac lowered her window. "The radio says it's all over the country. New York, Florida. Half the stations are just static. No power. No phones."

Hannah and the tan girl faced one another. The girl raised her hand as if to wave and then lowered it as if embarrassed. She drove away, hanging right, as everyone had to. Hannah pocketed her phone. A national outage meant something beyond failure. She inhaled. *OK then.*

The bridal salon owner walked outside. Tall, Eastern European. Her big chest and strong jaw augmented her short dark hair. Upon meeting, Hannah had guessed she might be transgender, but her buttery voice and small hands belied it. The woman's name evaporated off Hannah's tongue, but surely her own was lost, too.

"What do you think, Hannah?"

"Oh…it's probably nothing. The worst thing you can do is believe anything in the first half hour. What have you heard?"

"Nothing. I wondered if I paid my bill." Her teeth shone.

Hannah smirked. "Your phone is out, too?

"The cell, yes. I called my husband from the cord telephone, but it wouldn't even leave message." The woman scratched at her arm, looking skyward, then down the lane. "All of them bandits. You pay, you pay and what? Nothing works."

"Yes."

The bridal owner was already bearing it. She had a survivor's face, a dismissive shrug.

"My husband has plenty of food and water for us. My son, he's very smart with technology. You have protection?"

"Yes. I'll be fine."

"Good. They will- "

Two girls stomped out of the spa next to the bridal salon. A milky, butch-haired rooty blonde with dime-sized ring holes in her ear lobes tried not to look, like, scared, but her hose blast of profanity told more.

"Can you believe this fucked-up bullshit? These jack-off mother-fuckers just let the fucking power go out everywhere. Like nobody ever fucking planned for an attack from these assholes?"

The slight brunette behind her appeared ready to cry, arms tucked in. Her lips set in the dread of swallowing a mouthful of awful. In black *"Dreamland Spas"* T-shirts and black pants, neither girl could have been over twenty-four.

"It probably wasn't an attack," Hannah said.

The blonde's chin jerked up. "Think so?" From out of the spa another black-shirted girl emerged. Slightly older, Indian.

"I tried to call Meredith," she told the pair.

"She ain't gonna get it. And what's she gonna do? She's in fuckin' Farmington."

The Indian girl glimpsed at Hannah. *See what I deal with?*

"What should we do?" the Indian girl said.

"Whatever the book says," Blondie pulled a hard pack of ciga-rettes from her back pocket.

"There is no 'book' Ashley. You are the manager."

The brunette turned from the circle, but her sobs were not hidden. The Indian girl hugged the brunette, lips close to her ear. They walked toward the opposite, empty end of the parking lot, to the hedges. When the other three female faces drifted back to the pocket, blonde Ashley held the pack out to Hannah and the bridal owner. Both accepted.

Damn it, her name......

Hannah leaned in to accept the light, barely drawing the smoke. "I'm Hannah" she said, blowing out.

Blondie/Ashley pocketed her lighter as the bridal owner straight-ened, taking a smoker's inhale. "She's always such a crybaby. Like she's ever had to sweat rent or anything. Fuckin Daddy's Girl." The blonde girl shook her head. Why me?

Hannah smoked and exhaled, regretting the choice, but willed to finish it front of the others. Calm, she thought. Triage calm. *Dreamland Spas* was a recent franchise happening, serving up Serenity in 30 minutes. Hannah wondered what sort of mask blonde Ashley wore for the Rochester Hills wives. Was there any mask at all? Were the post-Zumba and lunch ladies satisfied with the price and pull-in convenience? Another discounted, degraded experience slapped down, unloved by those who served or consumed. Take it or leave it. At the door sound, Hannah glanced backward at Marion, coming out with the flashlight in hand, thankfully off.

"There's only a recorded message at the power company. I also tried my husband." Behind her glasses, Marion's eyes clicked from the cigarette in Hannah's fingers to Hannah's face to the other women.

"Want one?" Ashley asked.

"No. I...no. It went to my husband's voice mail," Marion said, moving closer to Hannah. "What's happening?"

"Terrorists. The whole US. They finally did it," Ashley said, close to smiling.

"Don't scare her," the bridal owner said. "What's wrong with you?"

"Who else do we have today, Marion?" Hannah took a drag.

Marion squinted. "You want me to call them?"

"No. You're probably right. But let's leave a message to reschedule. Their voice mails will get it eventually."

Marion nodded. "Certainly."

"The power's gone off before. You can go if you'd like. It's fine."

"There's a 3:30. The Farber girl. How long do you want to stay?"

"I'll manage. If they show up, I'll be fine. If not, I'll leave soon myself. The power's gone out before." Hannah repeated, behind a forced drag, the taste going truly foul. She could feel the other women listening. She looked Marion in the eye. Calm. New York calm. Corpse behind the next curtain. But smile at the young man you're examining as he coughs. That kind of calm. Besides, Farber was Münchhausen on gluten-free toast.

There was nothing wrong with the child.

"I'll make the call," Marion said. She walked back to the office.

"Don't worry, Marion." Hannah said.

She stopped at the glass door. "I'm not worried at all," she said. Hannah knew Marion enough to know her voice's truth. Some of the medical staff Hannah knew during the flu were very religious. Their fatalism and homilies could grate but their cool was welcome, whatever the source.

The bridal owner dropped her cigarette down the storm drain. "I have too far to drive. Don't wait here long, Hannah. It's not good to be alone now."

Hannah nodded, darting her own half cigarette into the hole. *Damn it*. The names wrong as they formed. *Nina, Eva…*

"Yes. Thank you. We'll see you Thursday."

She winked. "Yes. That is the spirit." The woman strode to the salon with confidence and yes, a lovely ass.

Over the blonde's shoulder Hannah saw the Indian girl lead the brunette back into the spa. The Indian girl then walked to her car and returned carrying a small, pink handgun. She clicked something on it – the safety? - and tucked it into the small of her back like a movie gangster.

"She's fine. She just needs to lie down."

"Well I'm outta here," Ashley said, regarding Hannah a moment. "You staying?"

"For a while. See what's happening. The roads will be worst now."

"Fuck that." The third butt went down the drain. "I'm in Eastpointe. I'm not getting stuck here in the dark. What should we do with the cash, Rina?"

"Leave it, I think. Everything is insured, yes?"

"This sucks." Ashley turned for the spa.

"We have tea and coffee," Rina said. "Would you like some?"

"No, thank you." Hannah edged away but stopped.

"Please be careful with that gun."

Rina's mocha face beamed. "You are sweet."

The water still flowed. Leaving the bathroom, Hannah found Marion at the front door, gathered purse and umbrella. All else unsaid, their hug goodbye was genuine. Hannah promised to check in before locking the outer door, knowing she was lying as she said it. Being the brightest space, Hannah stayed at the reception counter. Miraculously, one text to Joyce seemed to go through, but to no reply. The land line could connect to nothing alive. Recordings and requests for patience. She thought of Roger and Darla; clueless, black-shaded New Yorkers steering their rental car through northern Michigan two-lanes. By her guess, they left over five hours ago. She hoped they made it to Mackinac City or a safe room somewhere.

Not wanting to sit in her car for information, Hannah hit on the idea of calling radio stations. On hold, she could listen to the broadcasts over the speaker. Hannah busied herself. After the first hour straightening the counter again, spray washing the windows and pacing, the news stayed the same. The blackout was national, occurring simultaneously just past two Eastern. Nearly the whole continental US lost power. Within the first hour, it was officially announced a "cyber-attack of unknown origin" was responsible. The whole grid was not affected, most non-cell phones and other utilities were functioning. US forces were on alert but no other international action or terrorist attacks were being reported. In the second hour, the official warnings and advice were coming in. Check on the elderly, but then, the advice to stay off the phones unless an emergency. Conserve batteries. If there was any positive outcome of V-14, nearly everyone had built up their Code Red kits – food, water, batteries, medical and survival gear. The president's speech was brief but reassuring. Pockets of power were already returning in the Northeast with help from Canada. Everyone was working at their maximum to......

Hannah walked from room to room, unable to leave. Push/pull.

Strip the office or not? She had plenty of supplies at home - the same sample drugs, some of the equipment - but it was a question of theft. If this went on for days, even through the night, she could return to find the place gutted to the carpet. Even then, she had few boxes to put anything in, much less room in her Saab.

By flashlight, she found her brother's business card in her desk and returned to the lobby.

On the third ring, it picked up. "Sutherland."

"Dale?"

"Hannah?"

"Your phone works. What are you still doing there?"

"If you didn't think I'd answer why'd you call, genius?"

She drew circles on the pad. "I know you always wanted to die at your desk."

"Sorry to disappoint you once again," His exhale was weary, full of gravel. Kid brother nearing 50 and sounding it today. She hadn't heard his voice since April - Celeste's birthday. Then he sounded so buoyant and expansive, yelling over the kid's party noise. They talked of running 5Ks together, promises to make back it to Michigan or out to Chicago soon.

"How are you talking to me?" he said. She could hear him standing. "Where are you? You OK?"

"My office line. I'm OK. What's going on with you?"

"Sweating my ass off, watching World War III. So, you're blacked out, too?"

"It's nationwide. Aren't you going home?"

Dale huffed. "Well there's about 10,000 people packed down on LaSalle ahead of me. There's no way in hell I'm getting back to Glen Ellyn tonight. No trains. Forget a cab. Roads are impossible. People are leaving their cars and just walking down the Kennedy. It's, like, everybody leaving a Bears game at once, times a thousand."

"Have you talked to Maria? How is Celeste?"

"I wish I knew. We got rid of our land line years ago. Have you talked to Joyce?"

"No. Same thing. Technology, huh?"

"Probably the Russians, I bet. For that port thing. You don't fuck around with billions of dollars, man."

"Uh huh."

"It's getting kinda hinky here. We got shootings. Tons of looting on the south side. We can see the smoke. It's nuts." He switched the receiver to the other side of his face. "They're savages. It's like -"

God...Dad again. *Israel.*

"Sweating huh? So, do you have any windows to open?"

"I'm 28 floors up, ya goof. We got the stairwell doors open, helps a little. Everyone got out of the elevators, at least. Most of us are staying. All the train people. Us suburban whiteys."

"Don't trust Whitey. Lord loves a working man."

Laughing, he sounded younger. "See a doctor and get rid of it."

Hannah was glad. Humor accelerated calm. She smiled and drew circles. They both loved Steve Martin. *The Jerk.*

"Tuna fish on white bread, a Tab and a couple of Twinkies. That's about all we've got to eat" he said.

"Do you have food? Have you filled up on water, in case?"

"Water's fine here. We'll get through the night," he said

Fine Fine Fine. Dad and Dale's song. *Everything's fine.* She hated the idea of Maria and Celeste alone, worried insane about Dale being missing. But she couldn't advise him to go out there. How could she take him getting hurt on her advice? Hannah remembered daring him once - "pussy boy" - to high dive on vacation at Burt Lake. All summer in a cast. She x-d the circles on the pad.

"How are you guys set up at the house?" she said.

"We're good. Maria's got the shotgun."

Jesus. Frigging BOYS.....

"No, Dale, I mean like your generator, food, batteries, radio."

"I'm not 6-years-old Hannah. A little credit, huh? We're all set."

"Well…good then."

A cooling silence, then cupped muffles from his receiver. Modulating hums and replies.

"Dale? What's going on?"

"Nothing. We're gonna go downstairs in a minute for some air. We just got an eight o' clock curfew from the city. You gonna be OK, Hannah? You got a safe way home?"

"Oh, yeah. God, I'm out here in the sticks, remember?"

"Well, there's plenty of insane hicks, too. Just go, now, OK? Get back in that fort of yours. What, Fiddler's Green?"

"That was the zombie movie, asshole. Cricklewood Green."

"Just be careful," he said. "Thanks for calling."

"You too. Love you. My love to Maria and Celeste."

"You got it. Love you, Hannah. Bye."

After packing a spare medical bag, she finally locked and left at 4:45. At first the side roads and M-59 moved well. Even the freeway was reaching speeds past 35 around Pontiac. But the northbound finally slowed and halted just past the Palace of Auburn Hills arena. A frozen trail of red lights, gradually shutting down as people shifted to park. Before Hannah knew it, she was blocked, rearview filling in with cars behind the rise. A few abandoned cars dotted the road shoulders further up, blocking any flow. The southbound lanes were deserted. Tumbleweed and blowing paper deserted. Not even a stalled car. Finally, one state police cruiser passed south, leading a silent ambulance. Two wreckers passed carrying seemingly intact cars. The pain in Hannah's stomach reminded her of no lunch and the stash of candy in her desk at home. She shifted to park.

The radio reported some looting in Detroit, Madison Heights, GR, up to Flint. The governor had not yet deployed the Guard. At the breaking report of a sniper shooting at freeway traffic in Indianapolis she switched it off. Two cars ahead, a gangly tech-looking guy left his black Ford. His wrinkled khakis did a Texas Two-Step shuffle down the embankment, headed for the trees. He returned a few minutes later.

After a churning, finger-tapping, jaw-grinding half-hour, she opened the door and stood. An observing crow in the middle of empty southbound I-75 took wing as a wrecker came along. This time she noticed both of the towed Buick's driver's side tires appeared blown out, its windshield flash-smashed white, the burst air bag. A few standing and leaning souls in front of Hannah faced north, forward, as if expecting the arrival of a great sight. A sunrise or mushroom cloud. Hannah's low-sugar imagination was turning morbid. Like they were all parts and pieces being fed, digested, into something invisible around the turn. She forced herself to look away, south, into the windshields. Behind the closer ones, she could see set faces, refusing to meet her eyes, dreading she might stomp toward them, screaming the End was Near. Body Snatchers and bad reactions. Hannah thought of the Indian girl and her pink gun. Further back, the windshields were grey-sky mirrors, as the office windows had been.

She heard them first. Shouts. Two people on foot, emerging toward Hannah in the gap of the second and third lanes of cars. Both in all black, the male was dark, Hispanic, bald and in long shorts. Standing and leaning people turned to the noise. Tattoo's colorful on her bare arms, the girl was shouting short words and handing off checker-paper items from a large brown box in the male's muscled, tattooed arms. A sensation coming on like a cool breeze. Horns honked. Gleeful, toots of encouragement.

"Tacos! Free Tacos! Who's hungry?"

Encumbered, the male nodded to the gratitude, grinning above a skinny Pharaoh beard. The girl held a wrapped packet out to Hannah. She looked behind the pair. People were eating without hesitation. In the moment, Hannah met the girl's cornflower blue eyes and found trust. The box was still filled with dozens of the checker-wrapped wedges

"Who are you?"

"I'm Kylie. That's Jazzer. Our taco truck's back there. You want one? It's free."

"Yes. Thank you. You're wonderful."

She shrugged and smiled. "No problem. It's all gonna go bad anyway. Tacos! Free tacos. Take one."

Sitting inside the Saab's open door, Hannah tried tempering her lunging appetite, but inhaled the soft, steaky thing in four bites, gulping the water taken from the office. Lettuce, cheese, fresh tomato chunks. It wasn't bad. Within a few minutes, she began to think things may turn out alright. Others chewing faces around her were looser, more alert than alarmed. Hannah reached for the med bag from her back seat and locked the door. Free food was beautiful, but she could beat that.

Walking north in the road, Hannah bore the red canvass bag across her front, Red Cross out. The lab coat was back in the office. Her pink-patterned Saks blouse would have to convince them she wasn't crazy. None of the drivers and passengers knew the cause was when she asked. "*Accidents? Was anyone hurt?*" she said. Another wrecker passed south bearing another smashed car; ambulance trailing. *"Does anyone need any medical help?"* She stopped next to an 18-wheeler, the bearded driver looking down.

"Outta gas?"

Hannah held the bag up at him. "No. Do you know what's happening? With the traffic?"

The driver's shaded eyes stayed on her, snake-like. "It's almost clear. Some assholes spilled metal on the road. Tire poppers. A lotta blow outs and wrecks. Truck jackknifed. You a nurse?"

"Doctor."

"They're saying it's almost cleared out. If I were you I'd stay with my car, lady."

She heard Joyce in the trucker's drawl. Instantly, Hannah felt foolish, aware of surrounding, curious eyes. Walking back to the Saab,

Hannah avoided the faces. She heard Joyce. *Just be part of the group for once, will you? Relax already. Exceptional is annoying most of the time, and you're not so exceptional. Lady.*

Lady. Joyce's play name for her. Hannah unlocked the Saab, head down. She tapped at her phone. Acquiring…

The trucker was correct. Within minutes a tide of red tail lights advanced from the horizon. Cars and trucks came to life, inching forward. Quickly the road speed was a steady 45 mph and Hannah reached her exit, several miles past Clarkston. Slowing past the green sign, she recognized the man walking on the right side, suit coat fisted over his back. The walk she knew - a lurching, stiff-wind march, head pitched forward like a hood ornament.

She eased next to him, lowering the window. "Mike!"

The fuming glare of Mike Narlow dissolved into an orgasmic eye roll. His hands opened to a merciful God, shoulders falling in deliverance.

He opened the passenger door and pushed back into the air-conditioned leather. "Oh my God. Hannah! You have no idea how good it is to see you."

"What happened?"

Mike had left in the morning on a quarter tank. He'd fill up on the way home.

Hannah zipped around the two-lane's swoop turns. Shadowy, branched greenery hugged the vacant roadsides, vines growing up the power poles. With less request than notice, Narlow held up her water bottle, nodding once before swallowing the rest.

"I had to leave my car back on the shoulder, before the Palace. I been walking – fuck, I don't know – three hours? I got a blister the size of a quarter."

"Did you have a gas can?"

Air pushed out his lips. "I was waving that thing for I don't know how long. People pretending they don't even see you and I'm ten feet away from 'em. Like I'm some scumbag. I go out hijacking cars in a Brooks Brothers. Some Jethro in an F-150 laughed in my face. Guy in a suit, out of gas. Real funny, huh? I threw the thing away. I got the coverage. Let 'em tow it. I'm gone to China on Thursday anyway."

His eyes closed, head back, Mike's white shirt was past creased, tie missing, perhaps in the ditch with the gas can. She could imagine such a gesture from Mike Narlow. Looking like an asshole in a tie a fate worse than walking thirty miles. A scratchy, not-quite growl curdled in this throat. Her brother's sound. The national Tone of the Day for distressed men in suits.

"Thanks, Hannah."

"Certainly. I'm glad you're OK."

As he relaxed, Mike's recap pinged without pattern from boasts to agonies, then back to front. Worst Evers and Longest Evers and epic Dumb. Emotions finally evacuated, he didn't ask for hers. Hannah wondered if Kim would get the abridged version, now it had been released. She turned the AC a notch higher. Mike's morning Drakkar and mouthwash were well depleted. The Saab's interior hid the engine and road noise in zoomy peace.

"So, you're going back to China?" Hannah slowed on a curve as another car sped past. "What's it like?"

Mike didn't blink, voice drooped to a dulled report. "It's a shithole, pretty much. You can taste the air. Really. Did you ever get a mouthful of mosquito spray, or like, Lysol by accident? That's air in China. A month there and you forget the sky is blue. Clouds are white. Did Kim tell Joyce about my suits?"

"Yes. Joyce said you can't get them clean."

"They look clean, but the smell? Forget it. You gotta throw 'em out. Fuck, they probably end up back in China. Get sold here." He snorted at the notion.

"Check this," he said, straightening. "Last time I was there our escorts took us to see a taxi painter. We're automotive, so let's see how they paint cars…taxis. Whatever.

"It's this long garage, right? Shotgun-style." Mike's hand sur-vey-sliced forward from his nose. "We're standing back in this separate room, looking out through this long, plastic window. Like a car-wash win-dow, ya know? Plastic's filthy, barely see through it. So, a cab pulls in and these guys tape paper over the windows, headlights. 1-2-3. And these other two guys are standing there with spray guns. No mask, no goggles. They just start spraying the cab. Driver inside, engine running. Cover it in about two minutes. The other guys strip the paper off the windows and the cab takes off - right down the street. Wet paint. No ventilator in the place. No filter. Shit just goes right out into the air."

His face wrinkled in disbelief, bemused as if still seeing it.

"Another one drives in. All day long. They repaint the cabs every few weeks because the air in Shanghai eats the color off that fast. Like, those painters? How do they not die of black lung in a year? Ya know? *'Fuck it, get some new ones in here.'* They got it over us. That's for sure."

Hannah prepared to laugh in tribute, but the last bit stopped her.

"What do you mean?"

"They get it done there. You see it and you realize. They aren't a bunch of complainers."

The blistered heeled man just had The Worst Day of His Life.

"But you say it's a shithole."

"I wouldn't live there. Doesn't mean they aren't eating our lunch. They've got real discipline."

"Or pathology," she offered.

Tucking back, his head reclined, focused down his nose at the mov-ing road. Hannah could see conviction had washed out of Mike Narlow. What he was speaking was just two-and-two fact.

"All I'm saying is we've got a choice to make. Live or die. Die doing what we're doing or live doing something else. People don't wanna face it but this country's gotta adapt. Good, bad or indifferent. Look what happened today. The flu should have showed people. Nothing stopped over there. Here everybody thinks someone owes them something. They'd better get with the fact we don't really need you."

Today Israel was far away. Today Israel was on the other side of the world.

"What does 'we' mean, Mike? Who's all going to have to eat the bowl of what you're selling? Does it mean you or only the people who'll have to spray paint cabs?"

He chuckled, holding his wrists up as if cuffed.

"Yeah, I forgot. Straight, working white male. It's all my fault. Take me away."

Hannah slowed to turn right, taking Woodford Road to circle Trunk Lake, over the bridge to Orton Road.

"If someone doesn't have a future don't be shocked when they expound the hell out of their present," she said. "It might happen all over you. Us. We."

"Well, yeah Hannah. I – we - do a lot better than most people. And I worked my ass off for it. As I'm sure you did. This 'dream deferred' thing you're saying? If that isn't extortion, then what does extortion sound like?" His voice slurred to ghetto patois. "Fix my life motherfucker or I'll fuck yo' shit up."

The tires drifted right and bit gravel. Mike jutted forward, unbelted in the sudden stop. Mike Narlow's profile swung left. Full frontal, she saw the teenage boy he was - still. This toy wasn't working anymore. The scowl wanting it fixed NOW.

"Get out."

"What?"

"Get out of my car."

"Jeez, I take it back. I'm just talking, Hannah. I'm sorry, alright?"

She faced forward, as if thinking about it, while powering down her side window. Before Mark realized his suit coat had been scooped up it was balled on the road's solid yellow line. Before he realized, his right arm was cocked to punch. Hannah's side eye withered the fist open, drooping the arm.

"Gonna fuck my shit up, 'cuz I won't fix your life?"

Mike's face seemed to pucker. Stunned. It wasn't fair.

"You're nuts."

"Ouch." She was done looking at him. "Get out, Mark. You'll make it home. You've got discipline."

The door slammed. She ignored the rearview. Hannah didn't see another soul, all the way to Cricklewood Green.

****

Command wanted active patrols of all LifeForce posts. Situation reports (sit-reps) every thirty minutes. Profile and strength. The fax machine beeps repeated. Holding the phone receiver, Steve pivoted, plugging a finger in his ear.

"Yes, sir."

They ambushed a LifeForce patrol in St. Joseph. One dead, one wounded. Two guards were hostages. At camera, Mandel scooped dispatches from the fax. One ear of his headset keyed to the police radio, Mandel kept blurting the incoming messages over his shoulder, like some spastic parrot squawking ball game updates. *Barricaded gunmen in Troy.*

"No, sir. I still can't raise two members of our night shift." Steve said, lying about Joe Allen, confirmed on his way. On Steve's order, Venegas was on foot around the complex but not yet punched in. The whole afternoon had been a convince dance. "We're still three. I've had no contact with Sergeant Peltier. He said Flint, sir."

"Ho, yeah! They got the guys in Benton. Rescue! No casualties," Mandel said, wheeling, finger up.

In the kitchen, Tyce looked up from the generator manual to the TV, feet up in a lounged calm.

Steve seethed at the noise. "Say again...Yes, sir."

Hanging up, Steve booted Mandel's chair.

"What the fuck, numb nuts? I'm talking to battalion."

Facing up, Mandel seemed truly confused. "What you think I got blasting my ears? It's all command and police calls. We're in a firefight outside of Flint, yo. It could be Sergeant Peltier." Mandel thrust out some papers. "Fuck man, all we're getting are orders, frequency changes. All kinds of shit. Anyone getting re-deployed?"

Venegas pushed the door open, a hunk of tired and pit-stained dark blue, wiping at his thick hairline.

Steve tossed most of the fax papers, so faint you could hardly read them. *When was the last time anyone changed the ink? When was the last time they got a fax?*

"These are an hour old, Garrett. I'm talking to the man live. And no, not yet. They're calling back in 30."

Venegas entered his code, ready to thumb in.

"Wait, Juan. No overtime's been authorized. Wait until 7."

"What?" Venegas' mouth hung open. "People are getting shot and it's not 'excessive circumstances'. Gimme a fuckin' break, Steve."

"Talk to them about it. It's not me, Juan. I'm just trying to save you the write-up." Steve tossed the wasted faxes aside, evaluating Juan's red eyes. "Everything alright?"

"It's a joke. No one's outside at all. Look, I'll print in, OK? Say you didn't know. You're in the john. You're outta here anyway." Venegas stepped forward. "Come on, it's an hour already and I busted my ass to get here. Lemme get paid at least."

Steve walked to the kitchen, backhanding the decision. Whatever.

"Power's on in Florida and most of Georgia. New York's expected in the next hour," Tyce said as Steve passed.

It was good news. Without saying it, Steve had been trying to discourage command from dispatching anyone in the Green by claiming they were shorthanded. The captain hadn't mentioned the D-Plex, but Steve knew it was the local asset for LifeForce. The county wouldn't have the muscle to protect it. Knowing that, the manpower summary every 30 minutes had to be played right. ("Gonna need every swinging dick.") As Corporal, Steve could be required to work - no overtime. If played correctly, Allen would arrive as rank on post and Steve could skate.

Tyce hadn't made fresh coffee. Steve tapped one-minute on the microwave to heat the last of his cup.

Steve could imagine them moping around the D-Plex parking lot, sweating in the full kit – M-4, vest, helmet. Too many deployed dudes Steve didn't know, way too keyed up, especially with LifeForce men already killed. By midnight, hallucination would stack on rumor. Guys with the twitch, seeing crawling hordes in those dark weeds surrounding the blacktop, coming for the Pepsi and Huggies. One panic shot and it would be a giant Polish firing squad.

So far, the day had gone correctly. When the blackout happened, Steve notified battalion and ran the checklist. Steve, Mandel and Tyce conducted patrols around the complex every half hour. Reassuring, showing strength. He didn't have to justify a thing. A few residents came out to talk. Everyone was calm, grinning through it and squared away with their own generator power. The development's generator kicked on instantly. Excepting the 10-second blackout of the TV, inside the Barracks they would not have known the outage happened.

"Just go," Tyce said.

"I'm rank, Tyce." Steve tasted and spilled out the rest of the cup. "I'm pretty sure they're sending me to the D-Plex."

"No. Allen's rank, right? He'll be here soon. We'll say you went on a call," Tyce said. "Your shift's been up for an hour. You look fried, man. You did great. Just go."

"How come you're still here?"

"Well, just to tell you, I'm gonna sleep here tonight. So even if the Pakistani dude doesn't show – "

"Anish." Steve corrected.

"Yeah, Anish. You'll still have your full shift. They can wake me up if they need me. Don't worry. I'm not gonna fuck you on overtime. I won't clock in until tomorrow."

"I'm not worried. Why are you staying?"

"It doesn't matter." Tyce paused, looking away at the TV and back. "I had to move yesterday, unexpectedly." He half-gestured to his punched-up face. "All my valuables are in my truck. I'm not driving back into a riot for a bunch of clothes. I'll shower here and go back tomorrow night. I'll sleep in the cell."

Tyce's expression was passive. A lump of take it or leave it.

"Steve. Go already. Nobody's gonna ask."

Grey-soup sky inducing an early twilight, Steve pulled up to his parent's home on the northwest edge of Essex. Shutting the lights, he parked in the driveway behind his father's dusty green Ram – "JHD Construction". The step-stool now lived under the driver's door since the old man's hip surgery. Flashes radiated, thunderstorm-like, behind the living room curtains. Steve could hear the big screen's volume halfway up the lawn. Neither of his parents needed a friggin' hearing aid.

Inside the living room the lamplight gleamed on his father's sun-burned dome.

He pushed forward in the maroon leather recliner.

"They let you out?"

Steve glanced at the TV. A helicopter shot of a Detroit fire – 7 Action News Live.

"You got the TV working, huh? I thought cable was out."

Plugged power strips and unspooled, plaster-dusted yellow extension cords snaked over the brown carpet. Steve stepped around the cords, past his father and the chair. He peeked into the bright, empty kitchen. A halo of gnats and tiny moths orbited the ceiling light, more cord and power strips across the linoleum, leading out the cracked-open screen door. The trailer generator flutter-rattled in the backyard. Anyone can get motivated when the TV don't work and the beer ain't cold. Steve turned back to the living room. The cigar reek fresh.

"Where's Mom?"

"In her room. I had an old roll antenna in the garage. I unhooked the cable and attached it to a piece of coaxial. I got 2, 4, 7, 56. Same crap on all of 'em." His bloated, scarred hand reached for the can of Miller next to the ashtray.

"We have satellite at the complex. It's working fine." Steve said.

The old man twisted with his whole right side to get a good look at Steve. The red golf shirt tight around his belly. The right eye squinted, lip unfurled over his yellowed incisor.

"What's with the cop duds? You ain't been home yet?"

The call-bullshit expression, when he didn't buy the excuse. It occurred to Steve his father had never seen him in his LifeForce uniform. Maybe that was it. Maybe it was the hip, the arthritis. Maybe just pain.

You don't act Big. You don't show off.

"Nah, not yet. Just wanted to make sure you guys were OK." He sunk into the couch, belt gear bunching into his waist.

"Doug was here earlier. Henry called."

"Good."

"Doug said Jill had her hands full with Jason and Jordan today, but they're all OK. Doug was on a tile job up in Gavin, but the guys stayed with him. They finished it."

"Uh-huh." Steve looked up at the soft wire antenna duct taped to the ceiling, trailing behind the flat screen's stand. More fire footage. Lines of cops at intersections parting for fire trucks and re-grouping to escort-wedge formations.

"Figured you'd be working all night in the tear gas. Send you down to Detroit or Flint. Shines are already out on their shopping spree." He bless-gestured with the can and drank.

"They've got the D-Plex covered. The lot's blocked off. There's Sheriffs and a bunch of AUVs parked around it. This will be over soon anyway." A stab of spring moved Steve's ass cheek.

"Yep. What they're sayin'."

"Were you on a job when it happened?"

"No. Went with your mother to the doctor. We were on our way back when the radio went off. We thought it just broke. Then when we got to town we saw all the lights off, everybody outside."

His mother emerged from hallway shadow. "Stevie!"

Her legs were thick, pale, colored with vein under loose tan shorts. Dyed dark hair pulled back tight. Steve stood to meet her. The wobbling steps bothered him. He could measure the aging every time he saw her. Steve crooked down slightly for her embrace, hand cold on his arm.

"You look good, Stevie. I like this blue so much better. Better than that monkey-shit brown they used to make you wear. Are you hungry?"

"No, I'm alright."

"Bah. When did you eat last? Come on, I went shopping."

"Yeah. We got plenty of milk," his father said.

"Go fuck yourself," she muttered past the recliner.

"We get home and right away she has to go buy milk," he called behind them. "I don't drink it. She doesn't hardly. But we gotta have milk. She's gone two friggin hours."

"The goddamn kitchen is full of bugs, asshole," she said, pushing and jostling the screen door in vain against the cords. "Just leave it open all the way next time. Let everything in."

"We gotta keep the milk cold," he said.

Ice cubes snick/snacked into the glass she then filled with 7-Up. "He goes on all week about his hip and his hands and his joints." Steve's mother pulled lunch meat, a tomato, onion. She reached up for bread from the pantry. "But he drinks like the city sewer. If you can drink 70 beers a week, you ain't sick. We're out of mayo, OK?"

"It's fine, Mom."

"But say anything about yourself? *'You're so bitchy. You're so whiny.'*"

On the TV screen, through a cloud of fresh cigar smoke, Manhattan was fully lit once again. Pennsylvania, too. It would be OK.

Steve parked in his driveway and checked the mandatory landline (LifeForce Rule #63) to no messages. He unbuckled the belt, unlaced his cop shoes and collapsed into a two-hour nap. After showering by the ghosty-glow of Coleman propane, he took inventory of the still-cool fridge. Three eggs, some hamburger meat with not long to go. Butter. Ketchup. An ancient apple. Five beers. Chicken still firm in the freezer. He laughed at himself, toweling. No food means no food problems, right?

Pioneer-like with his lantern, Steve pulled a clean pair of jeans, briefs and socks from the drawer. He left his service .40 in the gun safe and considered bringing out his black Model 60 .38 revolver. The gun safe was sparse, like the rest of the cupboards. The 70s vintage Remington over-under 12 gauge had been his brother Henry's. The lever-action 30-30 Steve hadn't fired since his last time hunting, back in his first year on the Essex force, trying to be on the team. Off-duty, for if/when, Steve liked the revolver. No jam. Guys could talk all they wanted – housewife pop gun. Steve never got obsessions. Guys he knew growing up seemed to go from Ninja Turtles to everything X-Box, to fantasy sports and guns. Needing all the stuff, competing, the boasting and pointless argument. Besides, Steve reasoned, if he needed more than five hollow-points he'd need more than a pistol anyway. Steve decided yes on a jacket and the .38, checking the load, choosing the hip holster instead of the conceal flap. He picked the flashlight from his Batman belt for his jacket pocket, in case it didn't come back on.

He brushed his teeth, wanting dinner, faces, noise. He left on foot.

Essex was a festive town tonight. For once, everyone had a new story. Dozens of people strolled and clustered along Heller. Someone had set up two banks of 4-spot highway construction lights, spaced along the street. The adjusted high-pedestal floods bounced off the street and building front glass to create street light the whole length of the drag, back from the BP station. A few young girls were posing directly under the spots, vocalizing and hip-bump posing while their parents talked nearby. Nearly everyone had generators going in the open stores. Carol's was serving. Chairs on the sidewalk, the porches, the stoops. BBQ smell from someplace. Coolers of icy, floating bottles and cans. Steve nodded hellos and exchanged stories with those who spoke first.

His father had moved them to Essex from Taylor, Michigan when Steve was 11. By then his brother Henry was in the Air Force and Douglas had his GED, swinging the hammer for his father. Steve won his first new-kid fight in Essex, making the little fucker eat grass, though it bought him a year of counseling and court-prescribed 'behavior' pills through junior high (which his old man *loved*). He could play ball well enough and got along, but the Essex kids already had too many pacts and secrets. Obsessions. Never much interested in anything at all, Steve would always be off. In a way, he felt it made him effective as a cop, later. He was a known animal but not too familiar. When Steve had to bust them, there was no arm to pull on, yet he could listen and overlook when he needed to know something. Steve wondered how you couldn't be a little off and be worth anything as police.

The plastics plant in Gavin was still operating when Steve was a teen. The furniture mill; the aluminum stampers had two shifts. About

1,500 people lived in and around Essex. When he started on the force they were under nine hundred, the high school closed. The fewer people, the more problems. Break-in robberies. Some meth and dope. Jackpot and the Valentine's Day girl shook everybody. The Beckman kid disappearing, even though everyone knew the ex-husband did it. Then the town bankruptcy. Now Essex was like an old person in a nursing home, staring out the window. His grandmother in Swistak. Nothing much moved, nothing much said. Nothing would get better. Thoughts behind those yellow eyes were not petitioned.

Far past the noon-shine construction lights, outside Teddy's, seven men clustered under the door's cone of buzzing light. The crew's sidearms were buckled high on their hips. Walking in the street center Steve passed their curbed car's backseats and truck beds, the long gun's shapes discreet. Two stores further up a Ford Mini-van was slant parked to the yellow line, half-blocking Heller to hinder any westbound cars. By habit, violations clicked in Steve's mind and he slowed. The door crew returned his nod, watching Steve's lingering, scanning stares on the long guns and the parked van.

He stopped and approached. Filtered smokes coaled orange under ball-cap shadows. On Teddy's barred window sill, under the upside-down American flag, a box radio squawked the latest reports. There was no alcohol Steve could see or smell as he approached the shop front. Just energy juice, Gatorade and coffee. Like some geeky miner, Matt Malone had a pair of night-vision goggles flipped up on his head. The brick-sized hand radio clipped to the equipment belt of a buzz-cut, red-haired man crackled an insect's call and response. Others were posted somewhere, in the dark. Two pistol magazines were pouched next to the man's radio. Steve didn't recognize him.

"Hey guys," Steve said.

"'Sup Stevie," Robby Trella emerged in his Sheriff's reserve deputy uniform, vested. "What's goin' on?"

"Who brought out those lights?" Steve thumbed backward.

A few looked around. "Ain't sure."

"It's real nice, huh? Good gesture," he said.

"Yeah. It is."

"No doubt."

He peeked into the gun shop's open door. Teddy Gregg and two other men stood and sat near the register and glass counter. Unmoved, they stared back. Steve stepped away, looking down the length of Heller. He caught a fleeting whiff of skunk bud dope.

"Anything going on?"

"Nope. Nice and quiet," Trella said.

Casting his hand in half salute and kiss-off Steve told them to take it easy and squeezed past. He could taste the keyed-up tension. That hair-up tingle before an arrest, the charge in the air after a house party brawl. What he expected if he'd been posted at the D-Plex. The cursed murmurs back there bothered him. *Bitches are lucky I'm not a cop anymore*. Men he'd cuffed for choking wives and punching sons. Men he'd let go for pissing in doorways or arrested for peeping in windows and hauling poached deer. Men who knew it was Steve's fault. The bitterness worked him and for a flash Steve considered getting on the air to the State boys. If it didn't come back on soon, someone was going to get shot, for an equal mix of best intentions, "whoops" and little bit of somebody wanting to know what it felt like.

A squealing pack of young kids startled Steve, bounding down the middle of Heller; their flashlight beams popping like crazy fireworks. One of the slanted Ford van's rear stickers stood out in black - SECEDE.

Inside the Highwayman bar, Jim Cronc was cranking it full power. Steve passed a few doorway smokers, stepping up into the bar's dark wood warm-lit roil, packed with human hum and clatter. Steve worked the clowny hellos and jokes to reach the back elbow of the bar. His stool in front of the antique metal US Marine recruiting panel, speckled with rust.

The history of battles imposed behind the globe anchor ended in Korea. On the jukebox, Johnny Cash was getting busted down in Juarez, Mexi-co. Jim's place always shut out things out, even tonight. All the talking faces brought on a smile. For once no one was stroking on their phones. Steve counted twenty-two in the room.

Cronc inherited the bar ("*Since 1939*") and had done wonders. The food now bested Carol's. Duck fat fries, venison tacos. Cronc poured the drinks deep. The regulars stocked the CD jukebox – golden country and greasy rock. All chest and shoulders, Jim Cronc made it through Michigan State as a nose guard and played one season of special teams for Green Bay before the knee. But the Highwayman was hallowed Lions, Red Wings and Tigers ground from poster to flag to the cardboard drink coasters, save for Jim's old Packers helmet shelved by one of the flat screens. The man knew his customers. Someone who hadn't been working and looked hungry might get a burger and fries placed in front of him without a mention or a bill. Some Sundays Cronc would set the folding chalkboard sign out front – "Free Chicken for Lions fans". He'd cook all day, singing with the jukebox and cheering, longish hair tied back in a blue bandanna as he filled tray after tray with legs, wings and thighs. Unlike Steve's, no one ever said jack about Cronc's mustache.

Jim offered his knuckles to Steve. "Sarge. What's good?"

"Well nobody's shot out there yet." They knocked and stacked fists. "What's good here, boss? Hungry as hell."

"Got roast beef and peppers. Marinated ALL day. On the baguette. How's things? Figured you'd be out there." He reached into the tub, handing Steve an icy Molson.

"Nah. No big thing." Steve said. "Be over soon. How about you? You lose anything?"

"Food? No. I had the generator juiced in a couple minutes." Cronc's hands reached, washed, wiped and straightened but his face stayed unwavering on Steve's. If struck blind Cronc could work the joint, no spills. He walked off toward more thirst closer to the door, shoulders rolling and singing with Johnny. When he was a cop, Steve lunched there almost daily. To Cronc, Steve would always be Sarge, a kindness Steve couldn't reject despite a nag of annoyance. In Essex, Steve would always be what he was. He finished the beer in three more gulps. Some suit was on TV in front of sky-blue background, behind a government-seal podium next to a stone-face general. Reporters waving raised hands. The man peered at them, nodding and pointing. Eyes ready to Demand Answers from someone responsible.

Lorna Brusine's face eclipsed Steve's attention, near enough to smell her. A pure, cool force-field so beyond clean it made his showered self feel like day-long molt. Dark hair flowed off her shoulders, olive skin without a mark. Plush lips, gleaming eyes shaded in smoky dark green. The cut-sleeve black T displayed her mash-up arm tats in full glory - a cheetah pattern, tribal swirls, flowers and a Japanese geisha face. The bar candles sparked the short silver hoops in her ears. Her mouth spoke an alien language, repeating the question.

"Huh?"

"You want another?"

"Uh. Yeah. Please."

"You want fries with that beef, right?"

"Yeah. Please."

She drew the church key from her back pocket, popped the top and set the wet bottle in front of him. With his reply on the fries she tilted her head a touch. A pull to the corners of her eyes, a slightly open smile to say – *yeah, I know. And you know.*

"What are you doing here?" he asked.

"I could ask you the same question."

"I thought you went to college."

"I did."

Steve gestured to Chinese writing wrapping above her elbow.

"What's that say?"

Lorna glanced down as if a bug had landed. "Nosy."

"Old job habit. Sometimes I look too closely at things."

"Yeah. I've noticed," she said.

Her ass and flag of ravens-claw hair disappeared through the flap of kitchen door.

Steve drank.

Cronc's sister, Robin, brought the meal out to him. The foot-long beef and peppers *was* perfect, seasoned & soggy. Mellowed and full, Steve finished his third Molson while Lorna kept making her way back to the elbow for hit-and-run conversation. Meanwhile, four of Lorna's fans were front and center at the bar, throwing their best right down the middle at her, laying singles and silver down. A quick one turned into closing time because, well, maybe. *It's the way she looks at me, ya know…?*

The power was coming back on anyway. He'd napped. And he hadn't been out in a long time. Fuck it. Steve raised his empty green bottle to signal another, tossing the napkin onto his cleared plate. And here's Number Five.

Asshole.

******

This was a good one. A dud bomb landed in the middle of the compound and Hawkeye and Trapper had to crawl out to defuse it. It turns out to be the CIA's bomb, full of propaganda leaflets. To Ray, the old *MASH's* were the best. Ray looked over at Sherri in a pocket of lamp light, cat-curled on the sofa with her magazines. She didn't seem to mind the third episode in a row. Ray had a bunch of other things on disc. Mostly old movies - *French Connection, LA Confidential, Wild Bunch*, but he felt like something fun, easy. Cable still out, the radio said maybe after midnight.

Reclined, Ray sensed Mark huddled in the dark, by the kitchen.

Just like when he was a kid, wanting to ask for something. Ray reached down for his ice-weakened diet soda. He sipped and sucked his teeth, feeling Sherri's eyes up at the hated sound. The page turned. Mark stepped out, just enough into the TV light, gathering, pretending attention to the show. Mark's beard was gone.

"You shaved." Ray said.

"Dad, I need your truck tomorrow. Early. When it gets light."

"What for?"

"I need to go to my storage unit."

"Yeah? And what for? You were there two weeks ago. I told you – shit comes in, shit better go out."

"What does it matter?" Mark said.

"Jesus Christ. It don't matter to you, so it don't matter to anyone else, right? You think I can't see, or what? You think you're gonna move everything down there piece by piece and I'm not gonna notice?" Keeping his eyes on the screen helped Ray's tone stay even. The voices laughed at Frank Burns.

"OK. Well I need my black powder, my cartridge loader. Other stuff." He took a breath. "I think you'll be glad."

"Why, Mark?" Sherri said.

"Look, guys. I don't wanna fight...how we fight. Please."

Ray finally really looked at the kid. His eyes looked swollen, like he'd been crying. "But today is just the start. I know."

Ray swatted it. "The world ain't gonna end, Mark. Trust me."

"Did you see that on *MASH*? Or was it *Seinfeld*?"

"You wanna get cute?" Ray said. "No. There's your answer. Go anytime you feel like it. Why don't you move all your storage into the basement and then you can go sleep and eat there? How's that?"

Mark stepped in front of the screen, hands wide to hold the big ball of invisible.

"Guys, I've been listening on my short-wave receiver all day."

"I'm sure you have."

"– I've been hearing things – "

Sherri sat up. "Mark, it's OK. We listened to the news."

Mark half-circled in the bleed of TV light, as if he were turning from rain. Mark's fist knocked on the side of own head. Ray felt bad a moment but couldn't hold it back. It was always But. Always the threaded needle with Mark. If the uniform had to be green, Mark would wear green stripes because you didn't say it had to be ALL green. If you had to show up at 8:00 for something Mark would come tornadoing in at 7:59 with a 'how come?' look on his face when you got so pissed off, sure he was messing with you. But he wasn't. It was just Mark. Ray just never knew what to do with the kid.

"No, not like I'm 'hearing things'," Mark said. "You know what I mean. And I'm not talking about the news. Soon, maybe even tomorrow, things are gonna get really bad. They've been flying C-130s into Metro today, even before the power went off. For an entire day no one was paying attention to anything but traffic and looters and stupid distraction. I checked the news, too. Kids trying to get home from school. That's the crap they told you about. *Think*. No one's paying attention."

Ray's thumb upped the volume on the laughs. Hawkeye got in a good one.

"Look. I care about all of us." Mark said.

"Mark, almost the whole country has its power back on," Sherri said. "It was an attack, but nothing happened. A few crazy things. They fixed it. It's OK to be wrong. We don'-"

"I've got sources, people I'm connected with. They've been broadcasting the code words."

It put Ray on his feet, walking to the glass sliders as if swimming from the whirlpool of his son and getting sucked into hopelessly fighting it. Ray could hear Sherri huff and stand, feet across the carpet.

Count to ten. There was moon on the pond now.

"Mark, there's a million other things in this world I'll talk to you about. Pick any one of 'em. Please."

"OK, Dad. Let's talk about what you're gonna do when there's no more food. When they put your ass on a truck and ship you to some camp in the desert. When they kick in the door, in the last minute of your life. You're gonna wish you listened to me."

A wondrous, almost-laugh blurted from Ray, steaming the glass.

"Well I'd be pretty fucking stupid to waste my last minute thinking... thinking about," Ray said, head swiveling in the empty room. "Hey. I - I thought it was supposed to be when the flu - Mark? Remember? All those calls, telling me the same shit... Your 'people', your – "

"Mark?"

Ray was alone with Hawkeye and Trapper, shouting at the furniture. He stomped toward the front room, stopping when the dark grew too complete for the TV glow blot in his eyes. Turning, he felt for the door jamb of the foyer, squinting up at the moon glimmer on the hardwood stairs, then down at the blacker depth of the basement door. The TV laughter behind Ray brought a seething embarrassment. Mark was gone.

***

The wind had picked up, both guards thinking it best to go out now. Local news came on after Emergency Broadcast suspended at nine. The madness had calmed enough to give the weather guy's brown sport coat a few minutes, warning of strong storms after midnight. Power was on just east and south of the area. Nationally it was restored over 85 per-cent. Fires out, streets empty but for the red/blue flashers and spotlights of law. The guards shut the Barracks TV off before 11, when information repeated and expert's blame started. Joe Allen wanted some air. Tyce vol-unteered to come along, man the patrol car spotlight. Use the spotlights on patrol – faxed Battalion Emergency Order #37. Or was it #31? The amused men shook their heads. *Tyce, can you read that?*

Allen drove the LifeForce junior patrol car at a crawl. Houses were mainly dark inside, excepting a few upper bedrooms. But Cricklewood Greeners loved their outdoor lights. Flood beams tripped when the car passed. Lilliputian solar-cell lined the paths, beam directionals over the garages. Pinpoint highlight jobs along the brick frame gardens and chain-hanging purple bug zappers. Tyce had never seen the place at night, how bright it was. These people were paranoid.

Tyce cut the spotlight's hot-white tube through the trees, casting trunk shadows in bold black, dancing them off leaf undergrowth with the car's drift. The window handle was stiff and the light jerked as Tyce swept. He could still hear the fountain's hiss under the wind. Allen looked up out the driver's side window. A good night for stars, he said. Wind had taken the clouds. The storms would be strong. A cold front.

"What do you think he meant?" Tyce said. In the woods, a rabbit or cat's pink eyes bounced back at him, suspended before the beam passed.

"It ain't like Peltier to bullshit," Allen said. "I wouldn't worry it. Considering today, I'd say you're in good shape."

"How's that?"

"You stayed after clocking out. Tomorrow? Over the next week? They're gonna be refiguring all kinds of protocol. What went wrong, who fucked up, who came through. They'll love it. Gonna be a report this thick," Allen said, thumb and fingers spread. "You being out one day ain't gonna mean a thing. You stayed. It's gonna matter. What happened, if you don't mind me asking?"

"Me and my girl got jumped, coming out of the movies. They took my phone, Everything."

Allen thought it a shame and went on about tricks for moving up in LifeForce, the best postings for transfer. On a whim, Tyce aimed the searchlight beam up into the trees, the plush leaves taking on a concrete bake in the glare. No perched terrorists in the branches. He recalled run-ning from the cops as a teenager. They swept their lights all through the park but not up into the trees. They never thought to look up. Tyce and his friends right above them, breath held. There's cops for you. Jobbers.

At the braking, Tyce looked to his left, right hand easing to his hol-ster. A slumpy shadow stood back from a streetlight's coppery pool. The slash glint out the top of its shoulder unmistakably a rifle barrel.

Allen's fingers feathered Tyce's leg. "Cool."

"Mark. What's happening?"

"Hey, Joe."

The tall, heavy young man wore a red *'South Park'* T-shirt, his jaws working cud-like, head lowering to get a look at Tyce.

"Evening officer," he said, chewing.

Tyce nodded. South Park's hair a limp, dark sprout over his pushed-back night vision goggles.

"You washed your face."

"Huh?"

Allen's thumb and index finger scraped to a point along his own chin. "The beard."

"Oh. Yeah. I don't know."

"What are you doing, Mark? Hunting squirrels?" Allen's voice soothed easy. Taking a cue, Tyce shut the spotlight off. Besides the wood-stocked carbine off his back, South Park wore a holstered Glock pistol. The rifle something vintage, East-bloc.

South Park gulped down his mush, lips smacking. "Naw. It's OK. Just a little restless with everything. Nothing's chambered." His hands were visible, shaking bagged candy into his palm. Tyce noticed the finger-nails, bitten down to gruesome stubs.

"OK. Well, you take it easy, Mark. You see anything funny and you call us first. Before you do anything, uh, *rash*. Right?"

"Sure, Joe. Don't worry. I'm not worried." Mark pushed more

candy into his mouth. Allen nodded. After an eyeball pause on the kid he released the brake.

Allen said nothing. Streetlight reflections rolled up his eyeglasses.

"So, we're supposed to be protecting *him*?" Tyce said.

"Unless he shoots or violates someone's person or property or property of the development we don't have a thing to say." Allen's smile was amused.

They slow rounded the flat green space next to William Gallo's house, passing it and the house with the monster RV in the driveway. The big rig rolled in through the gate not an hour ago, the only traffic since evening. Tyce kept the spotlight off. The nervous, bright loud morning felt days away.

"What's the reg for a case like him?"

"Ah. Mark's just a big-ass kid. He's harmless. He never got over playing Army, I think. A lot of other really dangerous mothers live in this castle." Allen nudged at the house with the big willow in back. The German Shepherd barking as they passed. "If something like today really got out of hand? Long term? I'd stay as far from this place as I could."

"You'd rather stay in Detroit?" Tyce said.

"Straight up."

Allen's neck fidgeted. Tyce sensed him working the thought.

"See, I don't know what happened to you last night or where ya'll come from. But it ain't like you think. People – black people – we're just jealous of each other's shit. And that's our shame. But white people? You don't know anything about it, in general. That fear is just worked in you too deep. Yeah, there's evil motherfuckers in the city who'd take you off, kill you. Sure. And you'd better be aware. But mostly not. Like today? Where I live, it was cool. We did alright during the flu. 'Cause everybody had it the same. We'd look out for each other. Up here?" Allen's grimace and head belled toward not.

The rest of the slow drive was quiet but for wind. Allen pulled in at the pool house and rec room, head-lighting the brick. The first rain drops were coming in on the gusts. The car shifted to park. Curious, Tyce looked over at Allen, his arm out long over the wheel, bothered.

"Shit got taken tonight and places burned. And that don't sit right with me."

Allen faced him.

"All I'm saying is you – some - people do not deal with loss of control really well. Events – control, say - don't go the way you plan or expect and you panic. And the people up here got way too much firepower and they are *scared*. Look at all these lights. And they're inside a wall, with guards." Allen's head bumped back in the direction of Mark South Park. "They'd be killing each other over the last bag of M&Ms. Anything moving. Me staying up here? Shee-it. I seen that movie."

He shifted the car to reverse and turned toward the Barracks.

"What movie?"

"Whatever."

"I mean, what movie are you talking about?"

"I mean any movie," Allen said. "The nigger always dies."

****

It was over. Steve and Lorna walked away from the bar's buzzing neon on lamp-lit, wet sidewalks. He gave her his coat, insisting. The pair's steps clicked on the deserted, uneven cement. The flow of all the rain flushing into the sewers and the new, colder air made Lorna have to pee. She hoped he wasn't one of those guys who thought a short walk was, like, two miles.

At his side door, Steve pointed up. "North star. Can always find your way home."

"Wow. Cosmic."

Lorna followed him up the two cracked concrete-block steps into the kitchen. The microwave's under-light was on, clock flashing 12:00. The dim kitchen sour with boy smell, old garbage. She pulled the door closed as he set his keys on the counter.

Lorna swayed past him and felt her way through to the bathroom. When she came back he was setting the microwave clock from his watch - 3:19. She stopped at the stove and fridge, waiting on him. A few watery dishes in the sink, a pot full of gross floaties.

Arms crossed, Steve stood against the fridge, giving her space and time. Sometimes older guys were like this. Mostly they were takers. Setting her purse down, Lorna gripped the counter edge and pulled herself up to sit, jean legs and black Chucks dangling. This one had been a cop, but that could mean anything. Lorna's nerdy-looking Bio teaching assistant was a beast; all hands and hard, whispery orders.

"You got anything else to drink?" she said.

"Beer."

She fake orked. "You do anything else besides drink?"

Steve stepped back over to the cheap relic kitchen table and pulled out one of the two chairs, scraping the linoleum. His arms hung over the back of the ugly white and yellow pattern vinyl. "Nothing for years. Not even smoke. Sorry."

"No fun."

"You don't need any more, I think."

"Aww, Mr. Cop." She girl-whined her voice. Maybe he liked to play that way.

"You didn't tell me what the Chinese on your arm says."

"What do you think?" she asked, dreading the menu joke.

"Stop me before I get another tattoo."

Lorna's laughter was genuine, matched by his toothy smile.

"Aw, come on. You could use a little self-expression, Mr. Cop."

"I'm not a cop anymore."

She pointed to each character. "Power. Passion. Love."

Steve nodded. "Nice. I like those."

"Me too."

"Must have been expensive."

"Yeah. It took almost two months. I used all my high school grad-uation money. My mother didn't talk to me again until I came back Christ-mas break my freshman year."

"Funny."

"It was awesome. You never got any?"

"I do. I have a star on my right tricep."

"Really? A cop thing?"

"Maybe a little. I couldn't think of what to get. I just kind of set-tled on it. Me and two guys got them when we finished our certification. I'm sure it wasn't as special as yours." He chinned toward her arm.

His eyes cast down, at his cowboy boots. Lorna swung her legs out and back once, twice. He looked up, leaning back a little, face halved by the microwave light. The mustache did kind of work for him. The dim kitchen was sexy, conspiracy-like. Like they were planning a crime.

"I guess I could probably get myself home now," she said. "The rain stopped."

"Right. You have pepper spray," he said.

"Maybe more than that. You'd have to drive me back to get my bike, though."

"Your parents let you ride back every night by yourself?"

"Nobody *lets* me. And I don't work every night."

From dealing with her mother Lorna liked listening to language acutely. Words had power. Lorna looked for margins in meaning. Use any way in, around. She half-remembered a Zen quote about a flower pushing through concrete.

"Not to scare you, but do you know what happened out here?"

"I know all about Jackpot. I had to write English papers about it."

"I was first officer. The girl on Valentine's Day."

"What do you mean 'first officer'?"

"It means I was the one who found her."

"No kidding." Lorna leaned forward. "Oooh. Ghost story time."

They were hazel, large for his face. Cop eyes for sure when he wanted. Like now.

"I'm sorry. That was mean."

"Not mean. You shouldn't...people don't think things will happen to them. No one ever wakes up thinking they're gonna talk to a cop today. But there you are, in their life. It's usually bad. As police you learn to expect things most people don't."

"Tell me," Lorna said. "Finding her. What happened?"

"Whoever disposed of the body put a pair of red high heels in the middle of the road. It's why I stopped. That's what I remember the most, still. These shiny red shoes. It's Valentine's Day. So I stopped, got out with my torch. And they were placed together, like someone should have been standing in 'em. In the middle of the road."

Steve looked past her, eyes drifting like a blind man.

"I'm shining around - and it had been warmer, almost no snow. I shined over to the embankment on the other side of the ditch. There she was, nude. Stark white. Lorna, I'd never been so scared in my life. But that's where training is a nice thing. You're reacting - call it in. Observe, preserve the scene. Be a reliable witness. I remember the shoes. Another thing I remember, standing there, aiming my weapon around the dark, was feeling like they're watching me, aiming on *me*. I heard the sirens and it was like a movie. Really. Your head is praying so hard for them to come. *They're gonna shoot. They're gonna shoot.*"

She swallowed, thighs squeezed together. Fuck *me. That is so hot.*

"It wasn't Jackpot though, right? They never found the killer?"

He looked at her. "No. It wasn't Jackpot. The state police found out they weren't even hers. The shoes. They were too small. She was still warm, Lorna. It's like, you think, *ten minutes earlier...*"

"Isn't it funny about ghost stories?" she said. "It's the dark. You can't see, so you imagine. In the light it's, like, *so what*? You don't tell ghost stories in the morning."

"I guess so. She wasn't a ghost. She was a girl. Like you."

So, tag. You're it. She resisted the urge to check her phone. He suddenly stood. Lorna boosted off the counter, but he moved to the blinking red dot by his house phone.

"Hang on a sec," he said, tapping the lit number pad. She took her purse and walked down the hall.

Lorna sighed in the bathroom's ancient pink tile, staring at the mirror, pin-flecked with toothpaste. Her brush was gross with hair. She put it back in her purse, next to the revolver. *More than pepper spray.* God, fucking Cerestine. Her fingers parted her scalp, making sure there were no bare spots yet. Was he one of those small-town virgin guys? She reapplied, checking her teeth. One more minute, one more chance. Do you flash the guy or what? She could have peed again but was out of Kleenex. Next to the pot was an empty cardboard tube. She left the bathroom.

Half of Lorna knew it was his silhouette in the hallway; the other half deliciously, electrically frightened. His steps to her were deliberate slow knocks on the creaky wood. He seized her hair, pulling her head back, face up. Steve's bulk enveloped her against the wall. His kiss nothing but control. The gasp was the sound of worry – over the pills, over everything - vaporizing. Lorna's hands hooked up on his shoulders, to hang on and ride.

****

Wednesday, September 6th

It had been a while. Did his face ever just do this on its own? Grin all the way to his back teeth? Steve was loose in places he couldn't find yesterday. The computer cursor blinked at him like a middle finger, but he could grin as long as it could blink. After-action report? What action? You wanna hear about *my* action?

Tyce was right. Nobody asked. Nothing happened. Peltier's "report" order was the only morning dispatch. Never assigned to write one before, Steve thought on the language of police reports but was uncertain of format. The prospect of clicking through the 300-page PDF manual fucked with his mood. Nothing had ever happened in Cricklewood Green. He rested his neck against the wall, eyes closing. Just for a sec. Even showered, some of Lorna still clung to him. He drew breath, smiling.

Perfect timing. Exhausted, Peltier was taking the day off. He'd been deployed to Flint, all night chasing looters and blooping tear gas. ("Every swinging dick"). Steve listened to Mandel at camera, clocking in the D-Plex deliveries. Volunteering, Tyce left earlier to pick-up lunch in Gavin for them. (Manny's - real Mexican).

December was the last time Steve had gotten laid. A divorced 40-ish mother from Grand Rapids met on-line. A naked Christmas Eve and Day, her kids off at their fathers. A weird couple of days - glad, hot and sad all at the same time. He told his parents it was work and doubted he was missed beyond obligation. In his mind, Steve saw himself married one day, with kids, expecting it would happen the way things did. A years-old vision existed there. Himself old, white haired and weather faced, with a dog on a house deck overlooking Lake Huron.

Close to slipping out, he leaned forward. Do I dress it up? *"Perimeter patrolled safely and without incident. Any possible intruders succesfully intimidated. Got laid like a mof-fo last night. Sir..."*

A flash and skitter of sunlight snapped Steve's attention to the door. Vern Hapgood, without warning, unhappy and wearing a pistol. Steve's eyes drilled on Mandel's stricken profile, jerking off on his phone. Cousin Couldn't-Give-A-Shit.

"Mr. Hapgood."

"Officer Dominski. Do you have anything for me?"

Steve stood. "Sir?"

Hapgood appeared to nod, as if expecting a let-down. He glanced at the huge LifeForce Security decal on the wall, like he was thinking of buying the place.

"I need all surveillance files from last night." Hapgood said. His tiny, dark eyes and beak-like nose moved to Steve. The black/grey paneled sport shirt covered his girth, but not the low-belted 1911.

"Excuse me, sir?"

Vern stepped forward. "Officer," he said as if explaining to a child. "I need to see your video camera surveillance images from last night. From approximately midnight to 5:30 am. *This morning*. I also want to see the duty roster and activity logs of your officers last night."

"Mr. Hapgood, we've had no – "

"Consider this it," Hapgood said. A thick finger wagged at the desk computers. "Which monitor can I view them on? Or do I need to sit here?" He thumbed at the camera console - Mandel's phone, a torn open bag of Doritos and can of Monster.

"Sir, in the first place – "

The land line rang, Mandel answering.

"No. No." Hapgood's palms were up, pushing. The ugliest mime. "I've talked to your battalion commander. And your Captain. And the state police. I'm here to make sure evidence isn't 'lost.'"

"I don't know what you're talking about, sir."

"No surprise. Your Captain told me you were ranking officer last night. You weren't dismissed but you left your post. To…whomever. You'd be the last to know your 'troop' has cost this development thousands of dollars."

"Sir, what are you…"

Steve's eyes shot to Mandel, hand cupped over the phone mouthpiece. Steve guessed it wasn't Publisher's Clearinghouse.

The big man picked up some of last night's faxes from the closest desk. Hapgood's squint passed down the pages, imitating reading before tossing them to the carpet.

"This doesn't look like a very smart operation this morning."

Steve approached close enough to catch Hapgood's garlicish odor. "SIR. First, there are no video files. The server holds no data. It's a feed to corporate every 30 minutes. Secondly, any complaints or concerns must be filed as a formal report."

"I was told by your superiors the files were here."

"Well, you were lied to, sir."

The big man was getting to a boil.

"I'll file the report, then."

"Ordinarily we could. But first you must leave the building."

"I must leave," Hapgood said. A philosophy to be pondered.

"No firearms beyond those of LifeForce Security are permitted in the security center. S-"

"Don't 'sir' me again, kid. I know fuck off when I hear it."

Steve glanced at the hold light on the desk phone.

"I can furnish you with a copy of the agreement you signed. Sir."

A touché nod. Hapgood pointed to the desk phone.

"That man is going to ask you why the development facilities are using generator power, *not DTE power*, at this moment. Why the power room's connection to the DTE power line was physically disabled sometime last night. Why the lock and door to the power room is undamaged. And I'd venture he's going to wonder why you don't know what he's talking about. Son."

Unmoved, Steve watched the big man with khakis full of fat ass push the glass door open from its center with a greasy hand print. "The power company and a locksmith will be here this afternoon. The Sheriff I couldn't guess. They share a lot in common with your organization."

"More than one person has the key to the power room," Steve said. "Anyone could have done what you're alleging."

"Very good, officer." Hapgood said, one foot out. "That keen mind should have this solved before you file for unemployment. Or maybe they'll just blame *you*."

The door closed.

"Garrett, go to camera ten, on the power room, full screen."

The screen showed 24-inches of the power room roof, leaves and branches. The camera misaligned. Knocked up.

"What the FUCK? None of you noticed?"

"I didn't do it!" Mandel worked the adjust, marginally squeezing the shed's upper quarter into frame. "This camera got fucked with."

"Think so?"

Steve poised to touch the receiver, sweat dotting his head.

"Yo, Steve."

Mandel brought up last night's log on the console monitor. The log Steve hadn't checked, fuck-fuzzed on only 40 minutes' sleep. The power had hinked out again at 1:13 a.m. last night, going dark for under a minute, Venegas wrote. Lights, camera and action - zip. But the power came back on, right away.

Tyce. Tyce reading the generator manual. Tyce the spy. Tyce tempting him. *No one would ask*. Motherfuckers.

Everyone was going to ask. Every swinging dick.

******

There was no atomic-charred Hiroshima pocket watch to mark it, frozen forever at 8:16. Twenty-first century electronics couldn't mark their time of death.

Later some swore it was 12:40 p.m., September 6th on the nose when everything went dead. No, no, others said. It was just past 12:30 because their favorite talk show just started. There was bright faced applause over Ellen's monologue. Then a black screen.

For everyone a not-again dread. Two days in a row? Then came the sound.

For Robert Sanders, it was the wipe-out of 30 minutes' work. His introduction email to AeroMax of Houston was gone. A flung pen and curses to God. Fly paper....

For Joyce, it was the last straw, soap soaked to the elbows, Max in the wash tub. Billie Holiday zapped in mid-croon.

For Ray Dudek it was the fluorescents and fryers shutting down in

Burger King. He was slightly grateful in the groaning commotion of the line. Just as well, sign-from-God-like. Sherri would kill him. And yeah, he shouldn't be eating it anyway.

For Sherri, it was the snapped to black check-out screen as she paid for the 20-percent-off pearl nightgown she would never receive.

For Kim Narlow it was her edge-of-sleep breathing shocked by Sandra Rose crying out. The TV was off again.

For Mike Narlow it was the end of Vince Blackmon's power point. Mike would never learn the profit potential of manufacturing the K-switch ignition in Hunan Province.

For Joe Allen it was the traffic lights at Six Mile and Gratiot going dark the same time as his phone.

For Hannah, a bad moment. No window in the office bathroom.

For William Gallo, it wasn't so bad. When the TV went out he went to the kitchen for some more juice, knowing who killed the husband.

For Jim Cronc, his pen stopped on the inventory pad. The cooler's hum and cage light cut dead, leaving him in crypt-like darkness.

For Mark Dudek it was jarring. Lexi Belle's' straddling form became depthless void in mid-moan. He ripped the virtual goggles away, tucked, zipped and cursed his vulnerability in the basement's dim quiet.

For Lorna, the beginning was blissfully unknown. She was still asleep with no urge to go running.

Many remembered the sound. A soft crackle – winter sweater static or touching a TV screen after waking on carpet. A device-killing power surge. Nothing plugged into a wall socket ever worked again. Nor did the sockets, or the phones, the towers or the phone lines.

No souvenirs. No one would ever know for sure.

****

September 9th

Screeching crashes broke Tyce's sleep apart like ash. Boosted to his elbows on the blanketed slab, he blinked at the pulsing, single-candle light in the cell's corner. Silence. Phantoms. Exhaling, he rolled to pick up his watch. The button illuminating 4:53 a.m. Fuck. Forty-some minutes. In the duration his spine had gone Tin Man stiff. The blankets weren't much help against the slab. He winced, sitting up.

Oil can....

Tyce returned from the bathroom to the darkened office. Chin propped at the camera console, Dominski was awake if not alert. The police-band radio ran a cycling static. Part rain, part washing machine. The same noise as forty-some minutes ago, well after the thing had finished. Tyce reset the channel frequency, lowering the volume.

"You sure?" Dominski said, glazed eyes on the screens.

"He's dead. Probably lying on the key." Tyce said, wondering why they were both nearly whispering. "Sorry."

"I thought you were going to sleep?"

Dominski's free hand zoomed to a full screen outside the gate. Not quite daylight, the monitors still ran night-green, giving the office the feel of a submarine. They agreed on keeping it dark for themselves. Besides conserving power, it beat living a fluorescent purgatory in a shitty office.

"I did, too," Tyce said, walking to the kitchen. He yawned, turning the sink knob. The faucet's white noise flow caught his ear. Tyce concentrated on the cool water filling the cup in his hand, checking himself. Running water. *Appreciate this.*

He returned to the office with the cup. The radio's new frequency ran sparse civilian talk, some unknown codes and coordinates from law, most likely. Possibly just outside the wall or twenty miles away.

"Steve, if you wanna fall out it's fine. I'm up."

"No thanks. I'm staying on schedule."

Straightening his back, Dominski clicked to a six-screen shuffle. The yard's corral-post fences, the east loop blacktop, the driveways and woodline. This time of morning the houses and trees seemed smaller, huddled into themselves, unconscious-like.

Like a graveyard, Peltier had said.

"Have you ever heard anything like that?" Dominski asked.

"Yes."

"I never did. You heard the calls for DUI crashes, accidents. Guys hurry calling for the wagon. Not..." Dominski's attention drifted off the screens, head down.

"Here, take some. It helps you focus." Tyce offered the water.

Dominski sipped.

"You think he was there?" Dominski's agitated fingers selected Camera #3's long view down the pond and panned. The residents had disconnected the fountain and streetlights to save fuel. Tyce thought the dry, three-legged donut out in the water looked alien in the green light.

War of the Worlds. Germs killed the aliens.

"None of 'em should have been there."

"They weren't smart like us?"

"I'd rather be behind a stone wall than exposed in a parking lot for a quarter mile. Whoever..." Tyce left it unfinished.

"Maybe they weren't. You'd hope they got more prepared."

"I doubt Mandel was prepared for anything." Tyce said, regretting it as it came out. "Doesn't matter."

The camera panned the Brusine house. The Coors Light umbrella.

"You gotta look at it...cosmic. Sometimes," Tyce said.

Dominski's radioactive green face slowly swung a weird, clear-eyed look on Tyce.

"What I'm saying is, when I was deployed there were missions I lucked out of that got hit. The ones where I got hit, somebody else might not have reacted how I did. If you wouldn't have gotten fired, your ass would have been there. No offense, but, yeah. You would have showed and you would have stayed. It wouldn't have been..." Tyce realized the thoughts collapsing as he spoke. Brittle like ash. "You got the better deal. Not that I want to see...whatever. Let it go. It's always the other guy. You gotta stay here and now with me, partner. OK?"

Dominski grunted a laugh, head wagging. Tyce let it fall, in no frame of mind to judge. Sleep was needed. He'd been awake...22 hours now? 23? The punchy mood off Dominski convinced Tyce to try again.

"Right, Tyce. Partners. Cosmic. If you're Number Six, what number does that make me? The other guy?"

"What?"

"Nothing, Tyce."

"Look, man. For the last time - I didn't mess with the generator. I don't know what happened."

Seeming energized by the disdain, Dominski faced the screen. "For the last time – I believe you. I'm here. Go and sleep because I'm going down at seven." He clicked to the camera aimed down the east loop. Lawns like shag carpet. The row lines of driveways. All of them empty. People who had left. The Grutta's. The Fetter's. Chalmers and his wife.

Tyce rose and walked.

"We have to move some of the cameras today," Dominski called.

Tyce stopped, turning. "OK. What are you thinking?"

"We should move some to outside the wall. We'll know what's coming. If we have to defend a spot. Right?"

"Good idea. We'll talk to them. Get some ladders."

Tyce passed Dominski's cot, piled gear and clothes in the rear corner of the office, abutting the file cabinet. *Number Six? What was that shit?* That was all Tyce needed. Hurt feelings. Why did Dominski's white ass come back to the Green? They'd fired him the morning of the big meltdown. He lived in Essex and had mentioned family. Tyce was nothing *but* excuse. What was Steve's?

On his back in the cell, Tyce's mind heard it again. Like Little Big Horn, it lasted about as long as it took a hungry man to eat his breakfast.

The move-out order from command came on September 6th, a few hours after everything went black for good around Noon. Dominski had already left when Tyce returned with cold lunch. Mandel and Tyce were the only two guards in Cricklewood Green when battalion radioed the withdrawal to protect the D-Plex. All other posts in the vicinity were abandoned - Cricklewood Green. Tanglewood Estates. Burgess Township. *All personnel report to the D-Plex. No exceptions.* Mandel went hot-footed, pacing, warning Tyce of the hammer coming down if he didn't hop-to, invoking Peltier and contracts. Somewhere between Tyce's Fuck and Off, Mandel drove away, leaving Tyce a declared ass-is-grass pussy.

Tyce hung on alone in the Barracks, undisturbed and marveling at his full generator-power room, watching Emergency Broadcast chaos and drinking coffee, shaking his head at the radio calls from battalion. Tyce felt like a night-time winter-storm school kid, watching the snow pile up to the roof, doubting there would ever be class again, let alone tomorrow. He was pondering his sunrise move, toting the odds of the residents letting him stay, when after midnight Dominski showed up. His truck was stacked with flake board, plywood and tools. His possessions mostly in garbage bags.

Both men listened in on the updated LifeForce frequency through the 7th and into September 8th. The D-Plex protection force, about ten men they guessed, bitched about the promised National Guard relief. Bitching about no hot food, no water. How they should break into the place themselves, take the bank branch vault, take all the good stuff. Not even a porta-john. The ranking, Sergeant Dissette, neither of them knew. Mandel's name came up, a pawn pushed around the parking lot. Yesterday morning, September 8th, battalion was still slinging relief promises as the kitchen TV and the police-band promised murder. Curfews. Martial law. Constitutional suspension. Mutinous National Guard and reserve units reforming and declaring opposition. Fires, day looting, Bridges and overpasses blown up. Gangs of armed men. Shots fired.

Yesterday afternoon, twelve hours earlier, battalion went silent. Dissette called out to dead air. *Any law enforcement in the vicinity? Come in?* Tyce had to grab Dominski's wrist when he reached for the mic. The radio talk in the D-Plex parking lot took on a losing edge. Distant figures were observing them, the men said.

Vamos. Split. Run. Boogie, you assholes, Tyce thought.

With darkness, things came unwound everywhere. The music had stopped and it was time to grab a chair. Take the motherfucking chair. The Barracks picked up calls from the outskirts of Flint, Pontiac and unknown. A drowning pitch of *armed men, gangs of armed men, shots fired, rob-*

*bery in progress, gunshot victims. Active shooter. Shots fired. Sniper. Fire
out of control. Officer down. Active shooters. Request assistance. Gunshot victims. Mosque on fire. Request ambulance. Officers down request
URGENT back up. Suspects engaged by SWAT, eleven DBs. Gas station
fire at corner of. Shots fired. Looting at. Sniper fire. Officer down.*

At the D-Plex the attack came after 2:00 a.m. Tyce and Dominski
listened with sidelong eyes, flexing hands, nerves and muscles rebelling
- clenched and sprung at the same time. The flat rips of far-off auto-fire.
The closer, crisper rapid return-fire pops. Thuddy explosions. The calls.
Where are they? Brandon? *There!* Motherfuckers! Terry! *Left side! Go
go!* I can't…*Shoot at the flash!* Brandon? Mandel? You there?

Dissette was last on the air, still yelling for battalion, for names
not responding. The sergeant's returning gunfire stark and cutting within
his pauses. *Sergeant James Dissette of LifeForce Security under massed
attack at corner of Oakton and Heller Lake Road due north of Essex. Any
and all assistance. Nearly overrun.*

Finally, a cycle of static. Part rain, part washing machine.

Mandel, you there?

Tyce barely knew him. A putz, really. Another jobber.

Number Six. Like *The Prisoner* TV show? Did Tyce ever mention
it to Steve? Maybe? Fucking kid. One of those. Hurt feelings.

Tyce knew what was coming. Four full days after it all failed these
people were still talking it like a weekend disaster. Money lost, insurance
covering. Fed, state, Army and Johnny Law promises. When it would
come back on, yeah yeah yeah. Big fear to them was two or three Tyrones
or Pedros coming to take their stuff. What Tyce heard tonight was Big
Fear. A call back to his war year and ugliest self. What it would take.

Eyes closed, Tyce concentrated. After a few tries an old tune
hooked in. Tyce stayed on the song, feeling the drift of sleep like a tide.

Funny how the night moves. With autumn closing in.

September 12th

Watching the items passed hand-to-hand around the Activity Room's Last Supper-length table, William Gallo recalled his single stint as a juror, decades ago. The same short, stiff-back chairs, but no cigarette smoke this time. Then the faces were pinched, distracted. Then trying to make sense through nagging notions of missed work, dinner plans and wasted time. Boredom, foul breath and loosened ties. It had been murder. They put the boy away.

Today, now, the jury was not bored and the room only served to make the task stranger. The walls were a warm shade of tangerine in the delightful afternoon light. Breeze through the open windows. The bird sounds almost cruel. Gallo's eyes settled on the drained baby-blue swimming pool, listening to the chirps and fluttering notes.

Most of the exhausted people around the table bore the look of tornado refugees, Gallo thought. A moldy dampness clung to some, despite today's warmth. Sleepless, unsettled eyes. Slack lips a moment away from uttering 'what?', especially after they saw the pictures. Robert Sanders was a poised exception. Even his fingernails were clean. Like him, Gallo kept neat. Generational training, perhaps. No ties today. But the freshly delivered contents in their hands made them a jury, sure enough.

It had been a day of compounded unbalance. With the hours-ago departure of the Vanderkams there were now only 12 people inside the walls of Cricklewood Green, plus the two guards. John and Cindy Vanderkam's "supply" mission to Gavin was a punctuation of abandonment following the morning's shock. Gallo didn't believe the couple would return, despite being empty-handed in their Ford pick-up. Now an odious resentment hung over the table. The people with nowhere else to run.

Earlier, the 8 a.m. meeting had been underway with questions, rumors, theories, doubts. First, they heard it. Then everyone bungled out to the Activity Room porch to see it. Their absence from the meetings over the last day explained, Russ and Janine Leonard were standing across the way at the tennis court with their airport carry-on bags, looking up at the sound. Tyce came running with his scoped rifle, setting to aim on the descending helicopter before Russ Leonard saw him and waved Tyce to stop, running and shouting in his sunglasses and whipping grey hair. Finally, Tyce lowered the rifle and walked to the porch with the rest of them – all cringe-shielding from the slap of rotor wind. They watched the Leonards board the landed helicopter with their few bags, the blades fanning the lush infield grass. The machine lifted and rose above the height of the wall and treetops. It swung tail and flew west.

"Did anybody....?" John Vanderkam said.

No one did. Relieved from the helicopter's wash, they gaped at the flattened grass and the wall and the sky, not quite trusting their senses.

The young tattooed girl, Lorna, turned to all of them.

"How did they do that?"

"Mr. Leonard was a vice-president with AT&T before he retired," Vern Hapgood said. "Influence and a satellite phone, I'd presume." He walked back inside. Robert Sanders followed.

Mike Narlow approached Tyce. "What did Russ say?"

Gripping the rifle strap over his shoulder, Tyce squinted at the infield, the tennis court. It was off-putting, Tyce's day-dreaminess.

"Last one off the embassy roof is a VC," Tyce said, without humor.

Narlow grabbed the guard's free wrist. "No. What did he say?"

Tyce glanced down at Narlow's hand. By the time they met eyes, Narlow had released. "He said don't shoot."

"Nothing else?" Hannah asked.

"Fraid so, Ms. Sutherland. Maybe it's the Rapture for rich suburban whiteys," Tyce said, trudging back to the security building, singing something aloud. Tyce looked better, his face healing. Gallo watched him a moment before packing back into the birdhouse, cackling with brand new questions, rumors, theories and doubts.

Including Narlow and Hapgood, the afternoon jury consisted of Joyce and Hannah, thankfully calm and cautious. Ray Dudek and - was she his wife? – Sherri. Gallo liked Dudek. *It's All Bullshit* could have been his motto. Very East-Side, Gallo would have called him at one time. Robert Sanders was the final person to receive the packet of 'evidence'. Finishing with its contents he sat straighter and slid the packet to the center, removing his glasses and squeezing at the bridge of his nose. Contrary in a corner easy chair, denim legs tucked, Lorna listened more than watched. A lounged defiance - being away from the group, demanding to be part of it. Was I ever that insolent, Gallo wondered? In 1968 probably more so. The girl's parents left Cricklewood Green two days prior. Quite a scene, Joyce told him in private. When Lorna refused to leave with them, apparently, Robert Sanders went out to the melee in the driveway. Then Sanders' wife, Barbara, came out with *her* bags and *she* drove off with Mr. and Mrs. Brusine. Sanders returned to his home alone, Lorna to hers. No one was near enough to hear what was said beyond the girl's shrieked curses.

"This is insane," Hannah declared, looking over the packet's contents. "I don't believe it."

"Well, we better because it's fucking happening," Mike Narlow said, scooting back from the table. He was one of those who found toughness in profanity, not realizing it gave people the perfect excuse to ignore him. He walked to the window as if on guard.

The birds sang.

Only Mike Narlow and Vern Hapgood were visibly armed, with belt-holstered pistols. The morning of the fourth day, Vern came to the meeting boasting a machine gun. A fat strap bore the long weapon off his orange golf-shirted shoulder, the weight and ammunition bag supported by his keg-like girth of belly. Smirking, he heaved it over his head, setting it on the long table, bipod legs holding the barrel up. Gallo found the gun's supposed reassurance vulgar and intimidating. Such was Vern.

Yet, Vern Hapgood had been a revelation. He knocked on every door, rallying the whole development to meet twice a day, organizing, herding the cats. People were cooperating. Vern's boasted foresight to disconnect the compound's power system from DTE during the night of the first blackout was praised in every flushed toilet or glass of clean water.

Though the next day's attack (or 'the surge' or 'the wave') destroyed every home's electrical components, the comfort of fresh water, showers and the security cameras in the Barracks bought Vern deference, if not goodwill. Only Vern and the Dudeks were fortunate enough to have working televisions, but there were enough radios to keep everyone informed, if not knowledgeable. Unfortunately, the electricity in the home's generators was nearly as useless as the plastic in the resident's wallets. There was nothing to spend it on. The home generator's hard-wire juiced into surge-blown outlets. But, every basement generator in the Green did have two plug inputs. With enough extension cords, things were available and working. Portable radios. Old lamps dug out of basements. The blender in the cupboard. Hair dryers.

Anything plugged-in during the attack was cooked, including many cars and trucks. The computer-suicide bug which boiled nuclear reactors, blanked data servers and tricked powerplants and water pump stations into burn-out hyperdrive also a transmitted a kill command to any networked device. When Art Slavin turned the key of his Mercedes SUV the starter-motor bolt fired into the engine block, Russian Roulette-style. It took two days before the vehicle warning was broadcast over the EBN among the blizzard of rumors, contradicted rumors, advice, announcements and alerts. The Slavins had to leave Cricklewood Green packed in the Audi after disconnecting its radio, GPS, On-Star, everything.

Sherri picked up the packet's plastic-covered letter. "But what do they really want? It's not about the guards. It can't be. Trade? What does trade mean? I mean… it's crazy. Do the guys know?"

"Unlikely," Vern said. "The package was sealed when Tyce brought it to me. He said it was thrown over the gate by someone in a military vehicle. Former military, presumably."

"They're both gonna know because I'm gonna tell them." Lorna said. "I'm gonna tell them everything every one of you say."

"Look, hold it. Jesus Christ." Ray gestured, pushing. "I don't give a shit what they have out there. What about the real fucking army? The police? The Goddamn Law, for Christ's sake. I don't believe a word of this. Who are they to make demands of anybody? What we can do or where we can go? It's bullshit."

Gallo smiled.

"Steve is from Essex," Hannah said. "He was a cop there. He has to know them. He can -"

Sherri shook her head. "It's not Essex, Hannah. These are army trucks. From what they're saying here? *Remand* all LifeForce Security guards? And these pictures? It's revolting. Would *you* talk to them?"

"Of course, they know him," Narlow said. "They know every inch of this place. Who do you think delivers everything here? Cuts the grass?"

"I'm sure it's the grass cutters, Mike," Joyce said. "Please."

"You know what I mean," Narlow said.

Joyce's twisted mouth indicated she did. Or didn't.

"We've talked about this before, but don't we have a radio to try and call someone? The radio in the Barracks can't be fixed?" Sherri said.

"Once again - they both claim no," Vern said. "I'd like to be able to tell you more about what's in there. But that's your decision." Hapgood scowl-eyed them under brow. "Their handset radios have no range. That much is true."

Sanders lifted the plastic-covered case-file/manifesto/ultimatum and read aloud. He stopped periodically and looked at each face around the table. Gallo could not tell if Sanders' tone was a surrogate demand of the crazies or a faux-firm ironic disbelief. *Refusal to meet at the former Essex city building at Noon on September 14th would be seen as a hostile act. Your individual rights, property and liberty will be respected. But any movement outside of the walls of your homestead* ("homestead?") *will be trespassing and met with force, without warning. We look forward to meeting and discussing the future with you. We look forward to being good neighbors and partners in freedom and trade. This is not a threat. The choice is your own.*

His finger stabbed in exclamation. An absurd Uncle Sam.

Robert Sanders was a peculiar bird. Largely silent, typically only answering a question directly asked. But he volunteered - helping the guard's fix plywood and flakeboard over the main gate, for instance. Helping place cameras outside the wall the other day. With Joyce, he'd worked to transfer fuel from the vacant home's propane tanks to the development generator, even if it were by one tedious 5-gallon BBQ tank at a time.

(Joyce had learned the trick in Zambia). No one was sure where Sanders stood on much of anything, which made the incident with the Brusines and his wife more intriguing.

In a forced stillness the jury humored Sanders'…performance, their eyes meeting around him.

"Who cares what they want? It sure as shit ain't good." Ray said. "Probably sounds better when there's a gun in your mouth. Ask those dead guys in the pictures what they wanted."

"But it's not a threat," Narlow mocked, out the window.

"We have a right to refuse. That's what it's all about, isn't it? Rights and freedom. We have the right to starve to death here if we don't agree," Joyce said.

Their quips finally exhausted. Vern cleared his throat.

"We have to meet them."

Grumbles. Feints at rebellion.

"Yeah? Who's 'we', Vern?" Ray said.

"Hear me out, please. We have to presume they're logical people -"

"Oh, blow it out your ass, man," Narlow said, turning. "*Logical.* I'm not surrendering my home or the life of my daughter some to pick-up truck warlord, *Vern.* No fuckin' way."

"Let me finish, please. I can reach them in a way they'll understand."

"Understand what? If they want the Jews next? Or just the women?" Joyce said. "How is it logical to you? Do you sit out in the sun to warm up in the morning?"

A touch from Hannah put Joyce back into her short, stiff-backed chair. Vern watched her and them, his chin dipped, arms crossed.

"Very clever, Ms. Snyder," he said. "Now what?"

"Let me ask you something, Vern," Hannah said without stopping. "If these weren't white men who looked and sounded like you, would you consider these demands logical? If they were black, would y-?"

"No. Not for a moment. Correct. I'm a racist. Now what?"

He glared at them.

"Well? May I? I'm not talking about surrendering. I'm not allowing anyone onto my property. But we have to realistically acknowledge there's no way to defend the development against a true attack. Which is what we're facing. Even a dozen men, let alone these vehicles in the photos or heavy weapons."

"Where do they say that here?" Sherri said.

"Please, Ms. Mullins." Hapgood said. "I'm not naive enough to believe they won't try to remove us. But if we meet and parlay, we can buy time. We can gauge their demands, truly - until there's support from the police or whomever, which I'm not naive enough to believe in, either. Have you have been listening to the broadcasts? And *'I don't believe it'* does not help. Doing nothing is not an option. You're correct, Mike. It is happening. We should meet the problem, convince them we aren't a threat. But we need to demonstrate that we are organized. We will defend ourselves and it will cost. We can't cower."

The birds sang, wind tapping the blinds. Sanders muttered something about Chamberlain, appeasement.

"Really, Robert?" Vern's thick arms expanded a wide, mocking benevolence. "Let's hear from the other esteemed strategists. I love to hear analytical minds at work. What should we do, people? Those assholes out there sure are crazy. Yep. They sure are."

Gallo counted to 26 before Joyce broke it.

"If we can't call for help, some of us need to leave and go get it."

"The Vanderkams," Lorna said from the corner.

The mention was ignored.

"Say three of us?" Hannah said. "What's the nearest sizable place we could get to? Gavin? Someplace holding together. We've heard about Pontiac on the news, right? It's calmer now. They've got the Guard, the real Guard, there." Quavers of doubt and plea cleaved her tone of hope.

"This morning I heard a relief column was going to Flint, to open the highway," Narlow said. "That's pretty close. Maybe they'll send people through here. At worst, there's a safe corridor. We can try to meet them. We've got until tomorrow night to figure it out. Then noon, right?"

Sherri's voice stayed measured. "Yes. We've seen helicopters. Planes flying over. What if we signal them? Mark has a flare gun. There's still organized law, a government. We've seen it on TV. The United Nations. All these countries sending help."

Vern coughed his ridicule.

"No. What does a flare mean, Sherri?" Ray said. "Everyone's in the same shape. They won't trust anything. There ain't gonna be a rescue unless you know who to call."

"Exactly," Vern said.

"First, we need to ask the guys," Hannah said.

"Exactly," Lorna shouted.

Rigid, Ray leaned over at Lorna, hand raised to calm. "No one is saying that. We're not handing anybody over. Not gonna happen." He looked back to the table faces. "We bring them both in here any lay out every word of it."

"Fine," Vern said.

"What about Mark?" Narlow asked.

"What about him?" Ray said.

"Does he have a vote?"

"Same as your wife," Ray shot back.

Ray was touchy about Mark. Most residents seemed to chuckle regard him as a kind of mascot, not the stand-back oddball Gallo found him to be. A wrong child, skulking around with his weapons the way a 12-year-old would stalk frogs to smash. Gallo certainly favored the guards over Mark Dudek, or Vern for that matter. Gallo understand men of arms, men of law. The men of calm, not the displayers, the peacocks. Vern was still smarting over Officer Dominski's and Tyce's rebuffs, refusing Vern admission into the security building. A grateful early-majority had voted to let the two men keep the facility under their watch, as they saw fit. No one had forced them stay and guard the development.

"We'll invite both officers here tomorrow," Vern said.

Hannah shook her head. "No, Vern. We'll go talk to them now."

"As you wish. One thing to consider before your 'expedition'? The government 'help' you're seeking? The United Nations? Once again - the rights you thought you had, to protect you, are no longer. Ask yourselves this, Ms. Sutherland, Ms. Snyder. What if they're seeking the same thing our solicitors here are asking for? And if they wish to remand me, or Mr. Narlow, or Mr. Dudek? The white men? Would it be agreeable?"

Vern's snorty exhale was a spray over the silence.

"Well, ladies and gentlemen, I won't serve either master."

Gallo felt Joyce's hands squeezing his.

"William. Please. Say something. How do you feel?"

Last night over wine, Joyce asked Gallo how he could be so calm. Gallo told the ladies about living through the Detroit Riot in 1967 and more than a few ends of the world. V-14, he reminded them. Gallo's heart had sunk but calm was the only worthwhile face. This…Happening…was something new, as if a dry hurricane and hot riot had overwhelmed every square inch of the republic. No help was coming.

The faces pivoted to him. Gallo realized he was the elder at the table, now valued. They finally ask the Old. Gallo thought of the staggering amounts of knowledge fused to baked computer chips, cast up into the vaunted, evaporated Cloud. The library of Alexandria in ashes. Staggering amounts of knowledge forever gone. The Old. Metal and plastic, electrical circuitry and nothing besides.

How do you feel?

The question. The one he sought to avoid. When Gallo got the diagnosis at the beginning of August he decided to tell no one. He made the arrangements himself after the first few days. There was only his sister left and if he made it to Arizona for Thanksgiving (doubtful now) he would tell them he could not make it for Christmas. The pity? A living funeral swallowed by the drop? Gallo could not abide it. He'd had a grand life, seen and done so much, accomplished good.

Outside, the birds. Much like laughter.

Whatever wisdom he was about to salve upon them would mean as much as their pity. Nothing would change. Asunder and drifting. Humpty Dumpty. And all that.

***

Hannah was anxious having to knock on the plywood-covered door. The other day Tyce opened it before she'd walked up the cement ramp. She knocked again, headache pressing her frontal lobes. There were a few too many jokers in the deck today.

Scratching her arms, Joyce leaned around, peeking. The boarded-up gate, the corner to the small parking lot and the guard's trucks.

"Terrific. Are they even awake?"

The lock clicked and Tyce pushed the door open. "Hello ladies. Come in," He let them pass with their bags. "Welcome to World War III."

Hannah stopped, blinking at Tyce. *Her brother…*

"How are you guys doing?" Joyce said, passing around Hannah.

"Stylin' and profiling," Tyce said.

They were both shaved, groomed. Blue uniforms clean, if wrinkly. The dependable order of the full powered, bright-lit office slightly embarrassed Hannah, unshowered in scruffies. She felt a comfort, seeing the camera screens sort their cycles, like a clicked beat. Steve stood in the archway to the break room/kitchen area, arms folded at the loud TV news. Both women eased through to the round table, setting the bags down. Joyce stopped first, then the screen caught Hannah's attention as well. The sounds, voices, coming from the TV were unusual.

"They've got their own channel now," Steve said. "It cut in like ten minutes ago over EBN on Channel 7. It's on Channel 4, too."

She had been one of the girls on the network. Pretty, well-spoken, in a smart red skirt outfit with shiny legs. The background was cheap, but they had a computer graphic and a crawl. Freedom News. The truth about our overthrown country. She went to video of some senate and house leaders, speaking from undisclosed locations. Vowing to defend the constitution. This would sway people, Hannah thought. It was more pleasant to look at. The Emergency Broadcast Network was dour old men delivering grimly on behalf of.

Video of stripped, cuffed white men in a line, arrested for 'defending their community' outside Kansas City (tagged 'censored Occupational Regime content'). On the crawl, another state out west had formally seceded, but not yet aligned with the coalescence.

"Here," Hannah said, opening the bags. "We weren't sure how well you guys were set up. We brought you some soap, toothpaste, shampoo. Some vitamins. Some Tide for your clothes. We heard you guys were using hand soap for everything."

Gripping the bars of Dial, Tyce smiled, nodding.

"Thank you. Both. Very generous."

They kept the tiled space tidy, wiped down, not a dirty dish to be seen. The yapping TV noise backed Hannah out of the room, turning away. Even the office area was orderly. The sleeping area in the corner was stacked, blankets folded on the cot.

"Look at this, Ms. Sutherland," Steve said. She moved aside to watch him alternating the camera screens. "Those are the two we put outside the wall. We can see down the access road almost to Oakton now. And this one on the north part. It pans the whole north wall and the east wall. We can see anyone outside."

Joyce came around, over his shoulder. "Great. No progress on fixing the radio?"

"No," Tyce said.

"Can I take a look at it?"

Steve said nothing, sorting screens.

"Certainly." Tyce boosted off the wall. "Do you know communications equipment?"

Hannah watched Joyce squat before the wheeled rig under the console. "A little. We mostly used cell phones but there were still radios. For the planes and the helicopters," Joyce said, flipping the power switch to no effect. The same way everyone flipped the light switches sometimes, usually in the morning. A child's hope. Then anger when nothing worked.

Tyce pulled out the rack of equipment, loosening nuts and fasteners. "Please, take a look. I'm not sure exactly what the wave did." He removed the covering. "This has no single point of failure. See? If this were a 2200 model, like I had in the military, I could see it. These diodes? I think, maybe, an integrated signal did it."

Joyce nodded. It was garble to her, but Hannah knew the nod. Pretending to listen to the house special and getting the pasta anyway.

"Now, I checked the pre-selector here," Tyce said. "We could, maybe, replace the network switch. It might circumvent the break. But I'm not sure. And we'd have to go out to try and find one. Maybe from a law enforcement or emergency vehicle?

"Or it could be the flux capacitor." Tyce stood, smiling at Hannah. He offered open hands to the open-gutted box of electronics.

"See what you think."

Joyce's mouth moved, but at first nothing came out. "No. We need to talk to you about the meeting today."

Joyce moved to sit on a corner of the closest desk.

Hannah unzipped the canvas messenger packet. She pulled the contents, handing Tyce the digital camera. She looked the plastic covered letter again, to make sure.

A foreign-controlled force of hired thugs, LifeForce fighters have been committing crimes and killing citizens throughout the region. All around the Great Lakes, citizens, police and military forces loyal to God and the American Constitution have been defending lives and property. The images you see here are of LifeForce fighters who had seized control of the D-Plex marketplace known to you all. On confirmed Occupation Regime orders, they secured the supplies, food and material inside until a convoy could arrive to transport it to the ghettos of Flint and other cities. Patriotic forces have prevented that and secured the material for the local citizens stricken by this traitorous attack on our country.

She handed the document to Steve. In the kitchen, the letter had come to life on screen, perky with shiny legs. Starved for information and nothing but cotton candy, Hannah thought. As Steve glanced at the letter she was about to ask them to turn it off.

"Hey," Tyce said in a jolt. "Steve."

Steve moved to the break room, Hannah and Joyce following.

The televised images could have been blurry, streamed video from any third-world clan fratricide, once so common on cable news. Except for those green and white Michigan highways signs. Signs Hannah had been driving past her entire life.

Jumpy, hand-held video paced along the highway. Smoking, collided and wrecked military vehicles, ditched semi-trucks. Lumpen rag-like piles, some of the bodies on fire. They were using a captured Channel 2 news van, its antenna extended to the blue sky. A female reporter described. The column was headed to break the patriot's Flint blockades. If broken, Flint would flood the middle of the state with criminals, rapists and looters, attacking citizens like locusts. (They liked Biblical touch points). The reporter talked to a masked man in camouflage – 'Sergeant Nathan' – holding a blue helmet and stripped/scalped unit shoulder patches. Evidence of foreign invaders, he said. His black knit mask had a gruesome skull face painted on it.

"That's I-75," Steve said, pointing at the high flat-screen. "Right by Holly. It's like 15 minutes from here."

"Fuck," Tyce whispered.

A sapping vertigo came over her. Hannah could feel the fable settling, hardening. What this was going to do, setting everything in opposition.

"Please turn it off," Hannah said.

"This is going to turn into a war, isn't it?" Joyce said.

Hannah looked at Tyce. From her distance his eyes seemed moist, blinking at the screen, the ripped vehicles on the road.

"Yes."

"TURN IT OFF!"

Steve found the control. Within the silence, they sleepwalked to the office. A bad dream. The men looked over the letter and digital camera images as Joyce quietly related who said what in the meeting.

"Enough of this," Tyce said.

He powered-up the computer on the back desk. He pulled a USB cord from one of the drawers and connected it to the camera.

"You have a computer?" Hannah said.

Steve looked up from the plastic letter in his hand. "It was never recycled. Lucky."

Tyce brought the images up on the screen, full-size. Stopping on images of the LifeForce bodies in the D-Plex parking lot and their shot-up trucks and cars, Tyce found a pen and paper, writing.

"They want the water," Steve said. He dealt the plastic letter onto the desk and shaking his head showed them his dark blue back. Leaning over the console he clicked a cycle on the cameras. "That's my guess."

"The water?" Joyce grabbed the letter.

"When I came here the night it happened? The second time? There was no water in town. Like, anywhere." Steve straightened and faced them. "The water used to suck in Essex. It was brown. You couldn't barely drink it. They filled the wells in years ago and went to Detroit Metro water. My dad had one of the contracts. I'd guess if they know LifeForce guards are here they know you've got a well strong enough for twenty houses."

"So we shouldn't wait," Joyce said.

Hannah moved over Tyce's shoulder. "What do the red Js mean on the trucks?"

He continued writing. "Nothing. It means they're assholes."

The photo of the wheeled artillery cannon came up. A dozen soldiers in line near what looked to be a boarded-up school. Tyce muttered as he wrote.

"Stupid."

He glanced back. "Sorry, ma'am, Not you."

"Hapgood wants to meet them?" Steve said.

"Could you guys be ready to leave in the morning?" Joyce said. "The four of us could slip out. A few hours before anyone realized it."

"Oh, really?" Hannah straightened, hard-eyeing Joyce. "Where are YOU going?"

"It's what we talked about inside with them," Joyce said.

"No, it's not."

"Hannah, if you found out Vern Hapgood was talking to these vomits would you be shocked? How do they know so much? He would fuck you over for a can of tuna fish. He's ready to hang these guys. And Mike Narlow will, too."

"Oh, really. Joyce. Your bullshit –

"Bullshit? Maybe you saw something different around that table than I did. When they all got past the pictures of the bodies and the army crap? That was easy. The pictures of the stacks of food, there? The restaurant? I saw the looks. Hungry, scared people do all sorts of things. And the garbage in this letter? Well, I know *Jew* is coming up real fast in there someplace." Joyce thumbed. *"Get on the train."*

"What? Traipse through the swap for miles? Hope you don't get bit by a snake or snap your ankle? To go where? Hope you meet someone who doesn't want to murder you out in the sticks? Do you have a compass?" Hannah gestured at all three of them. "Do you? Are we going to use your GPS on your phone?"

"You didn't bring this up to the yokels," Joyce said. "In there, it was three of us, get to the police."

"You never asked."

Joyce walked to the kitchen. "Well, pardon me."

"The stuff in here is pretty specific. It is possible Hapgood's talking to them," Steve said, picking up the letter again. "He could have a radio. He probably does. Even a satellite phone. He probably thinks it's for our own good."

Tyce wheeled away from the desk. "Don't get paranoid, Steve. It could be one of those radio-control copter drones. I haven't been looking up. Have you?"

"No."

"Trying to game who might be your enemy and alliances like a fuckin' TV show - pardon my language - is a waste. Doesn't help. We have to deal with here and now."

"Amen," Hannah said.

Joyce returned, drying her hands.

"I think Ms. Snyder is right," Steve said.

"Please. Joyce," she said, waving. "Ms. Snyder was my mother."

"Vern Hapgood I don't trust. I'm not letting him speak for me, that's for sure." Steve said. "Leaving is a bad idea, Joyce. I say we wait."

"Yes. We can't get frightened," Hannah said. "During the flu, we learned. All of us. We got it done, wherever we were. And you know what? I live here. This is ours."

"Much as I hate to quote the Nazi, he's right." Joyce moved to the kitchen doorway. "Yes – but '*now what*'?"

After shutting the computer down, Tyce handed the camera to

Hannah. "We need to wait. We should meet with everyone tomorrow."

Steve went into the kitchen and came back out with a yellow Styrofoam package of frozen chicken.

"Here. I think we have the last working fridge for a hundred miles. But we want to say thank you. For being straight with us. We want you to have a nice, real dinner tonight. Whatever comes, know you're with us."

Tyce told them to stay moment, disappearing down the short hall. He returned carrying a handset radio, explaining the functions and frequencies to Hannah, the hands-free earpiece microphone. Hannah had not wanted kiss a man in a long, long time.

****

Pinpoints of evening sunlight watering her eyes, Hannah squinted lower into the green overgrowth across the blacktop road. Was there a hint of the pinkish wall far back there? You weren't supposed to see it. Only know it was there. She lifted her bare foot at the sensation. The melt from the chicken's bag had spread to her feet. Hannah rubbed her wet sole on the warm concrete.

Next to Hannah on the porch, Lorna exhaled another stream of dope pungency. Her fingers baton-fidgeted the metal tube. Lorna's face remained still, eyes flat to the west's lowering sun.

"How are your meds, Lorna?"

"All good. I started taking half yesterday. So far I'm alright."

The girl's voice was thick and mellow.

"You shouldn't alter the doses."

"Nah, it's OK. You wouldn't believe how much better I am with my mother gone. End of the world and all is well." Lorna stood, pocketing the vapor pen. "I'm gonna get a Pepsi. You want one?"

"OK."

Hannah couldn't imagine being high right now. Last night, after

William left, she and Joyce continued drinking. Three bottles of wine in pursuit of oblivion sleep, but all she did was kick through nightmares. Then to be Hung Over, watching the helicopter lift away miserable, high and mighty Russ and Janine Leonard. *The rapture for rich whiteys.* See a doctor and get rid of it. Hannah had to laugh. But she didn't laugh. For all its horror, V-14 was managed. After a few weeks, it was a known thing, with life flowing outside and around it. The power never went out. Law held. You couldn't go to restaurants, or really out at all. But they streamed the first-run movies all summer. Concert performances on TV every other night. You could sleep safe.

Now. The hideous, melting Now. Hannah felt as if caught in a brewing thunderstorm, the awkward instant before a lightning strike, yet sustained and infinite. Hannah feared the last seven days' exhausted tension becoming normal. Paralyzed/frantic. Reckless/second-guessed. To have a day off, 12 hours of good sleep….

Lorna handed down the warm can. "How's Max?"

"Thank you. He's OK," Hannah said. "He can feel things are wrong. He's been pooping inside." Hannah bunched her toes, sliding her feet on the warmth and concentrated on the sweet drink, savoring the three-seconds of relief. "We decided to let him sleep with us last night. Before, he never wanted to."

"It's funny about dogs. I think they're so much smarter than we think, you know?" Lorna's stoned eyes were opaque, placid. "Like, they just kind of let us take care of them. But they know things."

Sipping, Hannah was unsure if she were irked or envious of the girl. To nod and snicker along or slap her face.

"Lorna, I'm serious about your meds. Keep taking the full dosage. And watch the self-medicating. OK?"

The girl chuckled, as if in pity. "What do I do when I run out?"

"Don't worry about it."

Lorna shrugged, drinking.

"Do you want to talk about what happened with your folks?"

"I don't know, Hannah. It's, like, for the first time my mother was just totally full of shit and there's no way she could deny it. All her big talk just, like, evaporated for me. What she said just didn't matter. I laughed at her and she went nuts. She couldn't take it, Hannah. And my father's glued to her ass, so…no. *You can't make me go.* You know, it's not even like…the real estate company was my grandma's. She just gave it to my mother to run. Just to give her something to do. All my mother did was boss people around her whole life. That's all she knows how to do. Especially my father. He worked for her, did you know that? You can guess who's the S and who's the M."

"Where did they go?"

"They couldn't even tell me. Just the truth. She couldn't admit it. So, fuck that static."

Hannah dipped her voice. "Has Bob Sanders been bothering you?"

The girl's snorted guffaw finished as a whoop. The man cut apart in the way only a pretty girl can. Before there were ever words for it.

"Why did his wife leave?"

"Who knows? She was chummy with my mother. I don't think she was very happy with the mister."

Lorna pulled at a thread on her shorts, snapping it. She held the thread between her fingers, bringing it closer to her eyes.

"Has Bob said anything to you?"

"Huh? Oh, no. It was cool. He pretty much just stuck up for me. Not like I was gonna go anyway. The wife was ready to hit it, no doubt. She was *gone, baby gone*. It's all good."

Lorna looked over. "Will you take me with you when you go?"

Hannah swallowed. She watched Lorna taking its measure.

"I know Fat Fuck's gonna give us up to those freaks and I don't want to die beat to death and gangbanged. If you don't mind." She guzzled the rest of the soda. "The douches inherit the Earth. And dicks like

Hapgood'll be king."

"That's not gonna happen, Lorna."

The girl folded her legs Indian-style on the wooden Adirondack chair. "You know, it's really cool you're being nice and trying to make me not worry, Hannah. But I totally think you're wrong. I think we're totally fucked."

"I don't," Hannah said, pushing it into her voice. "No. There's millions of people like us who are helping each other and getting things working. Trained, smart people. Just like during the flu. It wasn't over then and not now, either. We might just have to get to them first. Don't think that way."

The girl's arm pitched up, voice a throaty howl. "U-S-A. Whoo!"

Lorna poured out the dreg drips from her can. She regarded it in her hand and, hesitating, tossed it into the flower bed, face mugging in mischief and embarrassment. Heresy for her generation, Hannah thought. The recycling nihilists.

"Do you want to come and stay with Joyce and I?"

"Nah., I have lights. Books. My Ipod's charged. My Dad already gave me a gun."

The sun had nearly dipped under the wall. Hannah stood, picking up the dripping chicken and sliding back into her Crocs. Another gun. Just what we need.

"How about food?"

"I've got enough."

"Well, if you want to, come over. We've got plenty of room."

Lorna's smooth face was radiant in the light, green eyes squinted.

"Um, do you got any tampons? Bitch didn't leave me any."

"Sure. I bring you some later."

"When are you gonna leave, Hannah?"

"Come to the meeting tomorrow. We'll figure it out then. We've already talked to the guys. They're with us."

Hapgood's shepherd barked in the distance. Both women looked up at the powdery rip of a blue-winged, blue-tailed twin-engine passenger jet, flying lower than normal. Hannah smiled down at Lorna in affirmation. All over the rest of the world people were working, having breakfast, joking and loving, kissing goodnight. *Up.* This was not the end.

"See?"

"Yeah. They're leaving."

******

His Dad's plod on the stairs. It wouldn't be her, anyway. Sherri only came down for laundry and she had already washed everything earlier in the day. When Mark woke up around 5:30 they were both gone to the afternoon meeting. He had to pull their stuff out of the big plastic sink to wash his own clothes.

Mark watched the bobbing flashlight spot on the wall, coming through the blacker shapes of his wet hanging shirts and pants. Mark went back to his desk work, waiting.

"What are you doing?" Ray said.

Mark looked away, hand blocking the beam in his eyes. He lowered the shortwave receiver's volume.

"Nothing. New batteries in my NVGs. What's up?" The goggles were within the few inches of clear work space. The desk lamp's light ringed a mish-mash of pliers, PVC tube, a snow mist of powdered aluminum, small screwdrivers, his soldering iron, maps, crumpled wrappers, shotgun shells, batteries, stumps of candles and an empty, spooned cereal bowl. More junk faded to the dim-dark edges. A week-old half-can of Mountain Dew and a scatter of plastic washers. Mark grabbed a fat, cut-apart skyrocket tube, emptied of its powder and charges, and threw it into the trash bag with the other cannibalized fireworks - fountains and bent, stripped sparkler wire.

"You eat?"

"Yeah," Mark said.

After sweeping over Mark's bed and desk mess, Ray clicked the flashlight off. Mark settled back in the chair.

"Going out?"

Mark's eyes stayed on the desk. His projects. "Probably."

"Why don't you stay in? There nothing going on out there. Let's have a drink. It's a nice night out. Let's sit on the deck."

"Since when are you drinking again?" Mark said.

"A couple ain't gonna kill me."

Mark opened the goggles, pulling out the depleted set of recharge-ables. The shortwave broadcaster, Blue Jay, talked about the fights on the Great Plains to secure the farms and fall harvests. The Feds were fire-bombing crops, Blue Jay said, preferring to let people of the heartland starve while European and South American cargo provisions were poured into the rat-hole cities.

"Why do you listen to this shit?"

"I'm trying to hear all sides. I listened to EBN all day. They say everything's gonna be fine. Habeas Corpus suspended. It's temporary, like a tax. All those Slovenians and Germans and Indians and Chinese coming in to help you are gonna go right home as soon as they fix us. They don't want anything for it, like your homes or anything."

"What are you hearing about around here?"

"A UN column got ambushed over on 75. Blue Jay said 80 killed. What have you seen on the TV?"

"Nothing else. Same." His Dad's tongue smacked the way it did when he was holding back what he wanted to say. "Just clean some of this up, will ya? The dishes? Come on. You know better."

"I will. Sorry."

Ray turned to walk back up, the clicked spot-beam on his bare feet.

"You know, you don't have to be the one who shoots first. Use your head, Mark."

"I won't, Dad. Anything new at the meetings?"

"No. We still got gas for the water pump and cameras. Everyone still here says they're gonna stay put. Nothing's changing. The guards have it handled, Mark."

"Until they don't."

Feeling it build, Mark rushed to put it down. He'd pushed too far.

"I'm not bothering them, Dad. I'm not bothering anybody. It's still a free country. At least in here, right?"

"Right, Mark."

It would hard if it was an American. But, Mark was pretty sure. If he saw a blue helmet or funky uniform speaking Aba-Daba, he was gonna do a Han Solo.

He would shoot first.

******

Trella was with them. His and a few other familiar faces clowned among the disciplined soldiers, the green six-wheeler trucks and machine-gun Hummers. Trella grinning like a tourist, monkey-gripping the open door of his prize, the Sheriff's Department desert war-surplus MRAP in the BP parking lot. Its blue was spray painted over with green and brown splotches. Red J on the door. So much for Call the Cops.

LifeForce was foreign-owned mercenaries, the letter said. *A foreign-owned midnight army in America.* Steve liked that one. A midnight army. He couldn't get to the notion of foreign-owned or what it meant anymore. To Steve, billions of dollars was its own country any way you sliced it. Billions of dollars was all pretty foreign.

Steve clicked the arrow for the next picture. Happy faces in Carol's, eating D-Plex meat and greens. Click. Moms and kids. Click. Stacks of canned and packaged food.

He shut the computer down, eyes adjusting to the dark around him. The ghost-green silhouetted Tyce at the camera console.

"Anything going on?" Steve said.

"Enos is out."

Steve walked to the monitors. Tyce had zoomed in on Mark. A slouched, tubby Martian in his night goggles, crossing the road, SKS carbine across his back.

"Enos, huh? Like *Dukes of Hazzard*?"

"Yeah." Tyce grinned at Steve. "*Dukes of Hazzard*. Going out?"

"Yeah. Do a loop."

"Keep your eyes open for dipshit. He's in the west woods."

"Uh-huh."

On his way to the HVAC/supply room he clicked the kitchen light on, running the cold water. Along with the 3-cell Mag-light, Steve opted to take the M-4 rifle. He loaded a magazine, checked the safety and put a spare mag in his back trouser pocket. He lifted the last spare hand radio from the charger rack and put it in his other pocket, for Lorna. His own radio was secured on his Batman belt with all the other weight. He filled a water bottle and shut the light.

Hunched at the console, Tyce concentrated, keying and zooming the south-end cameras. A blur of leaves, trees and funky road angles.

"Are you going to tell me the plan?"

"What do you mean?" Tyce said.

"You've hidden the note pad with all the things you wrote down today. When you were looking at the pictures? When the women were here? You were writing when you were looking at the military equipment. Then later you asked me where places are in Essex. All of a sudden you care where the school is. Fine. When I was in the shower I heard you going through the file cabinet. I checked and now the map discs are out of order. So, you've got notes on the assholes outside. You don't want me to see them and you're mapping, wanting to know where things are in town."

Steve's shoulder rested against the plywood-covered glass door.

"Some might call that planning, partner. Is this Rambo Tyce time?"

Tyce was not quite smiling. A confident card player's expression, on the raise.

"What you don't know won't hurt you, Steve. It's information we might be able to use, that's all. I'm not leaving and I'm not going to fuck you over. But, sorry. It's not a therapy group. I'm not gonna 'share' everything."

"Fair enough. Me neither."

Tyce scooted back, stretching his legs. "Since we're in therapy, if you have a problem with me lying about the radio and the phone just say it. Your little passive aggressive number with the girls? Did you think I would confess? Confess the error of my ways?"

"Maybe I did agree with it at first. But these people are depending on us. It's a little different now, isn't it?" Steve said.

"No."

"You don't think we need help?"

For show or not, the green-lit side of Tyce's face laughed. "You're gonna get it on the sat phone? 911? Come on, Steve. And the radio...."

Tyce inhaled, like he was about to perform a trick. His eyes fixed away before meeting Steve's, impatient.

"You know Ranger school? In the Army? You have to qualify?"

"Yes."

"They have an escape and evade course. You go in the swamp for two days with nothing. Your utilities and your boots, running from guys hunting you. The instructors will do things to fuck with you. Like leave a little Tac flashlight -". Tyce pointed at Steve's belt. "-by a path. Guy thinks, great, one of the hunt team dropped it. What an advantage. I can move at night. I'll make great time. So...stupid tired, starving, wet, he's gonna turn the light on. And the hunter team is gonna laugh their ass off before they tag him because he's just shown them exactly where he is. That's why I don't want them knowing there's a radio."

Tyce's right palm opened, empty. The magician's reveal. Nothing.

"You were a Ranger?"

Tyce rotated to the screens.

"No."

Hoisting the rifle, Steve unlocked the door.

"Tell her I said hello," Tyce said. "On your loop. Is that what you kids are calling it now? Do a loop?"

Steve froze.

"I saw you go there last night, man. I don't care. More power to you. She's hot. I guess I know why you came back here. Just keep your radio on, stud."

Steve's caught surprise found Tyce's grin. Each man's easy, aw-shit laughter gradually fed the other. The exhausted laughs spooled out of them, fixed to nothing, making them perhaps as close as they had ever been or would be. Two bullshitters. Midnight soldiers. High on the endorphin lift, Steve pushed the plywood and glass open, filling his lungs with warm, clear night air.

***

Steve passed only inches away from Mark. Steve's torch went right over him, la-de-da. Where *was* Steve looking with the thing? The objective of a light is to *look* where it's pointing. Mark wanted to jump up from the bush and shout, but he held still, knowing he was better than the cop. Mark could have knifed him. Anything. But Mark held his breath. Jump out and it's a perfect excuse for Steve to blast you, knowing and smiling evil at you in the last second.

When Steve was well down the road, Mark crept low, back into the east woods. Crouched, he checked the tautness of his trip lines, strung tree to tree in the clearer points. That's how *he* would come in. Over the wall, one or two at a time, SEAL-style. There was no way the cameras could monitor over a mile – a mile, Jack – of wall by themselves. The two of them in there had to sleep sometime. Living like kings, full electric. *Ace job on the patrol, Steve. Eagle eye.*

Mark followed the wall south, turning west at the corner. Through the electro-green NVGs Mark searched up for ropes or down in the dirt for boot tracks.

Closer to the gate, the undergrowth thinned. Knowing the camera positions, Mark walked easy and upright to the road, passing around the waist-high concrete barriers corridoring the entrance. The security car parked at a slant in the short lot, Dominski and Tyce's trucks beyond it. His eyes averted from the decorative solar lights bordering the lot, their harsh white distorting his night vision. At the metallic click, Mark snapped to his right side. Tyce stepped out of the Barrack's door. No light cast out behind Tyce, pretending to look up at the quarter moon.

"What do you think, Mark?"

"What do I think?"

"C'mere. I'd like to talk to you."

Mark approached the ramp, lifting the goggles. From the footlights Tyce was clear enough, leaning, forearms across the hand rail.

"Look, I can tell you care about this place. It seems like protecting it, protecting your family and the people in here, it's important to you."

Mark nodded, unsure what he was getting at. He expected Tyce to call him 'Buddy' next. Say 'we' instead of 'you'. Cop tricks.

"Yeah. I do."

"If you think Steve and me came off dickey to you the other day it wasn't personal."

Here it comes. Maybe it would be 'son.'

"Everyone's trying to sort this out. Steve and I still are. I'm asking you what you think. About this place. You're out in the woods every night. What are you doing that we're not doing? What are you looking for?"

Tyce's voice kept on.

"Look at me. I'm not messing with you. I'm asking."

"Cameras won't do it," Mark said.

"We know that."

"You and Steve patrol. Not in the woods. You walk down the middle of the road, knock on doors. What's that? You've got over a mile and half of wall and woods. That's what I'm checking."

"OK then. Good," Tyce said. "Keep doing it. Whether you believe it or not, me and Steve care about this place, too. You – your family – have been good to us and we're both taking this job seriously. You've probably seen and heard things are getting kind of ugly out there, Mark."

"Mark," Tyce repeated.

Mark nodded. "No doubt."

"Well, Steve and I might need your help. I'm on the side of the people living in here. I'm not on anybody else's side. Not whoever I used to work for. The same with Steve. And I want you knowing that."

"I hear you," Mark said.

"OK. Maybe you can help us with the cameras. I know you've got them spotted and figured out. So maybe we can position them better. Come to the meeting tomorrow afternoon."

"Yeah?" Mark faked a laugh. "Only owners allowed, right?"

"Well you come as my guest then," Tyce said.

"OK." Mark said, snugging the goggles over his eyes.

Tyce straightened up from the rail.

"You know your partner is out there sitting in the sand with his girlfriend," Mark said. "He's been fucking her this whole time. Almost every night."

Tyce laughed. "No shit? Sneaky bastard. I've been wondering where he's been going. Lorna tattoo chick?"

"Yep. Cameras don't catch everything, do they?"

"Guess not. Later."

Through the parking lot, Mark moved west across the grass toward the tennis court and cluster of trees in the southwest corner. There he rested. Lift the goggles, wipe the sweat. North-bound, he passed the pool, toward the west-side woods. Bats flitted through the sky. He crossed into the tree line, stepping right six paces where he stooped to check another tripwire in the undergrowth. Intact. Counting his paces, going left toward the wall, then zagging right and straight on again. No tracks or disturbed branches. No one had been through here.

Long ago, Mark's uncle had given him some books on the Old West. He loved the story of a scout who named himself after Tecumseh, the Indian warrior chief. One night Tecumseh's scouting party was attacked in camp while he was washing. The lone survivor, he ran naked for miles through the night. Afterward, all through the West, wherever he roamed, Tecumseh would hide a stash of supplies – water, food, powder, clothing. Where he hid them – buried near a huge rock or under the base of a tree - he marked the spot with a broad T – for Tecumseh.

Huffing breath along the wall, Mark slowed, seeking the wall marker. At the driven spike in the wall, tied with an orange ribbon, Mark went eleven paces right. Then northeast to the tall maple. The blindest of spots for his back-up bug out bag. Stuffed with his recently-added Glock pistol, ammo, energy bars and food, water bottles, clothes and socks and shoes in case he had to run out naked. In the long pack's zipper pockets, he had practical stuff like duct tape, a flashlight, Bic lighter, some medical supplies, pen and pad and a new Swiss Army knife in addition to a serious protection knife. A Marine K-bar combat blade – nine inches of real steel. The bug-out kit was also where Mark kept the LifeForce uniform he'd bought online. Mark was certain this was the blindest of spots because on the night of the first blackout this is where he changed in the rain. In his LifeForce uniform and patrol cap he climbed to knock the camera starward. With the old man's forgotten key from the kitchen junk drawer, Mark unlocked Cricklewood Green's generator room and disabled the relay switches to the public power lines. Thanks to Blue Jay, he'd saved all their asses with fresh water. Power for the Barracks, the streetlights.

Mark wanted to do it at the house, but all he could do was unplug their electronics - and his Dad and Sherri ragged on him while plugging them back in that morning. Because Mark was a dumb fuck. Because Mark was never right about anything. During the first night he couldn't disable the house's power relay. His Dad had locked the basement door to the generator. Those keys never left his Dad's pocket. Mark could have granted the house full power, everything working. A fridge, an oven....

After everything fried upstairs, his Dad took Mark's working TV from the basement. And Hapgood took all the credit.

Mark gripped the bark-pattern rope, feeling the bag's weight up in the branches.

Tecumseh, motherfuckers.

****

The filling meal made Mike Narlow want to smoke. He insisted Kim and Sandra Rose eat the chicken. He took one leg but went double portion on rice. They still had over 20 pounds of it, so Mike didn't think his agreed indulgence to cook a big batch would matter. The extra rice added to the girls' excitement over fresh chicken. It was nice to see. He closed the slider screen, walking out further on the deck. He stretched, lighting the cigar.

Mike was stunned by Hannah's gift. She wouldn't say where she got the chicken. It bothered him. He and the girls still had plenty of meals left. But, eventually, they would have to start trading....out there, with them. The gold Krugerrands, OK. Mike had snuck back some ivory from China, but what would it go for? With those hicks?

Distracted, Mike drew on the cigar, trying add-up the stock. The pantry and Tox Boxes - the dozen post V-14 aluminum bins he was damned glad Kim had filled.

Mike's eyes settled across the north edge of the pond and Hapgood's lit-up outpost. The shaded window lights making a freaky afro outline of the giant willow in his backyard. Fat fucker was probably eating lobster in there.

Frozen chicken. Vern having a working freezer would make sense. But he would never give chicken to Hannah. Vern couldn't stand her. Unless Vern was trying to play her. Hannah then giving it to him and the girls. Mike now owing her…

Mike's attention twitched right, to the Vanderkam house, at the grass line. He pulled the cigar out, squinting. A light moved. The light moved *inside*, behind the glass-block row at the lawn. White light. A shadow eclipsed past it, then the window block was dark again. It wasn't a reflection. The light was *inside*. It couldn't have been the Dudek kid. Mike had just seen him going the other way.

He squinted. A reflection? No. *Should have went for the eye exam.* Kim had some binoculars, someplace….

There it was again. White light.

They'd all agreed. No one goes where they aren't invited. Not into the vacants or the empty houses. No one breaks a lock here. Property rights will be honored.

Someone was in Vanderkam's basement.

****

September 13th

From atop the ramp Steve waited for the coming headlights, expecting trouble by the speed. Meet panic with calm. Training, he said to himself. Pretend you're on a bicycle rolling downhill. Feet out, brakes on. Balance. Slow it down. Slow. It. Down. Get control.

The mini-van jerked to a stop next to the Barracks. In the bluish half-dawn, Mike Narlow exited looking like a madman. Unshaven, a greasy smear of hair. Skittering white eyes in the not-quite morning. His ramble made little sense over the heartbeat 'bing' chime of the idling mini-van's open door. A familiar dread bore down on Steve. *Mike's wife and daughter. What he might find.*

"Mike. Relax. Turn the van off first, OK?"

"Steve, listen. I'm not fuckin' nuts. The cord is in the ground, going into the house. I didn't put it there. I'm telling you." Narlow's hands were live, tappy. "Come with me. Let's check it out."

From his higher spot Steve couldn't be sure of blood spots or rips in Narlow's clothing from struggle. Narlow was obscured, standing in the open driver's door crease. *If the hands disappear, I'll draw.* Narlow's known firearm was a Sig Sauer nine.

Slow it down.

"I hear you, Mike. Shut the car off. Come on up. Let's talk."

The man smirked and stepped back from the car, surrendering his palms. In grimaced nods, Narlow paused, shoulders drooping in the exhale, arms falling to his sides.

"I know. I come down here like a fucking maniac, right? You're right. I'm calm. But there is somebody in Vanderkam's house. We all saw them leave, right?"

The door binged.

"Right."

"Yeah," Narlow agreed with himself.

"How about you switch the car off, Mike?"

Narlow seemed to accept Steve's word, a truce with his own sanity. They'd all seem the Vanderkams drive off. Narlow leaned in and clicked the motor off, shutting the lights. Closing the door, Narlow walked around the back of the van, up the ramp. He was still fidgety, picking at his unzipped dark hoodie and green MSU Spartans T-shirt. Steve relaxed, eyes acting interested as Narlow explained what he saw earlier in the evening. There was no visible blood on Narlow. Barely sleeping, he had awakened at 4 a.m., he said. He crept in the dark and saw the cord, he said. The electrical cord leading from the street lamp post into Vanderkam's house. It hadn't been there the other day.

Steve remembered Tommy Bolger. When Tommy ran out of ketamine and turned to smoking a recipe found online he ran through Essex in the nude, fleeing attacking squirrels. Three cops, Tommy's brother-in-law and two stun guns at last secured Tommy into the wagon, still screaming in terror. They were all over him, chewing.

Steve would have check under the bed for Narlow. *No monsters...*

Telling Narlow to wait, Steve went into the Barracks to get a vest.

*****

Tyce watched the procession on the screens, Dominski in the dinky patrol car trailing Narlow's van up the east loop. A soldier's notion of luck and good signs came over Tyce. He'd wanted to do it around this time of morning and Dominski's nursemaid mission saved Tyce a walk into the woods and embarrassment if discovered. Tyce retrieved the satellite phone from its hiding place. He'd confirmed its charge last night.

The Colonel's business card was from last Christmas. Tyce and Colonel Wright had dinner together, not having seen each other in years. They drank long that night. Neither said it, but repayment, debt, gratitude, pride – all were present at the table. In Iraq, Tyce found then-Captain Wright fair and competent, in the higher middle of officers he had suffered through. Back in his 20s, paratrooper Tyce had been part of Headquarters company, communications – "Chairborne" to the combat jumpers. Dame Fortune discharged Tyce days before the Iraqi invasion of Kuwait. Ten-plus years later, with Tyce on the bad side of 35, she along with boredom, bills and another crashed boy/girl performance delivered Tyce to the Michigan National Guard two months before 9/11.

Captain Wright's contingent had been returning from a meeting with local sheiks. Second in the four Humvee convoy, Tyce was driving, Captain Wright the front passenger. Tyce's last thought passing the trash bundle with the fat cylinder across its top was "I wonder if that's a – "

The Captain lost his right leg below the knee and right arm from just below the elbow (very lucky to keep the elbow, they said). The Silver Star report commended Sergeant Tyce's actions - *pulling the Captain from the burning vehicle and stabilizing him. Pinned down by enemy gunfire, Sergeant Tyce helped return fire, called in the medical evacuation and directed the airstrike at great personal risk.*

Tyce was left with superficial burns, pinprick shrapnel and hearing loss that faded. Everyone lived who mattered. Those in the structures did not. Tyce's mother in Buffalo had the medal, as she should.

Tyce kept the business card in his wallet, the wallet that escaped her bathtub fire.

Luck. Dame Fortune.

The satellite phone was answered on the third ring. Good signs.

"Identify yourself."

"Is Colonel Wright available?"

At first, he thought the line cut off. Then another voice answered,

"Identify yourself. Who's speaking?" The voice was young, not him. Speaking into the phone felt odd. Everything for the last week had been handsets, ear pieces.

"Please tell Colonel Wright it's Landslide Six Delta. Over."

On the camera monitor Steve had parked in Narlow's driveway, following Mike inside. The cameras had automated to daylight view; submarine green brightened to color. He swept and zoomed as best he could with #7 but could see no cord leading into the Vanderkam house. The angle was poor, too low to the ground. Tyce switched to the roll shuffle of all 18 cameras in a block of six. The second monitor he reset to full-view, observing outside the gate.

"Who is this?"

The man's voice made Tyce wish in the finest margin he were there with him.

"Sergeant Tyce, sir. How are you?"

"Tyce?" There was a bump and shuffle. Steps and a closing door.

"Where in the hell are you? How are you calling me?"

"Still in Michigan, sir. Sat phone. You might say I've gone to ground. I'm amazed I reached you."

"Double for me," Wright said. "I had no idea my old line transferred here. How's your condition? Do you have any injuries?"

"Slight. My knee's banged up but I'll manage."

The old battalion code. A small discomfort meant a clean line. To be fine meant you'd been captured or couldn't speak freely.

"I have another number. Ready?"

Tyce wrote and re-dialed. The Colonel answered directly. His tone was not the whiskey warmth of Christmas. This was war and mission. Aware, Tyce condensed. LifeForce, Essex, the D-Plex attack (Wright knew), the enemy & the freeway ambush nearby (he knew too well). Tyce guarding fifteen-odd friendlies with only one other reliable man.

Colonel Wright was moving, other voices whirled as he requested and ordered. "Essex? You're pretty red up there, Tyce. Enemy country."

"Alamoed, sir. I've got confirmed enemy within Essex. Breakaway reserve, I think. I estimate approximately 50 men. Some from the highway ambush, I think. I've got vehicle numbers, sir. Confirmed two 120 mortars and one towed M-119 cannon. They're looking to seize the place I'm guarding. A gated development approximately six miles east. We have a well and fresh water here, sir. The town of Essex has no water service. That's also confirmed, sir."

Wright called for a sergeant amid the background motion. "Roger. I've got recent airborne visuals on your AO."

"My ass is in kind of a crack, sir. Can you do anything for us?"

"You say confirmed enemy, Tyce?"

"Yes, sir. I've got vehicle numbers."

"Copy. Your AO is a mess. We're at a skirmish line of M-59. We're not moving north without help. You know about Holly. We don't have the muscle to control any more than we've got. Actives are on the way. Until then, all I can advise is hold. If you have to move, head southeast."

"Yes, sir."

"What's your intel on those hostiles, Tyce?"

Tyce checked his notes, relaying the truck and Humvee numbers. He flipped the page.

Places.

The CD-ROM map had supplied Tyce the Essex street names and numbers. From what Dominski told him, Tyce had pinpointed the addresses of the school and city building, the old cop shop. One of the pictures had a .50 Cal Humvee at the elbow of the park and the bar where Heller Lake Road turned north. A good spot. Its turret could swivel control the north and west road approaches for a half-mile.

"How about air assets, sir?"

"Are you close enough to site targets?"

"Negative. But I've got street numbers of billets. Staging and supply areas. If you grid it from a civilian map I'm betting your pilots could acquire them easily, sir."

"What about civilians?"

"None, sir."

Tyce watched Dominski and Narlow walking the north loop of blacktop, westward to the Vanderkams. He expanded the whole first monitor on the pair.

"You're certain, sergeant? No civilians?"

"Yes, sir. Definite enemy. I've got a confirmed threat."

"Hold for my XO," the Colonel said.

Tyce relayed the streets and numbers to the executive officer and rogered, repeated back. Numbers grouped together becoming lethal, sentences of death for those beneath the pilot's released ordnance.

The numbers. That was all Tyce needed to say.

When it was done, the XO signed off and the Colonel seemed focused. One of the supply trucks was from their old battalion in Iraq, the

Colonel said. The Colonel was pleased, a well-done. He hoped a fire mission would relieve Tyce's immediate danger. Tyce thanked him. The men agreed to speak again if they could. With the arrival of the active Army the Colonel's forces would be absorbed. He expected to be unreachable very soon, relieved and likely administering back in the metro someplace.

"What's the bigger picture, sir? Roundabout?"

"Protect your people. Stay put, sergeant. We're coming. It improves every day."

Luck was wished. Tyce disconnected.

He yawned at the ceiling, tapping the phone on his thigh.

In the end, the mind subverted us. We so carelessly certain of control. Willpower was self-con. Your thoughts a passenger, to where those neuron sparks and chemicals were destined, all without You. Ask the schizos or the convicts living under Alzheimer's drip death. Life happened, simply.

Tyce realized his blurted word to the Colonel. *He* didn't say it. Something else said it for him. To him.

Alamo, sir.

Cricklewood Green was a fortress surrounded. A settlement, hostile to its terrain and its natives. Alamo. Dien Bien Phu. Hadrian and the Picts. Masada. Everybody dies. Sorry, Joe Allen. *Everybody.* One narrow way out.

But Tyce didn't believe in retribution anymore. One did what was needed, and that was it. The time Tyce touched it overseas, at the roadside, had frightened him. To call it retribution, or revenge, was pipsqueak. The awesome, soul-deep possession - beyond pleasure, beyond satisfaction - Tyce felt while kneeling, mouthing numbers into a tiny contraption of metal and plastic. Tyce so certain he controlled it. Then those houses disintegrated under jet bombs in the blazing Tigris sunshine, atomizing his ego. The enveloping, sand-sting blast waves knocked through him while his blood-covered hands fitted Captain Wright's shredded stump into the pressure cuff. Tyce ceased to exist.

The blast waves were an immersion whose depth compressed Tyce to a speck, taking the air from his lungs. For moments, Tyce was not himself. He was a clinging, terrified speck. A spark inside a tide. Infinity mocking him. *How dare you think…*

One did what was needed.

What would Dominski say if he knew? Sergeant Tyce, E-5, hadn't tried very hard to see it Dominski's way. Tyce knew, the moment he saw the pictures of the mortars, the Humvees. The LifeForce corpses. *Wait it out? And if you get shot at, shoot back?*

No. Airstrike. Communications. Tyce had trained years for this.

Good signs, connections, destiny.

Tyce stood, putting the satellite phone into the console drawer. Smacking his lips and thickened tongue in desire for… coffee? He'd only slept for -

The reports were faint, echo bounce-backs through the Barracks' door. Tyce jerked forward, inches from the monitor. His nerves ignited cold. On the monitor, Dominski was scrambling away on the Vanderkam lawn. He and Mike Narlow were firing their pistols into the house.

****

The only thing missing was the cigarette. In the still-night kitchen Kim Narlow's features and mussed hair were outlined by the pewter glint of a shaded side window. Her eyeglasses caught a scratch of brighter light from between the shade and window frame, jutted forearm holding up her chin on the breakfast bar. Steve's mother used to smoke this way, in the dark at the table while his brothers got ready for the paper route. He remembered as a little boy listening in the hallway, edging out to watch. The short, hushed words between his mom and them, a churchy weight to the sunrise quiet.

"Hey Kim, how are you?" Steve whispered.

"Been better. I'm sorry about this," she said. "Narlow is just...you really didn't need to – "

He shrugged, stepping further into the kitchen. He looked for marks, bruises. She was unmoving, shadow.

"How's your little girl?"

"Good. Thanks. Not easy without a TV, I'm not gonna lie. Do you guys have one? You do, right?"

Steve ummed and welled before the harsh whisper behind him. Steve twisted, seeing Mike leaning over the banister.

"Come up."

Following Mike Narlow to the master bedroom, Steve paused at the doorway of the daughter's room. Hearing her breathe untied a knot in him. Lace-filtered morning light brightened the wall murals. Blurs of pink and blue, a swath of orange. Dual fans hung from the pitched ceiling. The span between the cornered foam-block chairs, the TV stand and floor spread of toys was longer than his living room.

In the master, Steve noted the pump shotgun leaning next to a bureau. Cocktail tumbler, wristwatch and remote control. His side. Add drinking to no sleep for Mike Narlow. Opposite nightstand a lamp, tissue box, lotion and paperback. Her side. No phones. The contours of the mussed sheets and blankets in the darkened room were like the still-life of a storm at sea or a mountain range. Narlow handed Steve a ridiculously small set of binoculars, like opera glasses. Steve met Narlow's white, madman eyes thinking it was a joke. Narlow's head bopped toward the curtained window.

"Off to the side. Base of the streetlight. See the cord? It leads right into the house. Wasn't there yesterday."

And you could. A banana-yellow outdoor utility cord plugged into the streetlight base, a few feet of it threading across the roadside dirt toward the home - presumably - before it disappeared into uncut grass as

Steve's eyes followed left, before the hyper-focused brick corner of Bill Gallo's house cut off his view. There were a few covered outlets at the base of some of the faux Victorian streetlights. A legacy of the construction crews, Steve figured. He could see nothing of the Vanderkam house from the master window, obscured by treetops and Gallo's home. There were no lights or movement in Gallo's home.

Steve exhaled. He lowered the glasses. Everything was so far off now, the cord unseen. Miniature. The only visible part of the Vanderkam lot was the nose of their RV in the driveway. Narlow stared at him. Steve handed the glasses back.

"Sanders and Hapgood disconnected the streetlights," Steve said.

"The outlets are on the ground. It could be a separate line."

Narlow had an agility despite his desk-man jelly roll mid-section. It would be a fight. His teeth were bared, an expectation of action.

"Maybe. Maybe not," Steve said. "Did you check the other poles?"

"I didn't check any poles. I came to you. Who gives a fuck about the poles? It's there. It wasn't there last night. I saw the lights in the basement."

The first birds' breakfast conversations chirped through the window screens.

"You're sure – "

A bite of hissed air from Narlow.

"Mike. It's a not a crazy question. Nobody's sleeping enough. Everybody's nervous. Nobody's eating enough. You see things. You think things. You think you saw something." Steve forced his whisper. "What do you know about the Vanderkams?"

Narlow's voice stayed low. "Nothing really. They were from Florida. The bleach blonde wife, the tits. They took off a lot in the rig. One of those swinger-type older couples, ya know? But we both know they left and didn't come back, right? You're watching there at the gate. Right?"

"They didn't come back, Mike. OK – if someone's in there maybe it's Bill Gallo? Maybe it's Vern? What I mean is, you don't know who they gave a key to. They're neighbors."

"Well, then whoever's in there broke the agreement. And fuck Vern. No one goes into any of the vacants or the empties. Rules, right? And they're stealing power." Narlow's finger jabbed toward the house.

Steve looked out again. Slow it down. The black shingle slope of Gallo's roof blocked the view of Vanderkam's deck and most of their yard to the pond. So, there it was. Gallo probably, or Hapgood, powering up something or maybe cooking on the George Foreman grill. Using a little spare juice. No one would notice. Likely the cord had been plugged in for days, by Vanderkam.

Turning from the window, Steve walked. "I'll take care of it," he whispered, passing around Narlow to the hall and down the hardwood stairs. He was not surprised at Narlow dogging behind him.

Down in the now-brighter kitchen Mike Narlow unscrewed a water bottle and glugged. He declared he was coming along. Mike was bouncy, relishing.

"Just stay here, Mike," Steve said.

"What?" Narlow grimaced, head tilted, older brother style. He looked at his wife, still at the island, drinking a canned soda.

"Gimme it."

Steve was expecting the can when the woman lifted an automatic pistol, the Sig P226, from under the counter, blankly handing it to her husband. Narlow pulled the gun's slide, charging it.

"What are you gonna do with that, Mike?"

"What are you gonna do with yours?"

Steve looked at the polished tile, shoulders to the wall. All the time in the world.

"Come on, man. It's probably Bill Gallo in there. He's cooking Spam on the George Foreman grill. What's he done? You're gonna shoot him? Just stay here, alright?"

Narlow tucked the gun in his hoodie pouch. "Not me. But I'm gonna beat his ass for stealing power."

"You're gonna punch an 80-year-old guy?"

Steve's glance flitted to Kim in a bid of influence. She squinted at her husband, weary chin pressed by her small hand.

"You know, you can be really stupid, Narlow," she said. "I really can't believe you. The stupid shit you do sometimes."

"Yep. That's right." Narlow nodded at her, a confirmed disappointment. "I sure can do some *stupid* things, Kim. You're right about that one."

Her lips melted in derision, head shaking as she stood and made for the stairs. Fucking *men*.

The two men walked. Though the leaves and details outside were more defined, everything was still in a wash of blue-grey dawn. The large plot of grass between the Narlow and Gallo houses appeared a glossy blackish green, ankle high. In the gap, across the pond, Steve's attention went to Lorna's house. It would be an overcast start to the day. Faint sun like a flashlight through a blanket. A morning to spend in bed. Steve could feel Narlow close behind the knock of his cop shoes on the blacktop, pronounced in the quiet.

"That thing on safety?" Steve said off his shoulder.

"Yeah. Is yours?"

Steve stopped a few strides before Gallo's driveway mailbox and turned. Narlow's hands were jammed in his hoodie pockets. *What the fuck,* Steve thought. This guy makes four times what I do and he thinks to act like some movie thug is...

"Mike, I want you to understand something. I'm trained to use a firearm. I was a police officer for six years. You can stand in the street but you're not going into the house. You're not even going on the porch. I have a right to enter the house. You do not. If you try, I'm going to stop you. If you draw your weapon, I'm going to disarm you. If you resist, I will stop you. Do you understand?"

"I'm standing in my own street that I pay for," Narlow said. "You want me to say it, Stevie? You work for me."

"That was not my question. Do you understand what I just said?"

Steve blinked and breathed through the pout and roll of the junior auto executive's neck and shoulders. The next three motions were foreseen in Steve's mind. Wrist, twist. Kick collapse the knee. Face pushed to asphalt. Narlow's arms bent back and cuffed.

Finally, Narlow looked off toward the woods, scratching.

"Whatever. Yes."

"Stay behind me."

They passed Gallo's driveway and his lot's road-hugging hedgerow. At the lot's treed corner Steve stopped. In sight of the Vanderkam's pink brick two-level, he raised his right arm, halting Mike. The upper floors white/beige curtains were closed, the overhung porch empty. No back light through the thin living room curtains. Steve's eyes traced the yellow cord plugged into the lamppost about ten paces away. It went across the lawn about sixty-odd yards up into the slim, cracked-open living room window. Its companion slider-window bookended a broad, solid middle pane. What Steve's Mom would call a picture window. The white 6-panel wood door was closed. He focused. A few birds, yes. But someplace, barely, the tingle of radio voices, like a news report. Maybe from inside the home. The tan and brown profile of the RV took up half the driveway, another wall of hedge parallel behind it. Steve could sense nothing wrong. He lowered his arm and walked.

He passed the lamp and cord. Halfway along the lawn Steve abruptly looked backward. Narlow had stopped and bent forward. Steve watched him snag the cord from the plug and stand.

Like a caught kid in his baggy thug hoodie and spot-lit expression, Mike was suspended with the limp cord in his hand. The first pop and the crack of glass came simultaneous to Steve's ear, wondering what the hell Mike just did. There were two more close pops and cracks before Steve recognized gunfire from inside. Fluid, he dropped to one knee, drew his pistol and racked. He fired the Smith .40 three times into the wooden door and three into the picture window, crashing it like a sheared iceberg. To Steve's left, Narlow's Sig fired rapidly – seven eight nine ten – rounds busting glass and chipping through the Vanderkam's front room.

Steve dropped and rolled away until he was touch-close to the RV's bumper. Flat and facing the white expanse of garage door, Steve aimed on the visible portion of front window hole, fragments of glass fanging the frame. His eyes skipped to the curtained second floor windows.

There was no more firing from the inside.

Mike Narlow had backed up to Gallo's tree and hedge lot corner. Sitting, his back was to the house. His pistol aimed up to the treetop in his high right hand.

"Mike!"

Head bowed, Narlow patted at his crotch and belly with his left.

"Mike!"

Both of Narlow's arms spasmed, pissed-like. The Wolverines had scored and there goes his fantasy bracket. The pistol waved in his grip.

"Ah, Fuck!" The arms. "Fuck!"

"Mike!"

"I think I'm shot."

*****

Hannah kept trying to force Mike flat. Ray recognized shock. Slumped cross-legged half in the pebbly dirt and the blacktop, Mike was putty pale, sweaty, bloody hands and wrists draping over his knees. Mike's head whipped, checking himself, like he couldn't believe it. He thought it was a piece of the window, he said. Then the burn, like a needle.

"You guys...Ray. Got any water? Get me some water? Please?"

"Lay down, Mike. I need to look at you." Hannah said, trying to lead his wriggling shoulders. Her eyes connected upward to Ray.

"Come on Mike. Lay down. It's OK, buddy. Just relax." Ray said. He crouched, gripping and patting Mike's legs. Ray picked up the dirty, jarred-open handgun and flicked it toward the hedge.

"Yeah yeah. Cocksucker. I just gotta... just lemme -"

Mike heaved up, jolting free of Hannah's touch as he vomited explosively in front of himself, some bright blood streaked in it. Mike's eyes spun white as he collapsed backward, legs skidding into the slop.

Hapgood called out, behind the RV's windshield with an Army rifle. Next to him, Steve watched the Vanderkam house, talking into his ear mic radio, pistol aimed in his long, locked arm. Ray swatted, hoping Hapgood knew fuck off when he saw it.

Hannah pulled Mike's stained hoodie and T-shirt apart, probing. There was blood for sure, but not terrible. Down to skin, a dark pool oozed from a tiny hole in his abdomen.

"Open my bag. Get me a dressing."

Ray yanked the huge black athletic bag's weight, unzipping it. Full of bandages, packeted syringes, tape. Bags of fluid. Organizing pockets lined the inside, stuffed with tiny glass bottles, pills, pokers and digital implements.

"A dressing. The square one. Right there!"

Hannah's teeth ripped the paper. She grabbed Ray's hand.

"Hold there. Press."

He watched the doctor check Mike Narlow's eyes with a pocket light and test his pulse.

"We have to get him inside. Switch. You get under his arms. Like this. We're going up the driveway there, into William's house."

She taped the dressing and twisted toward the RV. "Steve! See anything?"

Steve shook his head.

"We have to move him."

"Go!"

Expecting bullets, Ray cringed. *Please please please God don't let it be Mark in there.* On three they lifted Mike Narlow and trotted as best they could around the hedge and up Gallo's driveway. There was no worry. The high hedge bordered the whole of Gallo's front yard. No one could see them from the Vanderkam's unless they were upstairs. As they crossed through the flowers and across the porch the lower muscles of Ray's back flamed, the sciatic pain stabbing ice down his left leg. Ray knew he wasn't shot, but he had just strained himself something awful. The bad back had kept him out of Nixon's draft lottery, now Ray was carrying a wounded guy. How about that one? From his arm strength Ray held the man, bare foot banging back on the wooden door.

"Open up! It's us!"

Bill Gallo's moony expression pissed Ray off. His zeroed mouth, catching flies. Like they were unexpected guests for Thanksgiving. He couldn't hear what was going on? He couldn't see? Crossing into the two-story foyer Ray smelled the shit in Mike Narlow's sweat pants. Huffing, Hannah looked left, right, then into Gallo's wide eyes.

"Kitchen," he said.

Ahead of their scraping and bumping, Gallo's arm swept the island's centerpiece and junk to the floor. The island was solid with no sink. From Narlow's folding middle Gallo helped boost him onto the dark green soapstone.

"Good," Hannah said.

From the bag, she pulled scissors and cut the rest of Narlow's clothing off. A spot had already soaked to the top of the dressing.

"Get something to raise his feet."

Gallo was quickly gone and back with two throw pillows. He pulled Narlow's tennis shoes off and set the pillows under the man's feet.

Gallo then bent to gather the torn and stinking shreds. Hannah had a bag of fluid out and was working the needle into the nude man's arm. Ray watched it all, unsure.

"Come here. Hold this up."

Standing with the bag, Ray watched Hannah fill a syringe and inject Narlow's other arm. Behind him, Gallo had opened the faucet full-blast and Ray could hear the sink filling with water. He glanced back. Gallo's fingers flitting through the pour, trembling.

"I thought hot water was for babies," Ray said, trying to joke.

"To wash him. Hannah, do you need to wash your hands?"

She dug in the bag. "No."

To Ray it felt like an embarrassed bad dream. Everyone was moving and acting the way they should and he was pinned at his feet. Hannah puffing the blood pressure cuff on Narlow's arm. Ray just…didn't know. Supposed to be there but not knowing why. Like the phony coach-ish encouragement he had been giving to the cussing, sweating Narlow before he puked and passed out. It didn't seem to matter to Narlow and it sure as hell didn't matter to Ray. Babble. Stuff he was supposed to say.

Please don't let it be Mark.

"Can you cut the bullet out of him?" Ray said.

Hannah didn't look at him, focused on Narlow's sprawl. Blood-smeared fist knuckled under her nose.

"No."

"Well, what – "

"Well what?" Her head snapping to him.

Ray swallowed. "I'm sorry. I -"

Her up-flipped hand carried more stop than OK. She went back into the bag, tearing open a small packet and pulling out a packet of tiny foam-looking strips. She pulled the dressing off the entry wound and with a scalpel cut the hole larger. More blood pooled down, spatting onto the tile. But then with a pair of clips she stuffed the strips into the wound and it seemed to swell closed; the bleeding stopped. Gallo watched while he washed Narlow's fouled legs. Hannah paused as Gallo moved over to slide fresh towels underneath Narlow's middle, blotting what blood he could. She thanked him, redressed the wound and taped it and asked for more towels and sheets to cover him. Backed off, holding the bag, Ray didn't know if it was a bigger asshole move to leave or just stand there.

As Gallo bent to wipe blood and gather the medical trash, Hannah stepped back, scratching her scalp.

"It's inside him. Internal bleeding. I don't know what damage it's done. Even if I was in a trauma center, I...."

"Can I do anything?" Ray said.

She took the fluid bag from his hand, still concentrating on the hairy body, chest inflating and falling. "Yes. Go get Kim and bring her here. Alone. If she wants to bring Sandra Rose, DO NOT let her. Even if you have to stay with her. And please don't say anything to anyone. William? Let's find something to hold this IV, please."

"Say what?" Ray asked.

"Nothing. Say nothing. Please. Go."

*****

Her questions came in a slow drip. From the U of over-stuffed couches in the basement Sherri and Kim Narlow watched Sandra Rose in their center, dip spreading water colors and setting neon plastic Legos around on the poster board. Multi-media.

"Does Daddy know who the man is?"

"Your father isn't that smart, honey."

Sherri ground her jaw, fist clenching.

Broad grey slants of glass-block daylight and Kim's candles shimmering the room's corners brought Sherri back to waiting out storms as a child in Florida. Later, the tropical storm and hurricane "parties" of her youth. No rules or chores or expectations. Those times could be another world, untouchable to the outside. Sherri pictured some of those people, how close she felt to them then - and did still. Forgotten but vivid, how were they during this crack-up? *Some storm, huh, guys?* She smiled at the young girl and her swaying bare legs. Sometimes it did seem like the floor was the place to be. With two remaining extension cords they'd plugged in an old dock player for Sandra Rose. Her music clicked and whirled and chugged along. Insulation-distraction.

Consigned to women-folk by the charging actions of their men, both women chatted above the listening girl as she painted and hummed. Aware of the big ears, Sherri demurred, mostly. Most uneasy for Sherri was the way Kim derided her husband in front of the girl.

"How come he's a bad man?" the girl said, kicking her legs flat on the area rug.

"We don't know," Kim said. "That's what Daddy is trying to figure out with the other men."

"But if he's in the other house how come we can't be upstairs?"

"Because they're trying to make us do work, Sandra Rose," Sherri said. "And if we stay down here we get to play."

"OK, but we have to go upstairs in a little while because everyone will wonder where we are and we'll have to find them and take the dogs. And we'll get lost and we'll have to sleep with the dogs in the forest and make a fire."

The women shared smirks, watching the frustrated little girl blow air when she couldn't get the color right, mashing the yellow and blue into green. At the doorbell's double bing Sandra Rose was up like a popped cork. Kim right behind her in a scoop.

"I'll go," Sherri said, laying a hand. "Do you want anything from up there?

Kim mouthed "cookies", free hand pecking to her lips.

Come on Sweetie. Let's clap with Gaga."

"No!"

In the foyer, Sherri's fogged worry while climbing the stairs was zapped clear by the bizarreness of Ray fidgeting outside the Narlow's door like some nervous date. His T-shirt and boxers were blotted with what looked like dry blood. Earlier, rapid gunshot echoes through their open windows had launched her and Ray out of bed, rolling, crawling to one another near the dresser. Sherri wasn't sure if she had screamed.

On the floor they had waited, hands together, listening. Finally, Ray warned her to stay put but she followed him downstairs, trailing his stomp around the home to peek low out any curtain and blind.

Bent and squinting out the front room verticals, his arm gated her back against the front door. "Shh. Stay back."

Sherri ran to get the revolver Mark had left in the kitchen, weighing down her robe pocket. They peeked, guessing and wondering. Through the living room window, they saw Hannah running north with her long, fat Red Crossed bag across her back.

"Someone's hurt," Ray said. "She's gonna need help. Wait here."

"Ray!"

And damn if he didn't run out after Hannah in his bare feet, T-shirt and boxers without a gun or a care. Breathless in the doorway, Sherri tilted between a blush of love for his bravery and stunned shock at his indifference to her. Locking the door, she crept down to the basement. Table fan blowing on him, Macho Mark, Mr. End of the World, snored. Then upstairs and around the rooms once more, Sherri could see nothing out of place – trees, hedges, pond, grass, road, houses. No people, a sickening quiet. Too wound up to eat, she washed and dressed. All of it happening in that direction, Sherri's thoughts filled with the young girl, Sandra Rose. On impulse, she went. Kim Narlow gladly let her inside.

Ray stepped back from the Narlow's open door. "What are you doing here?"

"I could ask you the same question," Sherri said.

His embrace was so total Sherri couldn't help but give in to whatever it needed, as if his gripping hands were accounting, making sure.

"Shh. It's OK," she whispered. "What?"

He muttered for her to close the door. They stood on the porch, Ray looking over his shoulders.

"You weren't at the house," he said. There was a rusty spot above his eyebrow, twitching.

She rubbed the spot away. Blood. Her fingertips steadied his cheek. "Are you OK? What's happening, Raymond?"

"Someone's inside Oompa's house with a gun. They shot Mike. It's...he's bad. Internal bleeding, she said."

Another of Ray's nicknames for everyone. Oompa as in *Willy Wonka*. 'Oompa Loompa' for the Vanderkam's orange tans, sunned hair, white teeth.

"Wait – what? Who said? Hannah?"

"Yeah. Steve and the other guard, they gave her a radio. And they called her. That's when we saw her running. I'm sorry. I know, I shouldn'ta without you. Anyway, Steve and asshole – Vern - are there now." Ray pointed.

"Who shot Mike? Are they still in there?"

"I don't know." Ray's voice caught. "Sherri, I was so scared it was Mark, maybe he went crazy. I had to go back to the house first, to make sure. And you weren't there and Mark didn't know about any of it. Son of a bitch." He hugged her again. "Goddamn I'm so glad to see you, babe."

Her hands pressed his chest. "OK OK. Where's Mike now?"

"They got him at Gallo's." Coming closer his whiskers brushed her cheek. "I don't know if he's got a long time. The bullet, it's up inside him. I think it might have hit some organs. From what it looks, I don't think there's much she can do. She asked me to bring his wife over but not the little girl. Mike was with Steve, I guess. They saw someone in there?"

"I know. Kim told me about it."

"She knows he's shot?"

"No, Raymond. How could she?"

"Look, can you go tell …?"

"Of course. Did you talk to Steve? Or Tyce? Is there anyone else in here? Is everyone else OK?"

"I don't know," Ray stepped back, gesturing at his filthy T-shirt and checkered boxers. Sherri was thankful he'd at least washed his hands. "We've been trying to save Mike."

"My God, Ray. Jesus. Who could be in here with a gun? They have cameras. Don't they know?"

"Maybe it's Professor? His wife left him and he blew his stack? Wouldn't surprise me."

Sherri placed her hands to his chest, hoping it didn't feel like a push. "Just, go back home. I'll take care of it. I'll stay here with Sandra Rose. Before – if - you do anything - anything else, Raymond, please come and tell me."

Under her touch she could feel him, almost…filling back into place. Ray nodded. Sherri caressed the back of his neck, bringing her forehead into his, amazed how in love she was with this big idiot.

After he vamoosed, Sherri watched him from the porch. She could tell by his walk. He'd hurt his back again.

Along the front porch Kim had planted tall stalk plants, wide rus-set fronds long limbed and almost tropical-looking in a graceful, wel-coming seven-foot sway. Cindy Vanderkam of all people had given the seeds to Kim from the planted cluster in her backyard. It was Yugoslavian, Cindy said. Sherri had intended to take some seeds for next year, before Fall.

At Sherri's feet Sandra Rose's chalk drawings had smeared to haze on the concrete. Faeries dust. Doorstep curses in colors.

Each time this had happened to Sherri she felt at war with Time. Every second she could stretch were so precious for the souls. They would never know about the time Sherri bought them, holding back the pressure, the necessity of Time. It was the only good you could take from being the messenger. The one telling somebody their sister was dead or Ramona had miscarried. The accident was too severe. Bobby wouldn't walk again.

For an extra few minutes Sandra Rose's not-too-smart father was larger than life and invincible, protecting her against the bad men. Sherri stepped around the cement, touching the solid stalks; pockets of fat, spiky seeds crooked in the branch elbows. They were lovely plants. She knew exactly where she would have planted them in the Spring.

At the door, Sherri blinked herself into a new face, going in.

*****

To Steve it was like being stranded in the middle of Lake Huron. Woozy, thirsty, scared and all of it. His raft was a walrus that wouldn't stop bleating, the breath you'd expect a walrus would have. Walrus was the nickname Tyce tagged to Vern Hapgood. But Steve needed the motherfucker's Belgian FN rifle and sidearm. He wanted some of the belted canteen, too, but wasn't about to ask. Vern was gnawing through Steve's patience, but to be alone in this deep water was worse. It happened to Steve on Lake Huron as a kid. The boat's motor was broken, rain and throw-up waves coming on while his brothers and father fought about whose fault it was. Ship to shore. Stranded. Come in.

Any law enforcement in the area....

Steve's radio checks with Tyce and Lorna had cleared everyone else in the development, even Mark. A stranger was in the Vanderkam house, armed.

Whose fault was it? It kept burping out of Hapgood, worded ten different ways. *Who are you talking to? What do you mean? Who's going to the Barracks? You need to position someone at the rear.* Orf Orf.

Steve slid closer to the center of the RV grille, twist pressing his head back on the windshield, trying to unjam the soreness in his neck. He rested his eyes.

"Your surveillance technique is outstanding," Hapgood said.

"Why did you lie to me, Vern?"

"I've had no occasion to lie to you, Officer." Vern's voice possessed two tones. Either lawyer-accuser or someone woken from a nap to flip a switch for an idiot. Vern had switched off the accuser.

"I got fired. I lost my job because of you. And you told everyone *you* disconnected the pump. And the power relays. You just straight face it," Steve said.

"What I said to the others was for their benefit. Giving them the impression things are further out of control than they are does no good." Vern flipped back to the courtroom. "The fact is - you left your post and those you entrusted allowed sabotage, even though it was beneficial. Thanks to your return, we have an intruder. And the likely death of Mike Narlow. Goody for us."

He could hear Vern inhale, licking his hairy lips.

"Your excuses are your own, Officer."

Pushing off, Steve stood to Tyce's call in his ear. "Yeah. I got it."

"Got what? What's happening?" Hapgood said, radio-less. In the swift play of Hapgood's grip the fold-stock, chop-barreled rifle seemed apt as a bludgeon.

Off to the RV's driver-side corner Steve watched for Tyce, emerging past the Christmas pine at the vacant house between the Vanderkam's and Hapgood's lots. He was weighted with long guns, vested, shotgun in his right hand and a school-size book bag down in his left. Tyce waved the shotgun once. Steve countered with his right arm.

"I can't see any movement in the house," Tyce reported in Steve's ear. "I'm coming in. Am I clear?"

It was about eighty yards diagonal across the grass. Steve looked upward, flush with the RV's driver side. There was some tree cover, but he couldn't be sure if Tyce would be concealed from the Vanderkam's upper windows. He pressed the ear piece.

"Which way are you coming in?"

Tyce looked up and around the branches.

"You tell me, partner."

"Which way? What's happening?" Hapgood said.

Steve looked over, about to shush, when Vern's profile set the FN to his shoulder, hairy forearm wrapping the strap. He aimed around the RV passenger corner.

"Wait–

Vern opened fire on the house in ripping, automatic bursts. Dropping to a crouch, Steve twisted away from the noise and spit brass, the home's upper windows shattering. Tyce crossed the front yard of the vacant house in a low trot. On Vern's fourth and last burst Tyce ran forward to the front of the RV.

"Mother-*fucker*!" Steve shouted. He holstered his pistol, poking-pulling his exposed, howling left ear and working his jaw.

"*I am he/as you are me/as you are we...*" Tyce sang, dropping the book bag. Tyce browsed up and down Hapgood, from the white cross trainers to the imitation vintage O.D. Army web belt louvered by his gut. Vern's XXXL black knit golf shirt bore two crossed putters over his puffy left tit – "Golden Bear".

"Good morning, soldier. Ready to go kill more Germans?" Tyce said. To Steve it sounded underwater.

Hapgood plucked his ear plugs and ejected the empty magazine from his FN. He locked in a fresh one, slipping the empty into his deep khaki pocket. He kept one eye on the house around the vehicle corner.

"Glad to see you're with us, Officer. What's your plan?"

Ignoring the big man, Tyce knelt, setting the Remington shotgun upright against the bumper. He unzipped the pack, handing Steve a water bottle. Pausing with one gasped *ahhh*, Steve finished it in three gulps, tossing the plastic shell.

"Shotgun's filled with six and there's a dozen more in the bag." Tyce said, handing Steve a protein breakfast bar from the pack.

"Who's monitoring the cameras?" Hapgood said.

Steve glared at Vern, drinking a short slosh from his canteen.

"What the fuck was that, Vern?" Steve said.

"Something. Cover fire for your comrade. How do you plan to take control of the house?" Hapgood snapped the canteen into its canvas and re-tightened the rifle strap around his left arm. "Who's monitoring the cameras? Who are your eyes?"

"Mark," Steve said, biting the packet open and chewing the nutty, grained chocolate. Hydrated, he already felt smarter. Barks from Hapgood's dog across the pond corner came in roiling, throaty spasms.

From the bag Tyce handed Steve a rear-view mirror.

"My truck." Tyce said, standing. The scoped Springfield rifle remained across his back. A black canvas sleeve around its stock held a spare magazine. "Use it. On the monitor you were peeking around the exact same spot every time. Lucky for you they don't know what they're doing or they're too scared. Or they're dead. I would have killed you twenty minutes ago." He looked straight at Vern. "Both of you."

"He's not dead." Vern eased behind the RV. "We talked to him."

"No shit?" Tyce looked to Steve for confirmation.

He nodded, swallowing the last bite of food.

"Yeah. He's Russian," Steve said

"What'd he say?"

"Don't know. That's what it sounded like. I shouted a few times for them to come out and they yelled back something like '*Nay baziti*' or '*potsiti*' I yelled back and they yelled back the same thing. I got a '*fuck you*' then something full of D's and P's and H's. It's an older male - like 30s or 40s. Not a kid," Steve said, checking the shotgun's safety.

Hapgood nodded in agreement to Tyce's skeptical frown. Tyce

moved to the passenger edge, cupping his palms.

"Koeinezhy! Veenyah oysachey! Kledyah!"

Tyce stepped back, facing the astonished men.

"You speak Russian? What did you say to him?" Hapgood said, beady eyes warming to something like respect.

"A bunch of gibberish that sounded Russian," Tyce said. "The same thing that fuckin' hillbilly in there is shouting at you."

"Why would anyone do that?" Steve said, standing. Irked foolishness went hot through his skull. Steve constantly felt a step behind Tyce. He believed Tyce preferred it.

"Why would you shoot somebody for pulling a cord? I don't know," Tyce said.

"The question remains. How did they get in here and what are you going to do about it?" Hapgood said.

"I don't know yet. How's that?" Tyce said, talking to the mirror he held out from the side of the rig. "It's gotta be one guy. He might be bleeding out. Realistically we've got *him* pinned down. Yeah?"

Tyce looked to Steve. Face to face they were able to start building the frame of what they knew (one guy, alone, small caliber gun from the sound) and how to do the damn thing. The shepherd's barks filled the pauses. In Tyce's expression, peeking at the edged mirror, Steve saw his own searching mind. This would have been the part where the state-accredited instructor would have looked out over the clueless, six-week police recruits, scowled and turned to the white board. This would have been the part where Steve called in for a TAC squad and Medical.

"You need to seize the house! Now! Remove the threat! Now!"

The two guard's eyes pinged to each other. Tyce set the mirror on the bumper, head ticking to Steve with the idea.

"We could light it up? That'd get him out."

Steve nodded. "Cover fire on the windows. Molotov through the living room and the upper floor. From the garage door, you're concealed."

"No!"

Steve's laugh was less at the walrus' puckered face than it was vocalized surprise at Vern's panic. It was like hearing a little kid swear.

"Really? Well, that's our plan, Vern. There's your answer." Tyce said, arms crossed. The hired help, smoke-break leaning on the RV's grill.

"That fire could get out of control." Vern said, pointing, trying to force fear as fact. Steve was enjoying Vern nakedly aware of how full of shit he was.

"I hope so," Tyce said.

"You have the responsibility of the safety of the people in this housing development. Not to destroy it."

"Really, Vern?" Steve said. "Put another twenty rounds into that house and explain destruction of property to me."

Tyce turned his back on Vern. "Good. Glad we figured it out."

"You've figured out nothing!"

Steve forgot what he was about to say when the motor buzz came from the east. He saw the approaching, spinning orange roof light of the LifeForce patrol car. Steve could tell without feeling his pockets. He'd left his keys in the fucking ignition. All three men's guns came up and the slow-rolling car braked before Gallo's property line. It jerked into park. Hands came up out of the opened driver's door.

"It's OK," Mark shouted. "I brought the car up. I thought you could use the help." He was in a black body-armor vest over a black T-shirt, green camo fatigue pants. Toting a black backpack and matte-black Mossberg 12-gauge. All in.

Both guards watched it like a tennis match. Vern marching away, west and Mark lolling toward them, waiting and peeking around the hedge corner. Mark grinning, puppy jumpy. *Treat? Who wants a treat?*

"You know where he's going," Tyce said.

Steve keyed the ear mic. On the third try, Lorna answered.

"Lorna. It's Steve."

"Yeah. I'm here. I can see both of you. I saw Mark driving but you said not to call unless…what's going on?"

"OK. Keep the back of the house on screen. Number four camera," Steve said. He glanced at Tyce. "Did you -?"

Tyce nodded. He held his palm up to Mark. *Wait.*

"Tyce showed me how to work them," Lorna said. "Relax. These are easy. I can watch everything. Where's Fuck Stick going?"

The name 'Fuck Stick' didn't narrow it down, necessarily. "Vern might be coming to you. Keep the door locked. Don't let him in. Don't let anyone in. If you see him coming, you call. OK?"

"Don't worry, I will. How's Mike?"

"We don't know. Hannah? Are you on?" Steve paused, finger off, waiting. "Hannah come in if you read. Lorna, stay off unless you see anything. Out." Steve said.

"What?" Lorna said.

"Out, over." Steve said. "Goodbye."

"You got your keys?" Tyce asked. "I think I left mine in the Barracks."

"In the car. *Fuck.*"

"Seriously, dude? Your girlfriend?" Tyce said, waving Mark on over without a thought to Russian snipers.

"Who else do you want in there? Bob Sanders? She's smart."

"I hope so."

****

It occurred to Hannah to open the sun room's side door, but she could not trust herself to keep from walking out. The room's floor-to-ceiling glass panels framed what may have been the best view of Cricklewood Green, straight down the center of the pond, making the trees and shrubs and decks of the backyards appear to be part of some grand estate, a play-land community of resort homes for the guests. The morning air was seized heavy with humidity. The stagnant pond a grey slate. Turning from the view, Hannah's eyes passed up at the ceiling fans. The thought – turn them…

William had taste. An overstuffed taupe sofa on squat, polished wood legs abutting the wall. A classic black leather Eames whispered in dust. Hannah's fresh steps were almost luminescent on the sun room's thick white carpet. On opposite sides of the archway seemed to be the swing of William's closeted life. One side, above the sofa, a huge, neo-psyche-delic Peter Max print - The Statue of Liberty. Vivid blues. The other side a smaller, sky-scanning, thorned Jesus awaiting the incoming inevitable. Fitting for a room to discuss death. Hannah's message for Kim Narlow was plain and practiced. Her New York V-14 script with new facts. There was blood in Mike's urine.

Kim came into the sun room striding, William not quite follow-ing, as if he had intended to lead her but she hadn't the use or time. Kim plopped onto the Eames ottoman. She patted wads of tissue around her nose, squeezed-out pink eyes behind her cat glasses.

"He's still unconscious," William said in Hannah's ear, handing her a cup of coffee. "There's about a third of the IV left." He backed up to the archway and finally turned, a servant in his own home.

Hannah set the cup on the low coffee table, knowing it would attack her empty stomach like solvent. She could still faintly hear Hap-good's dog through the glass. There had been a few seconds of machine-gun fire minutes ago. Still shaky from the noise, Hannah had to grip her left hand to keep it still.

Kim snorted and blew into the tissues. "Doesn't he have a bed?"

"What?"

"You can't make him more comfortable than that?"

"We shouldn't move him, Kim." Hannah said, sitting on the sofa arm. She recited the bad choices - Leave or Stay. Each of them funneling down to say goodbye before nightfall. Perhaps morning, but Hannah left that out. Any extra time would be to Kim and Sandra Rose's bene-fit. Explaining, Hannah's attention kept getting robbed by the bounce in Kim's knee, her averted eyes, her unhearing nods.

Kim finally looked up. "What if you tried to save him?"

Faces had typical responses when you told them The Truth. Some-times falling together in a stoic pinch or apart in a dam-break of tears. Sometimes the wet-eyed quiver became the bitter gulp. Or the laced-tight stare of disdain for the messenger (they would swallow later, on their own time, thank you). Not this. Hannah could see something coiled underneath Kim Narlow's squint.

"Kim, I don't know where the bullet is inside of Mike. It's dam-aged his organs and Mike has significant internal bleeding. I don't have the equipment. We don't have any blood to give him. I – "

"Yeah, I know. Drive him to a hospital. Wherever it is. I haven't been outside this asylum in two months. And I'm gonna take him out there? With my kid? Are you listening to the news? They're setting people on fire out there." The young woman's voice was odd, measured. Watch-ing Kim's eyes, the word *asylum* hung like a bell toll.

"Kim. Please. Listen. I did not say you should. In fact, I STRONGLY advise you against leaving. I was only telling –"

"So why tell me?"

"Kim…"

"Hannah."

The doctor looked away from Kim and her volatile grief. She stared out the glass walls at the desolate pastoral.

"What if we get everyone to donate some blood? I'll give a pint."

"I – what's Mike's blood type?"

"I don't know. Test it?"

Hannah realized Kim was trying to ape her tone, imitate her.

Hannah did have a test kit at the house. She stood and stepped to the door jamb, looking through the dark living room to the brighter kitchen and Mike's bare feet, already cadaverous. She turned to Kim again.

"You can't just put it in a Pepsi can. It's not only blood, Kim. Mike would need a trauma surgeon. And assistants. With equipment. Anesthetic. It's the only way he could survive this. Even if we had all of it right now…"

"Right, Hannah. I get it. But if he's dead anyway then try, at least."

Squatting to eye level, Hannah took Kim's hand. Hannah's were scrubbed, bleached but with rusty traces under her nails.

"Kim, I am very sorry. You can take Mike out of here and try to find a hospital. Which I advise you in the strongest terms not to do. Or prepare yourself and your daughter to say goodbye to him."

Kim Narlow tore her hand away. Shocked, Hannah went upright, rigid.

"I mean, you cut, you pull back, you feel in. You pull out the bullet. You sew." She looked up at Hannah, half her face a winked sneer "I mean, really? I'll do it." Kim's hands pantomimed slices and folds. A bizarre, invisible origami. "Try?"

"Kim…."

"Hannah…"

Hannah sighed.

"Why not?"

"You'll do it? Kim. Please. You're upset. You have no idea what you're saying."

Kim stood, uncoiled.

"Don't tell me what I am. And quit the 'doctor voice', Hannah. I know you. I'm saying I'm going to try to save him. Like you have something else to do today?"

Kim's yoga-pant leg kicked the low table's edge, planted foot knocking the coffee into an obscene spray on the white shag.

"Fuck you, Hannah. You couldn't even give him a ride the other day. Like I'm gonna trust you to break a sweat on your hairy cunt to try to save my husband's life? *My daughter's father.*"

Hannah marveled. *I know you.* After everything Kim had told Joyce about Mike. The things Hannah knew about him, them. Kim and Joyce - the work widows of the asylum complaining on the back decks about their absent mates. All of it there in Kim's sneering, shaking head. Everything Joyce had told Kim about Hannah. In New York, Hannah was behind the glass shield of Government. She was the Doctor at the Hospital who Said So. Oz's curtain. None of the death room grandfathers and guardian aunts knew Hannah's wife, Hannah's disappointments and what made her hurt. Those people whose faces Hannah forgot by the end of the hallway knew none of Hannah's night-wine you'd-never-believe-it secrets she'd whispered to Joyce in the nakedest confidence. Those now sharpened and poised to be run through Hannah by this feral-eyed girl.

"You'll cut? You'll sew? While he's punching and screaming at you in pain? What's your anesthetic? Are you going to hit him with a hammer?"

"You gave him morphine," Kim said.

"And say he lives? What about the infections? His intestines are hit. I can smell it. Have you ever seen anyone die that way? Any way, Doctor?"

"Oh, I know, Hannah. You're *smarter* than me. Like every expert in this whole fucking world. Ask them '*why*' and they lose their shit. '*How dare you?*'"

"Will you please shut up and listen, Kim?"

"You have antibiotics. You said so. *Hannah.*"

"Not enough – "

Kim's head thrust. "Not enough to waste?"

"Yes." Hannah could feel her teeth in it.

"Cunt."

On her exit, Kim whirled back. "I hope everything comes back on tomorrow and I can throw you in fucking jail. Doctor."

Hannah called to her walking, black silhouette. "Dream on. The nuclear plants! We'll all be dead of radiation in six months. You and your kid! There's your other news."

Hannah's fingers wrung to fists, balled soft sides pressing the glass. Kim's shouts echoed in the kitchen. Hannah could not shut her eyes any further.

"I'll be back, Bill. I have to tell my daughter Hannah thinks it's better for Daddy to die. She doesn't want to work that hard! He's not worth it!"

In the dark, William touched her shoulders. The sobs came. So hard they hurt.

****

The mist rain became enough bother for Tyce to radio request a poncho or trash bag or anything to cover his half-assed kill spot. Dominski said he'd work on it. Hannah the Doc had been quiet all morning, likely turned off, hands full. She hadn't responded when Tyce radioed how exposed she was, moving around inside the old guy's glass porch. Tyce wasn't sure what her exposure to the shooter was, but, like he'd told them in the driveway. If *he* were inside the house….

After they'd gotten Mark situated at the RV, Tyce convinced them he'd be best covering the back way with his Springfield. If Ivan was still alive inside Tyce could hopefully end it without them having to burn the schmuck out, which would blow up the fuel tank to the house, which would be…bad. So, Ivan had until an agreed 3 p.m. before bad-idea time.

Following the west side of the loop, Tyce scouted into backyards until he found something comfortable and concealed enough to wait out the rest of the morning. He knocked on Hapgood's door in a truce attempt, or at least estimate what the walrus was up to. No answer came except his barking, chained-up attack dog, dirt-dragging under the big willow.

The little lattice gazebo in the Fetter's yard had good sight lines across the water to the house. Taking one of the wooden benches Tyce could sit behind it and support the Springfield on the floorboards. Groomed-round pale shrubs border-blocked the lot south of Hapgood's, hiding Tyce from the dog. When setting up the bench, Tyce obeyed his sense and looked up, behind him. Sanders' shape, observing from his tower, slid away from the tiny window at Tyce's nod. Now almost 11 a.m., the radios were silent and nothing stirred the Vanderkam curtains.

At the repeat of his name Tyce glanced to his left. Tyce pressed the mic, seeing Mark hunt-stepping toward him. Mark's profile to the north in vigilance, Mossberg barrel pointed down, trigger finger out, stock tucked at his armpit.

"Steve. Mark's here. Over."

"Yeah." Dominski said. "Tag, you're it. Out."

Even the way the goof slipped out of his pack – not simply pulling the straps off – itched Tyce. Everything was off about the kid. The way Mark held his weapon, technically correct but with a weird, retarded crook to his arm. His turd-clench of a walk.

"Here," Mark said, opening the pack. He removed a steel Thermos and a baggie full of crackers. He set them on the bench next to Tyce. "Cracker sandwiches with peanut butter and strawberry jam. Chicken soup – Cup-a Soup. It's good. I used two packs." He stepped back, smiling.

"Uh…wow. I…" Tyce set the rifle flat on the deck. He hefted the steel tube and baggie mystified, like they were moon rocks. The Thermos was dented and dulled grey, old stickers on it worn to shapes and faint colors. The Dodge pentagon, an American flag. Two cartoon ducks fucking in mid-air – *'Fly United'*.

"It's for you. I ate already."

"Keep your eye on the house." Top unscrewed, the salty, hot smell lit Tyce's bulbs to hunger. Spoonless, he swallowed some and chowed three of the sandwiches, washing the sweetened peanut paste with more noodle soup. Damn, it hit the spot.

Mark had pulled a set of binoculars from the pack, his shotgun upright against the gazebo. He focused north on the Vanderkam house. Tyce capped the Thermos and shook mixed it.

"Thank you, Mark."

"Sure," Mark said. "We yelled at him a few more times but he didn't say anything. Steve said he sounded Russian."

"Steve's wrong."

Hair matted wet from the drizzle, Mark pivoted with the glasses, coast-watching along the pond. A movie line from "*The Longest Day*" came into Tyce's head, like they always did, but Tyce let it drop. He saved the last sandwich for the last gulp of soup and noodle sludge.

"I listen to this guy on shortwave. Blue Jay. Lots of Euro troops are coming in, he says. Feds brought them in to fight the seceders. They'll kill citizens easier than US troops will. Russian infiltrators could be with them. There could be more in the vacants. That's what I'm afraid of."

Chewing, Tyce pocketed the baggie and sleeve wiped his mouth. He picked up the Springfield. "Move."

Tyce leaned in, setting on the wood. He re-sighted the rifle, dialing in the optical's red circle through the Vanderkam's tall, rusty-leaf plants to the deck's curtained glass doors and vertical-blind living room to the left.

"Steve said you were in the Airborne. In Iraq".

"Michigan Guard in OIF. Airborne when I was a kid."

"Ya know, I had an idea. I've got a hundred armor piercing rounds for my SKS. Even if I used 50. We could just shred that house. It's all cheap brick wood-frame, every place in here. 7.62, dude. Like your Springfield. I've done it before. Right through cinder block."

"Unless he's in the basement," Tyce said.

Mark was silent a moment. Tyce heard him digging in the pack.

"Yeah. Well, then we'd have to go in, I guess."

Tyce raised the rifle a smidge, passing the red circle on the white-shaded upper windows. Tyce thought of white flags and surrender. Wishing.

"You should go talk to Vern, Mark. You have a lot in common."

A fucking pin-spot of rain found the scope.

"What did you do in Iraq?"

"Sweated. Drove around and got shot at. Bombed."

"What did you drive? Strykers?"

"Nope."

When pressed about his war-year, Tyce told people to think in terms of having a shitty job for 14 months. Asshole bosses and mostly boredom. Frantic, hyper-real moments flooding so much adrenaline you could feel it wilt from your muscle fiber later on. He never got the fetish some guys, like his lunch date, had for the hardware. To Tyce, an Abrams tank, an Apache helicopter or an M-240 machine gun were as interesting as a twelve-ton injection molder. The booming CA-CHUNK every five seconds, dropping out plastic air-conditioning vents for next year's Toyotas. All the same. Tools, bad noise and hazard for pissant money.

Tyce sensed Mark fidgeting. "Did you hear about the sarin gas? In New York?"

"Yeah."

"I have a mask," Mark said. "You know about them? Right?"

Be civil. He fed you. He didn't have to.

"I guess you do. How much time would you have to get deployed? With sarin."

"You're in luck," Tyce said. "Sarin will kill you without the mask. It gets in through skin. Something else you don't have to worry about."

"How about CS or tear gas?"

"If you smell it it's too late. Then if you manage to get it sealed we can call you Jimi Hendrix," Tyce said.

"Who's that?"

Tyce lifted from the scope. "Are you fucking with me?"

"No."

Mark's face was flushed. Blotchy. Stub-nail ring finger to his lips, pulled back from the bite. Tyce realized it had stopped raining.

"Mask-up too late and you suffocate on breakfast. Stop imagining, alright? You're not gonna get killed by a Russian. Or a Polack. Or an…Italian Marine. There's no sarin. You know what's going to kill you, Mark? You're gonna trip over your dick and blast your foot off. There's a guy in there with a weapon. And he's already killed Mike, probably. And we're probably going to have to go in. Get it? That's real enough for me. It should be real enough for you. Keep quiet and listen to what people tell you. Thank you for the food. That was kind of you. I appreciate it."

Tyce pressed the mic, looking at the boy in black.

"Steve."

"Go ahead." Steve said.

"Mark's coming back your way." Tyce watched him look away, picking up the pack and shotgun. "Over."

"Roger." Steve said. "Over and out."

"Hey. Mark."

The pack and Mossberg were drudge low in his hands. Tyce got the side-eye and a deflated half-turn.

"We need you, Mark. You're doing fine. Relieve Steve for a little bit. Let him take a piss, close his eyes a few minutes. He'll appreciate it."

Mark listened like he was on the way to the grocery, trying to memorize the list.

"A little fear is good. An edge is good." Tyce said. "Think about what you see and hear in front of you. Don't panic. OK?"

His nod and jumping Adam's apple did not convince.

****

With the sleep bandanna tied around his eyes Mark thought Steve looked like a hostage. Or like some Grand Theft Auto gangbanger, passed out drunk against the RV, arms out flat like he'd had a fix.

The bumper wasn't wide enough to sit on. Mark slid up to a half squat/lean against the grill. Dime-spot rain puddles shined in the road divots. Nothing would dry in the damp air. After palming his hair back, Mark frictioned on his camis until he had some grip. He felt the side pocket. Three of them in there, as he knew they would be. He just wanted to touch them. He looked down at Steve, almost snoring. Mark took them out of the pocket one at a time, carefully breaking the cellophane safety wrap from the fat, black aluminum Beller CS gas cartridges and easing the plastic red-loop pins sideways for easy pull. He hoped to only use two of them, keeping one reserve. If –

Don't imagine. What's in front of you? Was Tyce was telling him to do it? *Get it?*

Stop.

The drips down Mark's back weren't rain anymore. Sweat. Careful of the pins, Mark tucked each cartridge away in his pocket. Gripping his shaking thighs only moved the shakes up into his arms, like sitting on a bridge with trucks rolling over it. *Stop imagining.* But how do you see it? How do you know? What if you're too late?

He burped, the taste bitter.

What if Tyce shot at him?

Mark reached into the backpack and put his hand to the gas mask. Feeling both round air-filter discs calmed him some. All of it solid and sure. Protection. The three cartridges in his pocket and the mask. Tools.

We're going to have to go in and get him.

Setting the gas mask over his face, Mark pushed it for pressure like the instructions said. He breathed, like outer space, like a movie, and felt secure in the seal, glad he bought the full-face model rather than little eyeholes. Breath sounding through his skull, Mark felt steadier. The mask seemed to make it less real.

He picked up his black Mossberg and thumbed the safety button. The shotgun had a full load of rifled slug and buckshot shells and four more loose on the side slots, eight more shells in his right pocket. Plus, his holstered Ruger automatic and two extra mags. He could fill every room with death, piece by piece.

In the jump-off seconds Mark didn't think. Suddenly his legs were sprung, running up the driveway. Shotgun up and high. And then, with a hook of step onto the lawn, Mark's energy completely pissed out of him like a wasting battery. Going diagonal across the grass, over the yellow cord, Mark's steps became rubbery, huffed, nightmare lunges. In the mask, his breath came in a strangled, cave-like flush. Mark flopped forward in the last steps to the east side of the house, hidden from the front windows, almost crashing through Gallo's hedge.

Fat fuck. When is the last time you ran anywhere?

Mark's Kevlar-plated back pushed against the brick of the Vanderkam house. Heaving, afraid he might pass out. *No. No no no. What's in front? What's in front of you?*

Go go go. *The moment is always the same. You change.*

In the gap between the hedge and the house Mark turned and waist-aimed the long, heavy shotgun at the row of basement glass-block widows. He fired, racked and fired, blowing apart three blocks to a broken, dark mouth at the grass line. Mark marveled at the hole and the pulsing screech in his gun-deaf ears. The close quarters of the brick wall had double-nuked the sound. *Dumb ass, no ear plugs.* There was other gunfire, Steve's pistol from the driveway. Mark rolled and thumped back against the brick. OK. *Release! Release your hand!* Down into his side pocket his left hand grabbed one of the cartridges, thumb-pulling the pin. He held it out, staring, one two three four and then the sparking hiss of rocket fire out the top as the CS ignited in white smoke. Mark chucked the hot little fucker down into the Vanderkam basement. A kiss of burn across the soft skin pocket between his thumb and index finger.

Racking again, Mark swung around the corner, shoulder-aiming along the length of the covered porch. Aiming where the door would open and the Russian would come running out and he could crossfire the motherfucker into next week. Steve was on his feet by the RV, pistol out, hollering very far and small inside Mark's deaf skull.

The snap in front of Mark's face cut through it all. A second crack, just past his nose. A bullet and nothing but. Mark dropped hard to the porch cement and layered broken glass, mask fogging. The Russian was alive inside, shooting at him.

Mark's hand gripped a second CS cartridge. He rolled onto his side, pulled the pin and threw the piece through the shattered main window, into the Russian's pillbox bunker.

His ears screamed. Hand burned. But that was really fucking cool.

He pulled two shells off the side of the Mossberg and thumbed them into the tube. Everything went into his breathing. *What's in front? You can't pass out. Hyperventilation. Hold. Breathe. Hold. Breathe.*

Neck twisted up, Mark could see the CS burning righteous out the living room window. A whiter than white, fluorescent summer cloud.

With no other way, Mark flopped onto his belly, crawling forward, scrape kicking over the window glass covering the porch. He tried to lift his bare arms out of it, lifting the gun, boots scooting. He gritted the pain, hands trying to brush the glass away. Fuck fuck fuck. His bulk and the vest plate press-deadened his lungs, sucking for denied air like a goldfish on a sidewalk. Pieces of glass stabbed, needled, stinging, into his bare arms. Wheezing, Mark had to roll onto his back to gasp air, dropping the shotgun to reach for the blood-streaming cuts, razoring his palms, flaked glass slicing his skin. His cries sounded like an astronaut, far off tumbling into space. Mark's lungs had seized. He thought he might be choking. The gas. The mask wasn't working. Jimi Hendrix.

Tyce would find him and laugh.

Oh my God this fucking sucks. You stupid, fat, fuck-up.

Boots against the wall, he pushed himself along, on his side. Breaths came. He could keep his arms up, gripping the shotgun lamely by the warm barrel. At last, aligned with the white front door, Mark could no longer see the RV or Steve. There was no more shooting from the inside. The CS weaved out of the window like neon shower steam. On a ready 1-2-3 count and a whale inhale Mark slid up and stood against the short brick wall perpendicular to the bullet-holed door. A glass hummingbird ornament was strung, spinning, from the porch light.

Going back would be worse.

Mark fired the shotgun at each guessed door hinge. The slug and buckshot explosions fragmented and splintered the wood from the frame, propelling Mark's frustration into righteous fury. Directed down the barrel of his fantasies, realizing an enemy he'd sought his entire life, Mark leveled the Mossberg. He racked and fired at the door's deadbolt, so close a ricocheted hunk of buckshot stuck into his body armor. Arms up, Mark's leg mounted a kick. It big-bad-wolfed the oak door down to the castle's hardwood floor. The dragon smoke of CS flowing out the doorway like medieval times.

Through the clouded living room, Mark racked and fired blindly. Down the short hall into the kitchen more light and thinner smoke revealed a spastic man thumping against the sliding glass door, tangled in the white lace curtain. Mark saw a lab rat, a creature driven insane by some experiment. The man was choking for air, boiling out of himself, throwing himself against the glass with the handle right in front of him. Mark saw no weapon. The vomiting white man was older, thicker bodied in a weird pattern short sleeve shirt. A guy you'd see behind the counter of a party store or deli. Mark fired, racked and fired, racked and fired a third time into the man. The force shattered the glass, sending the man out and bursting the white-hazed room with arcing, chunked sprays of red. Wrapping the half-out-the-door man, the blotched gore shroud curtain caught the cross breeze. A fluttering, failed parachute dropping the man into the land of the Dead.

The blood, the meat. A rush of nauseous terror overcame Mark. Beneath the vest plate his core became gelatin, stomach rebelling. Dropping the shotgun, Jimi Hendrix turned and ran for the front door with a mouthful of bitter paste. Running from his bad thing, chased by an enemy he'd known his entire life. Clearing the house's threshold, through his facemask Mark saw Steve face-down stiff on the driveway, close to the garage door. Steve's arms were crooked, like he was swimming down the black-tarred driveway. His Smith & Wesson .40 in front of his paddling right hand. Mark kept running, over the lawn, to the road, the woods, away from the gas. More spewing bile wetted his chin and cheeks. Soup and crackers. His sliced-up, pumping arms spatting blood on his camo trousers and pin-flecking the mask, he ran on. Every man for himself.

*****

"They never show this part in the movies, do they?" Ray said.

Hannah worked a sliver of glass from Mark's forearm. He shuddered on the kitchen stool, face dipping further away from the bloom of blood. She dropped the piece into the white ceramic cereal bowl on the breakfast island. Her hemostats picked the swab from the other bowl, the alcohol in it pink with blood. Mark winced at the wet sting contact, neck cording as he swallowed.

"What's the matter, Schwarzenegger?" Ray said from the other side of the kitchen. "I thought you were Billy Bad Ass?"

Hannah set the clips down and dressed the wound from among the scatter of butterfly bandages and ripped wax paper. Hannah turned Mark's arm, peering closely for the next wound. The Dudek kitchen was dim. No skylight, unlike her own kitchen. A tear of blood pinpointed another pin-like piece deep in his flabby tricep. Mark's cowering energy reminded Hannah of her usual child patients. She could tell Mark was not used to being touched.

"How's it feel, Schwarzenegger? You got your kill, big man."

"Raise your arm," she said.

"How is Steve?" Mark muttered into his T-shirt, ringed with sweat.

"His nose is broken but he'll be fine," Hannah said, plucking the fine needle from his arm. Mark sucked in and shuddered. "The gas got to him, is all. He was knocked out when he slipped."

"He was trying to rescue your ass, big man. Big shooter. Shit, Doctor. If told you how many times a day this kid used to jack off, you'd never believe it."

Hannah stopped. "Shut up, Ray." She dropped the glass fragment into the bowl. "You're disgusting."

Behind her, Ray grunted, his steps fading to the living room. Hannah sensed Mark wanted to thank her, glad when he didn't. After a few more removed shards and thumbed-over bandages she warned him to keep the wounds clean. Shower, she said. More glass would probably force itself out. Neosporin. Hannah packed her aid bag, leaving the mess and the last of her ward of hurt boys, all losers at playing War.

***

Grimacing at the chemical odor, Sherri called a hello as she stepped over the red shotgun shell husks on the porch, past the busted-open doorway. The ruined front door was lying against the low white sofa. A fresh burn, like a torch mark, scarred the tan hardwood floor.

"We're in here," Tyce replied, far off.

Sherri had never been inside the Vanderkam home. The brightness of the kitchen and promise of fresher air drew her down the hall. The kitchen was done in gorgeous Kashmir white granite, its pendant lights stunning. Their blue setting off the island and the granite backsplash perfectly. The glass-face cabinets were a similar blue on the inside, highlighting the stacked white dishes, the hung wine glasses and glass tumblers. There were lights inside the cabinets. She caught herself reaching for the switch.

The wet sound of her tennis shoe's step put Sherri's attention down to the puddle and bucket. Both door-wall frames to the deck had been lifted out, curtains gone, the gaping way wide-open to the deck and the tall plants, to the pond. The white tile floor was still soapy wet and there were scrubbed pink spots on the walls and ugly holes. Outside on the caramel-toned deck a patterned Persian rug was rolled fat, a pair of brogan shoes exposed and cockeyed out the end. A body inside it.

"Sherri? Babe? Where are you?"

That must have been where he was, by the door. Trying to run, Mark shot him.

"I'm in the kitchen."

"We're in the garage," Ray called. "C'mere."

She found the side hall to the garage, passing the computer den and its bookshelves. The garage was swept and organized. Beneath a skylight panel Ray and Tyce were seated on two round stools at the workbench, almost like a bar. Instead of a sports TV and mirror it was a Craftsman drawer chest and pegboard hung tools. Both men had open cans of Heineken. Two stacked cases of it were under several cases of soda and bottled water. Tyce was studying two reddish/maroon booklets. Both men's chuckles hung in the stale, fumed air. They seemed fine with it. The front of Tyce's dark blue uniform was damp from soap water and spotted from human.

"Want a beer, babe?" Ray said, standing. Ray appeared dry.

"Sure."

"You're pissed off," he said.

"I'm not."

"Why are you pissed off, babe?" Ray said, retrieving and handing a can to her.

"Why not, Raymond?"

Sherri took a sip and stepped to Tyce puzzling over the booklets. Passports.

"Well, you won't believe what we found." Ray said, stroking her shoulder.

"I'm not sure what we found," Tyce said. "Other than he's the same guy out there as in these two passports. One I don't know. Something Balkan I think from the lettering. Serbian. Croatia? Bosnia? This one is Italian." Tyce handed the passports to Sherri and sipped.

"Where did you get them?"

"They were in his pocket." Tyce said. The Balkan one was to Zorin Jancovic. The Italian to Mariano Ruggero. The Balkan one, dated eight years earlier had several stamps – Turkey one of them Sherri could make out. Hungary. The Italian one was new, issue dated August 29th, a few weeks ago. It had two stamps. Leaving Madrid on September 4th. Stamped arriving in Toronto September 5th. The day of the first outage.

"That's when they picked him up, I bet." Tyce said, finger tapping the paper. "I remember they came back in the RV, that night. It was around two in the morning, after the power came back on. If you figure the times, it's about right - if he got in early. Landed, I mean. Toronto to here."

The man was younger in the Balkan passport. A glowering boxer's face. His balding head fringed in longish dark curls. For a man of 37 (it said) he appeared closer to 47. The Italian one put him at 49. Thinner in the face, a better haircut. A forced, coffee-dipped smile.

"I don't know how real they are. I don't know how real anything is here. Check it out" Tyce said, standing. "Take the flashlight," he said gesturing to a green 2-D on the bench. He looked and sounded exhausted. For the first time, Sherri noticed the rifle on the workbench. An old-looking .22 with a nubbin bullet clip. A squirrel gun. Her big brother and his friends at the creek, shooting crawfish.

"Was that his?"

"Uh-huh." Tyce said. "I think it was the guy's. Vanderkam's, from upstairs. We found more .22 longs for it upstairs, but no other guns. Glad Vanderkam didn't leave him an AK, I guess."

She took the flashlight and followed Tyce back inside the home, Ray behind her.

"Did you talk to her very much?" Ray said.

"Who? Cindy? Not really. It seemed like they were barely here."

Sherri thumb-clicked her light, adding to Tyce's beam. They eased down the stairs to the basement. She tasted more bitter chemicals with each step. Her eyes tingled.

"Well, now we know why," Ray said.

The chemical smell, flashlight beams and shadowy confinement frightened Sherri, even with Ray talking all the way. The two men had obviously been through the whole place. A battery lamp was on high glow in the middle of the green felt pool table. The table dominated the sparse basement, echoey from few furnishings and the sandalwood tile. A hunter-green leather sectional in the corner was abutted with end tables and a tall Art Deco 3-scoop lamp. Tyce explained how he saw it, Ray interjecting like a sportscaster. To Tyce it seemed the Vanderkams had cuffed the man to the pool table, based on the scuffed foot marks and scraped wood of one ornate leg. Spots of the leg were clear of varnish and fibery raw. The handcuffs were nearby, key still in them, disregarded like a chicken's egg shell. It certainly didn't look like the Vanderkam's were expecting a prisoner, Tyce said.

Who was this man? Why had they done this to him? To what did they think of their neighbors, Sherri thought. *Leaving somebody, with a gun in the house, knowing he was dangerous?*

The single key within the sprung cuffs was strung to a huge, otherwise empty loop. The loop was hooked to a rope made from strips of torn white T-shirt. The head of a wire hanger tied, as the hook. Did the Vander-kam's leave him these things when they fled, pieces of a puzzle he could do in time for them to get clear? Or was it some cruel game? Food trash was everywhere near the scuffs and pool table leg - scraps, paper plates and colorful wrappers, empty plastic bottles. They had fed and watered him.

Ray took her hand, livelier than Sherri had seen him in a week, a bouncing secret in his eyes, leading her away.

The flimsy, hollow door to the walled room was kicked open. Ray assured her this was how they found it. The Vanderkams had not locked him in there. The room's value was clearly greater.

The long side-room was home to dozens of cardboard boxes pack-stuffed with shredded Chinese newspapers. Inside and atop the boxes were strikingly authentic copies of purses, handbags, watches, women's shoes and electronics. Michael Kors, Burberry, Prada, Jimmy Choo, Marc Jacobs, Manolo Blahnik. TAG, Omega, Rolex. Ralph Lauren. Whelp, Apple. Hundreds of thousands of dollars in fakes.

"Is this your fantasy come true, baby? Or what?" Ray said, grin-ning.

"The RV?" Tyce said. "It's got a whole false floor going almost the whole length. There's a compartment behind the shower, even…."

"This is incredible," Sherri said, pulling out the bags, the shoes, most of them 7s and 8s. Her size. Tyce picked up a new computer pad with 3-D hologram feature, commenting on it. The Whelp T. The Vander-kam's decision to scoot in their gleaming new Dodge truck with nothing but their matching black-leather holstered pistols made sense to her now. How many homes, apartments and identities did they have? From here to any coast? Was Vanderkam even their name? Not before one last scam, taking hundreds of dollars in everyone's pooled money. *Supplies*, they said. Sons-of-bitches.

Ray and Tyce left Sherri to the goods, her fingers fascinated. It seemed the couple were smuggling everything else, why not people? Had the man been a courier they couldn't pay? Someone they had agreed to smuggle into the country, plans spinning wrong when the attack happened? Lifting a Marc Jacobs bag from a box, Sherri noticed a grocery-list pad inside the cardboard. A cartoon hummingbird in the pad's upper corner. The writing on the pad matched the style of lettering in the Balkan passport. Sherri took in a deep breath to call out. She stopped.

A compact, cramped, tilted scrawl filled eight pages, each entry separated by a big X. The number 7,500 stood out. On the last page names were listed, underlined, notes below. It felt and looked like a will, clearly signed at the bottom – Zorin Jancovic. USA and the year. Sherri put it into a Burberry she liked, buckling it. Whomever he was, he wanted someone to know what happened to him. Despite it all - Mike Narlow, Kim and Sandra Rose - Sherri decided to believe it. The man had been a prisoner. A monster, a maniac, wouldn't leave a testament.

The only other room in the basement revealed some more. A closet-like toilet and sink. He seemed to have spent his time down here, even when freed. It felt that way. Her light beam drifted over a bar of soap and balled towels atop the tank, dirty clothes corner strewn. He'd bathed. The flashlight animated distinct fingerprints on the mirror. Their mark of life backed her out of the water closet. Unnerved, Sherri quick-stepped upstairs with her new purse, gladly out of there. She gripped the handle with strange determination. The bag was hers. And the will.

She followed a long hall to the men's voices in the living room, past the den, the garage and mud room. Ray and Tyce were seated on opposite sofas, a 60-inch plasma on the wall next to Tyce. Sherri admired the grey brick fireplace next to Ray. A huge, round, gleaming brass sunman face was mounted to its floor-to-ceiling center. Mellow eyes and cherub cheeks ringed by tiny flames.

"Did you ever see *The Wicker Man*?" Tyce said.

"What?"

"The movie." Tyce gestured to the brass face. "Lord Summerfield."

"No."

Sherri leaned closer to the fireplace. Piles of paper ash. Half consumed spines of ledgers, unburned fragments of yellow paper. She sat next to Ray. Tyce's eyes were glassy, staring at the sun-man.

"Tyce, when did you sleep last?" Sherri said.

"Today, I think." Tyce huffed a laugh, sitting forward. "Yeah. Sorry. I'm not feeling too smart right now. Listen, I want to talk about your son."

Sherri could feel Ray flex inward, turtle-like. Head down into his beer can.

"I don't necessarily like what the kid did here. But I also can't say I'm unhappy with the results. We're pretty lucky with a lot, considering."

Sherri could sense Tyce's mind groping, as if he were trying to fit pegs in holes.

"He's 34," Sherri said. "He's no kid."

Squinting, Tyce tilted his head. "Where did he get tear gas?"

"I... I don't...I'm sorry," Ray said. "I wish I could – "

Tyce waved it off. "No. No. But I do think this insanity is going to end soon. The power is gonna come back on. Law will come back. And there's gonna be questions here. I won't guess how it's gonna be handled but I want you to know I've got nothing out for Mark. I don't want charges. But tell him we need to get a story together here."

This explained the cleaning. Tyce's idea. Sherri had never seen Ray wash so much as a spoon. Ray nodded again, inhaling. For Ray's benefit Sherri thanked Tyce.

"Good." Tyce said. "Ray. Sherri. You seem like reasonable people. I feel like I can trust you. I hope you both think of me, too."

Tyce paused. With their murmured agreements he got on with it.

"So, it's almost 4 o'clock. Hapgood and everyone are supposed to meet today, right? Well, however and when that happens –." Tyce leaned closer, coughing, voice hoarse. "- I don't think we should meet them in town tomorrow. We should wait another couple days. Ignore the demand...deadline crap. Support me with the others."

"What happens then?" Sherri said.

"Help might be coming. Let's stay out of it, bide out our time a little. Hapgood? If those assholes out there are going to harm us they're going to do it anyway. It's the water, by the way. That's what they want. The well and the whole system. Steve was going to tell you all at the meeting. But, I doubt..."

"You're right," Ray said. "I don't trust the cocksucker either. I say we stay put."

"Yes," Sherri said. "We should stay. But we should be ready to leave. I mean, we can't defend this place. Obviously." Sherri's palm went up. "I'm sorry. I didn't mean to go there."

Tyce's bleary eyes were unfazed. "Hey, it's cool. No excuse. And it's a point. If we have to move, we'll move. But your odds are better here than out there, on foot. That's a fact, Sherri."

"OK. We'll all meet," Sherri said.

Teeth tight, Ray stood. "Meet who? Mike's gone or gonna be. Hannah's with him. Gallo's with her. Steve's got a busted nose, passed out. Who the fuck knows where everyone else is? We find 'em and we tell 'em and we all tell Vern. Anyone wants a reason, they can kiss my ass."

Ray stopped at the turn of the hallway. "Maybe we should all pile into that RV and hit the road."

"Ray."

"Yeah?"

"While Steve's out I'd like your help in the Barracks, watching the cameras and things while I catch some sleep."

"Sure thing."

Picking up her new bag, Sherri stood.

"Come around in a couple hours," Tyce said. "You want the .22?"

Ray guffawed. "Nah. I'd start shooting people."

Sherri waited for Ray to leave. Despite the revolver at home, Sherri considered asking for a gun, her reply ready. *I was raised in the South.* Tyce's expression was blank, unfocused eyes miles into the carpet.

"Do you need anything, Tyce?"

Tyce shook his head, sniffing deeply, scratching. "No. I'm going to bury him and then get back to the Barracks. Thank you."

She thought again to ask for a gun but didn't.

His head turned to Sherri, an alert flash of purpose. "Check in on Steve, please? Tell him I'll see him later."

"I will."

In the hallway Sherri glanced back. Tyce gripped the arm rests, set to push like he was thinking of standing but couldn't quite remember how.

*****

By the first time Lorna had stolen money from her mother's purse she was already on medication. Every morning with her grape juice, before school. How old or what rules she defied to earn the pills, Lorna couldn't remember. But the feeling of stealing the five-dollar bill was like this one now. Shivery. Kind of glad, kind of scared. Lorna's fingernails scratched on the Barrack's ramp railing. She pushed, lift tipping forward, feet off the ground. The outside air felt good. She knew she should totally feel guilty for wanting to laugh. Her thoughts were slippery, but not storming. It was fucking *weird*.

A buzzing fly cut her daydream, planting her Chucks on the cement ramp, the broken Barracks' door behind her. She peered up the roadway to the split V of trees; pond shine between them. Nobody. Nothing.

It had been a cloudy, end of summer weekday just like this. School had just started. Lorna waited until her mother was in the shower and she took the five from her purse. Lorna remembered the big green 5 in the corner when she folded the bill and put it into her shoe. She could still picture her mother's unknowing profile on the drive to school, the revved-up feelings wanting to leap out of her.

A paralyzed kind of everyone-dead quiet. Lorna knew she could be terrified right now, if she wanted to be. *But she wasn't!* FUCK! It was rollercoaster cool. Almost like edging - masturbating and almost cumming but holding back. Heeling, her legs took her back inside the Barracks.

On automatic, the video screens ticked through long pans of the empty streets, the broad lane of dirt outside the walls. The big German Shepherd barked. *God, Hapgood's dog.* It barked, calling out. A delayed ripple through the open door. The barks weren't alarms. They were forlorn. *What about me?* Hapgood's dog. The sounds sank her energy. Suddenly cut low, Lorna wanted to sit but knew it was bad, sitting still.

No one was on the radios, or had been, since she watched the shooting happen - Mark Dudek going crazy and blasting his way into the house. Even though Lorna could call them now - could have called all day - she did what Steve said. What him and Tyce both said. She did what they told her, because she had a hole instead of a dick. Nothing to see on the cameras? Stay off the air. The exact words. She could quote them back. She did what she was supposed to do. And if she didn't? Well, then she didn't. She didn't see anything. So there. *Lorna has done her best.*

And, talk about orders? Well, she could have called anyone, and kept calling, on that satellite phone. She didn't. Steve would jabber for an hour after they fucked. His favorite lakes up north. Cop stories. The motorcycle he might buy someday, taking it cross country. But maybe telling her they had a working phone to call *some*body to get them out of this shit? Yeah. That might be something she'd like to know.

Lorna walked back to the threshold, the crooked front door she'd braced open with a box of paper. Keeping it closed was too much. Not that it would close properly anymore - the lock rattling loose, top hinge bent.

But she couldn't stay cooped up in there. She wanted to come and go, out and in. Not zombie-out in front of the monitors. Maybe if she could push some buttons and blow some things up, if she saw people coming. Maybe then. But no. No, the girl gets to call for help.

And well, she didn't. She didn't call.

Her father came home later - golf - and her mother hadn't picked Lorna up after school. The office sent her a note - take the bus. Using the key in the glove by the back door, Lorna was bouncing around the house, alone, wondering. Did she know I took the money? Is that why she wouldn't pick me up? Shivering.

Lorna had been asleep in the console chair when Hapgood came in. The crack and shove as the door banged open and there was Vern Hapgood, just as surprised to see Lorna. Crippled by surprise and trying to make sense of where she *was*, let alone Hapgood standing there with a mondo crow-bar in his hand. Lorna just reacted to his barked orders – *Up! Back! – Who else is here!?* It felt like crashing around in a fast river. Right quick, Hapgood had the satellite phone from the drawer, pulling out the radio gear from under the console, mumble cursing them, her, everyone. Lorna's brain was in full lightning, like smoking Velvet M, like trying to see your face in a mirror cracked in seventy pieces. God, she had totally cowered in front of Hapgood….

Lorna gripped the railing, pushed forward, leaned back, lowering herself. If she had been awake she could have called when she saw Hapgood coming. But Steve? Tyce? They wouldn't have gotten there in time. It would have just been her and Hapgood anyway. How different would it all have been?

Another fly buzzed past, zipping inside.

After yelling a lot of questions Lorna wouldn't answer about radios and other bullshit, Fat Fuck grabbed her and kept pushing her forward back, to the back of the office, into the hall, into the cell. He shoved her inside, looking down and around the open cage for keys. The bars locking when he swung them closed, yelling at *her* to shut up and stop yelling.

What would they all say? Bob the creepy engineer guy would have her back. Bob wanted to fuck her. But in the general way, like they all did. Like the way a guy wants to buy a motorcycle someday.

Later in the cell, snooping through Tyce's things, his notebook full of weird numbers and addresses, one CD - "BOB" (?) and other junk in the cell Lorna found a ring of keys under a dirty T-shirt.

Caught outside, spacing out on the ramp, Tyce's shout seized Lorna's attention. She back-stepped in fright.

"What the fuck?"

Another question Lorna couldn't answer.

Steve was walking behind Tyce, his bandage-taped nose swollen and red, both eyes blackened. He shook his head, stepping past her. Tyce set his rifle against the side of the Barracks. His hands worked the busted, hanging door.

Lorna's mother never mentioned the stolen five.

This would not be the same.

Opening the cell door with Tyce's keys, Lorna had barefoot heel-toed on the carpet, hugging the wall, making the right turn down the other hall, into the dark kitchen. After the longest wait, Fat Fuck got up from the console. Humming something. Actually human. She heard him fart, reaching to click the light switch. She hoped Hapgood's last fitting thought was of digging for food in the refrigerator. That the gun behind his ear - her father's stay-safe-baby snub six-shooter – never occurred to him. Truth? She didn't kill Hapgood out of revenge or hate or anything. He was a dick. And there was no reason not to. She pulled the trigger and he went off like a pinwheel into the table, the wall. Blood streams. A lot on the floor later…now.

Lorna showered it all off herself, leaving the bar of Dial in the shower rusty brown. She borrowed one of Steve's washed T-shirts.

She followed Tyce and Steve inside, standing over Vern's corpse the kitchen. Lorna's breath caught, fixed on Steve's scowl.

"I ain't fucking burying him," Tyce said, moving out past her.

She stepped behind Steve, hesitating to touch him. He crouched, peering. A dozen flies flurried around the body, the pooled blood.

"What happened?"

Lorna talked but Steve wasn't hearing. He stood, pacing the body, side stepping. His head shook, away from her. He went back into the office where Tyce sat on a desk corner, fingers raking through his hair. Ray Dudek walked in, curious eyes examining the busted door. Lorna stopped talking. It was only noise.

Tyce glared at her.

"I guess the meeting's canceled."

Ray Dudek's face blanked when he looked into the lit kitchen, walking to it. Lorna shivered with the surge, lips parting on their own.

They weren't going to do anything. It was funny. She could take it. They couldn't.

She looked at Tyce between the eyes.

"He found the phone" she said. "He was making calls on it and talking for a while. I don't think he could figure out the radio."

Whoa whoa whoa. Ray Dudek was behind her loud and clear.

"What phone?"

****

A fine relic. A soft padding of dark grey vinyl stitched into its Bakelite box by a thick white gauge. The metal-faced knobs had adjustable settings for MHZ from FM music to shortwave to trucker citizens band. Portable, Alan Shepherd solid-state technology Sanders' father had bought at an American department store, working just fine sixty years on. Tuned to BBC news, Sanders admired the radio atop the kitchen counter.

Imagine any radio, any appliance, for a hundred miles still functioning in another 20 years. Yes, this one.

Every effort was being made to contain the plant's leaking radiation, the report said. Water from Lake Michigan was being pumped in to cool the reactor core. The evacuation zone had expanded to 70 miles around St. Joseph. Most other nuclear facilities around the country had been stabilized and secured, some close to being restarted, the White House claimed. Technicians from all over the world were arriving to assist. But, at the same time, a pitched battle was engaged around the Grand Coulee Dam, the occupiers threatening to blow it.

Sanders ate another spoonful of cold beans from the can. Chewing, he walked to the living room, the reports echoing on in the kitchen. He paced the hallways and rooms, spaces dim-fogged by 10-watt fist-sized inflatable solar lamps. Sanders had a dozen of them among the disaster stores. There were more powerful lamps among the emergency equipment, but he preferred the dimness. Amazing, the human eye's capacity of adjustment. He strolled, round and round. Dining room, down through the family room, to the front windows, back to the kitchen, spooning from the can of Heinz beans. Texas had declared independence from the United States. Anyone wishing to leave had until Friday Noon.

The foreign news services were a tonic of calm, a tranquilizer from the harried EBN reports and looking-glass absurdity of the seceder's new Lunicasts, erupting over into the EBN signals as manifest schizophrenia. The American Nervous Breakdown dominated the coverage, but the world did keep turning. Hearing European soccer scores brought Sanders a smile. He stopped, leaning against the kitchen island to swirl the last spoonful. It's no wonder the government had lost control in so many places, Sanders thought. An unenforceable law is worse than no law at all. Respect withers. Without respect, there's nothing. But the revolting patriots would fail. They aspired to no standard beyond exerting control. Sanders' stockinged foot pressed the pedal and he dropped the empty can into the stainless-steel tube. Sanders then washed the spoon, washed his hands and dried them. He pressed the pedal and dropped the wadded paper towels into the can.

His eyes scanned the modern marvel of a room – the kitchen of tomorrow from some Jazz-Age World's Fair. It felt like a museum to him. Brown cabinets and brown speckled granite making it almost sepia in the lamp light. The kitchen of the past. Her kitchen. She had taken nothing. She wanted none of it.

To blank her, Sanders' mind went to calculations and figures in his notebook atop the granite island. The rate of the development's fuel use versus supply. With current patterns, the well would shut down by September 23rd, later if its filter processor was disabled. Water would not be a problem for him. He still had 60 sealed gallons among the stores. Food into December…no, April. Her half. During today's bloody bang-bang afternoon, using the blueprints of Cricklewood Green, Sanders had nearly finished the specs of a walkable escape tunnel which could be dug underneath the wall.

Monitoring the Crazies' communications on the radio was an assortment of horrors and insights. The other night Sanders listened to LifeForce guards dying off – plucked - in the D-Plex parking lot. Sanders could visualize where he had been parked in despair, days ago. The Crazies on the citizen's band were calm, directing massed fire and maneuver on the outnumbered guards. He marveled at the distorted pops, the agony, terror, the gross inequality of guns. Children made lethal. Though the Crazies were hardly children, the image propelled Sanders' rage as he listened. *Rotten little….*

Sanders told no one of the radio slaughter. To what end? He'd thought of the assault during yesterday's meeting, a soundtrack to the gruesome photos from the delivered packet. Knowing what he did of both security guards – Tyce and Dominski - they would not relent to the letter's demands, regardless. They were both strong men who needed no help from him. The same logic kept him inside today. Sanders knew he would be the worst kind of dilettante at armed resolution. When the determined-faced guard named Tyce came to his door around nightfall to check in, Sanders couldn't imagine how tragically ineffective he would have been at preventing or redirecting any of it. A child in the way. Tyce's demeanor in the doorway with his rifle was matter of fact and soldierly, reporting Mike Narlow's fading condition and the killing of the intruder by Mark Dudek. Telling of Vern Hapgood's death, Tyce's face changed, evaluating Sanders, somehow expectant. He dealt the details as if from a hand of cards, perhaps assuming Vern Hapgood was a friend. *Hapgood was shot. It was quick. Lorna killed him. Attempted rape, she said.*

Sanders mustered nods of comprehension. He hardly knew Vern Hapgood, a man who seemed to relish armed resolution, machine-gun and all. It was likely a final comfort to him. Some turgid, adolescent notion of honor, going down with his boots on. An exerter of control, Vern Hapgood was a stranger to Sanders, yet familiar from the first. Hapgood reminded Sanders of every man who ever fired him. As for Lorna's deed, Sanders' mind rebelled at the word "feelings". They were unmoved. He was certainly incapable of moving them. The girl lived inside of him as primal drive. A thousand pounds of pressure is.

When Tyce had stopped talking both men stared dumbly at one another in the foyer, Sanders unsure if they were finished. Finally, Tyce spoke again and Sanders agreed to Tyce's request. He would meet everyone else tomorrow at 10 a.m.

The BBC switched to jazz music, sending dedications and well wishes to their American listeners. Melancholy stopped his fingers on the off switch. To mournful trumpet Sanders turned and walked to the front window, clouded moon allowing little through the panes. The water. The food. The supplies. The equipment. Her knick-knack 'treasures". She had wanted none of it. Her last words.

I'm not going to die with you, Robert.

A nearby dog's faint, plaintive barking made him nervous. Sanders headed for the stairway. The single candle up there making a glorious moth's target. To the light, Metaphor Man, to the light. If he were that man, Sanders had an ideal sniper's nest up there. The walls could be re-enforced by kitchen slab granite, protecting him as he precisely zapped the Crazies when they finally came over the walls. The devolved, scurrying men below. Howling, crooked-tooth monkeys in caps and boots, hurling their feces at him in the form of automatic rifle fire.

Sanders opened the desk drawer and drank a gulping pull of brandy in the wavering, candle-lit shadow boxer's chamber. His black shape, the confines, the brandy's heat drawing down and out his capillaries. All of it made him ache for her.

He felt the thumps a fraction before he heard them. A pressure drop and muffled pop outside. Sanders went to the pillbox windows, looking out, sensing the distance. These were not gunshots. The west window's glowing horizon toward Essex stopped him. Sanders gasped at one, then two more mighty flashes in the area of town. Seconds later, he felt the explosion's slight waves through his breast bone. Sanders thought he saw a streak of lightning, or a missile.

****

October 17th

Sparky, orange squiggles traced unburned wood hunks in the fireplace. The embers reminded Gallo of undersea molten lava in childhood *National Geographics*. Storm wind still pushed at the windows. Head throbbing, Gallo hugged his blankets, shaking and uneasy over his weakness after a night's sleep. Laying on his right side, he squinted up at the mantle clock, blurry hands at nearly 4:30. The walls around the Narlow's fireplace and the flat-screen's imposing black mirror were uncomfortably bare; hooks and nails marking removed pictures. Gallo was uncertain if chills were coming inward through his pajamas or something inside him was giving way. Defiant, Gallo sat up. Slippers. Knees cracking as he stood, Gallo clenched against the tremors and walked.

Outside the rain-spotted glass doors, wind rippled the blue/black pond. Gallo's hand braced against the frame, fingertips tracing the door seam's fine draft. At this hour, already Robert Sanders solar lamps lit his top floor. Gallo could see no other light across the water. Only blocks of moon shadow and phantom obliques, tempting fear.

A long stream tangle of neon, green or yellow – it was too fast - blew onto the Narlow's deck. The color surprise made Gallo wonder what it was, where it came from, before it skittered away. Survey tape? A piece of parade float? Gallo accepted it as a blessing for the day, for whatever God had in store. At the very least he would get out from these damned walls. Cricklewood Green had become an asylum by any other name. A penal colony without outside contact since the day the package came over the gate. That day before the murders sliced open the thin membrane bearing the world Gallo had known. The blackout's first days of mindful, cautious vigilance had mired to a crushing, callow acceptance of madness. Kill. Take. Have a soda. Have a laugh. Who wants a purse? Who wants some whiskey? Questioning reality, if not sanity, had become a daily sacrament for Gallo in these weeks. Based on the radio broadcasts he was doubtful life was better elsewhere. Fratricide in God's name. Artillery and bombing by decree of Law.

Gallo was prepared for a reckoning from Him.

Kim Narlow had asked Gallo to stay the nights. The others took someone's twin bed into the Narlow living room for him. Gallo would arrive around dusk, sometimes for dinner. The talk would be pleasant, then a game or drawing pictures with the little girl. Kim and Sandra Rose spent their evenings upstairs. The mother gently reading to her or the giggling pair playing cards. Gallo would read by candle or solar lamp, building a fire on recent cool nights. *Moby Dick* was as boring as he had been told all these years. At sunrise he would make the bed, lock the door and silently return to his home.

Except for Sherri and Lorna, the others avoided the Narlow residence. Mike's burial had been a cringing afternoon. Kim's contempt was hydra-headed and omni-directional, spraying Blame in the vilest, blushing terms on everyone but Gallo. Curiously to him, Kim Narlow never mentioned Mike. Not once asking about the hours Gallo spent with Mike Narlow sprawled in his kitchen – bleeding, drugged, contorting, cursing. Dying. Still, Gallo was glad for the pseudo-guardianship – to be needed and for the distraction from a...countdown...of his condition. The little girl remained a delight. Whatever its delusion, his vowed protection of Sandra Rose from anyone was perhaps the most fulfillment William Gallo ever felt. He learned the importance of the pinkie swear. A watercolor sky should be green, not blue. When this newer, peculiar exhaustion came, like a toy winding down, thoughts of Sandra Rose lifted him. He imagined Sandra Rose the future grown woman, an astronaut in outer space perhaps, continuing on.

Gallo had been on bleary sentry at the door wall for a few minutes, contemplating coffee or more fire when he felt her steps behind him. He didn't move, not wanting to startle her. When Sandra Rose joined him at the glass Gallo waited, looking down in the margins of his sight, whispering.

"Are you alright, Sandra Rose?"

"Yes."

A flannel shirt of Mike's hung to her feet like a scarecrow overcoat. She had a sleeve up to her nose, watching the water. The sensory notion was certainly part of Gallo's heart. He had once kept a special lover's T-shirt until his scent faded.

Knees impossibly tight, Gallo eased to her level. "You should go back to sleep. Did the wind wake you?"

"No. I dreamed my Mom and me were with my Daddy and we were at a farm. There were dogs there and they all had wings."

"Come on. Let's get you back to bed. Do you want some water?"

She exhaled on the glass. Her finger smeared a five-point star in the fog patch.

"I saw a man outside," she said.

"You saw a man? When?"

"Downstairs. At the front. He smiled at me through the window."

"Oh, really now? And what did he look like?"

"He smiled really big. Like 'Krizma Cat."

"Did you smile back?"

Her green eyes met his. "Mmm hmm."

She was fanciful but worry tingled Gallo's head. There would be no more sleep.

He took her hand.

"Come on, angel. Let's get some water and go back upstairs."

"OK."

****

When the knocks came, Sanders rose from his recliner. Shoes on, he opened the door without hesitation. The Reaper, in whatever its form, would not knock. Behind Lorna's dim figure, first light had filled and defined the branches and autumn-tinted leaves back across the road. This seemed the best time to do it. This part of the morning was clandestine - and foolish. Sanders imagined sick gamblers seeing their fate this way.

Lorna entered the echoing foyer. He welcomed her polite smile. A complimentary drink from the casino.

"Hey Robert," she said.

Lifting his brown leather bomber jacket from the hook, Sanders noticed the silvery pistol slip from the pouch of Lorna's hooded sweat-shirt. Despite the denim jacket over it and her thin, sparkle-threaded scarf, she shivered. Not cold in the least, Sanders was unsure of bringing the coat. He looked into her unblinking green eyes, then down at the revolver in her open palm. An offering. He inquired if it was loaded.

She swallowed behind a quick nod. "Yeah."

He decided to take the coat. To be out there in shirt sleeves, with the gun, felt somehow absurd. Lifting it from her hand, Sanders gripped the whole pistol as if to throw it, nowhere near the trigger. He held the door open for her and followed. She asked a few perfunctory questions about sleep and the weather. Sanders answered friendly in the pitch and toss, walking down the wet driveway to the blacktop. Sanders zipped the jacket. The breeze did have a bite.

"I just can't do it by myself. I hope, I mean...." she said as they walked, looking back over her shoulder.

Sanders said he understood but did not. Lorna could do it, quite simply. Even accepting Vern's 300+ pounds had "tried' to rape her, Lorna's conscience – if Tinkerbell existed - seemed untroubled by killing him. Vern's murder – it could be called nothing else – concerned none of the Cricklewood Green moralists, outwardly. They appeared simultaneously amazed and disappointed entering Vern's home, postmortem. Disappointed by the puny "haul" and amazed Hapgood was technologically crippled. His home's wiring and the devices were all cooked to well-done, just as their own were. Considering his boasts and the all-night lights inside his home they were expecting NORAD's fabled Cheyenne Mountain. A bunker fit for a king and his court. But for weapons and cases of bullets, two drums of gasoline and a few other items, Vern had little of use. No communications equipment. One AM/FM. Not even a working television. They mocked the dead man's phony claims and arrogance – *"I have information you don't hav*e." A Spartan's worth of rations in his cabinets, enough for maybe a week. A few extra batteries. One flashlight. A set of night vision goggles. His beer, bourbon, cigars and, strangely enough, a polished-to-obsidian baby grand piano in the unfinished basement. Vern had never shown an inclination toward music.

Vern had two gasoline-powered generators in addition to the home unit. Noise be damned, the gas generator's plugs powered a table lamp in an upper window and a cage-faced hanging work bulb in his living room. He'd set foil dryer hoses from the exhaust ports to his chimney. All to maintain his full-power ego behind the shades.

The illogical imbalance of Vern's weapons still irked Sanders. Four pistols, automatic rifles, shotguns; let alone the machine gun? You could only shoot one at a time. The third rifle would make the difference? There was no evidence of contact with the lunatics outside unless it were in the den's computer and thumb drives. Within hours, everything desired was appropriated by the group as if it had fallen from the sky. The home's propane was extracted to the well generator, one BBQ tank at a time.

What was the old saying about insurance policies? Worth more dead than alive?

Many a truth in jest.

Could Lorna recognize the irony of their morning mission? When she asked Sanders for help, his weakness – the gambler – couldn't agree faster; anything to be this near or needed by her. Sanders wondered about Lorna's moral calculations, but they couldn't be called such. Calculation required logic and reason. Reason was not part of this, any of this. Thus, chaos. Thus, Sanders agreeing to help her.

At the Fetter's home, one house south of Hapgood's lot, Lorna stopped. She looked up at Sanders, expecting him to lead. He was caught flat. This had been the extent of the plan. Lorna never mentioned the execution of it, so to speak. She glanced in the direction of the dog, and then pouted down at her fidgety sneakers. Part of Sanders' mind broke away in the moment. If he just said it, gently cupping her chin, engaging her eyes? Leading. How differently would everything traject?

Recovering, he asked Lorna if she brought anything for the animal.

The cellophane crinkled in her grip, a handful of dried meat inside it. On the packet a cartoon image of a beaming dog and its red tongue. Something...*Bacon!*

To the dog, his master's last act of locking him to the giant willow tree must have felt like betrayal. The beast's training broke down as surely as any forsaken prisoner. Day and night the dog alternately barked or cried out, mournful. Sanders knew nothing about dogs but suspected the animal was becoming feral, matted in mud and its own waste. The short chain staked into the willow left little play. The animal had only mere yards of dirt to stalk.

In the first week several residents tried, several times, to approach it. But the dog's rage was demonic. Its growling barks were nearly strangled by the force of neck against collar. The clack of bone when its jaws snapped. Even the boldest among them would back-peddle, paled. Fearful the spike would give, Hannah, Joyce and the others satisfied themselves by throwing the dog scoops of food, which Vern had by the bagful in his garage. With a pole, Tyce forced a galvanized wash tub full of water close enough to it. Sanders had been there with Tyce and Dominski to watch the dog drink so much water that it vomited. Still, it attacked the next person who tried to get close.

Lorna was the one to stay, facing the throated fury. From the north window, Sanders would watch her sit. Fifty minutes, timed. Eventually the dog would tire, Lorna cross-legged in the face of it. The pair would stare at one another or Lorna would lay elbowed on the grass, smoking dope, watching the beast sleep. After a week everyone else had given up, assuming the role was Lorna's.

Six days ago, the animal got her in the leg, slightly, but Lorna rolled away before it could maul her. Boiling in adrenaline, Sanders could not recall how he got from the tower window down to the lawn. He picked up the bawling young woman - *touching her!* - in a cradle carry to the security building. How he babbled attempting to comfort her, even then failing. Speaking of infection. Dog's mouths are clean, Lorna. He's surely immunized. No danger of that. It barely broke the epidermis.

Epidermis. This he said to her.

Hannah swooped in to care for Lorna and they all thanked him, his inmate family. Sanders had come to understand the word tolerance as he never had. Tolerance for the dishonesty. The false, mannered camaraderie. But, the respect he felt from them went a long way toward tuning out their gossip; their venal analysis of the dead and absent - Hapgood, the Vanderkams, the crazy Narlow woman, the Gruttas, John Chalmer's ugly wife - as they dug and laid the joists and supports for the tunnel. Sanders was used to third-person references as he worked in silence right next to people. *What's Sanders' problem? Sanders - he never talks,* they said, as he sawed and measured. Sanders had nothing to say. Why give credence to their bile, waiting for his turned back, next in line for the magpies when he left for camera duty?

Besides the tunnel, Sanders contributed suggestions to the added defense features, like improving the road barricade. Cut gun ports into the wall, he said. Pieces of the brick face mounted with contact cement over wooden plugs. Except for his tunnel and the road barricade, the defense "improvements" were all bunk, never implemented. Nothing about Cricklewood Green was defensible, even to a tactical idiot like him. Too much to patrol. A rat-trap corner if the Crazies came in force. But the tunnel work kept the resident's minds off of the continued chaos outside. The labor served to unite them, somewhat. Perhaps the next person to be murdered for their value would be a tougher calculation.

Calculation. Today they were going out. Today was Vern's morning, a time-bomb prediction he had made weeks ago around the Activity Room table. The morning of *'now what?'* Things could be moving very fast within the next few hours.

But first....

There in the road Sanders sketched the plan's end to Lorna. He would go past Hapgood's house and come up behind the dog while Lorna approached the animal across the vacant yard, as she always did.

"Please Robert. Just, make sure. Before you have to. If? OK?"

He promised. He would only kill the dog if it attacked her.

Under the willow's stringy canopy, the side-sleeping dog was undisturbed by Sanders' passage. Hapgood's back yard was flat, without a deck. On one knee Sanders waited on the grey stone pavers, obscured by two evergreen bushes. The animal was just over 60 feet away. Sanders put the gun in a shooting grip, holding his wrist, and carefully cocked the hammer. He center-marked the steel stub on the dog's inkblot shape, juxt by panoramic gold sunrise and the sparkling pond behind it.

The chain rattle-snapped as the German Shepherd sprung, barking puffs of steam in warning at the girl, her jeans swishing the knee-high wet grass. Sanders could hear her murmurs of ease. The dog went silent, tail arced. In the last few days the animal was letting her get very close before it would growl and bare. Lorna unrolled the packet of food, pulling pieces as she walked. Sanders aimed, swallowed. Shivering.

Lorna kneeled, arms separating the grass, within inches of the dirt. She held out a handful of meat. Her cooed voice sagged Sanders' chest.

The shepherd's packed muscle strained the chain. It jolted and Sanders nearly pulled the trigger. The Queen moved forward one square. Her food hand reached.

Baron dug into the food. Sliding up, the flat of her left hand stroked the dog's head. Once, then along its neck. The animal sat, chewing as she caressed it, murmuring, offering more. Her knees slid forward, unconcerned of the filth, stroking its hide.

Sanders realized the tear blotting his right lens and lowered the gun. It felt so good – so unusual - he sat on the damp, cool stone and let the tears flow down his face, blurring his glasses. Sanders' laughter burbled out from nowhere. His mind surrendered to this surprise, hoping his body was smarter than he was.

****

Hannah inhaled cool air, making her feel expansive. Wind-sung trees and bright sun, her sweats and Nikes. For a few seconds, Hannah touched youth, getting ready to train for sophomore cross-country. Weightless and free of snares. The best kind of hope. No ifs. *When* everything worked this morning. *When* everyone came back from Essex, she would go running on this gorgeous fall day. The leaf sounds had changed recently from soft hiss to autumn rattle. Hannah liked it. An urgency and the warmth of the pizza tray in her hands got her stepping. The radio quiet. No one had called all night. No alarms.

Near the V in the road she noticed Mark walking north on the west loop. Joyce had already risen, dressed and left as it was just getting light, while Hannah was washing. *Going to the generator room*, the note said. The ersatz pizza had been Joyce's idea, leaving Hannah to kettle-bake it. Joyce was hardly looking her in the eye anymore. As Hannah kneaded and spread the dough, the EBN news reports from overnight were mixed. Hit and run fighting all through the Midwest and Great Plains over the fall harvests. The brightest spot being the last off-line nuclear plant, in Kansas, was declared contained. Contamination had been minimal, they said. It was Hannah's first willed swallow of the day, calling it Optimism.

At 1,000 calories per day, even accounting for hidden candy surprises, she and Joyce would eat their last meal on October 27th

Everyone OK with food? It was The Question, met with nods and stoic lips. Eyes locking with one another, a kind of warned agreement. No one going to the edge of the falls, when someone would say *"No. Can I have some of yours?"*

It was dark inside the Barracks but for the camera monitors and several candles. Sherri was seated at the console with her CD player. Cathy's Clown low over the soft pull of Ray's snores from the back cot. Hannah flipped the switch on the fluorescents. Sherri exhaled, cupping her palm over her brow.

"Good morning." Hannah set the foil-covered tray on the desk.

"Good morning," Sherri said. Under her keying fingers the console screen's boxes popped large, then reduced and rearranged. Pokes and enlarging swipes as if she were killing things in a video game.

"Is Joyce here?" Hannah said.

"No. I saw her go to William's a while ago."

"Did she go to the generator room?"

"Yes."

"I'm sorry. She knows she was supposed to relieve you at eight." Hannah stood behind Sherri, slipping off her med bag. "The kids didn't come back, I take it?"

"Not that I noticed."

"I made pizza. I wanted to make sure everyone had a full stomach going out. But it's for everybody."

Ray sat up, alternately snorting and clearing his throat. "Who turned on the goddamned lights? Jesus."

"Good morning Ray." Hannah called off her shoulder. "Stay right there."

"Well, I'm going to piss first. Whatta ya think of that?"

Sherri still wouldn't look at her.

"We didn't have the mozzarella, so we mixed a cup of parmesan into the sauce. I made pesto. We used the last fresh tomatoes and basil from our garden. We even had a can of black olives."

"I'm sure they'll appreciate a hot breakfast," Sherri said, zooming on the west yards, then tapping off to the view outside the wall, down the barricaded, deserted entrance road to the Oakton intersection.

"Oh my God. Stop!" Hannah leaned in.

"What?"

"Go back. Go back!"

Sherri brought the west yards up.

"Vern's yard. The dog! The dog escaped!"

"No," Sherri said. "Lorna released it."

"What? What do you mean 'released it'?"

"It's fine, Hannah." Sherri met her eyes. "Lorna has it now. Baron accepted her. It was sweet, actually. She took him back to Vern's."

Hannah pulled in a lungful and rolled her tongue, taking the pizza to the kitchen. "Well, it would have been nice to know, is all."

"Yes Ma'am. Next time. In triplicate," Sherri said.

Near midnight, hours before, Hannah was still at camera when five people – kids - approached the gate, seemingly separating from the foliage, layered in packs and bedrolls. Two boys had rifles. Beneath hoods and hats Hannah guessed them to be teens from their smaller frames and lurching motions. They stooped and circled, flashlight playing over the phony quarantine message on the gate as Tyce scrambled out the door with the goggles and one of the assault rifles, radioing Mark on the north end of the Green. Hannah, Ray and Sherri watched the split green screens in the dark. Tyce aiming on the gate from behind a tree, fitted next to the kids milling outside it. Sherri whispered, the "oh" so very small in her mouth. Hannah was nauseous, faint, standing over the electric green visual, answering both Tyce and Mark on the radio, jumping screens. A clash of radio jabber. *Were more coming?* Where? Status? *Shut up! Report. Report ONLY, Mark. Eyes open.* Do you see me?

Outside the gate the kids seemed to read, talk. Shine the quarantine sign and read again, backs together, facing out. Hannah zoom-focused on a short girl, perhaps 13-years-old, shrouded in a blanket, a hatchet down in her hand. Little Red Riding Hood as homicidal refugee. Tangles of hair like seaweed against the stun on her green face, eyes sparkling eerily. *Who was she to be living in the woods like this? Where was her family? What happened to her?* After ten minutes the bunch broke apart, absorbing back into the woods past the camera's range; rested enough or possibly convinced by the quarantine message. Lorna had created the quarantine warning with the office's computer. Hannah dictated the V-14 script from memory, substituting smallpox for V-14. They placed the printout inside the clear plastic Pool Rules mount. The hex worked. No one died. Hannah left at 1 a.m. and Valium kept her down until four.

Hannah poured out the cold coffee, jaw clenched at the waste. Four pots worth were left in the bag. She started a fresh one and washed her hands. She opted to leave the pizza covered on the kitchen table. Ray was already near the archway, sniffing.

"What is that?"

"Pesto pizza."

"Pesto?"

"Basil from our garden. It's good."

Hannah led Ray by the arm back to the cot. "Come on. Let's check you out, first." Ray let Hannah take him without insult, a sign more troubling to her than his wheezes.

"This whole thing is great for your figure, Ray. You'll be at a 36-inch waist in no time," she said, reaching for the pressure cuff. "Come on. Get the shirt off."

"Yeah, I'll look great in my coffin."

"You're good for another 50,000 miles, Ray. Shirt. Come on."

"It's too cold in here."

"You're fine." Hannah said. Some patients you caress to wellness. Some you jab. Ray's condition was another reason for the morning's outing. Nearly everyone was out of medication. Ray had swallowed his last half of Maxide tablet on Wednesday, Coumadin on Sunday. His blood pressure another red line among many. They had to go out. Ray's baggy, frog-like eyes looked her sweatsuit up and down as she pumped, squatting in front of him.

"If you're gonna be coach where's your whistle and clipboard?"

She ignored it but liked the notion. She felt like a coach to them sometimes. The score rose 150, 160 and climbing. Scope in her ears, she listened to his heart and lungs.

"What are you doing?" Ray's legs jerked as Hannah's hands slipped up under his pants, pressing his calves, swollen worse than Monday.

"Rest yourself today, Ray. And get yourself a bath," she said, bagging her items. "They'll bring back some medication. You still have some Diovan, right?"

"He does," Sherri said.

"Thanks for the prescription but we have shit to do, remember?"

"We'll manage." Hanna stood. "You're not indispensable."

She cringed at the metallic scrape of the still-unaligned door, having reminded Tyce to fix it days ago. William entered in his plaid cab cap, green jacket and scarf, greeting everyone. William's eyes twinkled as Hannah approached him, his cologne woody and subtle. William's weight loss alarmed Hannah, more severe than everyone else's. His skin had gone opaque and waxen, eyes defined like marbles beneath it.

"You're ready to make an impression, I see," she said.

"Why not? It's a beautiful morning. *Sunny/thank you for the sunlight/you give...*" He said, singing with Sherri's CD player.

William took Hannah in a laughing dance step, swinging her out. Hannah's hope soared. Momentum. She let go of William's hand.

"Come everyone. There's food and coffee in the kitchen. I want everyone to eat. And take one of those vitamins. Sherri, go ahead. I'll watch until Joyce gets here."

Hannah made a point to touch them - backs, shoulders. Ray was already in the kitchen.

Sherri stood, stretching. "One of those cameras is going, I think."

It took a few minutes for Lorna to walk down alone from Hapgood's house. She passed her home. Steve still sleeping inside it, Hannah presumed. The van in the Brusine driveway had already been packed with the water. Twenty-five gallons - the five Culligan bottles from the Barracks - capped and resealed in candle wax. Hannah gritted, faking a smile at the girl as she entered the Barracks, removing her black shades. Lorna's eyes were dilated and glassy red, like little unmoored boats in her face. How could she possibly have any marijuana left? Lorna didn't smell of it, unless she was stoned on something else. Some patients you handle like nitroglycerin.

"How's the dog?" Hannah said.

"He's great! Did you see it? I'm gonna wash him later. I can't wait." Lorna was manic. Good if it had to be one or the other. The words boosted Hannah. Plans for later from Lorna's mouth were a great step. She could hear it spreading in the kitchen. Optimism. Chatter. Even Ray. Good, good. Keep them up. Momentum.

"How's your leg?"

"Oh, it's nothing. I can hardly feel it."

I'll bet, Hannah thought. "You should go eat something. Take one of those multi-vitamins, too."

Lorna removed her sparkle-thread-scarf and denim jacket.

"You guys see the TV?"

"What? Why?"

"The bombs. There were bombs planted in government buildings and at army bases and stuff. Like all over. Pennsylvania, Columbus, Ohio, Kentucky. In, like really secure places. Like, dozens of people got roached. FEMA guys, this air force base hospital. They all went off at 7:07. The Fuckhead radio stations are creaming all over it. This one guy on a pirate station is calling them the Asshole Cocksu -"

Hannah faced the monitor screens, away from her eyes. Lorna seemed happy to tell it. Saliva on her little fangs. "Be quiet. It's the last thing we need."

"What do you think 7:07 means?"

"Who cares?"

"William's cute in his little hat," Lorna said, blind to his gauntness.

"Where's Steve?"

"I don't know. I took Baron back to the house. You should have seen him, Hannah. He peed like four times, sniffing everything. Then he laid right down by the desk, you could totally tell it was his spot and went right asleep. He breathed out and just…" Lorna blubbered an exhale in imitation.

"Vern's desk, you mean." Hannah faced her. Lorna wouldn't say the name. Ever.

Lorna's brow dialed in, mouth pulled tighter. Hannah swallowed, wishing she could take it back. They didn't need her infection of negative. Up. Up.

"Is Steve awake?" Hannah said.

"I don't know. I told you already. God, call him. You all have the radios." Hand swatting, Lorna went to the kitchen and the conversation dropped, chilled. Hannah cursed herself. *Damn it, Hannah. Fucking mouth.* She didn't want to bother Steve over the radio, having learned that lesson. Back in the kitchen the hum resumed. In a perfect save, Sherri brought up the dog, making Lorna the center of the questions and praise. Even better, Hannah could hear Lorna chewing between words. Hannah relaxed. They got the rhythm back. She sorted through the screens, looking for signs of people among the deserted homes and yards. Signs of Joyce.

Fifteen minutes later the conscripted Narlow van backed out from the Brusine's and drove up next to the Barracks rampway. Steve exited the driver's seat, Bob Sanders the passenger. Joyce exited out the sliding panel on the side. Steve apologized to the gathered, waiting faces, setting down the heavy duffel bag as Sanders and Joyce came in behind him.

"Where did you go?" he said to Lorna. "You said you were gonna wake me up."

She chinned at Bob Sanders. "I was with him. I rescued Baron."

"It's almost nine'o clock," Steve said.

"So?"

The question suspended, unanswered. True enough…

Joyce bumped past Steve, removing her tiny round sunglasses. "Enough with you two already. Let's get this going." She leaned inches from Hannah's face to a glass-cupped candle and blew it out. She went to the kitchen without a glance at her.

Taking a small rucksack, Steve disappeared to the back rooms while Hannah promoted the remaining pizza and coffee. Sanders declined, wedging the front door open. The tickle of cold breeze cleared the stifle.

"Should we wait for Tyce?" William said.

"No," Hannah said.

Sherri glanced at her, then William. "He just came off shift. It's fine. He knows."

"Mark's not coming?" William asked.

"No," Hannah said.

Ray asked anyone about the latest news from the outside. Lorna stood mute, sipping and looking away from Hannah.

In the office, Steve turned the CD player off.

"OK. It's time. Come here everybody. I need you to listen."

He set the duffel on the front desk, clatter betraying its content of guns. Steve's voice had the proper tone, Hannah thought. Brotherly. Tyce was more trusted than liked. He conversed cordially, but with a sting. Sardonic, William called Tyce, which Hannah thought polite for 'prick.' Some military men and women she'd known during the flu were similar. Tyce seemed to cultivate unease, indifferent to its wake. Hannah believed if it came to him or them, in the end, Tyce would cut the rope and leave them falling.

Plenty of bile flew at Tyce when everyone learned of the satellite phone and working radio. Tyce explained with the passion of a quarantine sign while Steve denied, claiming he wanted to tell the group. Absent pitchforks and torches, the group finally demanded and Tyce backed off, arms folded, as they rang 911 and number after dead number of every family member and government office they could recall. (It was striking how many numbers were lost to the dead phones. Nothing was written down). 911 was a recording, repeating EBN instructions, the curfew. *Stay in your homes, daylight travel limited to your zip code.* They were not sufficiently let down, so Tyce activated the police radio for them. Most frequencies were a dead, scanning signal, broken by a squelch and then oblique code letters and numbers. Words like quadrant, roger or a Babylon of curses and harangues – a clown with a police car radio and a message for all of you. Tyce and Steve related hearing the massacre of the D-Plex guards on the radio, giving words to those pictures on the long-missing digital camera the Essex Army had delivered. It was like hearing Custer's Last Stand, Tyce said. That is what a radio SOS will mean, he said. Coldly, firmly why. *Do you see my logic?* Tyce was firmly against going out today.

She could not abide Tyce's flip, forward look to Nothing. Whatever today might bring, Hannah valued its goal, its hope.

Steve had been suggesting it for the last week as things added up. There had been nothing from Essex, from anyone, since the letter and camera package weeks ago. Even the surveillance camera they posted toward the entry at Oakton Road gave them only blacktop, woods and grassland. A handful of cars had passed on Oakton or Heller Lake Road in four weeks. No tanks, no jeeps. No people. Helicopters were seen or heard occasionally along with high jet trails. One breezy day a blackish-grey haze drifted over, snowing flecks of ash and smelling of burn.

Unlike Tyce, Steve had abandoned the uniform. Today he was dressed in a black leather tab-collar jacket, its bulk stiff over the bulletproof vest underneath. He wore no visible LifeForce gear excepting the radio ear-piece. Jeans and hiking boots. Steve's nose had healed poorly, making his speech glottal and congested.

"Joyce and Hannah are both here on the camera and radio. You two radio Tyce or Mark if you need help. I already talked to both of them this morning." Steve said. "Ray and Sherri, both of you should get some sleep. Ray, first I'd like your help with my truck to move the road barriers. OK?"

"I'll do it," Sherri said.

"Fine. Good."

Yesterday Hannah worried it would be pulling teeth, but a crew assembled in seconds. Steve was the unquestioned leader. Lorna agreed to go, shrugging. She was a known quantity to most people in town, and sending a pretty girl is never a liability. William went eagerly, believing he could help with powerful state government names to drop, however archaic. (*"Where have you gone / Will-iam Milli-ken?"* Ray sang). Sanders appeared most glum at Steve's insistence. Sanders' why met with Ray Dudek's sharp why not.

"They'll love ya, Professor. Tell 'em your opinion of the school system," Ray said.

Steve opened the duffel bag, carefully removing guns. "We'll have to be close enough to talk back, but what's the radio code? Anybody."

"A hurt knee means there's no trouble," Hannah said.

"Yes," Steve said, looking up. "William, what's the code?"

"If you say you're fine, there's trouble," William said.

Steve pivoted to each face. "So, if Hannah or Joyce or anyone on the radio asks what's happening and there's no trouble, what do you say?"

"You, or Lorna or Robert has injured their knee," William said.

"Or you, William. Correct." Steve said. "A hurt knee means everything is OK. If it's bad or dangerous then you report things are fine. Does everyone understand? OK. Next. Here are your weapons. Emergency only. These are all to be kept out of sight."

William was handed a big, army-style pistol, Sanders a sawed-off double-barrel shotgun. William set his on the desk and stepped back.

"It's only for your protection, William." Steve said.

"No," William said, quietly, shaking his head. "No, thank you. I don't want it."

Steve held it up the unwanted prize, looking at the other two. From her pouch Lorna showed her own revolver. Steve set the handgun back into the duffel and pulled out sandwich baggies full of brass bullets and red shotgun shells, passing them around.

"These are rounds for each of the weapons we all have. So, if you have to use someone else's weapon you'll have a way to defend yourself. Or us. But no one raises a gun unless I say. Right? Is that clear? Everyone say yes if they understand."

He instructed Sanders how to open, load and safety the short shotgun. Hannah felt they all looked centered, even disciplined. The four were the right choice. Even Lorna. She could certainly charm and read people well and, Vern aside, Hannah didn't think she would overreact if counterweighted by three men. Second swallow today, calling it Faith.

"What about Kim?" Joyce said.

"Don't worry about her," Steve said, ignoring Ray's lippy jeer. "It's OK to be afraid but we all know we have to go out. Joyce and Bob ran everything down again this morning. Believe me, this isn't to scare you. But, we're gonna be out of power in less than 60 hours of use. There's no more fuel in here except for what's in your houses. Tomorrow we turn the well on for an hour a day. Even doing that we've got less than four days of electricity with our rate of use in here." Steve looked to Sanders' grim nod. "Then our water runs out and the only power we have for the camera monitors and the Barracks is what we get off the solar panels – if the inverters work right. I'm sorry, guys. It's numbers. I know we said we're going to try and rig -"

"Then why are we burning all these goddamned lights?" Ray said.

"Relax, Ray." Steve said.

Joyce commented on the transfer inverters, working between the generator and the panels on the Barrack's roof. They seemed fine, as did the camera batteries.

Sanders asked again about Tyce.

"Don't worry about Tyce. Any of you. Tyce and I are fine. Whatever you have been thinking and saying to each other. Look, this should go fine. Alright? No one's come in all this time, right? Maybe we don't see anything or anyone. If we do, we have the water to bargain with. It might work."

'It will," Hannah said.

"Right. They might have propane. We have water. We're nobody's enemy. We're going to my house and my Mom's house. Drive through town. See what we can see, trade what we can trade. And I do the talking for the group, right? Right? OK. Hannah, do you have the medicine list?"

Steve pocketed it, his voice pitching up, buoyant. "I heard a lot of good news this morning, guys. EBN said over 70 million people in the US have power up to 15 hours a day. Portland. Seattle. New York and most northeast coast cities are expected to have power 24/7 by next week. Some cell networks are already active in New York, New Jersey, Boston. Down south even, people getting fed up. They want all this civil war crap over with. It's gonna be over sooner than we think. We'll be back for lunch. OK? OK!"

Hannah clapped, calling out. Coaching. The group's smiles at her were derisive but contagious. She didn't care how they got there. Going to the kitchen Hannah kept her eyes down as they gathered, lifted, zipped, buttoned. Hannah resisted turning back, afraid she would never see the four of them again. Sherri asked for candy, if they could, for Sandra Rose. No peanuts.

*****

The guy on the van radio kept saying 'stalemate.' Lorna also heard it on Mark's radio at Hapfuck's house earlier, so it must have been someone's official new word. In the last couple weeks, radio stations were coming on and off every day. Crazy religious ones and billboard-type ones broadcasting messages from people trying to reach their families. Lunatic rockers and comics blasting ironic songs and cursing every other word. The dickhead radio and TV network was on a bunch of channels, coming from Texas and other states. When the government couldn't shut them down anymore it was funny how EBN stepped up its game, getting more like them, like TV was a month ago. The prof in Lorna's Media class had called it counter-programming. Some stations were sort of official but not, claiming independence, like they weren't trying to scam. Lorna recognized the guy on the idling van's radio. He used to be on Channel 7.

Lorna's hand almost went for her hoodie pocket. She smirked. Bored and reaching for the gone phone.

Hearing the revving engine and scoot of concrete Lorna turned to look through the van's rear window. Sherri driving, Steve's truck tires spun as the chain between his trailer hitch and one of the wedge-shape cement roadblocks locked taut and shimmied, straining. Getting traction, the barricade piece finally scraped toward its spot across the blacktop. Steve's hand flapping as he concentrated, *keep coming*. Hands in his coat pockets next to Steve, Sanders peeked over both shoulders, nervous. It would be a few minutes. Two more blocks to move.

Facing forward, Lorna zoned in/out on the straightaway blacktop, recalling the sensation of trees on both sides wrapping and closing up behind her, seeming forever ago, like she dreamed it. The buzz from her father's anti-anxiety Pelmycote crossed with two of Kim's traded Azalcets was rocking. Lorna always knew her parents smoked weed but when she found the cookie tin full of bud it really was Best Christmas EVER. After a few test batches, boiling it down and mixing the last of the butter, shortening, chocolates and whatever sugars, Lorna made some killer candies. One for breakfast, topped by coffee and she was untouchable. Gliding down the road behind five panes of glass. The judgment on their faces might as well have been raindrops.

"How come you didn't take the gun, Mr. Gallo?"

He lowered the radio volume. "Excuse me?"

"Why didn't you take the gun?"

"I've never fired a gun."

"What if you need it?" Above the seat, she could see the bill of his cap, his nose and the bump of his blue eye as he talked. Eyes don't grow, she'd read. The eyes are the same ones were born with.

Gallo scoffed.

"What if we're stopped and searched and they find the guns? Why hand a lump of red meat to someone like that? Why be a threat? Zen, maybe. I don't know. Of all my deaths I'd prefer not be executed at some ignorant checkpoint, thank you. If we're going to imagine what-ifs, I certainly couldn't have come up with all of this. *What if?*"

Lorna nodded, biting down a flash giggle. A handful of meat?

"I always said something like this was gonna happen."

"No, you haven't," Gallo said.

"What?"

"You're 20-years-old, Lorna. You've never 'always said' anything. Anything you've said or thought is someone else's. Your parents, your friends. Something you read on your phone. A perfect example of why we're sitting here."

Lorna sat forward. *What the fuck?*

"I'm young, so I'm stupid?"

"That's not what I said. And you needn't take things so personally, you know." He craned back, facing her. "Because a comment isn't a celebration of you doesn't make it an insult."

"Whatever."

"Indeed," he mumbled.

After more on the 7:07 bombs, the announcer went to a reporter up in Lansing. 'On the scene.'

While Lansing and the metro Detroit areas south of M-59 and east of M-23 are solidly in government control with a gradual, if minimal, return to order and services, other areas are not so lucky. Much of the city of Flint remains under siege, in effect, by heavily-armed gangs identifying with the racist, terrorist and secessionist groups allying themselves as the American Christian Republic. Roadways and rail links into the city have been cut. Hundreds are believed to have been killed, attacked by gunmen when attempting to leave the city. Reports from inside the city say the death has broken mostly along racial lines with the vast majority of the dead believed to be African American and other minorities. Sporadic explosions, some believed to be mortar and artillery fire, have been reported, causing fires throughout sections of Flint, resulting in more dead and injured. Food and resources have become scare and the last attempt by state and National Guard forces to break the siege in September was routed by terrorists, many of them believed to be former National Guard. In northern Michigan – "

Gallo tapped to other stations, stopping on Asshole Radio. They were talking about the same thing, but totally schizoid. Like the killers were heroes, urging 'patriots to resist wherever they can'.

"This reminds me of World War II propaganda."

"Flint's only like an hour away from here," Lorna said.

"Yes."

"Maybe all the assholes who sent the letter went up there. Essex will just be regular people."

Gallo chuckled. "Be careful what you wish for."

The Asshole News came at your head like flash cards, coming back to specific words - Roaming. Black. Thug. Gang. Rape. Murder. Women. Children. Defend. Lorna thought of a boring movie this guy made her watch once - her boss at the bookstore. The only good part in it was a montage, where words and images flashed after one another. Words like Me, Mother, Father, God, Love. The images switched to what you were supposed to feel when you saw the words, going from friendly and nice to sinister and then switching back and forth. Like Gallo said. Counter-programming and propaganda. Fear fear fear.

"Are you afraid, Mr. Gallo?"

"Of course I am."

Her hand slid in the hoodie. The pistol weight felt good. She was in the tube, behind the glass. Trees folding in. Untouchable.

"I'm not."

"Good for you, Lorna,"

*****

Steve drove southbound, enthralled. He'd forgotten the joy of movement. His spirits bubbled to optimism. Trees zipping by, like you could drive past – through – anything. Get away from it. But caution still nagged. How many people had the same idea once they started? Watching helicopter news video of the highway pile-ups and fires made you look around where you were sitting or standing, a little short of breath and glad you'd stayed put. Steve thought of his parents and Doug and Jill and their kids and he was glad once again he didn't go with them. Alpena, 200 miles. Impossible.

They'd traveled nearly three miles. On a slight rise under rust, yellow and brown canopy shade Steve gently braked. An orange diamond 'Road Closed' sign straddled Trunk Lake Road in a near distance. Fifty or so yards behind the sign was a bitten-out gap. Jody's Bridge.

Steve stopped the van and lifted Sanders' good binoculars from the dash. The ditch of Park Creek was an earthquake tear, trying swallow the bridge, broken in half and sloping down as if the concrete had been chopped by a giant's hand. There were no visible people on either side, only the back of another road sign in the spotty shade across the creek. They could not get into Essex from the south. Steve's plan already shot. No hope of getting to both houses before visiting the middle of town. He levered the Narlow's van into park and stepped out the driver's door.

The door binged.

"Hey Bob. Come on up here."

He handed the binoculars to Sanders. "Does that look like it was bombed? From the air?"

Sanders disagreed. No debris, no hole. It looked like a center demolition. Lazy amateurs who didn't want to waste explosives or do it right and send it down at both ends. This was not the area where he'd seen the flashes and fire that night, Sanders said. It was west, in town. Just as he had told everyone.

"They did put up a warning," Gallo said when Steve closed the door. "They could have let us crash into it. "

Steve nodded, half listening. He wheeled and drove back north. A bad mark. Essex cutting themselves off. They were afraid, barricading.

"Look in the glove box. See if there's any kind of music." Steve chinned at the CD player. "I want to let them know we're coming. "

Gallo pulled three CDs. Two were kid's music. The third was *"ABBA Gold"*.

"Oh, I loved this record," Gallo said, opening the case.

Steve glanced over.

"Uh-huh. Well, wait."

In view of the camera at the intersection with Oakton and Cricklewood Green, Steve stopped and waved for the camera out the driver's window before he turned left, heading west toward town. He tried the earpiece mic, calling Hannah. Her reply cracks of vowels, distorted. The radio was already out of range. *Lowest bidder, kid walkie-talkie, made-in-Bangladesh garbage.*

Past the third mile, Steve slowed to twenty-five, approaching a ditched silver four-door on the right side. Many bullet holes pocked the trunk and rear window, both doors flung open. Frozen, as if Steve could still feel the flashbulb shock of its crash. He could picture another time with every cop and piece of equipment in Essex. Everyone jabbering, poking around the scene. Snapshots. Talk of the week. Everyone asking….

They drove another bright mile in perfect football weather before clearing the rise up to Essex. The shell of the D-Plex came into view on their right through the trees bordering the parking lot. Steve reached for the binoculars. The huge structure was weirdly intact, not burned out but almost as if under construction. The entrance a dark cave, free of any glass; the door frames probably winched away to more easily truck out the goods. Damage-wise the massive D-Plex sign was target-practiced to green pieces and dozens of cars had been towed or pushed to the west edge of the lot like swept storm-junk at a sewer drain. A few carts were loose among the yellow lines. Some flotsam and cardboard boxes. No Lifeforce AUVs, no bodies. A slow magnet of grave sadness pulled at Steve's chest. He thought of what should be happening here on a morning like this. People shopping, little kids. The missing souls, a massacred future.

Look. Look, you son-of-a-bitch.

Fuck. The word pulled from his lungs as a gasp. Guilt.

"Steve," Lorna said. "Come on. Go. Please."

"I saw someone," Gallo said. "He was by the nursery. He's gone."

Steve realized and released the brakes, slow rolling to the upcoming intersection. "What did they look like?"

"Camouflage, green. I couldn't see a gun."

The woods on each side were thicker at the turn south onto Heller Lake Road. A half-mile distant Steve saw the orange blot of Burger King sign. He stopped the van.

A black plastic banner spanned the road about twelve feet up, tied between two telephone poles. They'd put holes in it, so the wind could pass through and not tear it open. White letters.

NO TRESPASSERS. RESIDENTS ONLY. WE SHOOT FIRST.

A door-size piece of plywood was mounted sideways to another pole further along.

TURN AROUND. SAVE YOUR LIFE!!! spray-painted in neon green on black.

Windows shattered, a dark grey van angle-blocked the road. Close behind it a white Ford Focus blocked the right side, forcing a zig-zag slowdown. Steve dropped to first gear and started popping the horn with the side of his fist. He clicked the flashing hazard lights.

"Play that CD. All the way up. Roll your window down."

At a 10-per crawl Steve steered around the first blockade, shouting over the music, warning his passengers to keep their eyes open. Beyond the high-grass drainage ditches the autumn-colored poplar woods were still heavy with undergrowth, dark and shadow only a few feet in. Steve's gut knotted, flight genes pushing the juice. *Slow it down.* Squinting through the glare, passing the two-car barricade, he took it up to fifteen, straining the low gear. Steve wanted to let anyone know the circus was coming to Essex. Horn honking, lights flashing. Just friends. All white. Just like the song. *Ha-ving the time of / your life....*

The Burger King's windows appeared completely, cleanly blown out. A layer of glinty snow glass around it. The few cars in the lot were shattered similar, two of them burned. Across the side street leading to the old school and the church and more homes, the city building and adjoining police station had been torn open by powerful explosions. The police station's entire south wall was collapsed to a charred interior. Two military trucks and a trailer-towing Humvee in the parking lot had burned a roasted black to their chassis, punctured by fist-size holes. The bottom of a red "J" was still visible on one of the green truck doors.

Further south, after more woods and a few homes, they passed the vacant Giant supermarket. Some of the windows looked damaged but its long, whitewashed glass had mainly escaped destruction. Don Wilk's auto shop seemed normal, one of the work bays open. Steve couldn't see anyone inside. Whatever hit the municipals looked precise.

Lorna shouted out over the music, tapping his shoulder. They saw their first people. Steve knew them. Penny Housley and her husband, walking their dog on one of the side streets, coming east toward them. In sunglasses, fall fleece and caps, Charlie shouldered a rifle or shotgun. The old couple didn't slow down or run, their small leashed dog trotting away, barking at the van. Steve tapped the horn twice. He remembered their son. Big basketball player. News clips and All-State.

"Should we stop?" William shouted.

"Not yet. Let 'em get used to us. We're not surprising anybody."

Coming up on the swoop turn at the park, Steve decided now or never. Eyes were on them, no doubt. Shapes changed behind sun-glared storefront glass. Curtains moved. They could have been shot to pieces already from the woods or any doorway or window. Foot off the gas, Steve drifted over to the curbside just north of the bar, about 20 feet before the right turn. He clicked the key back and stopped the music.

Excepting the hulk of exception in front of them, Essex seemed more normal than not. A few clean, intact cars were parked along Heller Lake Road. A few fresh-boarded windows, but the seven buildings in view looked whole. Forward and to Steve's left, at the road's elbow, Miller Park and the creek beyond it had not changed. The faded, rust-tainted crests of extinct Lions and Elks and Moose and benevolent town fathers abutted the entrance and the park rules. BBQ grills and picnic tables among the sparse trees, the swings and the merry go-round. The exception being Miller Park's brand-new war memorial. The armored Humvee from the pictures. Its .50-caliber machine gun turret was in perfect position at the park entrance, Tyce had pointed out. It could swing to fire down the road approaches from either west or north. Perfect if it were not a drooped, soot-coated wreck full of the fist-sized holes. Burned-off tree branches outlined its consuming fire. Blackened tree bark ranged twenty feet up to a thin halo of singed leaves near the top.

An air attack.

Steve had been passed out, nose busted, morphined. People heard thunder or far doors slamming that night. Crump/thump. Sanders said he'd seen the streaks, the flashes of bombs. Tyce said Sanders saw lightning, miles off in the low clouds. Tyce said he didn't hear anything in the Barracks. Tyce said it was thunder.

Tyce mapping and taking notes. The sat phone, the radio. Tyce in the Airborne. Communications. *Where's the school? Where's the city building?* Fucking Tyce. He'd radioed it in, somehow, to someone.

Tyce bombed Essex.

A reek of sewer, like a smelling salt, blew through the van's open windows. Steve looked at Gallo, his pugged expression an approximation of Steve's own. People approaching to his left drew Steve's attention. Familiar faces, they hailed him in good surprise. No soldiers were seen. Steve smiled, opened the driver's door and stepped out.

"Stevie!"

In her same satin Red Wings jacket, short and round Glenda Trebish squeezed Steve, toe-jumping to mark kisses on his cheeks. Steve's back stiffened to Glenda's hug, squirming from the pressing weight of the pistol in her hand, hoping her finger wasn't on the trigger. Steve looked up at the second floor of the faded maroon and white A-frame across the street, "For Sale" still on the covered porch rail. Glenda's older brother Danny Trebish stood in the de-framed window hole with a scoped rifle, behind some kind of wooden barricade, maybe a flipped table. Danny followed his shouted greeting with a wave. Steve waved back.

Next to Glenda, Dave O'Hara and his son, Matt approached. Steve figured Matt was about 12 now, bumping around inside what looked like an Army Kevlar vest in grey/green grid camo. Steve had drank with Dave-O a few times. His son liked to play hockey – street in the summer, frozen rink in the park all winter. Good guy, quiet, did auto body and car painting down in Pontiac.

Dave-O hefted an AK knockoff rifle with a curved magazine, pointed down. A thin brown strap was tight over Dave's black Harley eagle T-shirt, connecting to the bulge of shoulder holster under his dark blue down vest. Steve put his hand out. They shook.

"Good to see you, Steve," Dave-O said. The beard was new since Steve had seen him last, back around Labor Day.

"Hi, Matt," Steve said.

Matt glanced at his Dad first. Wide eyes circled dark.

"This is Steve," Dave-O said. "You remember him. He was a police officer. He's a good guy."

The boy's blaze-orange capped head looked up. "Hi."

"Alright" Steve said when Matt accepted his shake. "Now I know we're safe."

Glenda pocketed her handgun, brushing her straight, greasy brown hair off her acne-pitted cheeks. The fingers went up in desire to touch Steve's bent nose, her lips pursed in imagined pain.

"Sarge?"

Over his shoulder Steve saw Jim walk around the front of the van, wiping his hands in a belt towel. They patted in the embrace, grunts of affirmation. The hands communicated. *This*. They patted. *This was real*. They were making it, still.

Cronc's bandanna-wrapped head knocked back, hooting when Lorna stepped out of the van's slider. "Ahh! Nugs!"

"Jimmy!" Cronc's red "Marker's Mark" T-shirt bulk and tattooed arms enveloped Lorna and lifted.

"It's so good to see you," Lorna said. "I'm so glad you're OK." Setting her down, Cronc backed up, looking them over. "What happened to you man? Is Doug here? Wha…?" Cronc's expression slackened, preparing.

"I didn't go with them," Steve said, thinking - stay vague. He glanced at the park and the destroyed Humvee. Following to the right, along Heller he could now see one of the apartments over a vacant storefront blackened and busted-out. The sewage odor knotted his stomach.

"They really got you guys, huh?"

"Well, we got bombed, yeah. A few weeks ago. Where have you been, Sarge? Nugs. Jesus, I never thought I'd see you again."

"I've over at the development," Steve said. "Cricklewood. We brought you some water. Twenty-five gallons. More coming if you want."

"Alright. Well then you will find yourself most welcome, brother. You can smell spring the air, right?"

Comically inhaling, Cronc grinned, toothy and yellowed at Steve and Lorna standing next to each other. His gleaming, sun-squinty eyes connecting the dots. He glanced at Sanders and Gallo now standing behind them, nodding a welcome.

"Sooo you're both out at Shady Acres?" Cronc's smirk went sort of leery and sort of proud, hand to his hips, head shaking. "I figured you took off with Doug and your folks, man. Are they OK?"

"They all went up to Henry's in Alpena."

Lorna stepped in to hug Cronc again. "We got bombed, too. My mom got killed."

Knowing Lorna was stoned, Steve's mouth went dry. Glenda and Dave-O cursed betrayals behind him - government motherfuckers and the names of the dead, the wounds and the skin taken. Their own fucking government bombed them. Feeling Sanders' nervous eyes snag to him, Steve glanced short, hoping Sanders got the point to stay mute. The best Steve could muster at Cronc's uneasy stare as he petted Lorna's long dark hair was a matched shrug and a grimace. Thankfully, Gallo jumped in Elks Club style, glad-handing with the shake and introductions to everyone. Sanders followed, acting the part. Shakes and names. Glenda, Jim and Dave-Os faces seemed accepting of the groomed white men. Highwayman regulars Dave and Glenda seemed happy to see Lorna again, giving tighter hugs and sympathy for her loss. Thanking them, the dumb bitch seemed half-surprised at her own lie. Wishing for water or vodka, Steve's tongue and mind thrashed for a story, a means get in front of whatever

Lorna's fantasy could trap them in.

A shifted breeze briefly pushed the stink away. Far off, a chainsaw motor revved, slackened, revved and roared into something. In the saw's brief halt was an echoing, deliberate thump of hammer to wood. Steve became aware of puttering generator motors, like frogs at night, before the chainsaw started again.

"Don'tcha love the smell?" Cronc said. "The great outdoors, eh?"

"Sewer line?" Gallo said.

Cronc nodded, looking off a moment up Heller. "Yep. When they cratered the school and all the dudes in it. It blasted the sewer main open. We've got people out finally trying to get some help on that. It's funny. Bob Diskin was just talking about your dad and Doug the other day. We could really use them around. Hey, maybe we can use some of his equipment? Is it still all in the barn?"

Steve laughed. "I hope so. Bob here is an engineer. Can we take a look at it?"

Cronc squinted at the sun and glanced at Dave-O so quickly Steve couldn't read Dave's reaction. Cronc shook his head. "It's probably not a good idea right now."

The saw cut between the hammer's thumps.

"Water though, huh?" Cronc nodded at the van. "Thanks. That'll be good. Very welcome. Let's get you guys set up."

Cronc led everyone into the bar, assuring them the van would be safe where it was. Glenda came along but Dave-O said he'd be outside, thumbing to rifle to safety. He reminded Matt to say goodbye to everyone.

Stepping up into the music and smell of hot food Steve realized his hunger muscling all else aside. A full stomach would help him think and if the Essex militia were going to kill them, they would have already. The menu chalkboard promised Goose Stew and Rice while it lasts. TWO Drink limit per day. THIS MEANS YOU!!!!

Steve knew all five people in the bar, only one of them pushing the wrong button. Windows and the open doors lit the place well enough. Two visible firearms. One pistol on Mike Sylvester's hip and a pump shotgun leaning next to Don Wilk, the mechanic. Wilk sat alone further back, by the darts, just behind the side exit's shaft of sunlight. Randy Stubbs was into it deep with Mike Sylvester. Mike inhaled a Marlboro long, shaking his head at Randy's spiel. Mike's wife, Patsy, sipped from a sweaty can of orange Fanta. Steve had always known Randy as Stubby. Everyone did, and Randy grew into the aggressive flex and scowl of a man named Stubbs who was just kissing 5'7. Two grades under Steve and snow-white goatee already, Randy's silver wire eyeglasses made him owlish. His cigarette smoke drifted around and under the brim of the black red-eagle 'Ruger' cap tight on his crewed head. Randy's truck had a red J sticker in the rear window. He hung around at Teddy's. Randy was in the background of one of the threat-pack pictures. Stubby might be a problem.

"Bullshit. It's like they say about the water in Detroit. They say there's water. They've been saying it for weeks. That's what they're telling you, but you don't know. They tell you anything and you believe it. Everybody. Fucking sheep. Go get slaughtered." Stubby exhaled, dismissive, from Steve's favorite stool at the bar elbow, by the metal Marines placard.

"OK, so, Stubby." Mike blurted, trying to wedge a word. His silver-hair neck rippled. Mike was a long-haul trucker. Or had been. "Stubby. Did -"

Patsy turned to her right, wide face brightening upon seeing the group. Her wavy, greying hair was clipped back. Steve noticed her red stud earrings.

"Baaaaa." Randy bleated, whining. "Please just don't hurt me. Baaaaaaa."

"Shut the fuck up for a second. You ever see a Roman, Stubby? Like from Ancient Rome?" Mike said. "No, huh? How do you know they existed? How do you know there was an ancient Rome? Prove to me there was an ancient Rome, Stubby."

Behind the bar Cronc looked at the four travelers under brow, tipping in the argument's direction, side voiced. "This goes on all day. Different people, same shit. Over and over." He reached back and juiced up the CD player. Rolling Stones.

"Hey, look. The cops are here," Cronc called out, walking through the split doors to the kitchen. A handful of mirror-row bottles remained, spaced on the shelves and all less than full.

After the cut of silence everyone made hails and hellos. They all remembered Lorna but Steve's pressed finger into her thigh cut-off her opening mouth at the smile. Even Stubby nodded.

"I thought you were dead, Dominski."

"What makes you say that, Stubby?" Steve said.

"What I heard. The Lifeforce Corporation. You guys a have pretty low survival rate these days."

"Wouldn't know. I'm unemployed," Steve said.

Don Wilk's shape waved from behind the door light. Steve asked about the shop.

"Still standing," Don said. Steve's reflexes caught when Don stood, grabbing the shotgun.

"Tell Jim thanks for breakfast. I'll see him later," Don said to none and all as he left out the side door. The observing side of Steve churned, noting the exits and the bar mirrors for movement in the bright street behind him. Don rounded the corner, walking north. It was one rocket, Steve decided. Not a bomb. They got hit with one rocket. Lorna's mother and Mike Narlow were the two dead in the two dug graves. Not to be mentioned unless someone else did.

It's just a shot away...

Jim came out with four plates. A bowl of goose stew and seasoned rice on the side. Four cans of cold Lite. Steve dug in. Chock full of vegetables and potatoes, the stew wasn't bad, its warmth best. Lorna sniffed it, asking about goose.

"Finally solved *that* problem," Mike Sylvester said, laughing. "No one was sorry to see them go. Flying shit machines."

"Aren't you scared of the DNR, Mike. Where's your permit?" Stubby said.

Everyone ignored him.

"How are you managing cold beer?" Lorna took a polite spoonful.

"Oh, everything fried." Cronc's hand cleaved the air. "But they gave me four brand new refrigerators from the D-Plex. Carol's got three. I keep 'em on at night and I can make enough ice to keep things cold during the day. The J-Fucks only stole the diesel fuel from the BP. Gasoline-wise we're still pretty good. For the generators."

"Where's Robin?" Lorna said.

"Upstairs. She'll be down later. She's doing good. As much as anybody is. We're making it work."

"Good," Steve said.

"I'm sorry about your Mom, honey" Glenda said. "Do you remember Henry Poole? He got killed by the bombs." Her grey-blue eyes included Steve in the death notice. "Robby Trella, too. God, poor Henry. There was nothing left of him. I only knew because of his tattoo on his arm. And all those guys…"

"Bullshit, Glenda," Cronc said. "I'm not lighting a candle for Henry Poole."

"Nobody asked you to light a candle, Jimmy. That's cruel."

Cronc cracked open a Lite for himself. "He never helped anybody. He never paid any support for those kids. But he buys his new truck tires and drinks here and buys his fucking guns. Don't tell me about Henry Poole, Glenda."

"It is cruel, Jimmy. And disrespectful after all they brought you."

"And I'm feeding everybody with it. *Respect.* Fuck," Cronc said.

"I don't owe Henry or Robby or Margol anything but the truth. *Robby*. Robby was a dick and that's *all* he was."

Cronc stood in front of Steve. "Everything they stole from the D-Plex? They go door to door with food and radios and TV's and water cases. 'Oh, what great guys we are. We're the Christians, we're the Americans.'" He faced Glenda. "They killed all those guys. And you think they didn't kill those people back there on Roscoe? And those Bangladesh kids? And they had to fucking camp HERE. Was it worth your new TV, Glenda? And the cookies?"

"It should have sat in the store? The soldiers were just trying to protect us, Jim. You know how many laws we're breaking right now just sitting here? We don't have any rights anym – "

"Amen!" Stubby shouted. "We're an occupied country. And that's all we- "

Cronc leaned his head back, rocking his legs. "Oh, harder, Stubby. Harder. You know how I like it."

Glenda looked at the four travelers and shook her head, seeking sorry agreement. Steve forced a nod.

"Killing, stealing. I guessed I missed that in church," Cronc said.

"Yes. Feed the hungry. Clothe the naked. *They* did martial law. Then they bombed us."

"These people don't want to hear it, Glenda," Patsy said, zipping her sweater up. Her voice both butter and brittle. Patient eyes. "Nobody would have gotten bombed if those creeps wouldn't have camped here. Jim's right. They picked us so they could hide. Henry and Robby Trella and them loved it. Well, they got it."

"Hey," Glenda said, pointing to Lorna. "She lost her mother to them. They got bombed, too."

"I'm sorry." Patsy looked away, right hand lifting to her ear, tucking a lock of grey curl.

"It's alright. We got some payback this morning," Stubby said.

Lorna's lips parted. "It's…"

Steve poked her thigh.

The four travelers went into their stew and rice, letting the bar conversation volley, tire and fade. Cronc came out to clean Don Wilk's table. Glenda rose and hugged Lorna once more, kissing Steve on the cheek. "Nice to have you back, Stevie," she said. She bid goodbye to Gallo and Sanders, assuring welcome and walked out. Steve exhaled, feeling the bike slow down and control settle.

"How's security around here?" Steve said.

"I thought you were unemployed?" Stubby said.

"Fuck you, Stubby." Carrying plates, Cronc lifted the bar flap.

"Men protected their families before there were lawyers, Jim," Stubby said. "If I see some spooks breaking into your bar I'll read 'em their rights and call the ACLU."

Mike Sylvester sipped from his can. "Too bad there ain't zombies. Stubby'd be happy as shit. Mr. Walking Dead."

The stew grew gamier as it cooled. Steve reached for the salt. "But security wise people are acting pretty stable?"

A pause caught the room. All but Stubby looked down, away.

"We're safe. No break-ins or anything I've heard about." Cronc said, pouring Clorox into the work sink. "Except for Tommy Bolger."

"Cocksucker," Mike mumbled.

Patsy glanced over, hushed. "He cooked up, went nuts. He killed Katie. Cut her."

Steve's appetite vanished. He pictured the last time he talked to Katie Renfrow in the D-Plex. *Tommy Bolger*. Taser Tommy, the naked squirrel runner. Katie was a teacher in Gavin. Steve thought Tommy straightened out. Mandel was one thing, but Katie was Steve's first known death to this split-open vein of insanity. Worse because he could still see yesterday, see Katie. Steve pushed his plate. He could have. Should…

Hard to tell. When all your love's in vain…

"I guess it's good he did himself, too," Cronc said, taking the plate. Everyone had ceased eating. "Saved us having to deal with him. There's enough on people's conscience."

Mike nodded and stood up off the stool to lean and drop his empty Fanta can into the basket behind the bar.

"Lots of people itching to kill somebody," he said. "Good thing most of them got killed first."

"Is anyone else hurt?" Gallo asked. "We have a doctor."

At the mention of a doctor, the cases flowed from each local, expounding, correcting and overlapping. Blown-out hearing and injuries from the bombs. Injuries and burns from a propane explosion. Gunshot grazes and wounds. General sickness and infections. Gallo pulled a pen and pad from his green jacket, scribbling the dictation with sharp nods and raised fingers to slow them down.

He paused, looking up for the hook of his proposition. "We do need medications. Were there any left from the pharmacy?" Gallo said.

"Pharmacy?" Patsy said

"I presume they looted the D-Plex pharmacy when they took the TVs?" he said to various faces. "I hope. Unless they're still in there?"

"The Army medics got killed. Whoever the spies are knew where their clinic was. They bombed that, too," Stubby said directly at Steve.

"They had most of the drugs, " Patsy said. "Cheryl knows where the rest are."

"We gotta keep the pills locked up," Mike said. "Bet you didn't know how many junkies we have in town."

Steve knew. He had arrested them. He asked about Cheryl Peotgen. She was an RN, older woman, who worked at Gavin Hospital. Ash blonde and bubbly, a cawing laugh. Cheryl was most known for her affair with Bob Diskin the contractor back when there was a village manager and a police force and Diskin was a trustee. The saying went - *You can't sneeze in Essex without someone offering you a Kleenex.*

"Cheryl's doing her best," Cronc said. "But a doctor? That would be sweet."

Patsy bolted up, scooping car keys off the bar. "Wait here. I'll be right back."

Steve glanced over, surprised when Sanders asked unprompted about the sewer.

Leaning back, Cronc straightened. "Well, we've got the people with the know-how. They tried, but the problem is the heavy equipment. And the pieces. You'd have to bring 'em in on a semi and the fuckers blew up most of the bridges. Bob D, Gerry Schaefer and Harv Kosik, older dude from Gavin. You know him?"

Steve didn't recall the name.

Cronc poured a bucket of water into the sink with the dishes. "They left, what, four days ago? To get help to dig it out and replace the main - when they were asking about your dad and Doug? The last thing we need is cholera. You hear about that? Down in Mississippi and Florida, I think? Here people are getting creek water for their toilets. Told to stop flushing, too. But you can smell how that's going. Who knows with fuckin' people? Who needs laws, right?"

Steve finished his beer. "People are getting up to Gavin?"

"Sometimes." Mike said. "Sometimes nobody comes back."

"What are you doing for drinking water?" Gallo said.

"It's not bad but, yeah, we could use more. Some of the guys built distillers. And there's still pop and juice and stuff. Rainwater. I put a barrel out for the drain. I've been using rain for wash water," Cronc said, nudging to the suds.

"Well if you can get us propane I think we can set you up with water. As much as you would need." Steve said.

"There's a meeting every morning at nine. Phil Gallagher's still around. We'll talk later; maybe bring your doctor out? But I think that would work just fine," Cronc said. "You got a big well over there, huh?"

"Yep, we sure do." Steve said at Stubby right between the shine spots of his glasses. Stubby grimaced, eyes moving to the front door and stopping. Steve could tell what Stubby was doing, fooling him to look over his shoulder. Refusing the bait, Steve used the bar mirrors to make sure and he was right. There was no one behind him. Stubby's psych-out failed. Steve's eyes edged back to watch Stubby drop his cigarette butt into his Pepsi can.

"Phil, huh? Good. Where's Teddy Gregg these days?" Steve said.

Cronc snorted. Mike swung his grin at the four of them. "After the bombs he boogied with his family and the rest of the GI Joes. They all stripped that place to the bare nuts. There ain't a tent peg left in there."

Steve stood. "We'll bring in the water. Lorna, c'mere a minute."

Outside, as his eyes adjusted. Steve's instinct to take a lungful of cool air was put down by the stench. The van seemed untouched, gun duffel and his knapsack unmoved. Further away a skinny dog or coyote sniffed at the wide-open northbound road. The hammering and sawing had stopped. Danny Trebish was gone from the window. Dave-O and his boy were unseen. Lorna seemed jumpy. Steve sensed eyes on them.

"It's not too bad," Lorna said. "I thought it would be some *Resident Evil* shit here, you know? God, it feels good to be out. I don't want to go back yet. Do you?"

"Nugs, huh?"

"It's just Jim. Oh my God. Is that what this is? Poking me? Fuck you, dude."

He didn't want to look at her, but the burnt-up Humvee was worse. The drying, reddening tree tops beyond, across the creek, were bright in the sun. Steve thought on how many times he had stood in this spot, drove this turn. So many times and he could touch none of it. Like none of it ever happened. But it did.

"Why did you say that?"

"Say what?"

"About your mother."

Her voice dropped. "I thought we wanted them on our side? If you're in a Lions bar you like the Lions, right?"

Steve had never broken-up with someone. Thirds dates were his usual max-out. Getting ready after Lorna left him to sleep, Steve thought about how he would go off on her. Over the last few weeks Steve learned enough about Lorna to make it hurt, make her hate him. But under the sun he turned, resolving not to leave it childish. Lorna's squint and puckered mouth were trying to figure him in this instant. He took the satisfaction, leaving the comeback.

Like everyone, stressed hunger had wilted some of her features. But the fine-edges of Lorna's eyes, the assured set of her lips and graceful chin still wowed him. The vertigo of looking into anything you ever wanted at the cost of anything you'd ever have.

"Send Sanders out, would you? I'm going to my house with him. Stay here with William. Keep him out of trouble."

"Trouble how?"

"The way William's looking at Jim? I think he's in love."

*****

Sunk in metaphor, Sanders regarded the tract homes and sun-speckled autumnal yards full of poplar and willow like a convict in a prison bus. Dominski drove slowly on the pot-holed streets, without comment when the pair passed a white aluminum home appearing shot full of holes. Just folks 'round these parts.

The guard's eyes remained passive, watching the road. Sanders remained silent. All morning Dominski's attentions to Sanders were indifferent or overly condescending. Sanders sensed questions being a short ration in a place like this. Two granted per day. This means you. Sanders pressed back into the van's seat, rode the bumps and endured.

Dominski parked in the long driveway of an added-on ranch home, behind a double-rear wheel RAM work truck. The driveway extended past the gated back yard to a tall pole-barn. The house appeared deserted but locked-up, grass overgrown, flowers drooped dead. Dominski took the ignition keys.

"Wait here."

Dominski unlocked the door, entering and closing it behind him.

Inside the bar, Sanders had never been among people so placid, yet volatile. Brimmed with belief but without emotion. Whatever roles Dominski and Lorna were adapting, Sanders wanted no part of. Regardless of any forced kneeling he may do (oh, the metaphors) Sanders only knew he was an alien here. For all their petty jealousies and nursed grudges, in the end everyone in this town was allied. In the bar their babel of lies, fact fragments, proclamations and ghost stories compounded until Sanders' urges were pushing out of him in twitches. To stand and scream at them, pound on the polished bar. *No! No! No! That's NOT what was said! That's NOT how it happened! That's NOT what is happening now! You ignorant...*

When?

When did reality's certainty transmute into our nonsense fantasy conversations about faeries, elves, secret offices and Martians? When did nonsense parlor fantasy infect the conviction of reality and certainty?

He imagined some tribal whistle among them, a call-out Sanders would never here. Anti-bodies in blue denim erasing him, the alien, like a germ when it came time. He sat in the van tacitly bovine. A hostage. The conviction behind a swung hammer or pulled trigger mattered not to the nail or the target.

Nosed-up by the clanging, Sanders peered past the work truck. From inside the back yard Dominski opened its gate and returned to the pole barn. Looking around, Sanders noticed a few of the nearby yards had been mowed recently, within weeks certainly. Despite the faint whirr of generators any of the few low-slung homes among the wide, bushy lots seemed abandoned. Excepting the war damage, he could not discern which decrepitude in Essex was pre- or post-.

Sanders made no move to get out, watching Steve load two propane cans and a rolled length of heavy chain into the van's rear. He seemed to expect no help, slamming the door shut and driving in silence. After two more turns, finally seeing a few people and passing another moving car, Steve parked in the cracked driveway of a small, unadorned bungalow, its patch of scrub lawn so barren as to have been mowed yesterday.

Dominski's head tilted. "Come on in. Bring the duffel." He reached behind the driver's seat for his knapsack.

They entered through the side door into the kitchen.

"Give me the bag. Have a seat." Dominski gestured at the table and pair of chairs next to the gloss varnished wall.

Pulling one of the flower-pattern vinyl chairs, Sanders could hear Dominski rummaging in an adjacent room. Resting his arms on the cheap table Sanders could see the huge screen TV in the front room. The loveseat. An empty glass on the end table. Footsteps descended underneath him. In the creaking loneliness of Steve Dominski's kitchen, Sanders chuckled up at the stucco ceiling. Dickens, *A Christmas Carol*. This, Robert Sanders, is your future. This will be the fruit of the horrible choices of your life. The person, "Bob", who will be in this shack of a home with goose stew in his guts, worried about ammunition and plague.

Dominski came around from the hallway carrying a roll of chain-linked, triangle-spike steel. Mentally Sanders' nerves drew back from its points and shape. He surmised it was a tire blockade, an anti-vehicle device. Dominski set it on the floor and sat across the table from Sanders.

"I kept it after my department folded. I can't remember why. Nobody even asked." Dominski said, curiously eyeing the thing at his feet. Wincing, he reached backward and removed a black, snub-barrel revolver from the small of his back like a loosened cramp and set it on the scratched Formica. Its bottomless black eye toward Sanders.

"Did you ever do that, Robert?"

Sanders didn't understand, looking at the weapon on the table. His breath went shorter. The call would come. He would never hear it.

"I mean, do something and can't remember why you did it?"

Dominski's eyes remained on his boots, the spiked chain spool, the scuffed floor. He pulled a chocolate bar from his leather's side pocket and broke off a piece. Sanders declined the gestured bar.

Of course, Sanders said. Everyone has.

"Why didn't you leave, Robert?"

The chocolate bit rolled in his mouth, molars working.

"I think I know why. But I wanted to ask you. Alone."

Dominski's bland, tired eyes shifted to him, chillingly indifferent. Sanders glanced at the pistol and he felt the organs in his body slip. Iced, his being and thoughts grasped, to hold on, pleading with his own senses. *No. Wait.*

Blind trajectory is always a bad idea, Sanders told Steve. The known is usually best over the unknown.

Dominski's face profiled back down at the tile, smirking. "I know what you mean. But somehow, I don't believe it."

Sanders shivered. No....

"I mean, you packed, with your wife. You had bags. Your car was full of supplies. I mean...your wife?" His eyes flared in a kind of surprise. "I saw. I watched you."

Sanders wished to dissolve. Sweat trickled down his armpits.

"You were talking with the Brusines. You, them. Both of you had been loading supplies all morning. Then Lorna came outside...and all that. You just walked back into your house." Dominski squinted at him. "You didn't kiss her or anything."

Sanders' mind whipped. *Kiss?? Kiss who??* His tongue scraped in the dry swallow. No. Impossible.

"Because of Lorna?" Dominski's right hand slid over the table, near the gun, his thumb tapped. "Everyone can tell, how you look at her. How you act around her."

Sanders didn't know. Sanders closed his eyes, gripped and hoped.

"I don't either," Steve said. "I mean, reasons, right? That's the thing. My family told me to come with them, up to Alpena to my brothers. If they hadn't *told* me, I would have gone. It was the *way* they did it."

Sanders blinked and blinked again, Dominski's face was forward, voice murmured. "I'm not sorry I stayed. I would probably be dead now. I *would* be dead. God…" He shook his head and from his jacket pocket he slid the keys to the van across the table.

"I'm not going back, Robert. Take the van. Tell them I'm sorry. I've got my Dad's truck and I'll be by tomorrow morning. To get Hannah and…help, coordinate. But I'm staying here. Sleep in my own house, my own bed. I know it isn't much." He shrugged. "But it's mine, you know?"

Vision curled at the edges, Sanders looked up at the cobwebbed corners, gulping air. A faint, directionless whistling encircled him. When Dominski stood in one energized motion, Sanders tilted backward against the chair, fearing he might pass out.

"Let's get back," he said, gathering the spike strip and the duffel of guns. The bag appeared noticeably lighter.

Pushing on the table, Sanders got to his feet.

"Hey. Don't forget the keys."

"It'll be fine," Dominski said as he walked. "I know all the stuff I said when we first got the letter. But those guys are gone. It'll be OK now. The guys they were talking about? Diskin and them? I can deal with 'em. Phil Gallagher knows me. He was town supervisor. I'll be able to do the most good here. Really."

Outside Dominski loaded the items into the van and refreshed the turns Sanders needed to make. "OK? Got it? Good. Tell everyone I'll be by around eight am tomorrow to pick Hannah up."

He took Sanders' hand firmly. "Thank you for everything, Robert. And one last thing? Don't take this the wrong way, but she ain't all there. I'm just warning you. She looks great, yeah. I know what you're thinking, but you don't want any of it."

Dominski leaned closer to Sanders' face, peering in. His touch was gentle, slipping along Sanders' shoulder.

"Hey, boss. Are you OK?"

*****

Stand down, trooper. Fly some flags. We've got beans and tuna and carrots and radishes and colored peppers. Tomatoes and canned yams. Pounds of rice. Tyce's two plastic bags - *'D-Plex has Gone Green!'* - were double-share full of his own portion and the Narlow's. The weight of potatoes, canned soda and even four fresh eggs wrapped in bubble plastic. Everyone got an egg, but parceling the spread in the Barrack's kitchen Hannah decreed Sandra Rose should get two from the dozen and Nurse Ratched's will was not contested, even if Tyce had half a mind to drop them on the blacktop. Such a random, anti-social act on such a Nice Day. The clouds of recent days had passed and the mid-day north breeze was making the dying leaves hiss. Tyce stopped near the road V, looking into the sun. He closed his eyes, glow spot trapped on his retinas, listening to the wind. The Essex, Free America, Jamestown hicks were just like us.

Aw, shucks.

Tyce walked toward the clubhouse and the parked RV. Let's play house, girls. Put GI Joe back in his action vehicle. He smiled. Sometimes the crap in his head just never stopped.

Rather than infecting the victory party Tyce left, certain he was not missed. The Barracks became a blizzard of female mouths, talking trade, talking future and writing lists. The closest thing to shopping in a long time. The bartender was 'darling', Gallo said. The old white-haired

Rotarian was in *Hello Dolly* mode, buzzed and swooning. The bad men were gone. Dead gone. Even Joyce was with it, buying the line Gallo and Lorna were unspooling. Joyce was smug in the vengeance of Tyce's airstrike as they told of its damage. He saw it in her face, accepting the goodies as some kind of retribution, up-close inspecting the dowry in her ugly hands. Because she was smarter than Them.

Tyce's questions got no traction over their volume. He mainly pointed them at Sanders, back near the door, seeming shook-up. Knowing or at least believing more than he was saying, Mr. Engineer shrugged and syllabled, mentioning broken sewer lines, the smashed buildings. He said there were some cans of propane in the van. He would transfer them to the well tank. Half-hearing, the women didn't notice Sanders slip out while they went through the boxes and bags. No one was watching the cameras.

"While they are a tad edgy, in the end they're regular people," Gallo said. "With Steve as a mediator it's perfect. We met one of the men in charge, too. Phil Gallagher. He's reasonable. I'd heard of him. He was a convention delegate."

"It's cool. Like, Steve wouldn't have stayed if – ", Lorna said before Hannah said something over the top of her, opening the snap-plastic box full of medications.

Let's trade some of those Prada bags. Ha ha ha.

Now they were a man short and no one seemed to care; not even his girlfriend, who seemed glad to have traded him for a cold drink. Tyce had warned Steve, seeing right through it. Never stick your dick in Crazy. At least she didn't shoot him. Or beat him with an alarm clock.

Steve. Steve Steve Steve. Steve's there. Steve said so.

Steve who took just, like, took the satellite phone with him. Steve who just, like, walked. Quit without notice.

Fuckin' jobber.

Parked in the short lane to the pool and clubhouse, Tyce unlocked his new living quarters, the Vanderkam's RV. He set his Springfield in the driver's seat and left the groceries on the short table. He could feel his mouth pulled down and soured.

His right hand punched the cabinet. Mother*fucker*!

Tyce removed the radio from his belt and the piece from his ear. Things were different? Fine with him.

After a few minutes of pacing, Tyce put his Dylan disc into the RV player. Pouring a three-finger of bourbon from Vanderkam's full bar, he flopped back in the bedroom area. It was nice digs. Using Vanderkam's manual they cut or removed any possible network connections and reattaching from zero the RV started and drove. Glad for the privacy and a real bed, Tyce kept the big windshield facing the pond. It was a good response position, in the near middle of the complex. It broadened their cover of the place. At night, Mark watched the north end from Hapgood's upper balcony. Staring up at himself in the ceiling mirror Tyce half-remembered a quote. Something something 'the gift to see ourselves as other see us'.

This was Iraq again. Command's promise of brotherhood with the sheik up the road. Areas friendly until they weren't. Now the J-hicks were the Hajis and the granite/stainless/cherrywood citizens were Command. Smarter than Them.

Philosophy. The bourbon helped.   Steve Steve Steve. Fuckin' Steve. Last night it was Tyce Tyce Tyce. *People are outside the wall, outside the gate. What do we do, Tyce?* The precious, adorable 'we'. Sort it out, Tyce. Take the life. Or not. In the mirrored angles Tyce could see the D-Plex bags on the short table. How did Steve feel about those bags and what they meant? Tyce looked up, back at himself, his LifeForce uniform. Currency. We. We promise to Feel Bad if you kill some hungry, scared kids. Thank you for your service. Tyce sat up, downing the last swallow, muttering along with Dylan.

And you don't know what it is, do you, mister?

Kim Narlow's "hey" was lukewarm. Her ass swung back toward the kitchen, leaving Tyce to decide what to do with the open front door. She wore jeans for once, no sweats. Closing it, Tyce followed down the dim hallway with the bags.

Kim sat hunched at the granite island, like a perch. Across the shaded, darkened kitchen a portable antenna TV played the Asshole News, small screen radiating on the counter like some outer space artifact. It had been Hapgood's desk TV. Behind her glasses, Kim's white face eyed the bags side-long, not moving from her chin mount. The jumpy screen light danced over a coffee cup, a Bic lighter and cookie crumbs on the granite. The stone and tile wrapped the announcer's voice and sound of roaring motors in a tinny, jarring echo. In recent weeks any news irritated Tyce. The bad stoked his anxiety. The good, jealousy. Twelve city blocks in Boston with lights? They have hot food and water? What the fuck?

Tyce looked backward at the closed blinds.

"Should I say ho ho ho?"

"What's in the bags?"

"Food. Fresh veggies, soda, beans. Even eggs. Four of them for you guys."

"Who did you kill for it?"

"I wasn't there. We're trading with Essex now. They got back about an hour ago."

Her hair looked washed, T-shirt clean.

"Really? Nobody died, huh?"

Tyce couldn't tell if she was surprised or disappointed. He set the bags in front of her. Her eyes clicked up, annoyed.

"Those eggs are chicken coop fresh, they said. If I were you I'd make them tonight or tomorrow morning. Maybe hard-boil 'em? You could make a nice salad with all this stuff." His hunger sparked.

She backhanded, eyes on the screen. "Keep them."

"Well, I'm not a dietician but protein's pr – "

"Eggs are gross. Cholesterol, bad fat. Chickens are full of hormones, antibiotics," Kim said out the unpressed side of her mouth. Gunfire and mortar sounds skittered around the kitchen, serious voices scoring the dead and wounded of an engagement in Washington state, near SeaTac. She tilted a moment, looking at the bagged food.

"You eat any of this stuff yet?"

"No."

"Who knows what it's all been sprayed with? That would be pretty funny. A Trojan horse thing for all of you, huh? All poisoned?" Nothing in Kim's expression was amused.

Tyce pulled a stool, sitting on the far edge away from her.

"Where's Sandra Rose? There's Skittles and stuff, too. No nuts."

"I chopped her into little pieces," Kim said to the glowing object.

Her eyes flitted to him. A shaked pity, sneering. "God…all of you. She's upstairs sleeping. Wanna check?"

"There's soda. Potatoes. You're supposed to put in any requests."

Kim sat up straight. "Can I get shampoo?"

"I'll tell Hannah."

She seemed to ignore the mention.

"Hannah would like to see Sandra Rose. For a check-up."

"Or what?"

"Or nothing," Tyce said. "Nothing at all."

"She's not getting near my kid."

"It's not unreasonable, Kim."

Kim nodded at no one down the side hallway in fake understanding. "Oh, so that's the word now? Reasonable?" Her electro blue/grey face met him full on. "What happened to unstable?"

Tyce felt the need to keep talking.

"Steve stayed in town. He left us. How about that?"

She reached into the bag. "I always kinda thought he was an asshole, to tell you the truth. Type A, up everyone's ass. Like Cuntface."

Tyce stood and stepped to the small window next to the refrigerator. He pulled the cord, lifting the blind. Strangely, the flood of daylight made the wood and grey more unnerving. He had been in all 20 kitchens and to a toaster all felt like science labs. Like no one ever cooked there. Not in the sense of too clean, but soulless. And it flowed out from there along the hardwoods, up the archways and beamed and coffered ceilings down to the carpeted rec rooms. The bitter diminishment Tyce felt inside the houses wasn't envy. Picking through the homes, Tyce felt they were riddles of another species. Unfathomable monuments of people he didn't recognize. Peltier knew....

"They even met a local representative. Gallagher something."

Squinty from the sun, Kim plucked and opened a Diet Pepsi.

"Fascinating."

"I'm sure William will tell you all about it. He used to be on the County Board or something. Nothing to worry about." Tyce could ride her sarcasm. At least it engaged her forward. "They're not the same ones who wanted to execute me or killed the guys I worked with, I guess."

"The Friendly Assholes, not the Freedom Assholes?"

"I don't know," Tyce said, his appetite waning. The kitchen was airless, with a lingering order of something burnt. "Steve's there."

Kim drank. "You hear about the prison breaks?"

"No."

They loved to pile it on. Everyone in the office earlier, talking about the morning's 7:07 bombings. Guesses hardening to gospel.

"A bunch of the prisons up north got blown open. All the convicts escaped or broke out." She pointed at the screen. "Everyone blames the other one. I'd bet the rednecks did it so they could hunt them down. They probably like it, ya know? Like that movie?"

"Is there anything I can do? Anything you or your daughter need?"

"Aren't you sweet."

A dark thing came over Tyce. It could twist weaker minds. She had no idea of the simple on/off once you accepted it. What Tyce could easily do. Honesty was the only way to belay the thoughts and extinguish them.

"You know, Kim, you could be nicer to people trying to help you." She smirked.

"You mean reasonable?"

Tyce said nothing. Kim's' face went to the TV, now without mystery, so cheap-looking in the sunlight, an item waiting to become junk. Her nods nearly imperceptible, counting. She picked up the Bic lighter and flicked it. The flame a tiny, jumping genie at her fingertips.

"Yeah. Kill people, go through their houses, take their shit. It's cool. No problem. But Kimmy's not being nice?" She blew out the flame and clicked it to life again.

"That won't do."

Just as Kim stood from the stool Hapgood's television cut out with a pop, grabbing their attention to the void, then at each other. By reflex they looked up and around the room in alarm before the EBN news cut-in midstream, signal louder and cleaner. Dozens of freight ships were lined up outside a harbor. Cargo containers swing-lowering onto docks. "The armada of world aid continues to arrive…"

Tyce released his held breath. Kim had stepped closer to him.

"Peachy. What's the waiting list to get my house rewired? Five years? So I can plug in all my broken shit?" Stepping in, Kim squinted directly at the small window's light. Her wrist flick-snapped the shade, re-darkening the room.

"You wanna fuck?" she said.

The fine simmer in her eyes and curled mouth made it a dare, clashing her casual tone. *Wannna play cards?* When her head moved to his right, out of the TV light, she became a demurred shadow except for the glint off her glasses.

Tyce laughed. She didn't.

"It's…your girl's up there." Tyce chinned at the ceiling.

"Well, I do," she said. Cheers from the box, an exalted speech from some official.

For a few seconds they both held, face to face. When it passed, her breath came in a settling disgust. Grabbing her Pepsi, she moved around him, circling the island and snapped the TV off, stepping over the line of extension cord on the shining tile. Her steps up the hardwood stairs were deliberate, without pause. For a dumb second Tyce thought to follow her. He reached back, pulled the blind up and walked to the front door.

*****

Spaghetti-Os warm in his belly, Mark sipped Kool-Aid and watched Spider-Man do his thing in hologram on the bootleg Chinese Whelp player. The afternoon sun had shifted west through the glass sliders, its warmth creeping along the carpet, past his hand and the empty bowl, across his thighs, now into the living room to firefly the dust. Cat-content against the sofa, Mark thought he might doze again even with collapsing skyscrapers in his ear buds. The resolution and the colors were amazing. The arriving smell was jolting.

Mark's head swiped left. Ray had folded into one of Sherri's 'show' chairs - so uncomfortable you wouldn't want to sit in it anyway. His dad's expression was both tense and exhausted, eyes pinched, mouth hung open. Face a rotten pink, white T-shirt wet at the pits, down his chest. A sheet toga-wrapped his middle, over his bare legs. Mark was relieved when the old man blinked. He yanked the ear buds.

The smell. God, did he…?

"Hey. How are you doing?"

"For shit," Ray said, eyes someplace else.

Mark slid up off the floor and walked to him. "What ha…did you sleep at all?"

"Barely, then I'm wide awake." Mouth breathing, Ray's eyes finally rolled up to see Mark. "It's my head. It just won't slow down. I can't sleep. Then I can't wake up enough."

"Want some water? Some juice?"

"No."

"There still tons of alcohol in Hapgood's place. Want me to get you some? It'll knock you out."

"No." Ray's exhaled, head shaking in a resigned frustration.

Mark leaned in, clasping Ray's shoulder. The stink was awful.

"Where's Sherri? Can I get you anything? Listen, did you have... do want me to make a bath for you?"

"No. Let her sleep."

"Listen. Dad. What can I do?"

"What? I shit myself! You think I don't know?" His arm snapped loose. "Let go'a me!"

"Fine! Good!"

Mark went to the hall bath to brush his teeth. He filled the toilet tank with one of the buckets of pond water, washed from the clean water pail and noted to fill both buckets before he left for post tonight.

Sitting at the never-used dining room table Mark continued sketching the gun-stash map he'd begun yesterday. *Tecumseh, motherfuckers.* Hapgood's SAW was next to the wall, bi-podded on unfolded cardboard, for the sake of floor scratches and Sherri and his Dads' bitching. Mark concealed his joy when Steve and Tyce had no interest in it. Tyce trained him on the machine gun's tear down and assembly one evening and, after warning everyone, Tyce had Mark fire a few bursts. And it was just...*fuck*! You could erase a T-Rex with it. Hapgood had 1,000 rounds in four 250 pouches. One in the weapon, Mark kept two more in his pack and the last hidden in the trees near the tunnel. Mark banking on holding off whatever with the SAW so everyone else could escape.

Vern's chopped FN was hidden in the Vanderkam's house behind the couch. Mark stashed his own SKS and two hundred rounds under the stove in the vacant house next to Sanders. One of Hapgood's shotguns, with a bag of slugs and buckshot, was behind a bookcase in the Grutta's house. Steve stopped by before the town run this morning, approving of the plan. Mark smiled remembering Steve saying it was a good idea to spread ammo and weapons around if they had to retreat, fire and move. Everybody could get to something to fight with or help themselves. Mark would make copies of the maps for everyone. He could imagine some fuckers chasing Hannah or Joyce or William into a house. Then they come out blasting. The look on their faces.

Through the bay window Mark watched him coming, Springfield across his back. At the knock the old man shouted the question.

"It's Tyce!"

Unlocking the front door, Mark could hear the old man shame scrambling to the hall bath, hustling off to wash his ass.

Tyce seemed distracted, asking to talk to his dad. Mark said he was getting dressed. For a hot second he wanted to tell Tyce about the maps.

"They picked up pills for him," Tyce said, walking past Mark into the kitchen. From his jacket Tyce removed three baggies with about a dozen pills each with a paper note in them. "There's extra food, too. Back at the Barracks."

"What happened?"

They were all good news words. But whether in his hearing or Tyce's telling, Mark wanted to push back from them. There would be other people now. Mark imagined everything coming back on, everything returning like it was. He felt fuzzed out, queasy. Like wanting to hit a pause button.

"You and I still keep the night watch." Tyce said. "I'm especially going to need you with me, Mark, with Steve gone. You understand?"

Mark nodded. He'd heard it before. "What did they say about the letter? What happened to the LifeForce guys?"

"Ask them. I wasn't there."

Walking toward the glass door wall, Tyce stared at the pond. Mark wondered what it was about his own face that deflected people's eyes unless they were yelling at him.

"You don't trust them?"

Tyce pivoted. "Fuck no. And now they have a guy who knows this place to the bare nuts."

"You think he's going to say anything?"

"If they start breaking his fingers what do you think he'll do?"

"We might have better odds with them, though?" Mark said.

"Better than what?" Tyce stepped to him. Booze breath. "You wanna join the Js, Mark? You wanna go against mortar barrages? Getting corn-holed by some chopper jock's flex guns? All that fun shit? Those fuckers are all going to die. Badly. You said you understood me, right?"

He had to turn his back to say it. "Fuck you, Tyce."

Tyce laughed once. "You're right, Mark. You didn't do anything. I'm being an asshole. I apologize."

Mark faced him. "I'm with you. Are you with me?"

"I said I was."

"Yeah? When Kim and Joyce and Hannah and everyone talks about what I did?" Mark flashed on Cricklewood Green filling with cops and troops and Humvees. Dozens of uniforms and suits and ties, throwing their hands and fingers around. Radio calls and barked questions. Interrogations, faces and voices like Tyce's, fucking with him, using his answers back on him. Himself alone in some little room.

"Don't worry about it," Tyce said, looking away. "Hey Ray," he shouted. "I've got meds for you."

The return of imagined worry.

What had been pulling Mark around the last few weeks, after the

Russian, was somehow easier. Killing the Russian sucked. Mark felt the man's fleeing soul scream out past him, no-shit supernatural. But it wasn't a ghost, or a haunt. No nightmares. He remembered it precisely, could slow the movie to pixels. No, the thing pulling him around since then was a million years old. He was now part of a tribe in the billions. Killers. Bad - rotten bad – wrong doomed motherfuckers, all marching through time, unable to figure the thing, one hand on the shoulder in front of you, marching, pulled. Unable to solve or resolve, do or undo. Fucked. Dragged. But that was OK.

Mark realized then, since he killed the Russian, he hadn't been worried once. Now it was as if Tyce had told Mark he was being gulaged back to high school. Now it was all going to come back. Worry about money, time. All of it would come back on him. Whoever controlled his life, set prices and decided what and who mattered.

The old man had changed into a pair of his dress-up suit pants, but still wore the gross T-shirt, Old Spice wafted off him, hair wetted back. Sherri kept his dress clothes hung in the closet of the spare room where he'd been couch-crashing lately. His old man, in the archway under the phony tack millwork, chest pushed out.

Mark pointed at the unzipped, too big, clowny pants, laughing.

"What?" Ray said, going for the pill baggies among the never-paid bills and Sherri's tourist-trinket junk on the island. "You sound like an idiot. Don't embarrass yourself."

"That's not embarrassing?"

"What?" Tyce said.

"He shit himself. Before you got here. Like this is better?" His voice throated a funereal moan. *"Ohhhhh. I can't wake up enough."*

Ray's head stayed down, tremoring hands opening one of the baggies to read Hannah's note.

"Hannah said they didn't have one kind on your list," Tyce said. "But these orange ones are a substitute. It's all on there."

"Can't you smell him? He hasn't showered for a week. Sherri won't even sleep in the same bed with him."

Ray dry-gulped a pill. Tyce had backed up, silent.

"If I told you what he used to do to my mom when she was sick? She couldn't barely walk and she still had to make him fucking dinner, every day. Remember the time you threw the ketchup bottle at her?"

"Jesus, Mark!" Ray said, choked. "Be civil."

"You be civil." Mark mocked the huffing man, turtled into his shoulder blades, hanging on to the island with both hands. "She'd be throwing up all day. But if he was in a bad mood after work you'd better not say fucking word."

Tyce was looking down. Mark grinned.

"My ass. You don't know anything." Ray said, dropping onto a stool. His palm smeared tears off his cheek.

"Your ass is fuckin' canal water."

"What did you ever do, big shot? You're a grown man and you're still a baby."

"I'm not a big shot. I'm an asshole, right?" Mark said, stepping, taking on both men's avoiding faces. "I don't know anything. That's what I learned, didn't I? Or maybe I didn't? Maybe I didn't learn a fucking thing. Nothing. Exactly what I was told."

Tyce turned and walked, becoming a door thump. His dad's hands went for the other two baggies' notes.

Sherri tip-toed to the kitchen tile's edge, hair tangled and squinting at them in her black and orange flower robe.

Mark leaned back against the sink. "Hi, Mom."

****

The squad arrived at the Highwayman before twilight. Grimaced teeth and wide eyes, road-deaf shouts over the seceder TV news, shucking strapped gear and short packs onto the bar and wood floor as their legs reached out in kinked strides. They seemed breathless, though they had all been riding. Dirt bikes and four wheelers. Six men were in the posse, buzzed on pursuit speed and big-day sunshine. Buzzed on nigger, spic, A-rab, a chase ("Little fucker was quick, wasn't he?") and a paid-off quarter-stick booby trap. ("Shit, would YOU pick up a can of beets in the middle of a trail? How stupid can you be? What was that thing they used to have? Darwin awards?")

Two of them Steve knew, Gordon and Andras. Gordon was an Afghan vet, a little younger than Steve. Two of the unknown others were in bike club colors - The Vanguard. Two Harley pistons making the black V inside the white shield back-patch. One of the bikers, introduced as Gordon's cousin, wore an SS lightning bolt shoulder patch. Another rider Steve recognized from hanging around Teddy's. He knew the tall, red-haired man from the fuzz-squawking law-enforcement hand radio he had set atop the bar. Gordon and Andras greeted Steve with backslaps ("What the fuck happened to your nose?"). He passed accepted nods to the others. They had been curious about the Green, they said, figuring it abandoned. (first lie). The Green bordered the state land and the troopers had blown the bridge north of it. Patrols where the boys were "finding anything" were mainly northwest and west, even tripping up to Flint one morning to check out the action. The posse seemed glad for the water agreement, topping off their canteens from Cronc's pitchers, welcoming the talk of a doctor in the Green. Cronc reminded them to keep their guns off the bar and they complied with apology.

After Sanders drove away, Steve hadn't been down in his bed twenty seconds before he jerked up in fright. Lorna's smell was all over them. Then he realized he'd never changed the sheets from that night, a month ago. His mind/guilt/conscience was NOT conjuring her. Still, whatever was conjured proved stronger and he lasted only a few minutes in the bed, especially when the silver hoop earring stuck his thigh.

Stripped to his boxers, Steve stumbled his too-lazy-to-change-the-sheets ass to the couch. He crashed in the long afternoon sun for a few hours, but it was broken by zaps of panic, knowing he heard something, knowing he had to be somewhere. The quiet in his house was strange. Steve tried the satellite phone to his parents' cell, Doug's cell and Henry's cell, knowing but not knowing. The same way he still flicked a light switch now and then. He left it on the coffee table, stood and scratched.

He dressed and took a walk, saying hellos to any people outside tending yards, filling generators or blanking on their front porches. The citizens told daylight ghost stories; repeated, refried and blended from the radio and TV news they didn't believe but couldn't stop repeating. The Government did it on purpose. Poison gas. Concentration camps. Women being rounded up and sold to all of the Chinese and African laborers being shipped in. There were pulled-in, pointed whispers about missing people. The executed Bangladesh family. The Pakistani family who owned the BP? Known and unknown men with guns were guarding it but no one had seen the couple or their son for two weeks.

Do you know anything? Is it going to come back on?

A thirst in their questions. Things were running out.

Steve walked to his Mom's.

His parents had taken some clothes and little else, it seemed. Walking room to room the feeling came over Steve gradually. Objects at first - his mom's September copy of 'People' confected in fine dust. The old man's ashtray and half cigar. The elephant napkin holder in the kitchen. A hair in the bathroom soap. In every room the house was decidedly different – not abandoned but feeling of death. A feeling these had become dead people's things. Seized by it, Steve braced his forearm against the hallway, breathing. He imagined – pictured - their corpses roadside. A dreading, hollow ache collided against his memories. But it was more. More than memories. The smells and the sun color of every room this time of day, every accumulation in the walls and carpet, put him back twenty-five years. Slumped in the hallway Steve could almost touch the thought; almost make it a real memory. Like a frightened little boy shot forward twenty-five years to see, feel and breath this moment that wasn't happening then, but would, someday.

How? How did it go so wrong?

Feeling as if he were being followed, itchy and needing noise, Steve locked the place and walked swift to the Highwayman, looking over his shoulder more than once.

"This is better than real life," Andras said. Steve wondered about the patrol's wives, or the women who put up with them. What did the women or their kids think about real life in these last few weeks?

Lorna. The one-nighter that didn't end because morning never came. Wanting to fuck, staying stoned, playing music and worrying about the dog occupied her universe pretty well. Let the wheels come off and ride it. Whatever. Her motto. Everyone's.

Whatever.

Sitting with his third beer, (Cronc hadn't counted his "visitor" beer earlier in the day) Steve's thoughts of Tyce turned fond. Away from him, Steve admired Tyce's quick mind, his reliability and balance. A good sergeant. Steve had to admit he underestimated him. Tyce never complained. Watching the bar posse Steve wished he had Tyce there right now; someone to be back-to-back with in the slippery fog of Now, where law and order had become men with guns. One of them lifted out from under Michigan State Police body armor, laughing through his beard at Gordon's joke. He dropped the vest onto the bar floor and napkined his bald head.

So many dead. So he could be sitting here, right now, with Them.

Steve remembered his mother's saying about family, usually on tipsy holidays with the wedding and funeral cousins. *Family always remembers to forget and forgets to remember*, she said. He never knew if she meant it good or bad.

The handful of other mellow bar stoolies were watching the low-volume seceder news in the oil-lamp and candle light when Cronc bellowed last call. Everything shut down at dark. Despite the headache – he hadn't eaten since the stew – Steve knew to stay in his seat, look over at them now and then, stay connected. The posse had quieted as they ate, asking for hot sauce, thanking Cronc and his sister, Robin. Pointed, pulled-in voices among themselves, ripped laughs and hand gestures between bites of salami, hard-boiled eggs and what looked like fresh bread.

Cronc came over. "Where did you get the bread?" Steve asked.

"Carol's baking it. You got food at the house? I'll pack you some."

"Thanks, Jim."

Cronc came back with a stuffed D-Plex bag. "Come by around eight tomorrow. I'll take you to the meeting. You gonna bring your doc back tomorrow?"

"That's the plan."

His beer gone and the posse patrol crew not noticing or caring if he sang ABBA stripped naked or disappeared for good, Steve took his bag of bread, salami, apples, two bottles of water and two cans of beer out the side door. It was still light enough to see. He looked backward at the rising near-half moon before walking west. Wondering about clean socks at the orange and purple sky, Steve did not hear the bullet smash his upper chest as he passed Teddy's abandoned store. Steve Dominski never came out of the shock in the last forty seconds of his life on the cracked sidewalk as Jim Cronc, Glenda Trebish, Craig Andras and one of the bikers ran out of the bar, guns up, trying to stop the bleeding, looking for the shooter.

By then Randy Stubbs had pulled his Winchester .270 in from the window, picked up his brass, was down the stairs and out back through the high grass, late to the night patrol muster. Stubbs knew he killed a Fed spy – a Blue. The airstrike was no accident. Who knew the town better than an ex-cop? LifeForce, at that. He turns up and starts showing his ass, talking like he was Johnny Law? Randy's search of Dominski's house confirmed it. It was probably the same satellite phone he'd used to call in the jets. That was all Randy Stubbs would need to show them.

Besides, Randy never liked the better-than-everybody son of a bitch, no how.

*****

October 18th

Tyce asked who it was, on the radio. Bonnie Raitt?

Sherri half-turned from the monitor's night green. Tyce was at the back desk, behind a reading light, face up from his book.

"No. It's Emmylou Harris and Graham Parsons. Bonnie's coming up though."

"I like it. I never heard this version before."

Sherri smiled. "Yeah, Graham was something. My ex-husband met him once. Brilliant but crazy, like them all."

Tyce leaned back from the wedge of light, white smile defined as his stretching form dimmed. Sherri had to admit the man had something. Twenty years ago? Another time and place? Yeah.

"Joyce was telling me about him." Tyce went on to anecdote an intoxicated memory of her ex's one Big Hit Song. Where he was, what he dosed. Suburban whitey mythology.

"Yep. Fucked up. The best way to take my old man," Sherri said.

"Ended up bad, huh?"

"Not really, no. I don't have anything bad to say about Gary. He was really a great guy. I haven't talked to him in about 12 years. But I look him up now and then, what he's up to."

Tyce laughed. "Gary?"

"That's his real name," she said. "Dalton was his middle name. Works a little better on stage, don't it?"

"What was it like? Did you meet anybody famous?"

Bonnie Raitt came on. Angel from Montgomery.

Sherri's usual answer didn't come, the pat one she spun when people wanted dirt. Tyce's engaged eyes above the faint desk light, the bizarre green around the walls, the dark corners, made her feel confessional. Unfolding with the sweet/sad realization it might be the last time someone asked or cared.

"I always thought of it like protecting an egg. The little bit of image and the things Gary had gained, you get so sensitive to them. They're so fragile. You do anything to protect it and keep it going. So you pretend you're more successful than you are, you're more happening than you are. Pretend too long and you get twisted up. It gets sad. It wasn't a healthy way to be.

"What about you?" she said.

"What do you mean?"

"Your gal. Your exes. How come you're not with your family?"

"Nobody. Never married." Tyce closed the book, eyes down a moment. "I don't know. The sad of it for me is I fucked over every woman who I…conned… into thinking she could put up with me. I'm not a day at the beach, Sherri."

"Nobody is," Sherri said. "You do kind of remind me of Gary in that way. Defying yourself out of being happy."

Tyce smirked, head tipped. "I've defied myself out of plenty. Would you like some tea?"

A muffled thump pinballed against the home's angles and through the Barrack's front door. Too expansive for a gunshot. An explosive.

Tyce was on his feet.

"What do you see?"

Sherri tapped at the screens, sweeping through the green images. "Noth – I can't. It's not the front. I don't – "

The console radio crackled to life with Mark's call. "Barracks. First Squad. Someone hit a mine. It was right behind me, my right. The woods. I'm up in Hapgood's. Sev- eighty yards in. I see the smoke."

Mark had sown a handful of homemade flashbangs through the woods on ankle wires, full of fireworks powder and charges.

"What do you see?" Tyce said, inserting and pressing his ear mic.

"Nothing!" Sherri yelled, misunderstanding.

Tyce was behind her, scanning the monitors. He touched her shoulder. "Calm down, Sherri. Go easy. Camera Nine."

The panning west camera showed clear tree line and empty road onto the turnaround and doorway of the generator building.

"First. Squad. What do you see? Over."

"Movement!"

A faint rip of auto fire from Mark's SAW sounded through the door. Sherri zoomed on the position. She swung from the blaze flashes of Mark's gun in Hapgood's balcony to the wood line, but the camera couldn't pan further into the trees. They could not see what Mark was shooting at. He stopped firing.

"In the woods," Mark said. "They're coming south."

Tyce gripped Sherri at the shoulders and turned her, adrenaline fountaining. Her eyes were set, waiting. His mind stamped the phrase *'good woman'*.

"Stay on every camera and report to me. Lock the door. Anyone comes through? Get to the vault. Protect yourself."

"I will."

He was out the door, into the dark dimension of cool air and echoing machine-gun fire, carrying the night goggles and his Springfield. At the bottom of the ramp Tyce crouched and tightened the rig around his head. The dimension came alive as a green new world. Flushed confident, he set the rifle across his back, pulling the Smith & Wesson .40 pistol, clicking the safety and racking one. The pistol would be easier to fire with the goggles.

Tyce ran low along the Barracks shrubs, pausing to listen. He could see the clubhouse, the fenced pool area and the parked RV over the thigh-high wheaty-top grass. Mark fired another burst, but Tyce heard no return fire. A better sign. Armed, even the lamest hillbillies would have taken the machine-gun out by now. Hannah's radioed demands squawked in Tyce's ear, then Lorna's mixed in. Tyce told them to stay put, off the air.

Tyce Tyce Tyce.

"First Squad report. Over"

"No movement," Mark said. "Fuck, the barrel flash. My eyes. Should I – we- redeploy? Over."

"Negative. Stay. Watch the truck." Truck was code for the well and generator rooms. "I'm moving up, First Squad. Do you read me? Over."

"Got it. Out."

Two-handed on the .40, Tyce swished through the grass in one sprint to the clubhouse. He crept between the gap of the building's east wall and the RV's rear, the wood line in vivid, shimmering green across the sixty-odd yards of grass in front of him. Aligned with the brick he lowered to one knee and aimed. Far up front the brushed-back branches and foot-snaps paused. Someone was in the woods. To his right, Tyce could clearly see the blacktop road and southernmost houses. Half-moon on the pond. Tyce's mind was clicking, tactical. He could slip underneath the RV and shoot anything coming from the east as well. But no. The fuel.

"Barracks report. Over." Tyce whispered.

"Nothing. Nothing's moving. Over." Sherri said.

Tearing, blow-torchy gunfire from the balcony winked through the autumn-thinned treetops. The SAW was a ferocious little mother and Mark was working her like he should. Short cuts. One second of roar. Two seconds, pause, breathe. Then one more. He was firing nearly straight west across the woods. Hapgood had packed the ammunition four ball to one. The fifth bullet was a tracer round. The tracers were glowing flints of lightning, some striking the stone wall like welding sparks.

"One at least. Maybe more. Going south,' Mark said.

The machine-gun roared.

"I'm walking them to you. Over."

As Mark adjusted the weapon the rounds started chipping down along the wall, skipping off the stone like lazy, lost bottle rockets. As if a swinging gate, the SAW's cracking piss of bullets was gradually easing south, chasing the invaders. The lightning bolts gradually heading for Tyce, until he would be looking into the goodnight, star-flash of the barrel. And Mark would Feel Bad.

Tyce slid back around the clubhouse corner. He heard the fever in Mark's voice. Firing at any phantom motion in the night-vision scope, Mark wouldn't realize his fuck-up until the RV exploded. A Dylan song came alive in Tyce's head, a staccato 21st century mix over the SAW's rip.

Advertising signs that con. You're the one. Never done. Never won.

Fucking asshole.

Life goes on. All around you.

"Hold your fire, First Squad. Over."

The machine-gun went silent. Tyce peeked north, around the corner. Something was moving again through the twigs, weeds and vines in the sub-sea green. Tyce eased the Springfield off his back, ejected the magazine and cleared the chamber. He slid the empty rifle behind the RV's rear tire.

A bird-like whistle pulsed from the woods. It repeated. The human in the woods waited and whistled again, signaling.

Tyce aimed the .40 as best he could through the goggles.

A long-legged male emerged at the wood line, free handed. No weapons Tyce could see. This was no Essex redneck. No J-boy. Teen-ish, bony, bare arms. His bushy, woolly head sticking up through a sleeveless sweatshirt. Crouching just above the grass, the boy's' face twisted right-to-left, listening. Tyce comfortably blended in the wedge of shadow cast by the RV. The boy's unseeing face passed over him, whistling again. It probably saved his life, Tyce thought later. Instant choice, from kill to capture. Intel.

There were more of them.

Hunched, the boy sunk and knee-crawled east toward the houses, looking like the hump of an alligator gliding through green swamp. Tyce aimed on the last trees before the blacktop and fired the Smith three times, just above the boy's head. The hump dropped from sight behind the grass. Tyce fired twice more above him. Aiming during a ten-count, nothing else appeared. Tyce rose and advanced with the drawn pistol.

Closing in, he could see the boy, clawed into the earth. Tyce commanded the boy to put his hands on his head. He complied. Tyce circled. With his left, Tyce pressed the ear mic. Sherri and Mark saw or heard nothing. Mute, the boy refused to look at Tyce, face pressing into the grass. Ratty tennis shoes, no socks. Belted, filthy cargo pants hanging off his ass crack. Dark T-shirt under his neck-ripped sweatshirt.

Tyce kneed into the kid's back, cuffing him. Patting, Tyce yanked and snapped free a biker's fanny pack from around the kid's waist, fling-ing it to the grass. He grasped and tossed everything from his pockets. Food packets, a can of liquid, other items. Tyce rattle shook a bottle of pills. By touch he recognized a Swiss army knife. Tyce went to the bottom of a cargo pocket, knowing the shape and weight of a pistol magazine, his thumb playing over the smooth bump of a bullet. But no gun. Someplace close, Hapgood's dog was going crazy with barks.

Periscope-like, Tyce's goggles scanned left to right, listening for the other silent night bird. The one the kid had been calling to. The one who had the handgun matching the magazine.

****

It seemed a long time since Ray checked his watch. Now about 5:30, maybe? Past false dawn and now they were back where they started after walking all night. The kid's body, in the trees. In the near daylight, the shot-up body was like a pile of rags and garbage in the grayish leaves with somebody's old shoes tossed in.

Ray made the report direct into the hand radio, hating that fucking hearing-aid microphone. No surprises in the woods and they walked every inch of them. Him, Mark and the girl, Lorna. Flashlight beams swooping up, down and sideways, Mark guiding them around his fucking booby traps. Sherri responded. The Professor and the two dykes hadn't found anything either. Ray pocketed the radio in with the pistol Tyce had forced into his hand, demanding Ray take it. Despite fog breath Ray unzipped his jacket, feeling the hot flash and the wetness at his pits and down his back. Part of Ray wanted to keep walking. Whenever they stopped moving he felt shittier. Because of the pills he was a little better, even though it had to be in his head. It took days for pills to really start working. He was glad he'd washed and shaved. His selfish tantrum had become embarrassing. Be a man already. People were really dying, for Christ's sake.

"Well, screw," Ray said, clicking the light off. "Let's head back. We'll do better in daylight anyway."

Neither of them seemed to hear. Mark kept beaming up into the treetops with that big-ass, square nine-volt. Ray wanted a Lucky, a cup of coffee and a warm seat. Besides, he wanted a good look at the kid Tyce captured. In his gut, Ray felt the whole thing was over and the whole thing was a panic. A couple kids snuck in and one of them got blasted. The cameras, people guarding. It worked like it should've. If some bunch of assholes were going to really come and take this place, everyone would know it. People can't accept what they see. Everyone over-imagining shit. Too many goddamn movies.

Squatting with a pen-light in her mouth, Lorna pawed through the dead kid's pockets and scrawny body. He was sort of balled-up, eyes shut, one corner of his lip raised over an eyetooth, glinting when the hard light crossed it. Like the kid's face was lemon-sucking the pain. He'd caught some of Mark's bullets fair and square across his back. There was a mess of soaked-in blood and some rubbery pieces of him spit out his front, through the grey-patterned blanket-looking thing he was half-assed wrapped in like Clint Eastwood's poncho. A bullet of Mark's had nearly twisted off the kid's right arm at the elbow, looking like jerked chicken. Ray felt nothing for the poor dumb fucker. You don't trespass, especially these days. He didn't want to get close to the body. Lorna seemed like she was kid Christmas playing in it.

The kid was darkish, not quite Arab. Maybe Mexican? Who knows. Longish straight black hair. Teenage fuzz on his cheeks, crusty black nails poking out fingerless gloves. But the blanket looked clean, almost newer.

"Whatta ya got there?" Ray said, click spotting his light on her.

Lorna spread out the small pile of things, near the kid's head. She didn't look up.

"There. I'm giving it all to Tyce."

"What's in your pocket?"

The hate in her turned-up eyeballs went to Ray's bones. She could have pulled that silver jobby-do on him that fast, just like Vern. Showing those little snaggle teeth she pulled out a cell phone.

"You ever heard of these, Grandpa?"

"Very funny. You think we might want to know he had that?"

She tossed it at his feet. "Knock yourself out."

Straining to bend for the phone in the mucky leaves, Ray tried the swipe, hoping it would, knowing it wouldn't and it didn't. Lorna stood, exhaling and rubbing her eyes. The dead kid's stuff was odd. A hand-sized roll of copper wire. A Bic lighter. A cracked-handle flathead screwdriver. Half a packet of Planter's peanuts – honey roasted. One of those energy bars. A clean, sealed bottle of water. Ray picked up what looked like a purple balloon. A thick, jumbo-circus kind. A few drops of what looked and felt like water came out. Kinda smart, Ray thought. You could fill it up, drink it and collapse it.

A dirty white rag with spots of dry blood. A clean silverware spoon. A green triangle block of wood like you would find in a kid's toy box. A clean, new looking two-D battery flashlight. But no guns, no knife.

"Maybe he's like mentally challenged or something?" Lorna said.

Ray clicked the light off. "Who knows?"

"Like, maybe they weren't coming in to attack us or anything. They were just lost, hungry, cold."

Woozy, Ray needed to start walking or sit down. "Maybe."

"It didn't sound like Mark gave them much of a chance."

"Same chance you gave Vern?"

He got the finger from her. She imitated his wheeze. A sound Ray never realized until it was spit into his ear.

"Enjoy your heart attack."

With a snap turn she was marching. Ray watched her blurry shadow move out past the woods, becoming a sharp, black female shape against the brighter clearing, moving down the dewed, shining road. He zipped up. The chill had come back.

Mark moped under the same damned tree, jaw drooped open, pointing a tower of glare up into the yellowed branches.

"What in the hell are you looking for?"

***

Tyce had handcuffed the prisoner's arms behind his back. When the nude boy shifted, the cuff's short chain snicked across the squat, steel loop mounted into the wall. It was the near-exact distance allowing for a person to almost sit on the edge of the cement bunk, exact strain. Feet nearly touching the floor, the boy scooted for a comfortable position, neck corded. A starscape of blackheads dotted his twitching brown shoulders. To Hannah it seemed someone had constructed the bed, the loop and this cell with this very moment in mind.

Hannah flashed on her teenage class trip to Europe. Dachau. The guide described the refined structure of the death camp. She recalled there was a precise distance allowing for two men to grab and two-hand toss bodies from carts into the ovens without having to overexert themselves. Someone had planned every aspect.

Blinking to the now, Hannah sniffed deeply and rubbed her neck. She'd barely been asleep when the shooting started. With approximately six hours of sleep in the last two days, her focus kept blurring. Optimism was now a difficult math problem, all the more frustrating having known the answer yesterday. She set her stethoscope, placing it at the boy's back. His lungs were clear, breathing slowed. The injection had taken any fight out of him. He even accepted the thermometer under his tongue.

The boy had been living outdoors, but not for long. His vitals were normal. The malnourishment was obvious and a yellowing in his eyes indicated liver stress. No lice or skin sores and his nails were crusted but fairly short, even the toes. Numerous cavities, but there were three fillings in his teeth. Hannah guessed they had been brushed within days. He looked of mixed race, 16, 17. African American and white most likely. Despite the theories of some amateur eugenicists in the other room he was no African immigrant. Circumcision alone ruled it out.

His sour odor overwhelmed even from seven feet away. Escaping from Flint, days ago on foot, was not out of the question. His bushy head drooped, avoiding her eyes and the florescent light ringing off the white walls. His cheek had swelled. Blood on his mouth, drops on his chest, the bunk. Tyce had worked on him already.

"What's your name?"

He didn't move.

"We don't want to hurt you," Hannah said. "If you just talk to us maybe we can get those cuffs off. Get you some hot food. We can wash you up. Get you some clothes."

"So take the cuffs off," he said. The words thick, tranquilized.

His head lifted. The youthful voice juxt against his bottomless, gun-barrel eyes.

"How did you get in here?"

"I'm talking. Take the cuffs off."

"I said maybe."

"You afraid of me?"

"Yes."

"I could say anything, then."

"Make me unafraid, then. How did you get in here? Who else is with you?"

His plaqued teeth broke wide. A charmer's smile. "Maybe I'm Satan. I'm a nightmare you're imagining right now."

"I always thought if I met Satan he'd know how to wipe his ass."

He spit red onto the grey epoxy floor.

"What happens now is your choice," she said.

The kid's bony shoulder knocked her words away, brows knitted, having heard it before.

"Whatever, bitch. If you ain't gonna kill me, someone's gonna."

Carefully, Hannah stepped to the Barrack's kitchen to wash and hydrate. Crossing the 7 a.m. hour, the EBN played up the good. Limited phone and electrical service was increasing across the government-controlled areas. The television showed city blocks lit up at night. Commuter trains. Flowing water. Businesses opening. Cars and traffic lights, even though Army troops were at the corners. Hannah even saw a few seconds of LifeForce guards outside a bank. New NATO and US troops had arrived on the west coast. The California Central Valley declared secure. Crops being harvested. The rising bar graphs. The bad ran to cholera and TB outbreaks. Car bombs in Chicago and Atlanta. A truck bomb in Minneapolis killed a FEMA district director, her staff and 17 others, destroying the office. In the Michigan news, locally, the red and blue masses were little changed.

Cricklewood Green's area was still declared red, between the shrinking blue island of Flint and the slow west-expanding blue tide of Metro Detroit. The M-59 line just south of them stagnant. Excepting the blue bottom east quarter of the state and the island of Lansing, Michigan was mostly red. The rash was not responding well to treatment.

She ran the water and splashed her face. *My God*, she thought. They had a boy chained in a cell. A dead boy, shot out in the woods. And you could watch people laughing in Manhattan, in line getting coffee. Coffee. She opened the cabinet. Perhaps a teaspoon left in a baggie. She gripped the cabinet door, breathing, counting...

In the main room Lorna worked the camera sort, leaned close, panning. Tyce, standing, picked through a pile of items on the desk while Ray's lowering eyes watched, snapping open, gradually closing again. Mark seemed both catatonic and hyper, leaning forward in a chair, face down to the carpet, hands locked together, knee bouncing. Sherri was bagging the caged boy's clothes. Someone, probably Tyce, had turned the overhead lights on while the TV ran. Hannah inhaled. It was not a string she wanted to pull.

"We should burn those," Hannah said.

Sherri walked past, to the door. "I'll throw them outside for now."

"How did they get in?" Hannah said from the archway.

"The tunnel is secure," Tyce said. "Beyond that, who knows? Did he talk to you?"

"Briefly."

"And?" Tyce said, almost absently, moving one of the desk items. He was picking and arranging things into groups like he was taking a test.

"Curses, mind games. He's..."

Hannah's thoughts kept halting, voiding like a film melting on a projector lamp.

"Does he have anything? Contagious, I mean?"

"No," Hannah said. "How did they get in? How did this happen?"

"I don't know," Tyce said.

"That's not an answer."

"We told you a month ago. This isn't Fort Knox or a prison camp. These cameras were never meant for that."

"That's what you have to say? Wonderful. Wonderful job."

Tyce looked over his shoulder at her. "Is that what happens with doctors? A patient's lying there dying and you bitch at each other about whose fault it is?"

"What's that supposed to mean?"

He went back to the desk puzzle. "Whatever you think it means, doctor."

"I am a doctor. What are you? Why are you here?" Hannah said. "To what purpose other than eat and waste our power? Steve at least got us something. From you? What? Your military mystery bullshit? Your intimidation? A woman's a leader here, Tyce. Deal with it."

Sherri stood. "Listen. Everybody just – "

"If it's blame then give me your best. And I'll give mine." Tyce said, sitting. "I can't wait to hear your excuses."

Tyce shrugged in waiting welcome.

Ray's head lifted. "Tyce. Come on."

"It's not excuses. It's accountability," Hannah said. "I'm sorry you failed, Tyce. But you failed. Own it."

"A sheepskin doesn't make you Wonder Woman. And the only reason everyone puts up with your leader bullshit is no else wants it. And everyone in here thinks it's kinda sorry how much you need it. Including your wife. Wherever she is."

Seizing a water glass off the console, Sherri fastballed it into the huge LifeForce logo on the wall.

"Shut up! Both of you! Right now!"

Hannah moved first, into the kitchen, clicking the TV off. Tyce stood, glaring at Sherri as he flicked glass off his neck and shoulders.

To center herself, eyes closed, Hannah silently recited her favorite poem, "*Hope is the Thing with Feathers*" by Emily Dickinson. When she walked back into the office it was still ugly but calmed. Purge of anger.

Sherri was next to Lorna, whispering and pointed to a screen.

"I apologize," Tyce said. "I respect what you say about finding out how they got in, Hannah. But, first we have to search. I think there's another intruder. And we have to find the gun." He held a short, black metal bar. It took Hannah a moment to realize what it was.

"Why do you say that?" Hannah said.

Tyce told them about the whistles.

"There's your prisoner's stuff. There's your dead man," Tyce said. "So, each one of them had the stuff they'd been carrying, scrounged, whatever. Dirty, damaged. Then, each of them have this stuff. Like it just came off a store shelf. Where's this Glock pistol?" He pivoted to Hannah and Ray, wanding the 'exhibit A' bar, bullet at the top like a gold tooth.

Hannah stepped closer. The clean piles were a sealed bottle of Dasani water. A can of Red Bull. A protein energy bar. Two packets of peanuts, one opened and one half empty. A pair of clean, white socks. A roll of duct tape still in plastic. A disposable lighter ("This is full", Tyce said, flicking it to life). A spotless Swiss army knife (Tyce opened it to a shining blade). The flashlight was newer, clean. The dirty piles ran to a beat-up, cracked cell phone, a balloon thing, a wooden block, crusted spoon, a dirty and torn-label pill bottle. A small rubber-banded bundle of metal strands, oddly shaped and hooked. It looked like goofy junk.

"The one I cuffed? All the new stuff was in one leg pocket. The old stuff was in his other pockets and his zip pack."

"So?" Ray said. "They robbed somebody before they got here."

"Maybe." Tyce said. "One pocket means a hurry. It just doesn't fit. It's all too specific to one set, one bug-out bag. Why take a mag of bullets if there was no gun? Does any of this look familiar? From the houses?"

Hannah and Ray shook their heads.

"Mark? What about you?"

"No," he said, down at his shoes.

"Come and look," Tyce said.

"I saw already. I know where all my weapons are," he said, loudly. "I know where my food is."

Tyce frowned at Ray and Hannah, wagging the bar. "Well, the '*weapon*' is from the same kit, I'm sure. Maybe they dropped it. Or stashed it. Or someone else is hiding in here with it and more of these."

Tyce looked down into Ray's iron grey, greasy hair.

"You searched the dead one," Tyce said, declarative.

Ray looked up, bleary. "Yeah. It was all in the bag I gave you."

"You missed something," Tyce said, thunk-dropping the thing onto the desk.

"Hey. There is leaves and muck shit three inches thick out there. And we were out there all night, Jack," Ray said. He pointed to Hannah.

"What about her and the Professor and what's her futz? Where are those two? They were out just as – "

"Look, I'm not blaming anybody. I'm not saying I would have done better. You can have people hiding five feet from you in the woods and walk right past them. But there's gotta be a gun. There's gotta be another person."

"It isn't exactly a jungle. We're not idiots," Lorna said, turning.

Tyce picked up the rubber-banded metal sticks. "You guys know what these are? They're lock picks. This wood block? It's a shim to brace open a door or window. Just 'cuz that kid in there looks like he does don't think him and his buddies are stupid. It isn't military mystery, but I've got some experience with this. And we have to search. Every house. Every corner. It's gonna take all day."

"We've got Baron." Lorna said. "He could get the scent from their clothes and stuff, right?"

"Maybe. It's not a blood hound or a hunting dog. It's an attack dog," Tyce said.

"He can still help."

"You ha…fine," Tyce said, pocketing the pick bundle in his shirt.

"Did anyone check on Kim and Sandra Rose?" Sherri said.

"Yes. Robert and Joyce both went inside. William was awake with both of them," Hannah said.

Hannah's attention slipped left. Lorna leaned close to Sherri. She pointed out one of the square views in the screen grid. It was fuzzy and cutting out. "See, I think this camera? Number 12? It's going," she said. Hannah's eyes went hypnotic on the distortion. She snapped away from it.

"So we need to search. Lorna and I have to go to Essex when Steve gets here," Hannah said. "We could get help from the people in town. Lorna, what do you think?"

The dark-haired girl bit her lip. "I don't know. Those people? To bring 'em here? Yesterday, it's like…. you know how we wish everything would go back to normal? I got the feeling some of those people don't."

Tyce exhaled, head shaking. "Do what you want. But you bring those hicks in here? If they don't wanna leave, who's gonna make them?"

"Well, so what? No one's living in them." Hannah said. "Steve – "

Tyce laughed at her.

"Steve? Warn me before you do. You won't need me anymore."

Mark stood. "Let's start. We're wasting time."

"Sit down, Mark," Ray said.

Hannah slumped against the drywall, brain stalled. She had hard charged her thoughts over the cliff and Wile E. Coyote was falling.

"Listen, please. Everyone." Sherri's voice was clear and certain. "We are all very tired and very hungry. We can't make decisions like this right now. We all need to eat and sleep. At least a few hours."

In the silence, Hannah met a refreshing recognition in Tyce's face.

"You're right, Sherri" Tyce said. "We sleep. Who takes camera?"

"I will," Mark said.

"OK." Tyce nodded. "We all meet back here at say 11 a.m.? If Steve shows up, we let him in alone and he waits. Alone. That's my deal."

Hannah nodded.

Tyce faced them all. "We can talk about everything else later. Until then everybody be alert. Keep a gun with you. Keep your radios on. And let's make sure Joyce and Bob and Bill are here at 11, too. Kim should come. We need her."

Hannah agreed. "Sherri? Would you please talk to her?"

"I will," Sherri said.

"I'll go tell Robert," Lorna said, standing. "11 o' clock."

"11 'o clock," Ray said as he got to his feet. Mark moved around him, pulling out of his camo coat, going to the console.

"What about him in there?" Ray said, thumbing backward.

"He's gonna stay in there." Tyce said.

"He's got the answers we need."

"Wanna go *Marathon Man*? Go ahead. If I have to tell why it's a dumb idea..."

"So? What? Let him starve to death?"

"Let's burn that bridge when we come to it." Tyce said.

"You're gonna feed him out of your share?"

"Yeah, Ray. I'll be expected to kill him anyway. That's what I'm here for, right?"

Sherri stood, joining Ray. "Nobody said that."

Hannah shuffled toward the door's bright outline of escape. Still crooked. Never fixed....

"He won't starve before 11 o'clock."

******

Sanders guessed Joyce and Hannah had been dead several hours. There had been no answer to his knocks. No dog yaps. Sanders saw a body through the window he then smashed with the butt of the sawed-off shotgun. Over their living room window frame Sanders clambered in, clawing past the tangle of lace, tearing the sleeve of his bomber leather on the glass. My God and the called-out names.

Beneath the skylight, Hannah's noon-lit corpse was spread near the kitchen island. Soaked in it, almost black, like gear fluid. Her face of disbelief, reaching, voiceless in mid-scream. Bloody sprays were all around the bottle glass and wreckage of the kitchen, stab marks across her front. The meat of her whole right thumb area was nearly split-severed down to the wrist. She'd grabbed and fought. Deep, black wounds at her clavicle. One open, yellow-filmed eye toward the hallway signaled Sanders to turn. Joyce was down the hall to Sanders' right. Sanders locked the hammers back on the shotgun, stepping toward her body. The white and brown area rug in the hall was twisted, dyed in a rusty trail where Joyce had crawled. Blood patterns started on the walls and floor at the kitchen entrance. The death mural grew wilder and more terrifying – one planted palm print - further along until the abrupt spot where Joyce had collapsed. She'd crawled, now half in the gentle panel of sunlight coming from the powder blue guest bath. Joyce had similar wounds to Hannah's, at the base of neck, collarbone. Her hands were empty, the pistol she carried nowhere to be seen. Rusty shoeprints all around her. They must have surprised her, surprised them both.

When Sanders left Joyce just after 6 a.m. he'd offered to go inside with her. He had looked at her muddy shoes and walking away he thought he should have reminded her to clean them. Now 11:30 and Hannah wouldn't answer her radio.

They sent him.

Joyce's bare feet. Cold to his fingertips like a bath sink on an autumn morning.

The grandfather clock ticked. There was no sign or sound from their little dog. Sanders backed against the hall wall, sliding along it, eyes flitting for reflected movement in the hallway picture glass. Watching the long corridor to his left, toward the upstairs, Sanders gasped for air. White-gripping the gun he slid left past Hannah and the kitchen, around the corner and kept moving backward until he reached the front door, one-hand fumbling for the locked deadbolt. Sanders kept moving backward, shotgun leveled at the house and open front door. As the door shrank away, Sanders' panic vortexed. He could not get far enough away, the door a black hole, anti-energy, anti-life. In the driveway, his legs gave out to malarial tremors. Sanders threw up bile and crawled. On his knees in the blacktop street he waved his arms, looking up to the sky, to the cameras. To surrender.

*****

To speak, Sanders had to press his eyes closed and form words against the fibers of pulsing blood, left hand pinch-gripping the sides of his skull. They had driven up in the security car. Tyce and Ray Dudek, long guns, standing over him demanding a report on what he could never unsee. Sanders couldn't look at them and submit at the same time. He had to visualize the words to say them. In anger, he summarized.

Joyce's pistol, Sanders warned. Missing. Unknown. Be careful.

Sitting on the road, Sanders heard the snapping mechanisms of their guns above him. Tyce speaking into his radio. Now, more murder. Sanders' lifting head watched Tyce walking toward the open door with the raised, short black rifle.

"Robert. *Robert.*"

Dudek lifted him from under the armpits.

"Come on, bud. I'm sorry. I know it hurts, Robert. But you gotta get up. Let's go. You take all of it and let's give 'em it back."

Dudek's shoulder pats were encouraging. Sanders calculated but seethed. This was living. Cells group and they live. Eliminate the germ.

His truest self was now watching it, removed. The mortal, shaking empathy which sent him storming into the women's home was gone like steam. Sanders had never been amongst a corpse and yes, he had nothing but disregard now. He did not want to see the bodies ever again. The anger? Primal, blood-in-the-eye avenging man? No. Sanders trudged behind Dudek's stride weary of the bloody simplicity. Baby talk and murder. *'Now what?'* he could hear Vern Hapgood saying. Barbara would have loved this. Sanders could imagine her glorifying his role to surprised friends and family. Everyone so wrong about him all this time. Sanders knew he could kill the creature responsible for brutalizing the women, as he knew he could have gunned down a German Shepherd. At last his brand. "Bob" the Fearsome Executioner. The necessity of destiny.

This is how Kubrick should have ended his outer space film. The astronaut is not reborn. He is once again a monkey, smearing its ass on the refined, right-angle post of science. Content to beat his bone and howl in righteous fury.

Both men crossed the threshold, following Tyce into the tomb.

The stink had sharpened despite the open door and smashed window. Copper and rot. Above them the whumps and cracks and kicks of Tyce ransacking the upstairs. Ray Dudek went for Hannah. Sanders went to the right, to Joyce. Her eyes were closed. Had she tried for peace, knowing? A realist, Joyce was.

Sanders felt Ray behind him. "Cocksuckers," Ray muttered, laying a yellow dishtowel over Joyce's face.

After clearing the lower level rooms and the basement Sanders and Dudek made their way upstairs to the bedrooms and den, following one set of the killer's rusty shoeprints. Tyce was in the master bedroom, forearm braced above a slid-open window. Head resting on the muscle he was looking down, outside.

Dudek coughed but Tyce didn't respond.

"We've got no gun. The one Joyce had? We found the ear-piece, but Hannah's radio's gone, too. What do y - JESUS!"

Dudek's head snapped to the left, to Tyce and the window, cursing.

In his peripheral vision Sanders glimpsed a roast-like, bloody form near the open closet, knowing it had to be the little min-pin, Max. Sanders put his back to it, looking at Tyce and the open window.

Tyce sniffed, grumbling and scratched his head. "Come here."

The same stark, bloody tennis-shoe print on the carpeting marked the white window sill. New Balance, clear as a stamp. Sanders and Dudek joined Tyce in looking down. The thick and sturdy tree branch was only a short drop from the window. An easy jump and catch if one were wiry enough. Sanders could see the footsteps and brush-back in the high grass below, heading toward the next yard and the hedges vivid as virgin snow tracks. Toward the Slavin's house.

"We stay off the radio for now. Bob? You stay. Ray? Take the car. Go to the Narlow's. Take that M-4 on the bed with you. When you make sure they're OK, go to the Barracks. Stay there. Have Mark come here. Have him bring a shotgun."

Tyce's forehead slid off his braced arm to face both men.

"Have Lorna bring the dog."

***

"Why not?" Lorna said, the leash strained in her hand.

Tyce seemed unsure what to do with the bloodied rag when he moved it from the dog's snout. Baron certainly had the scent, its paw nails skittering on the cement porch, nosing the women's closed front door. Tyce finally tossed it into the broken window.

"Why?" he said.

Lorna sneered at the guard. Standing back, Sanders marveled how the child inside her could overcome the young woman. The weight loss, the poor diet dulling her hair and spotted skin revealed a peek of the woman Lorna would become. Brittle and cruel, an inflicter. Sanders was still thinking on true selves. Who was really who?

"Cuz she was my friend and I want to see her one last time?"

"Do what I tell you," Tyce said, removing his bulletproof vest. "Put that on and follow me."

Taking it, Lorna handed the leash to Sanders for a moment. The dog barked what could only be called a yes as Tyce walked to the rim of the porch shade, looking upward, pistol two-handed toward the Slavin house and the leaf cover between the homes. After she secured the vest, Baron dragged Lorna toward Tyce's alpha and the blood scent. Sanders followed. Lorna's pointless defiance seemed relieved, spared the sight of the women's corpses.

Tyce raised his left hand and Sanders stopped. Lorna yanked on the animal, whispering to stay, its tail up and arced. To their right, from his cover spot at the escape tree below the bedroom window, Mark nodded.

His shotgun aimed in the direction where the grass footprints disappeared - into the Slavin's rocky landscaping a hundred feet away beyond a row of bushes. The Slavin's basement had a sliding glass walkout on its west side, facing the water, closest to the four hunters. Next to the walkout, the Slavin's main floor maroon deck was supported by wood posts and lattice. They believed the killer was inside the home.

The three advanced. There was only one upper side window facing them. When the three of them cleared its view they paused against the home's tan brick. The dog remained jumpy, three commands from Lorna before it sat, panting as she rubbed its groomed fur. Sanders looked away, toward the home's front and the sunlight contrasting their wedge of shade. Disgusted for his jealousy of the animal.

"Anything?" Tyce whispered.

At the tree, aiming, Mark shook his head.

Tyce motioned Mark over, glancing to his right at Sanders and Lorna, his voice hushed. "Lorna, we're going to release the dog and follow it. We're going to watch what he goes for. Bob, you stay with Lorna. I'm going to follow the bushes, going wide. Mark, after me, you go right around the corner here, close. Follow what I do. Everyone check your weapons."

Tyce put one finger up with his free hand, pressing the ear piece. The two voices in both ears, live and in his radio, stirred the unreality for Sanders.

"Hey motherfucker. You hearin' me?"

Tyce released the mic to static, looking up and around. He peeked around the rear corner of the Slavin house and drew back.

"We know you've got a radio. If you've got any balls you'll talk to me. Come on, motherfucker. I know you got a Taurus .380 and bad motherfucking knife. You know where to stab, too. Don't' ya?"

Static.

"Here's how it is. We *know* we're gonna kill you. You ain't any good with that gun. Hearing me, sweetie? It ain't gonna work. It's gonna jam on you. You might hit one of us. You might even kill one of us. We *know* we're gonna kill you."

Static, hiss. A new universe fomenting in Sanders' ear. Tyce glanced away a moment, taken by a thought, a memory. The war? He almost looked amused.

Tyce nudged his chin upward. Hannah unclipped the leash. Baron charged around the corner to the Slavin's back yard, barking. Tyce swung out, aiming his pistol. The barks remained near, just on the other side, the back side of the home. Almost crab-like, Tyce strode sideways to the nearest bush, leaves gone brown and sickly yellow.

Mark whirled the raised shotgun around the corner toward the relentless, gnashing barks.

"Come out of there!" Mark yelled.

The shotgun blast cracked the atmosphere like a split of thunder. A cottony pain swelled in Sanders' ears. All became insect-like blurts inside his skull, more felt than heard by the concussed nerves.

"Throw the guns out, motherfucker! Hands! Show your hands!" Tyce dashed past the bushes into the Slavin's yard. Mark stepped forward, past the brick corner. The noise, the men gone and the sudden sight of his home across the water made Sanders blindly afraid. A vulnerable cell separate from the others. Breath held, Sanders moved along the wall to peek at the noisy hell around the corner.

Two dirty, raised hands were thrust out of the wedge between the Slavin's deck and the sloping ground. The three-foot oblong gap was the only part not girded by the maroon wood lattice, a roll of bright green garden hose nearby. Baron barked, neck feinting only a few feet from the hands and dark motion under the deck. Mark and Tyce slow-stepped closer, shouting with their raised weapons.

Lorna skirted around Sanders, yelling for Baron. *Come back.*

"Hands motherfucker!"

A skinny boy's body birthed out of the gap in a snaky wiggle, hands raised, flopping backward in retreat from the snapping dog. Sanders watched Mark and Tyce stop, silenced.

The pale boy's blue LifeForce uniform shirt was untucked, sizes too large for him. His skin, the blue shirt and blue, clownish uniform trousers were butcher-stained, darkly at the arms and waist. Blood stains spotted and blotched at the chest and up his scrawny, pale neck. His blonde hair tufted like moss under the LifeForce patrol cap. His peach-fuzz beard was smeared by his recent work. Sanders never connected with the boy-thing's tiny, sunken eyes. They were fixed on the two guns pointed at him. His pink palms were up, pushing back. It looked like he'd been rubbing on them. Guilty.

He blinked, and blinked again, knowing for a fraction before his lips uttered.

"Wait."

One blast from Mark's shotgun and four or five bullets from Tyce's pistol collapsed the boy. Lorna had frozen in her backstep, denim jacketed arms jutted out in shock, pushing air. In the moment Sanders looked down and away from the body he shuddered at the repeated shots from Tyce's pistol. Sanders jerked to see Tyce on one knee firing into the lattice. One two three. One two three. Mark dropped to the same position, racking and firing twice, the lead shot blowing the thin wood strips apart.

Making sure.

Lorna cursed, hustling forward to grab Baron and leash him, the dog's ears lowering as his body contracted inward when she touched him. Sanders jaw worked in the sudden quiet, trying to clear his ringing ears. Changing magazines in the pistol, Tyce stood and walked to the deck's surrounding gravel and stones.

"Friend of yours?" Lorna said.

"Not hardly. If this kid's 17 I'll kiss your ass," Tyce said.

"Can I see your light, Tyce?" Mark said.

Without looking Tyce snagged and passed the penlight off his belt. Mark clicked it on, scraping his bulk under the deck through the broken lattice, a blue/grey ghost playing in the dark. Sanders had not tasted a cigarette in over thirty years, but greatly desired one. Something for the shaking hands. Did any of them smoke?

His left side and arm well-shredded by the off-center shotgun blast, the boy was folded against the maroon supports and the low steps speckled in blood and tissue. His hands flat but wrists crooked, elbows tucked against his body, resembling a palsy or polio case. His tongue peeked out, like he was mocking a death pose despite the close grouping of wet bullet holes on his small chest. Divorced from empathy or revenge, Sanders marveled at how instantly a human body could become unreal.

"I know it's nuts, but doesn't he look like Jackpot?" Lorna said. "I mean, with everything…?"

"No." Tyce seemed to think about it. Sanders remembered the name, the killings in this region. During the trial, it was required national opinion. For many in California it recalled Tate-LaBianca. Sanders remembered the topic tangents - guns, drugs, parenting and poverty - to inane obscurity. What role did sugar in the killer's diets play?

"No. Jackpot's in his 20's now. He was bigger. He was up in Marquette anyway. This little worm…?"

"How come he'd wear the uniform?"

"Probably 'cuz he's fuckin' crazy." Pushing out a burst of breath Tyce looked up and around at the bushes and the landscaping, the upper floors of the Slavin home.

"Mark! Whatta ya got down there?"

"It's all good. I'm coming."

Sherri asked again over the radio. Tyce told Sanders to get it. Sanders reported the short version.

Mark emerged with a zipper knapsack, tossing the opened pack to the stones at Tyce's feet. "The Glock, the knife. Some clothes." He swiped the spider webs and flaky filth from his hair and bare arms. He tossed a handset radio. "This too."

Tyce crouched, examining. The radio had been smashed. The knife was a military combat-type, leather handle, eight-odd inches with a scabbard. Very durable, saturated in dried blood. Tyce unloaded the black automatic pistol but there was no chambered shell. He held it up to Mark.

"I don't want it."

"Sure?" Tyce asked.

"Yeah, I'm sure."

"I saw you with a Glock before."

"No. How many times I gotta say?"

Tyce threw it on the ground, pulling out a jacket, T-shirt, jeans. Some of them were the kids' size, filthy. Another sweatshirt, clean, was the same size as the XXL uniform. A red T-shirt with cartoon characters on it – 'South Park'. Tyce stood with the T-shirt, head shaking.

"Want this, Mark?"

"Why would I want any of it?"

"Because you found it. It's *yours*."

Tyce cursed and tossed the shirt atop the corpse, retrieving the thrown-out pistol Sanders recognized as the small gun Joyce had kept. They had found it in Vern's shower in a plastic bag. It was also unchambered to shoot. Tyce held it out to Lorna.

"Why'd he use the knife if he had those?" she said. She shook her head at the gun.

"Good question. He could have shot all of us. And your little dog, too." Tyce dropped the .380 into the bag.

"Where do you think he got the uniform, Mark?"

"There's a stack of you guys someplace isn't there? Custer's Last Stand, right?"

Tyce nodded, looking out over the water. Pockets of fast clouds were playing games with the sunlight.

"Yeah. That must be it. What do you think, Bob? Had all the fun you can stand?"

The words came from Sanders automatically but measured, as they would from a fearsome man. Perhaps from a Mike Narlow or the short, smoking man in the Highwayman bar or possibly Vern Hapgood. The point Sanders made to all three of them was of luck, which he didn't believe in, and probability, which he did. How much of this was now luck? If they believed in either thing, was it not perhaps better to shuffle the deck? Change the dice? For probability, abandon this place, which was quickly becoming a graveyard. The dead nearly outnumbering the living once the group anti-body massacred the boy in the cell, a fact as unsaid as the coming sunset. It was perhaps ten miles to the government line at M-59. Perhaps less by now. What to stay for?

"Are we gonna bury the girls?" Lorna said. She finally turned her back on the boy's body. All of them now facing northwest to the pond and bushes and trees and wild grass back yards. She started unsnapping the bulletproof vest.

"No, keep it." Tyce said, studying Sanders' face when they heard the buzz.

Back near the water a four-rotor helicopter drone hovered above at nearly eighty feet. They observed the tiny craft, maybe three feet across on a circle frame, for a few seconds. Enough time for each side to know they seen one another before the drone moved on, following the pond south, past the tall trees where the road split.

****

Lorna wondered aloud what Kim Narlow would do.

"Who knows, Lorna? I'm not sure I know Kim, if I ever did."

The two women passed Gallo's home, Sherri commenting how

awful he looked earlier, weeping about the women's murders. It was a now a little before 3 p.m. An algae bloom had taken over the pond. Swamp soup. Cattails and new strange weeds were popping up around it, all over the lawns. Dry-curled red and yellow leaves were stuck to the blacktop under their feet. Lorna glanced backward, trying to pretend it wasn't nerves. Bob Sanders words were still fucking with her. *A grave-yard.* Now a drone was spying on them.

"I bet she laughs," Lorna said.

She did.

She made tea.

In the center of the women's circle, Sandra Rose kneeled close to the battery lamp on the low table, painting her watercolors, adding a blur of yellow to the tie-dye Rorschach. Lorna kept her eyes on the humming, whispering girl

Kim snorted again, laughing, shaking her head at the basement's glass blocks. To Lorna it seemed the gesture was to the heavens, aimed for the Great Spirit in regret of having missed it.

"And she even had a gun. Stupid bitch," Kim said.

"She didn't." Sherri said into her cup.

"Stupid bitch," Sandra Rose said, dabbing for more green.

Scooching forward Kim kissed the top of the girls washed, pink-barretted hair. "Right, baby. Stupid bitch who killed Daddy is dead."

"Good. I hated that stupid bitch."

Sherri plunked her cup to the table. Lorna glanced at the older woman, but Kim made no notice, leaning in to Sandra Rose, compliment-ing. Her whispered question was returned with an affirmative hum and nod.

Lorna leaned off the stuffed loveseat. "You know, Miss Hannah liked you, Sandra Rose. That's not a nice thing to say about her."

The brush stopped in her hand, her chin tucked. "I'm sorry."

"It's OK. Because Miss Hannah is gone your mommy is going to have to go to work with us sometimes. But you'll be able to come to my house. Or Miss Sherri's or we'll come here to stay with you."

"Can we play with the doggie?"

"Yes, we can."

The girl's head swiveled up. "Where are you gonna work, Mommy?"

"Oh. Mommy's not going to work, Sandra Rose. They're just playing. Mommy doesn't have to do anything she doesn't want to do."

Lorna didn't want to look up. She knew this straining, ticking feeling in rooms, waiting for the rage. Look at those hands. The girl's little hands were so perfect.

"Nobody can do anything to us, sweetie." Kim said. "Can they make us leave our house? Can they make you not sleep in your bed?" Kim's voice rose in delighted exaggeration. Kim tickled the little girl's neck into shrugging giggles.

"No!" Sandra Rose said.

"No?"

"No!"

"If anybody does something we don't like, what do we do?"

"We kill 'em!"

Kim came in to kiss her cheek for the correct answer. "That's right, baby. We kill them. Bang bang bang. Ask Miss Lorna what we do."

"What do we do, Miss Lorna?"

Kim's face was pressed next to the girl's. In the girl's sweet smiling wonder at being included, Lorna could see the young woman Sandra Rose would become. The way Kim held her, there was no way to not look Sandra Rose in her green eyes.

"What do we do to people we don't like, Miss Lorna?" Kim said.

"We kill them," Lorna said.

"Bang bang bang!"

"Bang bang bang!" The mother and daughter hug-jostled with

each shot. Eskimo kisses and growls. Lorna felt hollow. The sadness wouldn't bottom out. What she told the little girl going on and on in some fucked-up canyon echo where it rolled over things Lorna hadn't thought of in forever. She used to feel it in the suffocating tension of rooms like this. A wrongness beyond anything, when her parents would turn on each other and things got ruined forever. No apology would unsay it.

Lorna could have easily shot Kim in the face if not for Sandra Rose. If not for Sandra Rose, Lorna wouldn't even be in this ugly basement, listening to Kim's demented bullshit. If not for Sandra Rose, Lorna would have never talked to Kim, another stuck-up, clueless cunt in the asylum. If things all went the down the same way Lorna might have shot her in the face anyway. Straight up. Some people just deserved to be set on fire.

Expecting fire, Lorna could find nothing in Sherri's eyes. Her face seemed so old and sorrowful in the gloom light. Lorna's attention flitted from the pair to Sherri and back for some kind of signal. But there was only a whip-tired disbelief from Sherri as she boosted up from the arm rests.

What to say when everyone has guns and no one gives a shit? Not enough or way too much.

"You keep painting, sweetie. Me and the ladies are going upstairs." Kim stood with her cup.

With hugs and goodbyes, they left the girl. On the way up Kim's hand went for the light switch.

"God, I still do it," she said back to the women, climbing.

"One good thing from all this? I bet the little kids are really gonna be amazing. Like the World War II kids? They'll be tough. They'll be able to rely on themselves. And good for them, ya know? God knows we fucked it up good enough."

The blizzard of words ran out as Kim side-stepped, herding Sherri and Lorna to the front door. It opened to cool wind. Lorna saw Kim's hand go to Sherri's back with the faintest push, beginning a goodbye. Sherri's right hand seized the wood door, slamming it closed. She grabbed Kim's wrist and turned it. The smaller woman crumpled sideways, porcelain cup crashing, before Sherri's strong right grip tugged her sweatshirt, bringing both women eye-to-eye.

"Don't ever put your hand to me.

"That woman did more in her life than you *ever* could. And how dare you poison your little girl with that shit? Hiding behind her. And HIM? Your husband was a pig. A bastard. He was *fucking* that Chinese girl *right in front of you*. And you act like he was a saint. We are *ALL* you've got and you had better start respecting and helping us or I will beat the white off your ass. You spoiled little bitch."

Lorna guffawed. "*Ohmigawd.*"

Sherri yanked. "Tell me you understand me."

Kim shuddered in terror. "I do. I do."

Sherri released. "Get Sandra Rose ready. Put a sweater on her because it's chilly. Be down at the security building in thirty minutes. I'll have a snack for her. Don't make any plans the rest of the day."

Unsure if they would both get shot in the back, Lorna and Sherri were nearly to the street when Lorna heard the door click closed.

****

Sherri felt the sunset, red and cloudless, on her toweled skin through the second-story bath window. A few wet drops tickled her neck. Bob had never turned on the water today, so Sherri contented herself with a fireplace-heated pasta pot full from the rain buckets. They had barely any gas left in their home tank. She would let Ray come up with the reason to waste it.

Janis played. Sherri repeated '*Call on Me*' again, humming with it, lifting and pushing the drooped, withering goods at her reflection. Not bad for the first week, the new diet had forced Sherri from her preferred plumpness. She'd made the decision for a beautiful face over a rock body long ago. Ray would use all his cheesy lines when she would play with him about her belly or her widening ass. *Meat's for the man, bone's for the dog*, he'd say. *A woman should feel like a woman. Curves. If I wanted a teenage boy I'd move to San Francisco* - whatever that meant. But plush and solid had gone to folds of fallow skin. In another week she'd be borrowing clothes from…Hannah.

She went to her product cabinet, picking the lavender lotion. She put a leg on the bowl's closed lid, working it in. *Call on me, babe, and I'll come to you.* She was finishing her shoulders and upper arms when she heard the steps.

"Ray?"

"Yeah. It's me."

Embarrassed, she wrapped by the time he'd clomped up to the doorway. He looked so drained, so cashed out.

"Whelp, we took care of everything. I brought her medical stuff here. Tyce figured you'd be the best one."

"OK. How do you feel?"

"I'll be alright."

"Did you bury them?"

"No. We wrapped them both up and nailed the place shut. We didn't find anything else – anyone else I guess I mean. Christ, I'm beat." He leaned in the jamb, avoiding his reflection in the broad mirror.

"What about him? The…"

"Tyce said he dug his last grave. Can't blame him."

"You left him out there?"

Ray shrugged.

She came closer and kissed him. The embrace long.

"I'm dirty," he whispered.

"I don't care. I love you, Raymond."

"I love you, darlin'. More than you know."

His throat cleared. "We, uh, found. It's kinda funny. In one of Hannah's drawers…"

Sherri backed up. "If this is smutty I do not want to hear it."

"No, no. You know how she would go on about losing weight and how, oh, we have to all keep our calories under a thousand. Well, you wouldn't believe all this candy she had hid. Little baby Almond Joys and Reese's cups and M&Ms. I don't even think Joyce knew about it."

They laughed a bit, tossing bits of things Hannah had said and Joyce would say back to her. Tears flowed. Ray's arms wrapped her, setting kisses to her neck.

"It's OK, baby. Go ahead."

"Oh Ray…."

The music changed and snapped Sherri out. *Thunder Island.*

"Do you wanna eat?" she said, sniffing.

"Later, before we go back. What do we even have left?

"There's the eggs. Those veggies we got from town. We still have rice, some cans. I've got us set for a few more days. Did Steve come?"

"No. Not yet. Let's cook up those eggs tonight. Tyce gave me the ladies, too. And some other stuff of theirs. I just wanna lay down for now. I got another pill to take, I think?"

"Yes. At six. I don't know about the eggs for you."

He grimaced. "A little late in the day, don't you think?"

"I know, it's just…how were Kim and Sandra Rose?"

"Kim's OK, quiet, doing the cameras. The kid loves it. She's running all around, singing her head off," Ray said.

"Wait. Is the one still in the cell?"

"No."

"You mean…?"

"I don't know." Ray shook his head. "Tyce moved him out after you left with Lorna. It was before the little girl got there. It was bad. We had to... anyway, the light's out, the bars are shut. The kid won't see any of it. Whatever Tyce did...no one wanted to ask and I don't think he wanted to say."

She sat on the closed pot. "Maybe we should have let him go?"

"Come on, Sherri. You should have seen the shit he was saying and doing in there. Kid was an animal. Just forget about it. Let's go lay down, huh? We'll watch something."

Sherri held her head. "Raymond, you know there's going to be an accounting for all this?"

"Well, right now I'm accounting for all our asses. And I'm not apologizing for it. Come on, babe. Not now."

"Go ahead. I'll be there in a minute."

He coughed. "You know, Tyce thinks we should leave. I'm not crazy about it but he might be right. We don't know who was watching us with that drone thing, or how long. And food? Like you said?"

"I don't think we should. Out there walking through the woods? Really, Raymond. On the news, there's power and phones coming back on all over. They'll come. Maybe the drone was the military?"

"Then we won't. Everyone thinks we should at least wait and hear from Steve before we do anything."

He came in to lift her chin and kiss her. After Ray left she stood and could hear the souvenired 3-D Chinese computer in the bedroom, tinny through the small speakers. She shut her CD off.

Brushing her teeth, a sound brought her to the window. Calls of distress. Across the water, in the Fetters yard, Tyce had the naked prisoner. The boy was writhing in the weeds and grass, the last of the sun casting long shadows. His legs looked tied together, hands behind his back. Tyce was standing over him, near the gazebo. Tyce kicked him forward like a log, closer to the water. The boy's cries were a vibration, leaking in.

The TV laughter behind her sounded like static or electrical shocks, broken by the hummed tones of the characters. Like people were answering questions and getting shocked. Sherri couldn't be sure which noise was the boy.

Past the weeds and cattails, into the water, the boy fought to roll up and away. Tyce kicked him once more, finally bending to shove him in deeper until Tyce was in the water to his uniform's knees.

Static. Tiny shocks. Wasp laughter.

Tyce was holding the boy under. His sleeves rolled up, arms locked. His left arm pulled back and punched into the splashes and rippling muck. Tyce's force and weight bore down from the shoulders onto the wriggling, flapping shape like a wash woman.

It hit Sherri like leaping free of a bad dream. A caught-breath moonlight startle. Sherri turned from it, fleeing the bathroom. Coming closer, the video static formed into distinct voices. Humans and fun. Wanting to be there, Sherri stepped in and closed the bedroom door, knowing no one had seen her.

****

October 22nd

Clicking the cell's overhead light off, Gallo wheeled the bucket to the bathroom and poured the rust-colored water down the shower drain. Bleach fumes tingled his eyes and nose as he wrung the mop as best he could, breath held. After days of everyone commenting, Gallo knew the cell wouldn't clean itself.

The man at the window. *A big smile. Like a cat*, she had said.

Gallo left the mop and bucket in the open supply room, the mop upright to properly dry. By the time he walked to the office he needed to sit again, starry. The open front door brought in most of the room's light, all of the chill. Candles and battery lamps were on the desks and console. Marks's shape came through the door, the machine gun and bag of ammunition born across his front by the fat strap. Mark was bearded again, as Vern had been.

Gallo's mind went to Sartre's Hell. No exit. Forever trapped.

Mark and Tyce discussed the tunnel's condition after yesterday and last night's severe rain.

"It's not bad, about four inches deep."

Tyce's shoes were up on the camera console. "Did you go inside?"

"I stick measured it." Mark looked from Tyce to Robert Sanders, seated at the first desk with the plugged-in battery chargers. "Everything looked sturdy, straight. None of the supports shifted."

Sanders did not react from his pad and scribble.

Tyce looked back at Gallo.

"The cell is clean."

"Good. Thank you." Tyce's pursed concentration was familiar to Gallo, with individual variations on each face. Gallo knew they were seeing him like a faded hieroglyphic, guessing. Seeing the disease overtaking him. "You didn't have to do that, Bill. How are you feeling? Are you up to going?"

"I am. Where is Lorna?"

"She's outside." Feet dropping, Tyce turned to shuffle through the screens, muttering a curse at the #4 camera mounted on the clubhouse, another one failing, cutting out to mostly static. It was the erratic power, Sanders said, looking up. He asked Tyce to come over, glancing again at his pad. Tyce told him to speak up.

"Each man is a leader, here, Bob. No more of that antiquated system." Tyce half-smiled at Gallo, who turned his puzzlement to Mark, who passed his puzzlement to Sanders. Tyce often did this, uttering peculiar phrases he expected others to understand.

"I mean lay it on us, Bob. We've got all we need, right?"

After pumping this morning's trade water there was enough generator fuel left to pump approximately 10 minutes of water, probably less.

But the last day's rain would help, the gutter buckets and tubs were full for the most part. At 13 kw the battery from the roof's solar cells would power the cameras at the current rate for maybe 12 hours with no additional input. If they planned to trade any water they would need the fuel to pump it. And sunny days for the cameras and Barrack's electricity.

Yesterday had been the third day without word from Steve. They had decided to combine and plan all the food. Not including the certain stashes and hold-outs on everyone's part there were two meals a day until November 5th.

"Well, hot damn. I thought we were in trouble," Tyce said.

Lorna entered the Barracks with Kim and Sandra Rose. The young girl struck a pose in her pink raincoat, flowery dress and yellow rubber boots. Fists on hips.

"William! Where have you been?"

"Cleaning, darling."

***

It looked like they were Kentuckian Prohibition smugglers hauling moonshine. The van's floor was packed with clear liquid bottles and jugs, plastic and metal, pint to gallon. They'd removed the van's middle seat, Sanders squeezing in, not shutting up about driving. *Fucking guys*, Lorna thought. Always wanting to do too much for her. She preferred to drive and how many times and ways do you have to tell a person no? And Bob Sanders wasn't exactly a guy you had confidence in if things got jammed up. At least Gallo wasn't saying anything. He'd stopped shaving in the last few days and the snow scuff was working for him. In the plaid cap and scarf he reminded Lorna of a fisherman.

She clicked the wipers once, clearing the speckle rain. Fog pressed the treetops. It was hard to tell what felt different on the first four miles driving to town, but something was off, not just the weather. Trees were trees, another abandoned car. The shot-up grey car with the open doors. Lorna slowed the van. At the rise further ahead, a giant steel dumpster blocked the right and most of the left lane. Painted an earthy brown, it matched the dirt, wood and cinderblock debris stuffing out the open top. 'Independent Recycling Services' with a phone number, yellow banner next the logo encouraging to RENT ME. As if explaining an art exhibit, the orange-frame construction sign in front of the dumpster flipped its green-letter messages on repeat.

WARNING SECURED AREA   SLOW/STOP FOR SEARCH WARNING SECURED AREA

Things felt like they were about to get jammed up.

"What do we do?" Lorna said.

Both men said to go on. Lorna crawled the van around the sliver of left lane and the gravel shoulder, branches scraping the side. Lorna rolled down her window, remembering something Tyce said about bullets and glass. No glass is better.

Past the dumpster, the road was open. Lorna kept it ten per. In the distance, an 18-wheeler semi was back parked to the D-Plex's gaped front, some camo/soldier figures casually near it. The lot was still trashed with pushed-back cars, driveways now blocked by yellow construction barrels, six or seven deep. The kind you'd see at highway exits, always full of water when cars slow-motioned into them in movies.

"Lorna. Watch the road," Gallo said.

At the T-intersection where they could turn left into Essex or north/right toward Gavin and Flint and Hell, cement barriers like they had outside the Green now cut off the right-side blacktop. Another green flip-letter sign warned them. They were about to be stopped and searched.

She braked. 'What IS this shit?"

"We have to go through. We know the names." Gallo said.

Lorna made the left to Essex.

More of the cement barriers and long, seven-foot-high mounds of dirt made the road an obstacle course, radically built up beyond the couple of cars of a few days ago. Right side blocked, thirty yards, left side blocked. Again, then again. Puttering around the S-turns Lorna's eyes picked at the thick woods on each side, for the animals she sensed watching them. She caught an Army truck's shape back in the woods, autumn branches stacked over it, machine gun pointed at them. Black shoe-boxy looking things were fixed to the front of some barriers, wires leading out of them. Lorna didn't doubt they were anything but what they looked like. She clicked the squeaky windshield wipers again.

"Ask for Jim," she said, turning the wheel. "Jim'll stick with us."

"Be quiet. Just stay calm."

After the last set of barriers, the road was empty for a while before the black line in the road became clear. It was a steroid version of the spike strip they had back home. Steel pointed Xs two feet high and six inches around chained from tree to tree across the road. Beyond them, a hundred feet of open road lay before two more massive, long dirt mounds broken by a thin middle passage. Beyond them Lorna could glimpse the Burger King and a big-claw yellow and black construction crane under the fog. In the woods, to the van's right, another Army truck and another machine gun with a clear plastic cover and metal plate shield. This truck was closer. She thought she could see someone in there, behind the fog-cloud reflection on the plastic.

She stopped in front of the spikes and jammed into park.

The woods popped with sound. A cop's pull-over bullhorn.

"Shut the vehicle off."

Lorna complied, pocketing the keys. She put her hands in view.

"Listen carefully and exit when you are told. Everyone will slowly step out of the vehicle with your hands raised as high as you can. Walk forward to the front of the vehicle, facing forward. Do not turn. Leave any and all weapons inside. Repeat. ANY and ALL weapons IN-SIDE. Leave your doors open. Flash your lights once if you understand. You have ten seconds to answer."

Lorna clicked the lights.

"Exit the vehicle."

Lorna left her silver gun on the dash and flipped her hood up for the mist. Stepping down she could hear Sanders open the slider. There was barely an instant to glance left at the rustling and rushing bootsteps.

"Eyes front, Ma'am. Face forward," a helmeted face said, slipping behind Lorna. Others came. She could hear them in the van and sensed more aimed guns. Her breath puffed to steam.

From behind one of the two-story mounds a helmeted, grey/green uniformed soldier walked to them as someone pat-groped Lorna ankle to tit. The approaching soldier didn't carry a rifle but wore a pistol on his pouchy, packed utility belt. More stuff was rigged to his shoulder straps. Stripes patched on his sleeves but black tape hid his name tag. Lorna saw a new red J patch on his bicep and thought of the Sneetches on the beaches with stars on their bellies, changing marks and changing sides. Wrap black shades hid his shaven face. He was white. Lorna wasn't surprised.

Pungent wood smoke. She could not smell sewer anymore.

"She has body armor, sergeant." The voice behind Lorna was younger than her. The voice had pimple scars.

"I have to give it up?" Lorna said.

She could sense a squint behind the black lenses. "No."

His voice ordinary, a hint of wonder why she asked the question.

"The vehicle is clear, sergeant. Water and two firearms."

The helmeted robot eyes moved to Gallo and Sanders. "Lower your arms, gentlemen. What's your business here?"

"Trade." Gallo said. "William Gallo." His right hand sprung, met by the sergeant's. He accepted Sanders' shake as well, without comment.

"All of these obstacles are new to us," Gallo said. "We were here the other day, trading with the town. Mr. Cronc. Phillip Gallagher told us to return with water to trade for food and fuel."

Looking to the side, the soldier's nods were those of person hearing correct answers.

"Where are you from?" he said.

"Nearby," Gallo said.

"Not the distance, sir. Where?"

"Cricklewood Green."

The black lenses passed over the three. "Wait here a moment. Eyes front. You people can relax. You're in no danger."

He walked back behind the mound. A radio voice behind Lorna crackled and a female soldier answered it with bit-spit code words and numbers. From the balls of her feet Lorna fought the urge to turn, wondering if she was the groper or the pimple-voice boy. Lorna went to this clusterfuck straight, afraid she might freak out if she were too high. Pretty funny. Without faces to go with the soldier's voices behind her and the clack and jumble of equipment and the van's shutting door and unseen scrapes of bootsteps Lorna's nerves were jump snap sizzle sparking like a crashed down power line inside a big puddle.

Lorna's hands went into her pockets. The roadside execution, sophomore year Ethics class. It must have felt like this. She tried to remember names of people in the class, trying to push back at the world collapsing behind her, like boxes folding together as her brain stormed, rocking on the balls of her feet. Lorna wished someone would try and touch her again and she could swing at them.

Sophomore year, her Ethics class ran a mock trial. Soldiers on trial for killing women at a roadblock. They were nuns doing hospital work. No, they were revolutionaries with a wanted terrorist in their car. No, he was wounded and they were taking him to a hospital. No, they were spies. No, it was murder. The professor said it was based on a case in Central America, a long time ago. In the Cold War.

Rocking on her feet and running names, the collapse finally sucked

Lorna in. A canvas bag pulled over her head turned everything dark.

They were like blind elephants, bumping along, grasping trunk to tail, led by polite keepers. Head bagged, Lorna's grip stayed tight on Gallo's cold hand in front of her. He squeezed back in assurance. Tiny, Chinese lady steps, scraping.

The soldier's touch was gentle, his soft voice guiding them on the turns, nine steps down, Sir. A railing on your left side, Ma'am. *We regret to inform you the situation requires we shoot you in the back of the head.* Lorna could tell they were in a basement, smelling mildew, old wood and furniture. Bootsteps and voices above them on the upper floor of the house they had been driven to. They were told to sit. Lorna's back and ass sunk into a leather loveseat with worn springs. The bags came off to reveal a small rec room lit by two electric lamps. It was drywalled and adorned with a framed sunset poster of 'Cabo San Lucas' in swirly yellow letters. A big screen TV had been moved against the wall. A shelf full of DVDs and a small fridge. No sunlight. Hair skewed, Gallo was next to her. It took a moment to realize the difference, but his shakes were of anger, not chill.

One soldier was already tromping back up the stairs. The one watching them held his rifle pointed to the ground. If you looked quick his index finger near the trigger seemed to be flipping you off. He had narrow blue eyes and a wide jaw, 30-ish, broad chest. Bulletproof vest and stuffed pouches. A black metal square thing on the front of his helmet.

"Would you like any coffee, water, soft drinks?" he said. His voice was scratchy, like he'd been shouting. Lorna and Gallo shook their heads. The trooper looked away from them, keeping them side-eyed.

Another few minutes of generator hum and creaky footsteps and mildew smell passed before the man came down in quick steps, entering like a game show host. Camoed, ashy buzzcut with a smallish head pronouncing his grey eyes. It was the face and head military guys had. Like he'd once been a regular guy but had been shaped, shined, processed. Fitted into a part. Even Tyce still had a little bit of it. This one had a name tag - "Haffner." He offered a hand. Sir and Ma'am again. Captain Haffner. He asked their names. No, full names, please, he said. For a second Lorna thought to give a phony name but didn't. The older man was limber and quick like somebody younger. He pulled a wheeled office chair from a darker corner and sat in front of them, leaning forward, forearms over his kneecaps like a coach or someone with a good secret.

"Weren't you offered anything to drink?" Haffner glanced over his shoulder at the standing soldier. His boots were polished. A gold wedding band. He didn't have straps and pouches, only a belted pistol and canteen.

"We were," Gallo said. "Your men were very courteous, captain. Considering." Hannah had said Gallo was a lawyer once and this sounded like his court voice. Butched up for use everywhere back in the day, probably. She was glad Sanders stayed with the van.

"Precautions have to be taken, sir, unfortunately. Regretfully we're in a state of conflict and this could become a forward area, very soon. The UN airstrike here was precise. When a LifeForce employee with knowledge of the area arrives, with satellite communications, it grows suspicion. The bags were necessary. You understand."

Lorna looked at her Chucks. Regretfully. Steve...

"Are you with the United States Army?" Gallo asked.

"I am."

"Serving under the command of the President?"

The captain's lips curled, thinking this cute. "A parlor talk for another day, sir. If you're unfortunate enough to encounter the troops of the regime that's overthrown our constitution and country, you won't be given the courtesies you've been shown by my command, Mr. Gallo. You and the people in your compound are still enjoying your freedom and personal property. If this battle line shifts, it won't be the case."

"If you're defending the Constitution by what right do you have to search and detain us? I'd like to see Mr. Gallagher. We have business."

Haffner twisted his lips, roll sucking on words before speaking.

"My rights come from God, sir. Endowed by my Creator as specified by our founding fathers in the United States Constitution. The document I've sworn to defend." Haffner twisted to pull a matching camo knapsack looped over the chair's back support. He dug for two hand pads of paper and two pens, handing one each to Lorna and Gallo.

"We'll honor your trade agreement this time, but the water needs of Essex are now being met. Mr. Gallo, please make a list of the items and amount you need in equal compensation for the water. Then, Miss Brusine and Mr. Gallo, please make a list of the names, sex and approximate age of each person living in Cricklewood Green. Do this separately." His eyes pinched, imitating a smile. "No sharing of work, please."

"That's absurd," Gallo said.

"We've extended courtesy to you, sir. We're asking for the same."

Gallo's pen went to work, stabbing and scrawling. Lorna lifted her thin pad with a Comfort Inn logo at the bottom and got started. These motherfuckers were nuts. This was the time where you don't miss breaking the rule by an inch. You fucking *MISS*.

She heard men's easy laughter upstairs. Food was cooking, fatty rich and spicy. Lorna's stomach seemed to come alive, spasming. Her pen continued, lines and scrawls.

The captain's eyes scanned completed Gallo's list, lifting to read the other page. His almost hairless brow turned down. "You have a 95-year-old man in your complex?"

"He may be even older, with dementia who can say?"

"Horst Wessel?"

"European. You'll like him, captain. He's a supporter."

Lorna handed her pad to the married-gold hand. Haffner's eyes snake struck on Lorna, crumpling her sketch of a hairy, big-lipped vagina. They stayed on her as he spoke.

"We'll accommodate most of your requests, Mr. Gallo. My executive officer and a group of my men will accompany you to your compound. First there's something I'd like to show both of you. You especially, Miss Brusine."

From the bag he activated a computer tablet, handing it to Lorna. The slow scroll rolled photos of shot and maimed bodies in the wreckage of buildings and streets. The outdoors. One in a car. Black men and women. Hispanics. Some whites. Spatters of blood and gore. He talked the way someone would tell you about their vacation pictures.

"Notice their tattoos. Many of my men and women have tattoos. I have one. But notice these. Demon and devil imagery branded into their flesh. Their clothing."

A white kid's Slayer shirt, 666. Fire. Pagan symbols older than history, Haffner said. A black man with a gold plastic chain of dollar signs was sheared apart below his ribcage, face peaceful. Idolatry, Haffner said. All of it convening. Satan's many masks converging. One picture shocked Lorna. A red-haired young girl. Total kid, with a faint wash of freckles on what was left of her face. She wore a black hijab, blood shined. A military-style rifle with a hunting scope was still gripped in her hand. Haffner had stopped talking. Lorna looked up.

Haffner held out a small book to her. She passed the tablet to Gallo and took the book. It was a Koran in English, blooded.

"That's what we found on her. The girl could have been one of daughter's friends. I would never know it. Would you say she's older than 14, Miss Brusine? She killed two of my men and wounded a third in the groin. He'll never walk again or father a child."

Lorna imagined Haffner in a summer knit shirt and his board shorts and flip-flops, cheering at some soccer game. She didn't like him there either. A dick all the more because he thought he was such a great guy who loved his kids. No fucking doubt.

"My men and I come to our duty with a servant's heart. None of the deaths you see there are celebrated. No bodies have been violated and there's no torture tolerated under my command. And as I said, this is all regrettable. We had chances to stop it for years but the fig tree is in bloom and we cannot deny the harvest, how bitter. It is not too late for you. It's a choice you cannot evade Miss Brusine. Mr. Gallo. Darkness or light."

"You're certain?" Gallo said.

"I am, sir."

William set the tablet on the floor, wiping his hands on his trousers. "Tomorrow belongs to you, captain. There's no doubt about it. But I'm ready to meet my God. I've never needed a killer's word to sell His grace to me. And if you wish to challenge me on scripture I'll undress you right here. You have the power and ability to bend us to your will, but His word has nothing to do with it. Let's be clear."

Haffner blinked and held his hand out for the book. Lorna handed it back, knowing the prop would be used in the next show, somewhere.

******

Starved of sight, Sanders concentrated his hearing. Touch, - the wet air on his skin - was less focused a sense. After bagging his head, the soldiers zip-tied his wrists at the front and Sanders was led and spun around by a young-voiced soldier who eased him up into the van's passenger seat. Buckled in, someone drove Sanders for a measured count of 183, turning and reversing several times before the van backed to a stop. While mute workers unloaded the water, Sanders' mind constructed the picture. He built tree branches above him, dripping onto the metal roof. He could hear and smell the wet molt of soil under their boots. The near vehicles - diesel fuel and gun oil, the stink of machinery - were hidden under trees. They were afraid of the skies now, what had happened before. On his left, through the van's open driver's window he could hear distorted radio calls echoed inside what he visualized as a large war machine. A tank or armored car, perhaps. He built a square, boxy shape. The radio-responding soldier would be sitting.

The van's rear door had closed. Sanders was left for many minutes, long enough that he had to fight sleep and the void it would leave him in when he awoke. The shorthand of military language was familiar enough to Sanders. There were plenty of former servicemen at NASA and even Ford Motor Company. The radio exchanges Sanders heard sketched out a problem. People were being tracked but had been lost in the close vicinity. Two posts - picts - Echo and Sierra, were not responding to calls. Hotel came back negative. Juliet came back negative. Someone outside the armored shell suggested going "there" but was cut off at the verb. Sanders could imagine the hand swipe or finger to the lips. A drop of discomfort cut the operators voice, asking for Sierra again. Someone opened the driver's door and the van's windows powered up. An iron door clanked and that was that. Only wet drops on the metal roof. Three barks of a dog somewhere, back...there.

Sanders' head went into *why me*. Would the real American Army attack and kill him in this van, thinking he was allied with these lunatics? This thought led him to chase another fear. Had they wanted Sanders to listen? Had it been theater this whole time?

After more minutes the van's rear door opened. He could hear cardboard sliding in, liquid in metal cans, the mash of bags. The reek of gasoline.

The van started. They drove. After the van stopped the tie was cut from Sanders wrists, the bag removed. The driver was already gone before Sanders realized where he was, mind momentarily retreating from the sudden unclog of it all, infantilized. Those are trees, this is a road. The road. I am in the van, pointed east toward home. Outside of town. The brown squat dumpster, up ahead. Sanders twisted to look backward. Yes, food in boxes and bags. Red cans of gasoline. Two cans of propane. Outside the rear window, Lorna and William's hoods were removed. Their glassy, zippy eyes met his own without knowing it. Three helmeted, combat-loaded soldiers were near them. The roadblock sergeant in the sunglasses was speaking to Gallo, who nodded like a man just sprung from a wind tunnel, mouth agape, stunned.

   The group stood in front of a green camouflaged, armored Humvee. A helmeted trooper stood high in the turret, looking around at the fall-colored trees on each side of the road, the menacing machine gun casual under his forearm. A similar painted, tall Army truck with a canvas back idled in chorus behind the Humvee. More combat men were legging up and into it. Sanders unbuckled and scooted behind the two front seats. He secured a place down among the goods, awaiting the countdown. Even before their doors closed Gallo and Lorna were jabbering at each other like chickens. Lorna started the van and they slowly rolled forward.

   Tyce tell them radio warn them what the fuck quiet we can't asshole fuck they know Steve they killed shut up Steve and fuck fuck fuck. Lorna spitting to fight, Gallo hoarsely barking for calm. The pair had not looked at Sanders. He was not even sure they knew he was in the van. There was a leaping bump of speed as Lorna wheeled around the dumpster barrier. She floored the accelerator, knocking Sanders backward.

   "What are you doing?" Gallo yelled.

   "I don't know!"

   Sanders' felt a screaming pressure through his spine…….

***

   The explosion behind them shattered the van's rear window inward, the other windows blowing out. To Lorna it seemed like a giant toddler had lifted the van and slammed it back down, snapping its frame. A shrieking ache warped her deafened skull, mouth lapping for breath that wouldn't come. She felt four inches high. A doll inside a toy. Giants around her.

"Tuhh. Tuhhhhhhhh".

Her lungs had seized.

"Hunnnnh. Hahhhhh."

Lorna pushed against the steering wheel of the stopped van. The world had ripped open to a tantrum of giants. The toddler was kicking and pounding the van, kicking its sides. A wailing in her ears, eyes blurred. Lorna unbuckled and collapsed between the seats.

Another shock wave of explosion quaked through her. She realized bullets were cracking around her, banging metal, shredding the van's interior. Lorna felt a momentary, swelling relief when air finally bellowed her lungs, but the stink of gasoline came on strong. Rising to lizard her way out the passenger door with or through or over William, the toddler outside cracked Lorna in the center of her back with the fist of fucking Zeus. She'd been shot. A million spidering volts of more breathless pain, flattening Lorna over William's unbuckled, limp broken-neck body. Shot or not, electrified terror flexed Lorna's fingers and kicked her feet and FUCK YES they all worked.

Gasoline….

GetOutGetOutGetOutGetOutGetOut.

She yanked the passenger door lever and shoved. A hand grabbed her shoe. She shuddered. Lorna jerked to see Bob Sanders, as if through a film of grease, pieces of the van bursting apart behind him. A stream of blood leapt from a hole in his throat. Glasses bent, he reached for her, burbling.

"Wait."

Lorna kicked his hand free and rolled over William's dead body, leaving the droop-armed old man half out the door. Breath still gone, Lorna wormed over the wet blacktop to the gravel edge. She rolled through the high grass into the ditch, cold jolted by the water. Sobered, sloshing, the wetness swirled her fears of bleeding under the vest but there was no way she was tearing it off. Getting to her knees, Lorna peered through the grass, eyes level with the road. The van was fully burning now. They – whomever - seemed to have stopped shooting at it. Behind it, the Army jeep with the machine gun had been blasted open, flaming bright orange and oily black. Smaller clumps of fire all over the road. There were still a few popping gunshots, way back behind the brown dumpster. The canvas truck was on fire, stuck between the dumpster and the now burning trees. Fire brewed inside a crater middling the gap between the van and the Army jeep. Lorna realized that by punching the gas she beat the timing of whoever bombed or missiled them. They were going to get all three rigs as they squeezed through, only getting the back two. Her head throbbed, ears buzzing, sensing a humming above in the fog, around her. Afraid she might throw up, Lorna huddled against the grassy bank, teeth chattering as she lifted her feet out of the freezing water. Under the vest a bite of pain came with ever inhale. Wait here. Just for a second. Just a second.

There were far-off shouts. Or ghosts. She flopped over and looked east, toward the Green. She would have to crawl, but the ditch was too narrow, too full of water. Hugging the top edge Lorna moved only about ten feet before her weight slid her down the slicked weeds. She tried bracing but her right palm slipped. Crying out, Lorna dunked under. Pasted in brown slime she coughed water and finally vomited, dizzy. Against the bank, Lorna wiped her mouth, crawling as high as she could on the side like some dumb, shaking crab. She could not be here when the J-fucks came looking and their trophy cameras found her tattooed pagan ass.

Up inside the fog, Lorna felt roaring jet planes behind her as she crawled east. Her back twitched from a bomb's shock wave, ears popping again. Tasting mud and bile she kicked and clawed, moving faster.

DontdieDontdieDontdieDontdie…

*****

October 26th

Like a lighthouse, Mark's flashlight beam swept the room one last time. His idea on the walk down was to torch the Barracks, leave them nothing. But standing there looking at the dead monitor screens, the console chair pushed back, waiting on someone to sit the shift, Mark just felt tired. There wasn't a drop of gas left in the walls and the clouds didn't cooperate. Mark was there yesterday morning to watch the solar battery go below 3 percent. The monitors went first, then the desk lamp a few seconds later. Of course, the horizon was coming on bright today. It looked like it would be a sunny day. Anything else they could use they had cleared out yesterday afternoon before the party. Mark taped his enveloped letter to the monitor and closed the Barrack's boarded front door, still off-align.

No one ever fixed it.

The party had been Sherri's idea. For the last night they all went to stay at Kim Narlow's house, to try and keep the little girl as comfortable as possible. The girls spent the day decorating. The Christmas lights came out, strung beads, candles and scarves. They put Hapgood's two gasoline generators outside and ran the power cords inside. Everyone brought out the last of the sweets and the unpacked food. It turned out Sanders still had quite a bit in his house. Beers and some booze. Everyone got to pick some music from Kim's 16,000 song player and the RV's music dock. Sherri's order for the night was no sad stories, no toasts to the departed. Only fun and celebration. Sandra Rose had a fashion show of all her costumes. Lady GaGa was rocking those phony bags and posing for the cheers. Mark had to say Kim did a good job with her. The kid was calm and listened when she was told, using really big words for her age. Truth? He complained more than she did. During the party Mark found himself actually laughing and forgetting for a few minutes. Watching the fashion show Mark thought of his sister Colleen and her daughter. He had a niece he'd never seen in person. He was an uncle. He'd never thought of the word for himself. The girl with her boas and sunglasses made him look away and take a long sip. He looked at his dad, smiling tightly at the girl. Did he feel it? About his granddaughter? Mark couldn't tell. His dad danced with Sherri to old songs. Lorna didn't say much, looking out the windows all night.

Tyce stayed outside with the SAW and the night vision. He came in once for a few minutes and a toast, smiling and joking.

It was a little after seven, the sun nearly up. Mark wanted one last lap, going to the left to walk the west side of the loop. Tyce had moved the RV, parked it at the top of the loop, near the tunnel, close to the Narlow's. Mark kept the SAW and a pistol for the walk. Each of them kept one pistol for last resorts but the rest of the guns he buried. More guns than they could shoot and thousands of rounds but what Mark wouldn't give for a

Whopper with extra mayo. He could fantasize about some meat, a real meal, and make his mouth flow like a river and his head go swirling.

Hundreds of feet in the air a rushing, crackling flutter drove Mark into a crouch. It was like a coming train and falling tree all at once. The mortar round, cutting the cold air and exploding someplace in the woods outside the wall. The previous round came in around 4 a.m. This one made eight all together since the other night – hours after the four men tried to breach the roadblock with the Cherokee and Tyce cut them down. Only one mortar so far exploded inside the walls, in the southwest corner. They didn't know what they were doing, Tyce said. Lorna was probably right. The soldiers were gone or dead, moved on. This was the locals. Clowns didn't even know what a mortar was for, Tyce said. A tactical weapon. Dumbfucks treating it like some hillbilly V-1.

Tyce called it the Haji clock. One round every few hours to fuck with your sleep.

To whom it may concern,

There are bodies in this housing complex that deserve burial and notifying of next of kin. In the house at 306, in their bedroom there are the bodies of Joyce Sutherland and Hannah Snyder, owners of the house. They were killed by an intruder who was then killed by other residents. Marked in the northwest corner area of the woods are the marked graves of Michael Narlow of 314 and Vernon Hapgood of 322. They both were killed by intruders who were killed by other residents. Any other bodies found in the complex are either not known to us or deserving of any recognition. We have no knowledge of the final whereabouts of anyone else who lived in Cricklewood Green.

Sorry about everything.

The RV idled, puttering exhaust steam. Inside, Tyce was pouring hot tea into an insulated mug. Music going, some weird hillbilly-sounding song. *It's all-rahgt mawww*. It sure wasn't what Mark would play to get himself pumped up. More Weird Tyce. Tyce's full backpack and his Springfield were on the dining table bench behind the spread map.

"You can read a compass and a map, right?"

Mark nodded. The topographical map had been Sanders'. The Boy Scout compass was found among old man Gallo's things. A sash of merit badge patches and a Scout handbook from the 1950s.

Tyce drank from a regular cup, setting it down next to the topo map. "Alright. You're gonna be point man." Mark stepped up to study, joining Tyce's lean in. It didn't need to be asked. "We're gonna stay off the roads. We have to go straight west until we can find a place low enough to cross the creek here. Then we can hang south but this looks swampy, so – either way I'm pretty sure we're getting wet. From there it's you. I'll trust you, Mark."

He stood upright. "Only you and me have radios. You'll be about forty yards in front. They'll group together even if I tell them to spread out, so we'll just let them. I'll be in back and off on the sides, covering so nobody follows us. You see anything shady in front, call me. You hear anything in back, on the side of you – DON'T shoot. OK? It's probably me. If anybody fires on you, you lay down with the SAW and open up. Right?"

Mark nodded and smirked. It didn't need to be said. He knew what Tyce expected. Which was good because Mark didn't know how to tell Tyce he couldn't read a compass or a map. But he'd never killed anybody by rushing into a house either or shot people or laid booby traps or had people use his guns and knives against him because he was too fucking stupid and left it up in the trees. Before this Mark never had to lie like he had – every day and constant since the three got inside the wall. And it all worked out to this anyway. Tyce thought was he a fuck-up. And Tyce was right. So what would be different out there?

******

Arms drawn in and pressing her layers against the cold, Sherri marveled at the little girl. Crouched and up to her wrists in the creek, clearing, smearing leaves from a rock flat. The deers and animals needed a clear place to drink from, she said.

Ray had saved Sandra Rose the wet, freezing feet aching the rest of them, saddling her on his neck most of the way. Much of the walk was swamp and stumble, waiting and watching. Tyce had to fire his rifle in the air once but the unseen followers did not come closer. Sandra Rose hadn't even squeaked. Before they went into the tunnel Kim had taken her off to the side, caressing her face, kneeling close. The little girl's mouth flat, nodding. Brown bangs under her knit cap, her yellow rain boots. But Sandra Rose's eyes now were just...not what they should have been.

The sun was about an hour from disappearing, pink-dyeing the tops of the bare, skinny, pole-like trees. The layered golden, brown and red pattern around them seemed fresh, unbroken by feet or hoof. Anyone who had been in the trailer behind them hadn't been out here since the leaves had all fallen from the rains. Sherri's arms reflexed together, elbows flattening to her ribs, bone to bone, except for the pad of paper in her sweater pocket. Zorin Jancovic's diary and will. A truth Sherri would Hail Mary into whatever truth remained if/when they found other people.

Sherri considered memory, its limits. Being cold was the same as hunger, neither there until it is. Could you be full and imagine being hungry, truly? Sweltering and lazy on a humid summer night, imagine shivering with soaked feet and an aching back? You think you can, Sherri mused, but until it's there? You can Think, Believe or even Know. Then real immersion on your nerves makes imagination so tiny, useless. Sherri recalled what Bob Sanders said one night. Hubris, he said. That word.

"Events do not happen for us. That's only our hubris," he said. Sherri realized she missed Bob. She'd never really talked to him. He was a smart man, now gone. Hail Mary.

She walked closer to Sandra Rose.

"Are your hands cold, honey?"

"Uh uh."

"Stop now, Hun. Come up here. Let me warm them for you."

"No, if you don't mind, please." Sandra Rose looked up. "I don't get to do this very often."

The girl's words and expression was a meal itself. Sherri leaned her head back against the bark, up at the loose clouds. They were getting very close. Tyce said they were only two miles from I-75, yet the trailer could have been in the Tennessee hills 75 years ago excepting a TV antenna and the green corrugated plastic flap over the dirt porch. They had circled around to the front of the trailer and watched it for over an hour. It had no address, no mailbox at the end of its two track where it met the dirt road not on Hapgood's map. After a few minutes inside Tyce and Mark declared it safe for the night but asked Sherri to keep the girl outside for a while. Ray and Kim were called in to help while Mark strung his trip-wire traps on the road and the paths. Lorna and Barron went off walking. Lorna had not talked all morning.

Sherri's eyes stayed on the green glow cast on the porch table and two chairs, drawn to the color after starving on brown and grey and tension all day.

Ray slid a window open and called out to her, waving in.

"Let's go inside and eat something, honey."

Sandra Rose splatted a handful of something into the water. "There was something bad in there, wasn't it?" The little girl said.

"Yes."

****

October 27th

All morning they heard the sharp/dull *whump* of helicopter blades. Many of them. Tyce radioed Mark to keep them going south, following the creek toward the sound. Around 9:30 Tyce spotted the UAV overhead and pulled the white towel from his pack. He hollered for them all to wave up, cheer whirling the towel over his head. The UAV passed. They were getting close to a perimeter. Tyce hoped they would not be surprising the outer picts. He expected a patrol anytime. Tyce radioed to Mark, whom he could not see. He saw the back of Kim Narlow in flits between the trees. They were still in lower land but rises were all round them, worn dirt paths visible. To Tyce's surprise the group listened and had not bunched up, even when they were being circled yesterday. He supposed the guns helped. Superman's cape. To Tyce's greater surprise they did not shoot at the footfall noises, respecting what he had told them.

Mark didn't reply. The radio batteries may have finally cooked.

Mostly Tyce remained a hundred yards back, doing cloverleafs to the left and right, watching and crouching. After ten minutes he moved on and caught up to them, huddled and halted by the flushing, rolling water sound. Ahead, the trees ended like an open curtain before a low set of cement dams; a railed wooden walkway bridging them. In a pack they stood, rigid, at edge of the tree line. Helicopter and motor noises beyond.

"Where's Mark?" Tyce asked.

Mark had told them to stop and went on, Ray said.

It was on Tyce's lips, to call out, when they heard the auto-burst. Pop pop pop. Sherri grabbed Ray at the chest to keep him from running. The dog erupted in barks.

"Mark!" Ray yelled.

From behind, Tyce heard rapid steps and the command to drop his weapon. The command was accented English. European, then another American voice.

"Arms out. All of you."

"Mark!"

In flummoxed, pissed surprise at how well they had flanked him, Tyce flexed his left straight out and dropped the Springfield. Something taut inside of him gave, an exhausted relief. He wouldn't be responsible for it any longer. This had never been him.

Ray cried out again. Sherri fist-clenched his jacket to restrain him from running but Ray's feet never quite moved, quivering and flailing.

Four helmeted, camo-fatigued men surrounded the group.

"To your knees. On your knees. Arms out to the side. Now."

One of them shoved Tyce to the ground, warning him to stay still. Kim's body wrapped Sandra Rose as they dropped. With all of her backbone Lorna tried to restrain the dog, yelling commands. Tyce watched one solider raise his downward FN's barrel and snap two rounds into the growling, bounding shepherd. Its whelped, dying cry made Tyce nauseous. Lorna's arms sprang up as she backed away from the executed dog. In the sudden shatter of quiet, Ray collapsed to his knees, simpering under the slushing hiss of the dams.

After the group was disarmed and searched, the Dutch soldiers marched them a few hundred yards to a staging area. It had once been a park, with a rocky dirt parking lot and a picnic pavilion where troopers were eating and waiting among the tables and a few trash-can fires. Tyce felt no comfort. The Humvees, Bradleys, trucks, command tents and platoon formations of moving troops made Tyce weirdly resentful. No one hates like family.

Tyce fumed. *How could he have missed all of them?* The whole group could have been wiped out and Tyce never saw them. Fucking Mark. What could he have done....

The Dutch patrol and their American E-5 lead the group to the lot. Adamantly yelling at the American E-5, Ray and Sherri were separated from the group, Ray demanding answers for his son. Tyce watched three of the Dutch in their smear-style 80s-looking camo admiring his Springfield, talking in yahs and ahhs of throaty gutter. Shouldering aside, the E-5 ordered the rest of them to sit.

Over his shoulder Tyce watched a thumping Blackhawk helicopter circle-cut back and land beyond a stand of trees. When Tyce faced front again Ray and Sherri were both gone from behind a shifting screen of camoed limbs and vehicles. He started to call out but there was nothing to call to. He looked to the side at a medic and two female soldiers surrounding Sandra Rose and Kim with crouched, gentle touches. One offered a steaming paper cup to the little girl. As the soldiers stood and led the pair away Kim met his eyes a moment but Tyce looked away as the nodding, little capped head and yellow rain boots disappeared behind a truck tire.

Lorna's face was hidden by her hood, crossed legged next to him.

"I'm sorry about Barron," he said. The dog bothered him. The drowned kid had meant nothing.

Lorna looked at him. "What?"

"I'm sorry about Barron."

She nodded and reached out to take his hand. There was a snatched kiss to his cheek. Tyce wasn't sure if he imagined it.

One of the Dutch soldiers pulled a cell phone from his thigh pocket and snapped a picture of Tyce and Lorna. His thumbs worked to send it someplace.

Another female soldier led Lorna away. While she was looking back, pointing at Tyce and complaining, the soldier shook her head, taking Lorna by the arm toward one of the tents. Fuckin A, Lorna. Always and forever telling them where to shove it.

Some other Chairborne-looking E-5 came along. He was hot about the SAW. *A military weapon, where did you get it?* Weirdly enough, he seemed to accept the truth from Tyce and finally Tyce was allowed to stand. He was searched again and led to a walled command tent. A 30-ish 1st Lieutenant and his E-7, about Tyce's age. Perhaps what Tyce could have been if he had stayed in, back in the 1980s. Other troopers in the dim corners listened while they pretended to work. A command radio buzzed with calls and a female trooper rose to plot points on an old-fashioned hung map. Someplace another radio played the EBN news.

The patrol E-5 handed Tyce's wallet to the LT. The kid officer snickered and read the word 'LifeForce" with the conviction of 'ballerina', giving Tyce's uniform a cop's once-over. Tyce had no notion of where his keepsake military ID had gone.

The LT had a small scar over his left eyelid and bulgy pupils, wide and dark from the dim quarters. "You get what you pay for, I guess," he said to his E-7. The weathered grey sergeant grunted. He eyed Tyce with amused, familiar disdain.

Tyce felt cliff-dizzy since they'd been led into the camp's motion, like an ant colony in its doubtless execution. Shoot, move and communicate. Realizing how out of shape and half-speed he was, Tyce felt like an Iowa Corn Queen, prettiest girl in Ukiah Township, in the 5th Avenue bottle-service club with the Manhattan models. An old dog knowing what happens to old dogs.

The company commander was away, but the LT wanted to know how Tyce survived in the deep red for two months - how and why. Tyce was cursory, slipping in his experience casually – MOS, former ranks and certifications, bases trained, Iraq and Colonel Wright and the SAT phone and the airstrike.

If not friendly, the postures and faces relaxed. When the LT asked who in Cricklewood Green knew about the airstrike, Tyce said he received no official clearance. He just thought it up and did it. The E-7 laughed out loud. Tyce smiled. *Apocalypse Now.* Someone had finally gotten one.

Tyce was directed to the map. He told them what he knew. Neither of the men knew Colonel Wright. This was mechanized infantry from Kansas. What hadn't defected of the Michigan Guard had been sent west, to Grand Rapids, north Indiana and the radiation zone on the lake. They returned Tyce's wallet. The LT called for Specialist Wolding. A smaller, muscled black trooper stepped forward, 22 maybe.

"Specialist, take this man into Dwyer. See he gets a place to wash up and some hot chow before processing."

Tyce looked to the E-7. "Top, I was tight, through a lot, with these people for two months. I'd like a chance to say goodbye to them."

The LT turned his back. Didn't like it.

"You'll see them all in processing. Specialist get going."

He circled a point on the map of Essex.

"My rifle, Lieutenant?" Tyce said.

"Get him out of here, Specialist."

****

A Dutch trooper drove Wolding, Tyce and a roof gunner into Dwyer on autumn dressed two-lane blacktop, past houses and driveways and people raking leaves and kids playing in front yards. Some civilians didn't pay a notice to the Humvee. Some dry-sniped them with an evil eye Tyce had seen once before, when the faces were browner and the hot air stank of burning cars.

The hilly town of Dwyer spread over into strip malls facing I-75, flowing with trucks, military and even civilian car traffic. Among the one-story buildings Tyce mostly saw military and government bodies in blue FEMA windbreakers, but there were civilians. Working and building, getting out of cars, going into stores and emerging with bagged goods. Outside the FEMA shower station where the Humvee dropped Wolding and Tyce a new cell phone tower was being crane-raised. A massive orange generator with German wording on its side passed them, taking up nearly the entire back of a semi-trailer. Wolding told Tyce he had ten minutes. Towels and everything were in there. Tyce was alone in the eight-stall FEMA shower. He washed hot and shampooed and washed again. His skin alive and humming. Tingles of relaxation were coming on, up his back bone, tickling, releasing out his fingertips.

For chow Wolding took him into a Burger King, removing his helmet. Wolding paid with a blue card he swiped into a counter machine Tyce did not recognize. On its small screen Wolding's picture, name, rank and serial number appeared with a charge amount of zero. The old woman in a polyester brown uniform handed over the bag with a smile and Wolding handed it to Tyce. Everyone working looked well past 60.

Tyce sat in the plastic booth. At a table to the side Wolding ate nothing, watching Tyce inhale a Whopper and fish sandwich and double fries. It all tasted as Tyce remembered. The ceiling speaker's music cautioned of a witchy woman, flying high.

"What's the card?" Tyce said.

"Ration card. The banks are still all fucked up. No money anymore, yet. You'll get one when you process. Military gets an open account most places." A woman and two kids walked past with their trays and Wolding moved his leaning M-4 off the tile floor up to his lap. "You gonna re-up?"

"Don't know," Tyce said. He asked Wolding about the action he'd seen. Fighting around the gas refinery in Whiting, Indiana, Wolding said. Indianapolis had been bad. Lots of civilian dead. The Js were crazy. Troopers had to shoot kids dropping firebombs from roofs. Wolding was glad to be far from the nuke plants. They were calling them safe, but...
Wolding asked him about Iraq. Tyce sketched a few incidents, telling how he'd felt like old man in the reserves then. Let alone now, at 51. A nightmarish vision formed. Marching back through that swamp with Dutch troopers, having to clear Essex.

"You might get rank back," Wolding said. "LifeForce is still active, some of the calmer parts south of here. Get your gig back. Otherwise you'll end up in a detail."

"How's that?"

"Man, you ain't under 16, a woman with kids or crippled you're on a work detail or you ain't keeping that blue card long. And if you think about flexing those rights you used to have they've got places for you, Sergeant. Believe it."

Tyce crumpled the wax paper. The ceiling speaker wondered about Pina Coladas and getting caught in the rain.

Wolding stood. "Ready?"

At the former warehouse, Wolding handed Tyce off with wished luck to an ear-pieced and radio-belted woman in blue FEMA golf shirt. They moved to her station among a dozen rowed, curtained cubicles. Walking, Tyce did not recognize anyone among the few people seated in front of blue questioners. The entire structure was nearly empty of humans. Hollow echoes. It felt like arriving at the end of a missed concert. After they sat, the woman, Estralita, aimed a camera, cabled to the laptop. First the picture. Head on, then a profile. A tablet was slid over the plastic table top. Tyce put his palms down as instructed and they were scanned.

"Do you have any documents?"

The woman accepted the Lifeforce ID and his Michigan driver's license, entering the clicks and clacks. "Is this your current address?"

"No."

"What is your current address, sir?"

"None."

"Is there anyone you wish to alert or contact?"

"No."

"Place your index finger here. It may sting." The prick and then she handed him an alcohol swab. O+, but he could have told her that.

"Wait here a moment."

Among the muttered voices humming down from the corrugated metal ceiling Tyce began to feel very alone and small. Like a toy inside a big doll house.

Keeping his other IDs, the woman handed Tyce a laminated picture ID card and a blue ration card with flag and eagle and Unites States of America printed in the pattern. "Two hundred points of rations per week, you can use them anywhere you choose. There's more information in these documents." She passed him a half-dozen logo-ed paper hand-outs.

She pressed her ear piece.

"Process. PK-1"

"What is 'PK-1'?"

"You'll be told, sir."

"This way, sir." A field-capped trooper hovered behind Tyce's shoulder. Eyes on her screen, Estralita wished him luck. The radio beeped. She answered her ear piece, swiveling to the side.

"Hey! Yes. How are you?"

Outside, the lower autumn noon sun had emerged, agitating Tyce's eyes. He greatly wanted to freeze everything happening around him.

Wait.

The field-capped trooper escorted Tyce to an idling, canvas-top Army six-ton truck in the parking lot. A sergeant and two troopers with M-4s lingered by its lowered back gate. The sergeant held a long-strapped keypad. Something like it had once been a UPS manifest reader or something to read the power level of a water-well generator.

"PK-1," the capped trooper said, walking back to the warehouse.

"ID." The sergeant said.

Tyce passed the card and glanced inside. He could make out five white-eyed shapes through the faint sunlight. What they used to call in Iraq MAMs – Military Aged Males. They glanced at Tyce, then down or away. Passengers. The closest one to Tyce wore a white, long-sleeve button-down office shirt, one hand gripping a pair of broken eyeglasses, the other shaky hand held a handkerchief to his bloody nose.

Tyce looked at the sergeant, name-tagged "T. Jones." He swiped the ID card through the keypad, handing it back.

"Where are you taking me?"

The sergeant's jaw motioned to the lowered tailgate, the darkness behind it.

"Get in the truck."

Made in the USA
San Bernardino, CA
25 May 2020